BROKEN RED SKY

BROKEN RED SKY

ANNA KIRCHNER

ISBN: 979-8-88785-037-5 (Paperback)
ISBN: 979-8-88785-038-2 (Hardcover)

Library of Congress Control Number: 2024938242

Any references to historical events, real people, or real places are used fictitiously. Names, characters, and places are products of the author's imagination.

Original cover design by Nem Rowan.
FMP book design by Allison Chernutan.
Edited by and Carol Kudeviz and Emily Kudeviz.

Printed in the United States of America.

First printing edition 2024.

emily@fracturedmirrorpublishing.com
Fractured Mirror Publishing
Knoxville, Tennessee

www.fracturedmirrorpublishing.com

To all those dreaming of a better world—
Keep on fighting. Keep on dreaming.
Let's make it happen.

LANGUAGE GUIDE

Please note that some Polish sounds (for example *c* or *y* or *ś*) don't exist in the English language. In these cases, the closest approximates are used.

NAMES AND PLACES:

Beata – Beh-ah-tah

Bieszczady – Bee-eh-shcha-di

Bydgoszcz – Bid-goshch

Chors – horse

Cyprian – Tsi-prian

Dawid – Dah-vid

Dudzik – Doo-djik

Eliza – El-ee-za

Elżbieta – Elsh-bee-eh-ta

Jagoda – Ya-goh-da

Jelitkowo – Yeah-leet-koh-voh

Koniewski – Kon-yev-ski

Laura – L-oww-ra

Ludmiła – Lood-mee-wa

Mariusz – Mah-ri-ush

Marzanna – Mash-an-na

Mateusz – Mah-teh-oosh

Nowacka – Noh-vah-tska
Ogiński – Oh-geen-ski
Potocka – Pot-o-ska
Regina – Ray-ghee-na
Rydgier – Rid-gheer
Strychalska – Stri-hals-ka
Stanisław – Sta-nih-swav
Tadeusz – Ta-day-usz
Tomasz – Toh-mash
Wiktoria – Victoria / Wiki – Vicky / Wiwi – Vivi

SLAVIC MYTHOLOGY AND POLISH FOLKLORE:
Baba Jaga – Baba Yaga
chmurnik – hm-uhr-nik
diduch – dee-dooh
gumiennik – gum-in-nik
Jare Gody – Yah-re Gho-di
Jawia – Yah-vee-uh
latawiec – lata-vits
Leszy – Leshy
Nawia – Nah-vee-uh
Nyja – Nay-ya
płanetnik – pwa-neh-tnik
rusałka – russ-aow-kah
Sława – Slava
Sława Ci – Slava Tsi
Sława Wam – Sława Vam

Szczodre Gody – Shcho-dre Gho-di
Święto Plonów – Sh-vi-en-to Ploh-noov
strzyga – st-sh-iga
swaćba – sva-chi-ba
Twardowski – Tvar-dov-skee
upir – uh-peer
Węgliszek – Ven-glee-shek
Weles – Veles
wiła – vi-wah
Wyraj – V-rye
żmij – zh-mee

SUMMARY OF BOOK TWO
TALL WHITE TENEMENT

The story picks up a day after *Little Black Bird*'s finish when a demon attacks Wiktoria at school. Tomasz helps her and takes her to the Clavichord Café which gets visited by the Guardian of Gdańsk. He accuses Zuzanna of instigating magical accidents in his territory and demands that she send Artur and Wiktoria to be tried by the Guardians' Assembly. Zuzanna refuses to send them away. Wiktoria shows her the letter from her mum, which explains how to break the curse on the Kromer family.

Wiktoria's dad catches her when her magic slips. She convinces him to follow her to the Clavichord Café. Zuzanna shows Wiktoria's dad the letter but his memories are vague because of the deal with the devil, he remembers only that there was an important reason why breaking the curse is a priority.

The sorcerers celebrate Dziady, where they feast with the souls of the ancestors. During the celebration the ghost of Zuzanna's father gives her an ominous message: "If you turn your back on your own blood, you'll be as good as dead."

Wiktoria and Artur stumble upon a powerful demon just outside of Wiktoria's home and she decides to remind her mum about magic. Her mum doesn't believe her. Wiktoria channels Tomasz's hypnotic powers to run away.

Artur and Wiktoria are at odds about whether they should side with the Children of Weles or help Zuzanna break the curse. When they meet Klara's shadows, Artur tells her that they suspect they're a part of the Circle of Four and they need to find the other two members to make the transition to the Guardianless system easier. The same night, Wiktoria starts getting visited by Baba Jaga in her dreams.

The sorcerers are attacked at Zuzanna's father's funeral. They are saved by Zuzanna's girlfriend, Aysun, who turns out to be part-irshi, a demonic protector who has chosen Zuzanna as her human to protect. Artur is kidnapped and Tomasz and Gabriella try to stop Wiktoria from going after him.

Wiktoria learns that Karina is still half-possessed by the demon and that she is likely a part of the Circle of Four. The Children of Weles help Wiktoria save Artur, but they make it clear that they see her as a liability.

At home, Wiktoria is attacked by a demon. She saves herself, but her mum sees the fire and gets terrified of Wiktoria's new powers. Wiktoria tries to once again tell her about magic, but her mum rips the letter she's written.

Magic in the city gets wilder and Zuzanna hosts a meeting for the sorcerers, but they turn against her. Ordinary people begin to notice that something is wrong— people stock up on food and hold religious processions. The domowik tells Zuzanna that her family is cursed because the Guardians abuse magic. He also tells her that if she rejects her Guardianship, she can still survive the curse. However, Zuzanna wants to hold on as long as possible so that Wiktoria has a chance to complete the Circle of Four, find the Twardowski's scriptures, and end the Guardian era once and for all.

Wiktoria, Karina, and Laura go to Poznań to meet Laura's brother, Damian, to complete the Circle of Four. Because he's never been welcome in the magical community, he's reluctant to join but after he learns that they are trying to overthrow the Guardians, he agrees to help. The Circle of Four summons a devil to find the Twardowski's scriptures. The devil tries to make them change their mind but eventually he agrees to give them the Twardowski's scriptures in return for four bargains. When they accept, he says that the scriptures had been destroyed centuries ago and the Circle of Four is left with a strange purple egg and a high price to pay.

Wiktoria has to collect an old debt for the devil from Tomasz. The devil takes Wiktoria's blood and Wiktoria is saved by the Circle of Four. The egg hatches and the Circle of Four become parents to what looks like a baby dragon, which they name Arrow. The devil grants Tomasz his side of a bargain—a page from a diary of a seventeenth-century alchemist who created the Guardians' rings. She warns about the gods' wrath when the Guardians fall.

Klara tells the Circle of Four that the Guardians' Assembly has a copy of the Twardowski's scriptures. Damian makes Wiktoria realize that the Children of Weles want all the Guardians gone, which includes her.

The city is attacked by gryphons and Zuzanna confronts the Gdańsk's Guardian. Later, she meets again with her sorcerers which ends in violence. Zuzanna is saved by Aysun. The Guardians' Assembly appoints the Guardian of Gdańsk to replace Zuzanna, but Zuzanna uses her remaining powers to seal off the city so that the Assembly can't take over.

The Circle of Four learn that the devil bargains have a physical manifestation and if they are destroyed, the bargain is broken. They set out to find the bargain between Wiktoria's mum and the devil. They find a chest filled with figurines but they decide not to destroy them as there are hundreds of them and they know that some of the bargains might be protecting the city.

The same night Wiktoria, Karina, and Rafi sneak back to the tunnels and find the figurines destroyed. They are cornered by a basilisk and barely manage to escape. Wiktoria runs to warn Zuzanna, but she finds her nearly lifeless. She saves her with her magic and convinces her to finally reject her Guardian heritage. Wiktoria gets the Guardian ring and Zuzanna and Aysun fly away.

Wiktoria is struggling to keep up the protections between the realms. The magic is too much for her mum to comprehend with the devil blocking her memories, and she's unresponsive. Desperate, Wiktoria talks to a rusałka. She sees a memory of her parents planning for the Circle of Four and learns her mother's true name.

Wiktoria and her friends encounter a god, Nyja, who possessed a human. The god is violent and powerful, but with Damian's help they manage to put them to sleep. Then Wiktoria and Tomasz go to talk to her mum. She agrees to do a ritual with the Circle of Four which starts to bring back her memory.

The Circle of Four performs a ritual found by Laura to strengthen the protections over the city. However, the opposite happens—the protections disappear, the sky cracks open, and powerful demons make their way to the city. Arrow chases after a firebird. When Wiktoria makes her way to the Guardian's tenement, she encounters Artur's mum who accuses her of murdering Zuzanna. Wiktoria blacks out and in a dream, Baba Jaga tells her that it will help her patch up the sky if Wiktoria passes a series of trials.

Wiktoria is taken to the tunnels by the Children of Weles. Laura tells Wiktoria that she gave the Circle of Four the wrong ritual on purpose, to save the magic. Artur finds Wiktoria, but the Children of Weles stop them from escaping. Klara tells Wiktoria that they have been ramping up animosities between the Guardians on purpose and that the Children of Weles have been responsible for everything they'd blamed on the Gdańsk's Guardian–chasing them in Gdańsk, attacking the funeral, and even kidnapping Artur. The Children of Weles want to bring back the god of magic, the guardian of Nawia—Weles.

The book ends with a mock fealty of Wiktoria as the last Guardian of the City.

ONE

MAGIC ROAMED FREELY IN THE TUNNELS UNDER THE city. My skin tickled under its touch, its warmth burning my overstimulated body. I didn't flinch, I didn't move, conserving my energy to stay conscious.

What day was it? How long had I been here? I had no way of knowing; time didn't make sense in the tunnels. Maybe the world outside ceased to exist. It wasn't too far of a stretch. The last time I'd been outside, it'd looked like the end of days.

I shifted, trying to get more comfortable, as if that were possible, and winced when pain shot up my numb legs. The centuries-old stones bit into my knees, their coldness a startling contrast to the burning hot magic in the air.

My hands were tied to a tall dark crystal that speared the floor and rose all the way up to the low ceiling. The candlelight danced on its black surface. Magic rushed through me into the crystal in a steady flow, making my hair fly around my head. The red cloak of the Guardian of the City clung to my skin, clammy with sweat. I didn't have much room to move—my ankles had been shackled to the floor ever since I'd kicked Filip so hard, I'd broken his nose. I could only kneel and resist the temptation to rest my head on the hot crystal.

Shadows danced on the walls, constantly shifting and morphing into grotesque shapes, making sure I couldn't forget they were there. Their movement made me nauseous. I squeezed my eyes shut to block them out.

Klara had promised I'd be able to protect the city as the Guardian, but not even in my wildest dreams had I dreamed up this torturous magic. She turned me into a living conduit with magic of the tunnels rushing into me and through me into the crystal, which kept the nearby area as safe as it could be during the end of the world. Or so the Children of Weles claimed. It was a pretty ingenious device, channelling the energy of a magic-user to protect the area around. I didn't know its reach, it wasn't like I had a chance to stroll around and admire its effects, but we were still alive. While in theory anyone with magic could use the crystal, I had more magic at my disposal than any magic-user we knew and was the only person we knew who was fed by the city magic. Anyone else in my position would have been drained in minutes. I could stay there as long as my body held on, the magic flowing from the tunnels through me to strengthen the city wards, making me feel less human with each passing hour and day.

The Children of Weles couldn't force me to conduct the Guardian rituals. But they could chain me to the crystal.

Klara had also ensured I knew who'd helped them design the device and as much as I tried not to dwell on it, my mind wouldn't leave it alone. I felt a deep stab of betrayal every time I thought her name.

Laura.

Laura, whom everyone liked, who always had flowers in her hair, whom I'd never expect to hurt a fly.

Laura, who had given us the ritual which had shattered the barriers between the realms.

Did she know how the Children of Weles were using her crystal device? Did she care? Or did she think my life was a reasonable price for restoring the magical balance?

My heart hurt thinking about her, but could I blame her? What was one life in exchange for countless others?

With a squeak, the door behind me unlocked. I opened my eyes but didn't move, my muscles tensing in anticipation. I couldn't wait to leave the crystal room but I didn't want to face Filip again.

"How is our dear Guardian doing on this fine day?" he asked.

I didn't answer. His steps pounded, each sound like a thousand needles stabbing into my exhausted brain, as he walked around the small room to face me. The ceiling was so low that he had to bend over, dark hair falling into his face. He wore his black sorcerer's cloak as usual. His nose was crooked from when I'd kicked him—apparently, there wasn't anyone around to set it straight for him.

I didn't feel super bad about it.

"Still not lowering yourself to talking with us commoners, I see," said Filip, crouching in front of me. He held a vial filled with yellow potion. "Are you ready for the evening snack?"

I couldn't believe he wasn't over it yet. We'd done it so many times before. I'd tried to keep count, to help me measure the passing time, but my brain was too mushy to comply.

Filip brought the vial to my lips but I kept them resolutely shut. I put all my hatred into a stare and looked into his eyes. I knew it was pointless. Filip clamped his fingers on my nose, his touch, his closeness revolting, my whole body balking at the touch, but I couldn't move away. I held on as long as I could but, eventually, I gasped for breath. He used this chance to pour the rue potion into my throat. I gagged and sputtered, but Filip pressed his hand to my mouth, still clamping my nose shut until he heard me swallow.

"Aren't you tired of this game? You know you'll never win," said Filip as I gasped for air. But he didn't sound exasperated—he enjoyed this game, no matter how many times we played it.

On the other hand, I was more exhausted than I'd thought possible. If not for magic, I probably wouldn't be alive anymore. But there was a tiny grain of hope that maybe, one day, Filip would forget about the rue potion. Maybe he'd unbind me while I could still use the magic, and I'd break free.

Besides, and I felt gross admitting it even to myself, Filip's hands were always ice cold and after the constant burn of magic, they felt like heaven on my skin. I hated having him anywhere close to me but I was desperate for any sort of relief. The contradiction made the whole thing even worse.

Filip crouched in front of me, his cold hand on mine, feeding off my magic as the rue potion started working. I wished I could punch him, to lock him in this room and never have to see him again, but I was still bound. I glared at him, my skin creeping at the contact. Soon, the burn of magic disappeared. The crystal was still hot to touch but the flow of energy was blocked and I sagged in relief, exhaustion settling into me.

Filip unshackled my feet and hands. He knew I was too tired and that, without magic, I posed no threat. It took all my energy not to slump to the ground once I wasn't tied to the crystal, and he had to heave me up. My muscles protested and my brain screamed even louder at having Filip's hands on me, but I was so, so tired. The days of me kicking him in the face were over.

We stumbled out of the room, Filip's hand wrapped firmly around my arm. Magical vines climbed on both sides of the ancient stone tunnel, reaching for us as we walked a few short steps to my cell. Filip kicked open another wooden door and pushed me inside. I tripped and fell onto the thin, firm mattress on the ground.

"Get some rest," he said, slamming the door and locking it behind him.

I had about four hours to eat and sleep. Maybe. The time flew weirdly in the tunnels but in the outside world rue potion usually blocked my magic for four hours. Filip had left me a paper plate filled with kluski covered in sugar. It was a simple dish, little balls made of flour and little water and boiled for a few minutes. I devoured them quickly with my hands.

How was the food situation in the city? Before everything had transpired, the Clavichord Café had been the last place which regularly sold bread and pastries, as everyone else suffered from the lack of electricity. Dawid had grown vegetables and our meals were simple, but I hadn't gone hungry, which I suspected was a problem for many others.

I didn't think the Children of Weles would try to starve me. They needed me. No, most likely they either hadn't found Dawid or he'd refused to help them and now they lacked food. It wasn't surprising as Dawid had been on the Guardian's side. Or was he? We'd met when he'd followed me on Stanisław's orders, but he'd refused to kill me. He'd worked with Zuzanna afterwards but maybe it was gay solidarity more than support of the Guardians. After Laura's betrayal, I wasn't sure of anything anymore.

My head hurt trying to think about it. Or maybe it hurt from exhaustion.

I had a small plastic bowl filled with water and, after I'd licked the last of the sugar off the paper plate and gurgled down a full water bottle, I put my hands into it. The water wasn't cool but it was still a relief to my skin. After a couple of moments, I splashed some of it on my face and brushed wet fingers through my greasy hair. The Children of Weles had even given me a toothbrush.

I leaned on the cool stone wall, stretching my muscles, making sure they remembered how to work. It lasted only a few moments before exhaustion won and I curled up on the mattress and passed out.

It felt like I'd only just closed my eyes when I the door to my cell slammed open. I jumped and sat up, my head swimming. I hadn't gotten nearly enough sleep. I never did. I didn't know if the Children of Weles wanted me exhausted or if they didn't want to risk me being away from the crystal for too long, but they never allowed me more than a few short hours of sleep.

"Breakfast time," said Filip, placing a paper plate and a water bottle on the floor. "Eat up, you have five minutes."

My head was still swimming and the nausea made eating difficult, but I needed food. I'd declined food only once and having your magic brutally harvested on an empty stomach was even worse than normal. I'd been unconscious before the Children of Weles had unshackled me.

I relieved my bladder in the bucket in the corner, splashed some water on my face, and forced myself to eat some plain barley wheat and drink water.

As soon as I was done, Filip reappeared and took me across the corridor to the room with the crystal. I let him drag me, I didn't have the strength to fight. My whole energy went to making sure I wouldn't throw up.

A cook-a-doodle-doo reverberated down the corridor as Filip was closing the door behind us. I would have dismissed it as my imagination playing tricks on me but Filip stiffened. I shivered.

"You told me you'd taken care of the basilisk," I said, my voice croaky.

"We did," growled Filip, his fingers digging painfully into my arm. "But I didn't say it was dead. So, if I were you, I'd make sure never to wander these tunnels on my own."

He threw me to the stone floor and shackled me back to the crystal.

Everything hurt. Every time I opened my eyes, the world swirled. But the basilisk had given me much needed hope. I needed to wait until it crowed again, until Filip lowered his guard again.

Because it was always Filip dragging me between my cell and the room with the crystal. Maybe no one else wanted to bother with me, or maybe he was extra sadistic. I had no idea what the Children of Weles were doing while

I was stuck there. I didn't know what the world outside looked like, if there was still any world outside at all, if there were any more Children of Weles left. These were all question marks I only acknowledged in the rare lucid moments. The only thing I knew was that the magic in the tunnels continued to grow or maybe I was growing more sensitive to it.

It took four more crystal sessions until finally, one time, on my way to the crystal room, the basilisk crowed again. Filip froze, his hold on my arm going slack for a fraction of a second, and adrenaline spiked through me. I elbowed him in the stomach and ran.

I didn't think it through. Adrenaline wasn't enough to make my poor body work. I stumbled but kept going, tears stinging my eyes, as I forced my numb legs to move, my arms to reach for the stone walls to keep me going.

I didn't get far before an ice-cold shadow touched my leg and wrapped around my ankle. I fell face-first into the stone floor. I caught the worst of the impact on my hands and they burned, scratching against the floor. I kicked and punched, desperate to free myself from the shadow-grasp, but my energy was depleting fast.

A sparkle of magic ignited inside me. The rue extract was wearing off and the magic in the air streamed towards me, feeding my magic. I pushed it out, desperately trying to free myself as the shadow clung to my ankle.

Please, I pleaded in my mind. Where were the devils when I needed them to make a bargain?

Light. I needed light, powerful enough to banish all the shade.

But I was useless at controlling magic. Even as it rushed out of me as a powerful force field, keeping Filip at bay, it did nothing to free me from the shadow.

Another shadow wrapped around my wrist, rolling me to my back, and I screamed in frustration, which quickly turned into sobs that made it hard to breathe.

Slowly, my magic died down. The shadows kept me pinned to the ground as Filip approached, his heavy steps echoing down the corridor. But it wasn't only him—my screams had attracted a small crowd of the Children of Weles. I recognized Paulina and Agata, the two sorceresses who had helped Klara stage the ruse of kidnapping and freeing Artur to get us to trust them.

"Do you think that maybe—" started a sorcerer I didn't know, but Paulina interrupted him.

"No," she said firmly. "She is the worst sort. She not only leeches away our power—she can *use* it herself. To think that's who would have been our leader in the old world."

"But she's Aleksandra's daughter," said the sorcerer and my head snapped up.

They remembered my mum. The memory spell must have finally properly broken. Who else remembered her? What did they remember? Mum had worked with the Children of Weles, maybe it could be enough for someone to help me, to get me out of here.

"Just think about what the Guardians have been doing

to all the magic users for centuries," said Filip, squashing my seedling of hope.

He crouched beside me. I wanted to punch the stupid, self-satisfied smirk off his face, but the shadows held me firmly to the cold stone floor. I was helpless, once again at his mercy, and hatred burned in my veins.

"Come on, Guardian," he teased. "Don't you want to make sure your magic-users are safe? Don't you want to protect your city?"

Tears streamed down my face and I shook my head, unable to speak. I just wanted it all to be over. I didn't want him to look at me, to talk to me. I wanted to disappear.

"Too bad. It's not like any of your ancestors bothered to ask us if we're willing to sacrifice our magic, either."

ᛏᚹᛟ

IT SEEMED LIKE I'D BEEN SHACKLED TO THE CRYSTAL forever. I was nauseous and my head pounded, but oblivion wouldn't come. The push of magic forcing its way through me to the crystal was unrelenting. I couldn't stop it, no matter how hard I tried, no matter what desperate pleas I threw into the darkness around me. It was too bad for the devils that my magic kept them out as I would have given anything to get myself out of there. My hands stung from the constant heat and magical stimulation and for the first time I started to wonder how long I could take it. Time didn't make sense in the tunnels and I'd lost count of how many crystal sessions I'd endured. It must have been days in the outside world. How much more could I survive?

Some part of me agreed with the Children of Weles. Didn't I owe them protection? I'd messed everything up over and over. I'd broken the sky. Wasn't pumping my magic away the least I could do? I was uniquely suited to it. The tunnels kept giving me more and more magic that I could channel into the city defences as long as my body held. Maybe it was what I'd been meant to do all along.

The question was, how long *would* my body hold?

This time, when Filip forced me to drink the rue potion and unshackled me, he didn't drag me back to my cell. He walked past it, his hand clasped on my arm. I didn't realize it immediately as my eyes were shut and I struggled to contain my nausea. But after we'd walked more than I had in days, I lifted my head and looked around, making myself even sicker. Odd sconces lit up the ancient tunnel enough for me to see the shadows dancing on the wall, forming eerie, nightmarish shapes with horns, their long claws reaching for me.

I'd thought this morning had broken me but I'd been wrong. Dread filled my heart as if the shadows' icy fingers wrapped around my insides.

Filip opened the wooden door with a creak that drilled into my exhausted brain, and, before I could put up a fight, pushed me into the dark room.

"Wash yourself, you stink," said Filip and the door clicked close.

I blinked, trying to get used to the darkness. In a small ray of light falling from under the door, I managed to make out a big bowl of water on a wooden table, a bar of soap, and another Guardian's cloak.

I didn't need to be told twice. The water was cool, a balm to the scratched skin of my palms that felt burnt from all the magic, but not too cold. I splashed my face and washed myself as best as I could with my shaky hands and without taking off my clothes—it was too cold and I didn't trust Filip not to walk in on me. Besides, if I'd taken off my worn-out clothes that I'd sweated through multiple times, there was no way I would have put them back on.

I was glad to exchange the Guardian's cloak for a fresh one, though. The red fabric didn't feel right to me and I would have loved to abandon it altogether, but the magic woven into the threads kept me warm.

I still felt sick but, as I leaned on the table and left my hands in the water, letting its coolness soothe me, I decided I might be able to hold on some more.

Filip shouldered his way inside the room and grabbed my wrist.

"Perfect," he said, dragging me outside. "Dinnertime."

For the first time since my fake Guardian's fealty, I was back at the main lair of the Children of Weles—a large room, filled with maps and pillows and a huge symbol of Weles on the wall. There was a row of candles under the symbol, because naming themselves after the god of magic wasn't symbolic— the Children of Weles anticipated the god's return.

I hoped he hadn't returned yet. The day before I'd ended up here, the day before the failed ritual, we'd faced another chthonic god, Nyja. They'd only possessed a human but they could still make the ground shake.

I didn't want to meet any god in their true form.

The room wasn't empty. Klara, Paulina, and Agata sat on the pillows in the corner, all wearing their black sorcerers' cloaks. In front of them laid a simple feast of freshly baked bread, blackcurrant jam, cheese, gherkins, and olives. There was a jug of water and a bottle of wine, together with five glasses.

My stomach growled.

Trap, trap, trap, said my brain.

"We're dining tonight in fine company," said Paulina.

Trap.

Filip led me to the pillows. Hesitantly, I sat between Klara and Paulina, every fibre of my body screaming I shouldn't be there.

"Will you dine with us, Guardian?" asked Klara, her tone mocking.

The shadows wrapped around my legs, making me shiver and my stomach revolt. The bread smelled delicious and the spread, while simple, was the best food I'd seen in a while. Millions of times better than the plain kluski and kasze I'd been eating in the past days. But everything in me said I shouldn't touch it.

"Not lowering yourself to eat with the sorcerers," said Filip, sitting opposite me. "Just like any other Guardian out there."

I didn't speak. I sat in silence, fighting nausea and trying not to collapse onto the pillows. I was starving, yes, but I was also exhausted. I needed to stay alert among the Children of Weles, but I struggled just to keep my eyes open.

They ate the food and every crunch of the bread made my stomach growl more. I took sick pleasure in staring as they ate bread with cheese and jam and drank their wine. Not enough to get drunk and lose their focus, but enough to make it look like a fancier dinner.

I could eat. I wasn't punishing anyone apart from myself.

"I gather your god still hasn't shown up," I said, my voice hoarse, trying to distract myself.

I received four nasty glares.

"We would have traded you to the Guardians' Assembly if you didn't know too much," said Klara.

"I don't think they would have traded with you," I said.

"I wouldn't be so sure. I imagine they aren't happy you've broken the centuries' old barriers between the realms, bringing the world back to the way it used to be. Back to the way it should be. They call you the Skybreaker."

Guilt bubbled in my chest, but I pushed it down. I couldn't let them get under my skin.

"I thought you need me to keep you safe. Because apparently the Guardians aren't as useless as you thought. Otherwise, you wouldn't be hiding in the tunnels."

"You aren't fully a Guardian," said Klara, swirling the wine in her glass. "You're a hybrid. You're uniquely suited to serve as a bridge between the Guardian and the sorcerers' era."

I didn't have energy to continue the conversation. It didn't lead anywhere nor raise my spirits. I didn't learn anything new. I couldn't even enjoy being out of my cell or the crystal room because my head kept pounding and every little movement made me feel sick.

"Speaking of Guardians," said Filip, glancing at me with a malicious gleam in his eye. "I wonder how our other non-Guardian is faring. Or if she's still faring at all."

My head snapped up. Zuzanna. Did they know something about her, what could have happened to her after she'd rejected her Guardian heritage and flown away with Aysun?

"She should be long dead," said Klara. "She stupidly bound her lifeforce to the city and we've broken the devil's bargains, destabilizing the city, pushing her past her limits."

I remembered that night too well. Zuzanna lying lifeless on the floor in the Guardian's flat, Aysun crying over her, the domowik trying to comfort her. I'd pushed my magic into Zuzanna, I'd woken her up. I'd given her a chance to pass on the Guardian's ring to me. But what if it hadn't been enough? What if it had been too late? What if Zuzanna had died trying to buy us more time, trying to protect the city which hated her?

My hands shook and I fixed my eyes on the floor, trying to ignore Filip's stare.

"She made it too easy," he said, his eyes boring holes in me.

I don't know how much longer I sat there, trying to not collapse but also wishing for my brain to stop thinking about how I'd failed Zuzanna. How I'd failed everyone. I was too exhausted to feel much but it didn't stop my mind from spinning.

At last, Filip got up and gestured for me to follow him. I heaved myself off the pillows while Klara, Paulina, and Agata continued lounging and snacking on the food. Filip pulled me out of the room and down the narrow, dimly-lit tunnels. Magical vines reached for my hair and snatched my cloak, but I didn't have the energy to fight them.

"Don't think you're getting anything else to eat tonight," said Filip, his fingers digging into my arm.

I didn't expect to. I just wanted to collapse on my mattress and sleep forever.

We were close to my cell when Filip's grasp around my shoulder loosened. He fell to the ground with a loud thump.

I took a step back, staring at his prone figure. Was he dead? What had happened? I looked around, my head swimming, nausea rising in my throat, but the shadows on the walls stayed still.

Was it a trap?

I walked a few more steps away but I was so dizzy I had to stop and lean on the wall. I took a couple of deep breaths and when I opened my eyes, Filip was still unmoving on the floor, the shadows motionless.

Leaning on the wall, I walked deeper into the corridor. I could barely remain upright, exhaustion making me sick. At least my magic was blocked so I couldn't feel it pushing at me from everywhere, because then I surely would have thrown up or collapsed on the stone floor crying.

Steps echoed behind me and I forced myself to speed up. My hands were shaking, but adrenaline filled my body.

I couldn't let them get me again. Not again.

Run, I told my body. *Please, run. It's your only chance.*

Ignoring the pain, I ran, shoes smacking loudly against the stone, heart hammering in my throat. My body didn't feel mine, desperation propelling me on. I could do it. I could lose them, stay low, and then find my way out of the tunnels. The alternative was too unbearable to consider.

I waited for shadows to reach for me, to wrap their icy fingers around my limbs, but they didn't. Instead, my legs gave out and I fell. My heart skipped a beat as I braced myself for impact. Just before I collided with a floor, two strong, warm, human arms wrapped around me and pulled me upright.

THREE

A HAND MUFFLED MY SCREAM. I BIT IT AND TRIED TO kick but I didn't have energy to pull myself free. My muscles were too weak, my head spinning. It was all over. Gods, how stupid I was to think I could escape these tunnels.

"Shh," said a familiar voice my ear. "Don't scream. Everyone should be asleep but we shouldn't risk it."

Blood was roaring in my ears and it took me a moment to process these words. The hands let me go and I turned around and threw my arms around Rafi's neck. I couldn't find any words, shaking all over.

"We'll get you out," Rafi said, hugging me close to him. "But not this way. You were running in the wrong direction. We don't want to get lost in the tunnels and encounter the basilisk. *Again.*"

I managed to walk two steps before my legs gave out

again. Rafi caught me, but my whole body was begging for rest.

"Can you walk a little more? I don't know how much time we have before they wake up, and Damian has something that should help you keep your strength up."

Damian. Damian was here, too. What were they doing? Did they want to get stuck underground? The last thing I needed was having to worry about Rafi and Damian being here, too.

"Come," said Rafi, wrapping his arm around me for support. He was a head taller than me so it was uncomfortable, but we managed to stumble back towards the Children of Weles' lair.

A dark shape appeared down the tunnel and my fingers bit into Rafi's arm, certain that the shadows were moving again. I was ready to plead with him to run, to get out of here while he still could, but he squeezed me to his side.

"It's Damian," he whispered.

But my heart stopped hammering only when the boy was within eyesight. His eyes looked a little wild, emphasized by dark bags underneath, his dark hair a mess. He pulled a small bottle, filled with amber liquid, out of the pocket of his jacket.

"Drink it," he said. "It's temporary but will give you enough strength to get out of here."

My hands were shaking too badly, so Damian unscrewed the bottle and helped me hold it, making sure I wouldn't drop it. The liquid didn't have a taste, but it burned my throat and filled my stomach with warmth. Heat radiated to my limbs and soon I could stand on my own. I was still lightheaded and my legs and arms didn't feel like my own, they were strangely detached, but strong, and that was what counted.

"Let's get out of here," said Damian.

We scurried down the tunnels, Damian leading the way, lighting it up with a torch. Every loose pebble we kicked, every flicker of the torchlight made me jump and look around.

"You didn't eat any food, did you?" asked Rafi and I shook my head. "Good. We added sleeping potion to the food, but we didn't expect them to invite you for dinner. Damian was trying to pass the message to you telepathically, but the bond between the two of you isn't very reliable."

"I could feel it," I said. "Not really hear, but I knew I shouldn't touch the food."

I didn't know we could do that but we'd never tested our bond.

"How did you manage it?"

"Long hours of stalking. Most of their food still comes from the Clavichord Café storage and Klara's shadows patrol only the tunnels."

Damian pushed a door open with his shoulder, and I winced at a loud creak. He nodded at us to follow and we found ourselves in a wooden staircase, climbing the stairs two at once. As we made our way to the door, the hall flooded with red light. Damian reached for the doorhandle but it was locked. He swore, then put both his hands on the door. After a couple of moments, there was a crashing sound, like someone chewing on ice, and Damian pushed the door open.

We emerged onto a street a few blocks away from the old market square. It was dark and there were no lights neither in street lamps nor in the windows of the low tenements fencing the street, but the cobblestones were painted in an eerie red glow. High above, a long line split the sky nearly in two, the unnatural light flooding through it and illuminating the night sky.

The colour of the red light matched my Guardian's cloak perfectly.

I knew the hole in the sky wouldn't close itself but the sight still froze me. Maybe running away was a horrible idea. Maybe the Children of Weles were right and channelling my magic into city defences was the least I could do. After all, if not for my ancestors, the past Guardians, none of it would have happened. And if not for our Circle of Four, the sky would be whole now.

"Come," said Rafi. He put his arm around me and pulled me down the street, melting snow crunching under our feet.

The cold bit my nose and I could see my breath but none of it felt real. Maybe I was dreaming, maybe I'd lost consciousness chained to the crystal. Rafi and Damian couldn't really be here.

We made it to Aunt Eliza's blue Opel. Rafi opened the back door and I slid in, followed by Damian. Rafi took the driver's seat.

"You can't drive," I protested, buckling up.

"I'm still a better driver than Damian. Besides, it's not like there's a crazy traffic around here." He turned on an engine and released the clutch too early, throwing us all forward. I put my hand to my mouth, trying not to throw up.

On the third try, Rafi managed to get us rolling towards the main road.

"Let's go home."

"Home" turned out to be our summerhouse, a tiny, one-room cabin not far from the city. I didn't have the energy to question it—my body was demanding immediate sleep and two-week holiday on an island where it's always sunny and warm. The only protest I made was when the boys offered me to share the sofa bed—sleeping trapped next to someone else in the crumpled space seemed like a nightmare. I quickly washed myself in a bowl of water heated up with Damian's magic, changed into some old clothes, took out a sleeping mat and a sleeping bag, and almost immediately fell asleep next to a crackling fireplace, while Damian walked around with an incense, whispering spells under his breath.

I didn't sleep long before I sat up bolt upright, screaming murder. My heart hammered, my body begging me to run but I couldn't move, couldn't move, couldn't move…

I gasped for breath, struggling to break free. The fire was slowly dying but cast enough light for me to see that I was in the summerhouse. That I'd only tangled myself in the sleeping bag. That, for now, I was safe and alive.

Damian got up from the sofa. Rafi was awake, too. Of course. My screaming wasn't exactly subtle and we were all jumpy.

Neither of the boys asked if I were okay. It would have been a waste of breath.

I tried to untangle myself from the sleeping bag. Damian threw another log into the fire, and the flames hissed and sparkles blew. I flinched and struggled to find the zipper, frantic to get out, my heart racing.

Damian walked over, kneeled by my side and unzipped my sleeping bag in one move. I felt stupid. Useless. Unable to do even such a simple task. But his eyes fixed on my forearms, the deep, angry red welts around my wrists left by the crystal, and the badly healed red scratches all over my forearms and hands from when the latawiec had attacked me in the forest.

"I have something that can help," Damian said. "And you're sleeping on the sofa. There's enough space for us all."

He helped me to my feet and I followed him to the window, where he'd set up his witchy equipment.

"Give me your hands," said Damian, reaching for a glass jar full of sticky green poultice. I hesitated for a moment, then forced myself to extend my palms towards him.

He wasn't going to hurt me. I could trust him.

Probably.

"Look, it smells nice," he said, extending the jar towards me. I sniffed it obediently, taking in the calming rosemary smell. "It might feel a little cool."

He took a big dollop of the poultice on his fingers and smeared a thick layer over my arms, paying special attention to my wrists.

"I'm going to bandage it, okay?" he asked, retreating a few steps to the kitchen to bring a long piece of gauze.

I nodded and he wrapped it lightly around my forearms and tied a loose knot.

"Now, let's get some sleep."

Everything afterwards was a blur. There was the heavy smell of burning wood and herbs, the first reminding me of the endless, carefree summers spent in this summerhouse with Rafi and Kari, the latter of the protection rituals I'd done with Zuzanna. I was warm, covers piled on top of me, often nestled next to someone. I was never alone but in a good way, looked after by people whom I trusted.

I slept and slept, and slept some more. I woke up only to drink water and eat porridge or rice, then fell back to sleep.

Until one time when I opened my eyes and didn't feel the need to fall back asleep again. The summerhouse was blanketed in darkness, the only source of light a crackling fireplace. Rafi and Damian sat in front of it on a sleeping bag, playing cards.

The sofa bed squeaked when I moved and the boys looked up.

"Do you need anything?" Rafi said, getting up to his feet immediately. "I'll get you some water. And more rice."

"No," I protested, my voice croaky. "I mean, yes, please but I can…I don't want you to…You can't keep running around for me like that."

Rafi ignored me and went to the kitchenette. He poured me some water from a big, five-litre bottle and put some more plain rice into a bowl.

"You don't have to jump to my side every time I move," I said.

I pushed myself to a sitting position and my head swam. I took a deep breath, steadying myself.

Rafi put the glass into my hands and the bowl on the table next to me. I held the glass with both of my hands, its cool surface grounding me.

"You need food and rest," he said.

"No. I need to…" I trailed off, unsure how to finish the sentence.

I wouldn't be here if I hadn't been arrogant enough to believe I could change the world. The barrier between the realms was broken and now that I wasn't channelling my magic into the crystal, probably all hell was breaking loose. Even before the sky had broken, we'd seen a god take up a human form. What if now they could cross into Jawia in their divine forms?

What about Artur and Karina? What about my mum?

What about the city?

My hands were shaking so much that I had to put the glass away, magic slipping away from me. To my surprise, I didn't hate feeling its warmth on my skin. There was no foreign magic invading mine and no one was taking it away from me. It wasn't overwhelming.

But I still had no control over it and the glass on the table exploded into a million pieces, the shreds of glass raining around us. The fire in the fireplace roared louder.

Damian came to my side and extended his hand.

"You don't have to," he said, as I stared at his outstretched hand. "We can find a way for you to spend your magic yourself."

"I can't control it," I whispered, blood roaring in my ears. Something else crashed and I flinched, my eyes wet with tears.

"You can," Damian said. "We can strengthen the wards around this place."

"I can't," I repeated. I closed my eyes, trying to stop the tears threatening to burst free and reached blindly for Damian. He caught my hand and intertwined our fingers, but he didn't pull on my magic. His hand was warm but normal human warm and not warm with magic. If he felt mine, he didn't show it.

"I won't take it from you," said Damian. "But if you want to share it, I'm here."

I pushed my magic into him. I couldn't hold it in anymore and I couldn't risk burning the place down or blowing something up. I couldn't worry about that, too.

Tears ran down my face, my breaths coming in shallow but I kept pushing my magic away. It wasn't at all like in the tunnels but I didn't like being reminded that I was just a conduit for magic. The sofa bed squeaked as Damian sat next to me. He put his free arm around me, pulling me in, until I was sobbing into his jumper. He ran his hand up and down my back, but neither he nor Rafi spoke.

FOUR

I WOKE UP CUDDLED INTO DAMIAN, HIS ARMS WRAPPED around me. For the first time, his skin was tickling with magic but it wasn't the violent push I'd felt in the tunnels but a pleasant, warm tickle of a magical bond that I knew so well. If the magic in the tunnels felt like holding your hand too close to a fire, our bond was like hot chocolate. And because of its comfort and familiarity, pain sliced through me, crushing my lungs.

I couldn't feel my bond with Artur.

My eyes were puffy from crying, my head pounding. I disentangled myself from Damian's arms and propped myself up. Where was Artur? Why couldn't I feel our bond? What had happened after the shadows dragged us apart?

"Water?" Rafi asked.

"I can get it," I said, but before I could get off the sofa bed, Rafi returned with a glass.

My throat was parched, and I gulped its contents down in one go. Rafi extended his hand for the glass, but I cradled it against my chest.

"Please, stop," I said. "You can't jump at my whim."

"You aren't a burden," said Damian.

"You had to rescue me," I said. "I forced you to perform a ritual and it broke down the rest of the barriers between the realms, and then I was stupid enough to run straight to the Guardian's tenement and you had to get me out of there and now I can't even get myself a glass of water."

"No one forced me to do the ritual," said Damian. "If I hadn't wanted to do it, I wouldn't have. You were trying to save as many people as possible and when that failed, you tried again, and again. The least we can do is to offer you a glass of water or a hug."

"But we can't go on like this. It's bad enough if it happens once or twice but you can't keep doing this."

"Well, hopefully, it won't last forever," said Rafi. "But we can bear with you for some more time. Would you like some tea for a change? I could drink some tea."

I nodded, still feeling miserable. I didn't want them running around me like that. Especially the two of them. Rafi always did that when I was particularly low and it was bad enough, but Damian?

"Witch boy?" asked Rafi. "I could use your magic hands."

There was a fraction of a smile on Damian's face as he obediently went to the kitchenette. The electricity wasn't working—it was always shut off for the winter, not that it mattered since I didn't think the city had electricity now, either—so Rafi poured water into three mugs and Damian wrapped his hands around them until the water inside bubbled and steam rose. They reused the same teabag for all of them, and, after a few minutes, added honey and raspberry syrup which Aunt Eliza had made from the berries growing in the garden.

"You aren't a burden," repeated Damian, handing me a cup of tea.

"What day is it?" I asked, trying to change the topic.

"The twelfth of December."

I ran numbers in my head. We'd performed the ritual that had broken the sky on first…second of December? I'd spent days in the tunnels, at least a week, depending on how long I'd been in the summerhouse. Three days? Four?

Time made no sense and the calculations were useless, either way. A lifetime had passed, everything had changed. There were more important things I needed to know.

"Do you know what happened to Karina? And Artur?"

Damian nodded, but he didn't elaborate.

"What have you been doing all this time? Were you hiding out here? How did you find each other?"

"When our ritual failed and the barriers between the realms fell, I was in the middle of nowhere and it took me forever to get back to the city. I knew it was stupid but I didn't know where else to go and I needed to find out what happened to the rest of you."

"You should have run," I murmured.

Damian smiled weakly. "Things got really bad before I got back to the city. People broke into supermarkets, fighting for food and medicine. The military was on the streets, threatening to shoot. And I knew where Karina lived and it was on the way so I decided to check there. But she wasn't there, only Rafi."

"My mum was freaking out and Karina was nowhere to be found, which didn't help," said Rafi. "I had to tell her what was going on and she didn't believe me, but then Damian came in and performed all these protective spells in our flat and they helped. And then griffins flew outside of our window and Mum couldn't pretend they were just overgrown pigeons."

"We waited for Karina," said Damian. "She came back just before it got dark; the car had run out of petrol. We wanted to head out and look for you and Artur, but your mum and Tomasz came. Your mum was still pretty out of it after the ritual, but they hoped to stop us before we went after you. They said that the Children of Weles took over and that if we weren't careful, they'd capture us, too."

"We weren't sure they had you, but it was a pretty safe bet," said Rafi. "We knew you'd run straight for the Guardian's tenement to try to recreate some protections and we knew Artur would run after you. We tried to come up with a plan and Mum was getting more and more weirded out, because your mum wasn't behaving like herself at all. Suddenly she was all about magic, demons, and realms. Not to mention that she brought Tomasz with her. But as much as they wanted to get you out, they insisted that the four of you can't be caught together. It was bad enough that the Children of Weles had you and Artur, and they also knew about Damian. We had to keep him as far away from them as possible and make sure they wouldn't find out about Karina."

"Your mum remembered she had a secret hideout in the city centre. An old house near the court."

"No, she doesn't," I said.

"It was your dad's."

"My dad doesn't have a house in the city centre either. Come on, he emigrated so we wouldn't have to choose between paying bills and getting groceries."

"He means Zuzanna's brother," said Damian.

"Oh."

"Yes. So, we divided time between there and Rafi's flat, making sure we wouldn't draw too much attention to ourselves. We also scouted out this place, to make sure it was liveable. And, of course, we tried to find out what happened to you and how to get you out."

"Your mum wanted us to bring you to her. But I didn't think it was the best idea. That, maybe, you'd like to recover first without dealing with her, too."

"Thank you," I said.

Just the thought of talking to my mum made my throat clench. It was counterintuitive. For so long, all I'd wanted was for her to remember about magic, to tell me what to do. But the mum who talked about demons and realms and magic sounded like a stranger to me.

"So, Karina is with them," I said and Rafi nodded. "There is one other person you're awfully quiet about."

Rafi looked down, inspecting his thick woollen socks. They were purple, pink, and blue—the colours of the bi flag, knitted by Karina. Damian glanced at me but he looked away immediately, unable to hold my gaze. My stomach squeezed painfully.

"What about Artur?"

The boys exchanged glances.

"We know where he is," said Rafi slowly, measuring each word. "Do you maybe want more tea?"

The deflection stung. My heart beat faster, my lungs constricting. What wasn't he telling me? Where was Artur?

No matter how hard I searched, I couldn't feel our bond.

"You're not helping," said Damian. "He's in the tunnels. The Children of Weles got him."

I squeezed my eyes shut and pressed my shaking hands against them. My mind spun, memories of Artur pushing Klara away and the shadow holding him down before we could escape inscribing themselves on my eyelids. Klara had told him she wouldn't hurt magic users, that they needed everyone to build the new world, but when he left, she called him gullible.

That's why I couldn't feel our bond. The strong magic in the tunnels was masking it.

"Why didn't you get him out?" I asked.

"Because he's been turned to stone."

My heart stopped.

"What?"

"The Children of Weles secured cooperation of the magic users through intimidation. Whoever defies them faces the basilisk."

I swore and slumped forwards, energy fleeing my body. The tunnels were the last place I wanted to be, but I had to free Artur. Only how do you save someone turned into stone?

Damian put a hand on my knee and magic sparkled between us. I looked up at him.

"We'll help him," he said. "We'll get him out, but we need a plan."

ᚠᛁᚢᛖ

To my disappointment, we didn't leave immediately. Instead, I got bribed with the best bath in history. It was an old metal tub on the terrace, filled with water heated up to a nice temperature with witchy powers and with balls of light levitating above. It was the most marvellous experience.

Or it would have been, if not for the dread settling in my stomach, every fibre of my body begging me to get Artur out, and the red slash tearing the sky in two. I lay there, vapour rising around my tired body into the freezing cold air, staring at the sky above, anxiety coiling in my stomach.

That night, when I fell asleep, I dreamt for the first time in a long time.

I'm at the familiar riverbank, not far from the summer-house. The sky above me is a patchwork of cracks, with the same red light streaming through it that now lights up our own sky.

"Do you want to save your mortal world, sorceress?" asks the Baba Jaga. I don't startle at its voice; I expect it there. "Do you want to earn your dream cloth and patch up the sky?"

It was something I dreamed about after the failed ritual, the last dream I had, just before the Children of Weles captured me. The Baba Jaga told me about the cloth it'd woven from my dreams, a cloth that could patch up the hole in the sky.

"Yes," I say, turning to face the demon-goddess.

Like the last time, the Baba Jaga is fully corporeal. There are deep wrinkles in its face and moss on its teeth. It's wrapped in a sheepskin, its hair covered by a scarf decorated with a folk pattern. Its gnarled fingers are wrapped around a wooden stick with a head of a żmij carved into the top end.

"Very well," says the Baba Jaga. "I have something of yours. Come and find it in the forest. We'll see if the magic is right about you."

"What am I looking for?" I ask, but the Baba Jaga disappears and the world around me blurs and vanishes.

I woke up to a scream. I sat up, head swimming, heart pounding in my chest. It was dark outside and the fireplace was once again the only source of light. Next to me, Damian sat up as well.

"Rafi," I said, my voice shaking. "Where is Rafi?"

He wasn't in the small room or in the bathroom. Damian glanced outside but I knew it was all for nothing.

"The Baba Jaga has him," I said, wrapping my arms around myself.

"What?"

"I dreamt of the Baba Jaga. It hasn't visited me since the Children of Weles got to me. But the last time it told me about a cloth it wove from my dreams. It could patch up the hole in the sky and save us. But to get it, I'd need to pass the trials. And the next task is to retrieve something of mine."

"Like in a fairy tale. A hero on a journey encounters a Baba Jaga and must pass three trials to prove their courage or cunning."

"We need to go."

Damian shook his head. "You need to go alone. It's your trial. And I need to redo the protections here. If the Baba Jaga got in, we don't want to know what else can wiggle through."

I pulled on my shoes and Damian's jumper and jacket, while he spelled a lantern for me, sprinkling herbs onto the candle and whispering spells over it. He passed it to me together with a bottle filled with amber liquid.

"It will help, but don't drink more than a mouthful."

I took a swig of the liquid and it burned my throat, filling my body with warmth. I put the vial in my pocket, grabbed the lantern, and left the summerhouse.

"Wiki," Damian called after me. "The forest isn't what you remember it to be."

It was deathly quiet outside. Cold wind and a flurry of snowflakes blew into my face and I zipped up Damian's jacket. I walked across the half-frozen garden, the red light catching in the frost on the grass and branches. Nothing felt real, it was like a fairy tale, and between that, my frozen skin, and numb-from-disuse muscles, it perhaps made no sense to wander off on my own into danger.

I took a deep breath and momentarily regretted it as the cold winter air stung my lungs. I coughed as I exited the garden onto a narrow, sandy path between two rows of summerhouses. I made my way towards the forest, my heart hammering in my chest.

I quickly understood Damian's cryptic warning. And it was an understatement. The pine trees were at least twice as tall as before, stretching a good fifty metres up, so tall that their snow-capped ends seemed to brush the gaping red hole in the sky, and so thick I'd have had a problem embracing one of them. I hesitated for a moment, but only for a moment. I needed to get Rafi back.

Once I stepped onto the forest path, magic cocooned me tighter, like a rough blanket. The magic felt different here, wilder, unused to humans, The branches of the pine and birch trees creaked and cracked, and soft, unintelligible whispers sounded from the darkness. I kept my eyes on the path in front of me, trying to focus on the warm, yellow light of my lantern and not the red light of the tear between the worlds.

The forest was filled with whispers and giggles, the snow and the tree branches rustling and crunching. I was in a demonic world now. Every once in a while, a shadow shifted along the edge of my lantern light, causing shivers to run down my spine. Klara's shadows chasing after me? Demons hunting for their dinner? And was it bad I'd rather be dragged by demons further into the forest, maybe even into Nawia, than for Klara's shadows to take me back to the tunnels?

Something screeched in the bushes, then soft fur touched my legs and I gasped. I stepped back, trying to put distance between the thing and me. The demon looked at me, two red eyes gleaming amid shiny brown fur. It screeched again and skittled under the bushes.

I stared into the dark forest. Going off-path was the worst possible idea, but leaving Rafi there alone wasn't an option.

I walked between the trees. Snowflakes fell slowly to the ground, the eerie red light seeping from the tear in the sky making them look more like drops of blood. Frost crunched under my feet but magic in the air latched onto me, keeping me warm.

It's just magic, I told myself, trying to keep myself steady. *Magic itself isn't either good or bad, it's just energy.*

It was difficult to remember this as I was on a rescue mission to find a cousin abducted by an all-powerful demon.

A howl ripped through the night and my heart stuttered. The demonic whispers intensified and was that crunching of the snow? I didn't wait to find out. I broke into a run, the flame in the lantern jumping as I tore through the snow.

But I didn't make it far before my head swam and my weak muscles shook. I tried to go on but my vision went spotty and I leaned on the tree, fighting to breathe.

Snow crunched and I had to force myself to look. Two golden eyes gleamed in the dark. I remembered what Artur had told me weeks ago, about going to the forest after dark. If you made it back, it meant that the god of night, Chors, was looking after you.

Some believed he needed a blood sacrifice.

And ever since the sky had broken, we'd known the return of the gods was imminent.

I didn't have a knife but I was desperate. I brought my palm against the tree and scraped it, hard, against the bark. I hissed in pain but warmth blossomed down my hand.

"Please accept my sacrifice, Chors," I whispered into the night. "Please keep me safe in the forest tonight."

Blood leaked down my hand and I held my breath. Was it a mistake? Would the beast attack? But the golden eyes blinked and the creature (animal? demon? god?) retreated into the darkness.

I put snow against my aching palm and walked on between the trees. The demonic whispers hushed and I walked with renewed confidence. Hopefully, hopefully, I had divine protection now.

Hopefully attracting the god's attention wasn't a mistake and wouldn't backfire.

My instincts guided me ahead, pulling so strongly I almost started questioning it. Wasn't it too easy? What if

Baba Jaga was misleading me on purpose?

The trees grew denser, their massive trunks so close together it was difficult to walk. I meandered between the trees more slowly, moving away the branches that kept smacking my face and clothes.

I almost missed it. A low gurgling sound made me stop. I spun around and I saw toads. There were at least ten of them and they were *massive*, so big I wouldn't have been able to wrap my arms around them. They stared at me, gurgling and groaning, and I took a step back, colliding with the tree.

The toads were brooding eggs. The eggs looked like regular chicken eggs, so at first I didn't notice them under the toads' massive bodies. Each toad was sitting on dozens upon dozens on eggs, and the eggs stunk of something rotting.

They were brooding basilisks.

I took a step back, shaking, and stumbled over something. I caught my balance and looked behind my back. Half hidden in the overgrown underbrush was Rafi. He lay on his stomach in the snow under a huge bush, squeezed next to a gigantic toad, his dark jumper and hair making him almost invisible in the night forest.

My heart thundered as I moved towards him. The toads turned to look at me as I approached, gurgling and groaning. Magic prickled my skin as I stepped carefully, trying to stay as far away from the toads as possible.

"Rafi," I hissed.

The toads gurgled louder and I flinched but my cousin didn't move. I touched his leg. No reaction. With effort, I rolled him onto his back. His clothes were soaked through with snow but his chest rose and fell gently, his breath misting in the cold air.

"Rafi," I whispered, shaking him.

He groaned and opened his eyes a fraction. He stared at me for a couple of moments, then he sat up suddenly, almost hitting me with his head.

"What the—" He stopped, staring at the toads.

Rafi winced and touched his head. Then he giggled. *Giggled.*

"Toads, Wiwi! Look at these massive toads!" he called, his voice echoing down the forest.

"*Shh!*"

The toads gurgled and groaned, shifting uneasily. Rafi reached forwards and almost touched the closest toad before I snatched his hand.

"What are you doing?" I asked, but my cousin laughed louder, folding in half.

It must have been part of the Baba Jaga's trial.

"Okay. We need to get out of here," I said. "Can you walk?"

Rafi kept on laughing and I sighed. I stood up and clutched his hand, trying to pull him up. But Rafi only pulled me down in the snow. The toad next to me groaned loudly as I spluttered snow.

"This isn't funny. We need to go, now."

I pulled myself up to my feet and tried to drag Rafi after me. This time, he got up, but he couldn't walk straight. I caught his arm just before he barrelled straight into a toad. I put my arm around Rafi but he was a head taller and much stronger than me, so whenever he side stepped, I was pulled after him. It took us a good couple of moments to get away from the toads.

They didn't try to stop me. They just kept on gurgling and groaning.

But…the eggs.

I looked at them. There were hundreds of potential basilisks here.

Rafi giggled again and I shook my head. No. I wasn't here to deal with it. It wasn't my place to intervene. The Baba Jaga had made it clear I was supposed to retrieve what was mine. The trial wasn't to destroy the basilisk's eggs.

I hoped.

Manoeuvring in snow, in narrow spaces between huge trees, with a cousin behaving like he was drunk, took forever. Rafi kept giggling and dragging me into bushes. We fell more than once and we were both soaked by snow and shivering.

"Nap?" suggested Rafi as we fell for the third time.

"Absolutely not," I said, pulling on his hand to get him up.

"Just five minutes," he murmured.

I smashed snow into his face. Rafi spluttered and pulled me down next to him. I swallowed a scream as he pushed snow under my jacket. I smacked him and we rolled in the snow, Rafi laughing, me fighting hard not to push him away with my magic. He didn't know what he was doing. After a few moments, Rafi got up and we walked on. The demons hid from us as we crashed through the forest, making too much noise.

I wanted to cry when we made it back to the summerhouse complex. Instead, I looked up at the moon, dimmed by the red crack in the sky, and whispered:

"Thank you, Chors."

I dragged Rafi back to the summerhouse. Damian was pacing by the fireplace, but he stopped when he saw us.

"You made it," he said, relief plain in his voice.

"DAMIAN!" shouted Rafi, tearing away from me and throwing his arms around Damian's neck, drenching him, too. Damian swayed under Rafi's weight.

Damian looked at me terrified, his eyes wide. Despite my shivering, I managed a shrug.

"He woke up like this," I said.

I wanted to collapse on the sofa but I needed to find dry clothes first. Damian beckoned me to him and he took my hands in his. Magical warmth flooded me and my clothes steamed and dried within seconds.

"That's a really cool trick," I said.

"It is. I haven't felt cold since you've shared magic with me. Alchemy is amazing."

I plopped down on the sofa. My eyes were closing, my muscles screaming for a reprieve, but we needed to take care of Rafi.

"You're so beautiful," he said, twirling Damian's hair between his fingers.

I raised an eyebrow at Damian.

"Should I leave or…"

"Shut up and help me."

It took at least an hour for whatever was wrong with Rafi to wear off. An hour of him dancing around the house and singing, and making googly eyes at Damian who was pointedly ignoring him.

Then, like a switch turned off, the energy left him. Rafi dropped down next to the fireplace, his shoulders sagging, his eyes drooping close.

"Feeling any better?" asked Damian.

Rafi laughed but it wasn't the same recklessly happy laughter as before. He sounded tired. "You call that better? Because for a few moments here I felt happier than I had in weeks. And trust me, coming back to reality isn't fun."

"What happened? How did the Baba Jaga get to you?"

"The Baba Jaga? I don't know. I was asleep and the next thing I remember is you waking me up and everything feeling weird."

It was nearly dawn now and none of us felt like going back to sleep. We made and ate rice with strawberry jam.

"Feels sacrilegious," said Damian, looking at the meal.

"Don't you eat rice with fruit in the summer?" asked Rafi.

"Pasta with blueberries and sour cream. Not rice with *jam*."

Despite his protests, Damian inhaled his meal fast. We were lucky Aunt Eliza loved making winter preserves in the summerhouse and always made sure we had a stash of non-perishable basics. We had a camp stove, a witch, and an alchemist. But what about the other people out there?

"We could leave today," I said once I'd inhaled all my rice so fast, I nearly choked.

"You need more time to recover," said Rafi.

"I'm fine," I protested.

"Liar," murmured Damian.

"Fine," said Rafi. "Whatever you say. But *I* need more time, too. At least another night of sleep. We're safe and peaceful here, we have enough food to stay a bit more."

I looked at Damian.

"Are we safe?"

He shrugged. "As safe as we can be."

I gritted my teeth. My heart felt heavy, my stomach squeezed with anxiety. I could feel Damian's presence through the bond now but I hadn't forgotten my other bondmate.

"We can't just camp here and enjoy ourselves while Artur is in the tunnels."

"He's been turned into stone," said Damian. "Not ideal, but I don't think it should make much difference if we free him tonight or a week from now."

"And how would you know he isn't aware of everything or in pain? How much research is there about how it feels to be turned into stone by a basilisk?"

Damian huffed out breath.

"I want to get him out as well, okay? But we need a

plan. We need to be able to get in and out undetected and, most importantly, we need to know how to un-stone Artur. Also, unless you're eager to get caught, you need to get your strength back first."

I shook my head. It was taking too long. There would always be reasons to wait and Artur was stuck there, turned into stone, going through gods knew what. I hoped he wasn't aware of what was going on, stuck in some magical sleep, but what if that wasn't true? What if he was conscious, unable to move, or in pain?

"Stop doing it!" snapped Damian.

"I'm not doing anything, that's the problem."

Damian brushed his hand through his hair, pulling on it.

"Your mind is spinning and it's driving me crazy."

His eyes were shut, his face twisted in a grimace.

"You can feel my emotions," I said.

"Unfortunately."

There was a beat as my mind rushed to understand what it meant.

"I'm sorry," I said. "I can shield it, I'm not as good as Artur, but it's something. I just didn't know it was necessary."

I didn't know you could feel them, I finished telepathically.

"That would be appreciated," said Damian, his head still cradled in his hands.

Can you hear me? I tried again, but got no reaction, so I asked out loud:

"Can you read my mind, too?"

"Gods, no, thank you."

Slowly, I reached out and touched Damian's shoulder. Magic sparkled between us, warm and comforting.

"You can feel that, though, right?"

Damian nodded.

"Could you look at me?"

He nodded again but it took him a moment to lift his head. When his eyes met mine, for a moment I thought they were his usual dark brown. But as our eye contact held, slowly, specks of gold appeared in his irises, mesmerising me.

"It's getting weird," said Rafi and I let go of Damian's arm and twisted around to face him. "Just a reminder that we're sharing these twelve square metres together, the three of us. Three. And she's my cousin." He pointed at me.

"I'm gay," said Damian, rising his eyebrow in a challenge. "A magical bond doesn't change that."

I marvelled at his certainty. The bond between Artur and me often confused me, made it hard to understand my feelings. But there was no hesitation in Damian's voice. The day before we'd broken the interdimensional barrier when we'd talked about attraction. Damian had been certain of his feelings, too. He could distinguish between attractions and knew that he'd only experienced romantic attraction once, without hesitation. How could people be so certain of their feelings, especially when magic was involved?

Then again, I didn't feel attraction towards Damian, either. I felt comfortable around him because we'd made it clear we weren't compatible at all and nothing that wasn't purely platonic would ever happen between us.

"Lie to me," I said.

"Winter is my favourite season, I love cold," said Damian. His words felt like someone pushed needles into my skin and I flinched.

So, I could sense his lies.

"But your birthday is in winter," I said.

"The worst timing, because it's basically Christmas and no one bothers to celebrate it properly."

The birthday thing made me realize something. I turned back to Rafi.

"We missed your birthday!"

Rafi shrugged. "Happy seventeen to me. Glad to have made it through my sixteenth year alive."

"When was your birthday?" asked Damian.

"Last week. The ninth of December."

Rafi usually made a big deal out of his birthday, claiming the whole week before and after as his birthday weeks, which served him as an excuse for being extra loud and over-the-top as well as eating lots of cake. But now it seemed like he couldn't care less, and Rafi wasn't the sort of person who could hide his emotions.

"We'll catch up when the sky is fixed," I promised.

SIX

Rafi drove us the long way around the city, staying in the forest for as long as possible. The trees everywhere grew on magic, doubling in size, reaching so tall and their branches so thick that they were blocking off most of the gaping hole in the sky. Only slivers of the strange light made it through, lighting up the road in grotesque red. The gnarled branches of the trees stood guard on both sides of the road, the shadows they cast in the headlights terrifying.

I kept expecting the shadows to move, to grasp me, drag me out of the car kicking and screaming, for Klara to emerge from the shadows, but nothing happened. I grasped the car seat tightly, magic humming on my skin as we rode through the darkness in silence. Even Rafi, who usually talked enough for the three of us, was quiet, eyes fixed on the road in front of us.

It made sense now why for the longest time people had been deadly scared of the forests and wrote so many fairy tales revolving around the beasts lurking there.

"How do you have enough petrol to drive so far?" I asked. "I'd imagine it would be one of the first things to go during apocalypse."

It was already difficult to get it when the barrier between the realms was only weakening. People had been hoarding for weeks and now they couldn't count on any imports from the outside. We were cut off from the world.

"Alchemy," said Damian.

"Took a bit of trial and error and almost ruined the engine but now it's working," said Rafi.

"If you mean you can turn water into petrol or something like that, you could get insanely rich," I said.

A movement on the side of the road drew my attention. Before I could open my mouth, Damian screamed:

"Watch out!"

The car swerved as a deer jumped onto the road in front of us. Magic rushed out of me, unbidden, and the car bounced off an invisible barrier and back into the road before we could crash into a tree.

"Jesus," said Rafi, his hands shaking on the steering wheel.

The deer stopped in the middle of the road, staring at the car. Just like the trees, the animal looked much bigger than any deer I'd seen before, easily the size of a moose with equally massive antlers. A shiver ran down my spine as I realized that green ivy climbed up one of its antlers. For a second, I thought its eyes flashed red, then it jumped on into the forest, disappearing between the trees.

"You're better than an air bag," said Rafi, but his voice trembled.

"I can try to drive," I offered.

Not that I had any driving skills but I didn't want to feel useless anymore and Rafi didn't seem in a state to continue.

Rafi sat still for a couple of moments before nodding.

A long while later, we made it in one piece back to the city. When we got to the outskirts, we turned off the headlights and hid the car in the bushes on the side of the road.

The city was quiet as we walked down narrow streets, manoeuvring between buildings and trees, trying to stay as invisible as possible. The streets were lit up only by the red light streaming from the broken sky. The windows in the buildings we passed were dark, with only an occasional flicker of a candle betraying that the city wasn't abandoned. No cars, no streetlamps, no flashing signs on stores. No signs of life. Only the disturbing red light, magic warming up my skin, and thawing icy snow under our feet.

Soon, I was out of breath and a stitch stung my side, but anxiety propelled me forwards. In the forest I'd been scared of powerful magic and demons. Here, I was scared of humans. And the difference was that with the demons at least there was a benefit of doubt whether they wished me harm.

With humans, there was no doubt.

I understood why Rafi and Damian had been happy to stay in the summerhouse for as long as we could. The forest looked like something out of a dark fairytale but the city was purely apocalyptic.

Aunt Eliza's place was the closest to where we'd left the car but we'd decided it was too risky to go there—the Children of Weles undoubtedly knew about it. Instead, we made for the mysterious house left behind by my biological father, sticking to the backroads.

As we walked down the dark, empty alleys, the silence was broken by a loud rumble of a car engine. Rafi pulled me further into the shadows, behind a corner of the nearest building.

"The city is under curfew," boomed a powerful voice through a megaphone and I jumped. "Anyone found outside after dark will be subject to the martial court."

"Something you forgot to mention?" I whispered. Rafi looked away.

We waited for the sound of the engine to drown in the night before Damian waved at us to move on.

By the time we got to the mysterious house, I was glad Damian and Rafi had insisted on me regaining strength before leaving the summerhouse. The stitch in my side grew stronger and I could hardly catch my breath but I made it without faceplanting into the pavement. My muscles were shaking and I was just walking, while Rafi and Damian carried heavy bags filled with jams and preserves from the summerhouse.

We turned off a narrow road into an even narrower path leading into a park. We were on a side of a hill towering over the old town, not far away from the court, as the boys had mentioned. The Guardian's tenement was maybe a ten-minute walk away.

"Hold my hand," said Damian.

"Why?" I asked but I put my hand into his while Rafi grabbed the other.

"Because the house is only visible if you have the key. And you gave it to me."

I didn't know what he meant, but I held on to Damian's hand and let him guide us to the house. I couldn't test the house invisibility theory either as I could only make out the brick walls in the darkness when we were just in front of them.

Damian propped open a metal gate with his foot, and we walked through a wall of dense magic. It seeped under my clothes and ran along my body, touching every part of my skin. Its warmth and intrusiveness reminded me of the tenement's magic and I shivered, my body begging me to get out of there. Damian squeezed my hand harder, our bond more recognizable than ever, a steady, warm link between the two of us. Rafi stepped ahead and, using the key that Damian handed to him, opened the door.

"It's the keys you gave me," said Damian. "The keys to the Guardian's tenement? Except not only. We wouldn't have gotten here without them."

"I'd gotten them from the domowik. He'd said it's so I can always get home."

At the time, I'd assumed he'd meant the Guardian's tenement. But what if he'd meant this place?

Quietly, we walked into a dark hallway. A clock ticked loudly, the sound reverberating off the walls. I pulled the door closed behind us and we stood in complete darkness. Rafi put down the bags he was carrying and I flinched at the noise the glass made connecting with the floor.

I didn't let go of Damian's hand.

There were footsteps and a flicker of candlelight and I held my breath. A shadow appeared on a wall as the footsteps grew louder and I squashed Damian's hand.

"Hi, Aunty," said Rafi.

Mum walked down the last couple of stairs, a candle levitating in front of her. She wore a black knit jumper and a pair of jeans and her light hair was pulled back into a ponytail. She stood still at the bottom of the stairs, assessing us a for a minute, as if making sure we weren't just an illusion.

"Hi," I said, shifting from one foot to another.

Mum crossed the space between us in few fast steps and enveloped me in a hug. Damian let go of my hand, giving us space. Mum's magic hummed on my skin, and I had to force myself to hug her back.

"You're back," she whispered, her voice breaking. She didn't sound the way I remembered, there was something different about the cadence of her words, but maybe it was only my imagination.

She kissed my temple and brushed the hair out of my face, her magic uncomfortably warm on my skin. I stayed still, letting her have this moment, trying to convince myself there was no reason why my own mum's magic should make me feel sick when Damian's felt good. There was no reason why I shouldn't want her to touch me.

Mum brushed her hands through my hair, and my scalp burned, the magic on my skin too much. It was as if I were back in the tunnels again, magic pushing at me from all sides. I drew back and Mum stared at me, her hands still reaching out towards me, her eyes big, her expression crestfallen. I wasn't used to her face being so open.

I felt like the worst person in the world.

"Your magic…" I said, but I didn't know how to continue.

Because I knew that my main problem with my mum's magic was that it existed in the first place. She'd used to hate my magic and now her memory and, apparently, magic was back, and she was a different person.

"I understand it might be a tough adjustment," said Mum, her tone gentle.

She didn't have the slightest clue.

I took a deep breath. Magic still vibrated around Mum but now that we weren't touching, it was bearable. It was different from other sorcerers and it made me wonder if magic recognized people close to you or if I were oversensitive.

I wished I could ask Artur about it.

Pain sliced through me, jolting me from my misery.

Artur.

"You've done it," said Mum, hugging Rafi and Damian. "You've disappeared for so long. We worried that the worst had happened."

"We needed to make sure no one would follow us here," said Damian.

"We stayed at the summerhouse," added Rafi. "And we brought more food."

"You're amazing," said Mum. "Let's get it to the kitchen."

The bag which Rafi had put on the ground rose into the air and flew towards the kitchen, and I took a step back. It was surreal. It was one thing to know Mum was a sorceress but another to see her use magic so freely, without a second thought. And especially since it was telekinesis, the power she'd hated so much in me…

Mum looked over her shoulder and her expression fell again when she saw me standing wide-eyed. But she didn't say anything as she followed the boys into the kitchen.

The candle remained with me, suspended mid-air, wax dropping to the floor.

No. I couldn't just stand there rooted. I'd wanted Mum to remember all along, I'd fought so much to find out what she knew. What was the great plan that she, Dad and Igor had come up with before I was born. Now I had a chance to find out, I could ask her and she would have all the answers. So what if it was weird?

But also, I had other priorities.

"I need to get Artur out," I said, following Mum into the kitchen. It was spacious and old, but clean and well-maintained. "But Rafi and Damian said he's been turned to stone by a basilisk."

Mum didn't look surprised. She held my gaze while, behind her back, the preserves took themselves out of the bags and into a cabinet.

"Then the only option is to kill the basilisk."

SEVEN

I'D GOTTEN MY OWN ROOM IN THE HOUSE AND, UNUSED to the new space and consumed by conflicting emotions, I didn't fall asleep until early morning hours. By the time I made it to the kitchen, the sun was setting, the world full of deep shadows and the eerie red light seeping from the crack in the sky. Through a window framed by a white curtain I saw an empty garden, full of dried grass and melting, muddy snow. It was surrounded with a tall and simple metal fence, but, when I looked at it, I also noticed a sheet of shimmering, silvery magic. Protection magic, I hoped. Beyond the fence grew naked trees, which, similarly to the ones in the forest, rose impossibly high and grew so thick I couldn't see beyond them.

I hoped the kitchen would be empty, but Mum was there, sitting at a table and scribbling in a notebook, while dishes cleaned themselves over the sink.

I took a step back but the wooden floor under my feet creaked, alerting Mum to my presence.

"Wiki!" she said, a small smile on her face. "You're up. Would you like some tea? I'm afraid we don't have coffee but, if you close your eyes, a strong tea is almost as good."

I nodded and Mum went to a gas stove and put on a kettle.

The silence between the two of us stretched, filled only by the rattling of the kettle. I shifted my weight from foot to foot, pulling on the sleeves of Damian's jumper which I still wore. I could feel the sparkle of Mum's magic and my own magic rose to my skin, demanding to be let out.

"Where are Rafi and Damian?" I asked. "Are they still asleep?"

"They left earlier," said Mum. "It's not a good idea for too many of you to be together. In case something happens, we don't want all of you to be attacked at the same time."

I froze, my hands shaking. I pulled Damian's jumper over my hands to hide it.

They'd left?

Magic pushed harder at me and I slammed it down. Not now. I couldn't let it out and I didn't have Damian to take it from me.

I hadn't expected them to leave without a goodbye.

"I thought this place was safe?" I asked.

"We can't be too cautious."

The kettle whistled, and I flinched, the magic on my skin almost unbearable. Mum took it off the stove and poured the boiling water over a teabag.

"There you go," she said. "Do you want something to eat, too? You must be starving. We have some fresh bread baked by the domowik."

"Domowik? This place has one, too?"

"It's the Kromer's domowik," said Mum, cutting two thick slices of bread for me. "Well, yours, too, I believe. He's been taking care of this place the whole time, ever since Igor got it, keeping it clean and functional, until we remembered it. He'd been storing food, making sure we can come in anytime and stop for long. And doing that alongside taking care of the Guardian's tenement. Poor demon has a lot on his head."

Was the domowik responsible for missing supplies from the Clavichord Café? Had he been preparing us for the apocalypse all along?

"He can bake?"

"Of course. The domowik takes care of his family as long as we take care of him."

She placed the plate with bread on the big wooden table, together with an open jar of black currant jam. I reached for my mug of tea, but magic rushed out of me and the cup exploded, scorching tea blasting around. I shielded my face with my arm just in time.

"I'm sorry," I whispered, my hands shaking, magic unbearably hot on my skin. "I can clean it up, where is the—"

Before I could finish, a broom levitated towards me and swept up the broken pieces of glass onto a dustpan. The door to the cabinet opened and I stepped back as the dustpan emptied itself to a garbage can and a cloth mopped up the floor. Once the mess was cleaned, another mug took itself out of the cupboard, a teabag plopped inside, and the kettle rose and poured more water over the new cup of tea, which then flew over to the table where my mum was sitting and set itself nearly next to my plate.

I stood frozen, starting at Mum's display of magic.

"There," said Mum with a smile. "You should practice your magic. I talked about it with Tomasz, and I find it hard to believe you wouldn't be able to control it at all. At least telekinesis would be useful but I want to understand your channelling properly. If you could use the abilities of any sorcerer, that would be an incredible advantage."

I swallowed. I couldn't do it. I couldn't just stand here and pretend it was all good, that Mum and I always discussed magic in such way, that Mum had always seen it as something to be cherished and not hidden and condemned. That it was a power and not a symptom of some strange illness. That it was something to be used and honed, like a weapon.

I fisted my shaking hands and shook my head.

"I can't handle this," I said, my voice weak.

I took a step, then another, and left the kitchen, my stomach still growling.

I was hiding in my bedroom. It was big enough for an old, squeaky, queen size bed covered with a heavy patchwork quilt, and an empty wooden wardrobe with a door which wouldn't properly close, as well as a small desk and a chair by the window. A flickering candle illuminated the pale green wallpaper.

I sat curled up on the wooden chair, my knees close to my chest, playing with the sleeves of Damian's jumper. Mum had brought a pile of clothes from home for me, including a winter jacket, but Damian's jumper was the little piece of comfort I needed now. While the house was supposedly safe, I didn't believe such thing existed anymore. I packed the clothes in my backpack and left it by the door so I could pick it up and run at a moment's notice. After some hesitation, I bundled up the Guardian's cloak and put it inside as well.

I knew I was hard on my mum, I knew I was unfair but feeling her magic, seeing her use it so freely and then encouraging me to use mine...it was too much.

But I needed to get a grasp on myself, especially since it looked like Mum was my best way of getting Artur out. I wouldn't be stupid enough to try to kill the basilisk on my own. And I couldn't condemn the world because I didn't want to talk to my mum.

The longer we waited, the more time I had to panic about returning to the tunnels. I had to free Artur and I could hardly think about anything else. But there was enough room for doubts to creep in.

I'd barely gotten out last time. I would never have done it without Rafi and Damian. Just the thought of going back to the tunnels, of feeling all the intrusive magic made me nauseous.

My magic pressed at my skin and it took all my focus to keep it contained. I tried to breathe evenly but my breath hitched every time the flame of the candle expanded, my magic testing its limits. At least it was warm and in the freezing cold house it was a small blessing.

The door squeaked open, and I didn't move. I didn't want to face Mum. But then arms closed around me and the push of magic lessened and I noticed the familiar dark hair with fading blue tips.

"You're out," said Karina. "I was worried sick about you."

"You came."

"Of course I did. You're my best friend, my family, *and* we share a magical bond. I have triple responsibility to make sure you're all right."

"Should we be in the same place at the same time?"

Karina walked around to face me so I could see her roll her eyes. She wore a thick ink-blue jumper and a comfy pair of yoga trousers. She flung her backpack onto a floor next to the desk.

"I don't think isolation is a good idea. Besides, I was stuck with my mum for days in our flat. Which, don't get me wrong, I love her, but spending so much time with someone in a closed space? Without Rafi to keep us company? And with a cat who's still scared of me and Mum having so many questions about magic I can't answer? Yeah, not fun." She stopped and glanced at me, guilt flashing in her eyes. "Well, I guess it was nowhere near as bad as your week."

"Honestly, I'd much rather complain with you about your boring and awkward times."

Silence stretched between us. Karina played with the candleflame, touching it, then retreating her hand before the fire could burn her.

"That was one of Gabriella's alchemist exercises," she said after a moment. "With enough practice, I should be able to walk through the fire without it burning me. Or jump into ice-cold water without freezing to death. Thankfully magical tricks are a good distraction, otherwise I would have gone crazy with nicotine withdrawal. Or worrying about the demonic possession."

I didn't know alchemists were capable of these things. I knew that a month of intense preparations to become a Guardian of the City couldn't make up for a lifetime of knowledge but I still felt a pang of guilt. This was supposed to be my world, my people, I was supposed to know these things.

"Have you seen her since…since the ritual?"

Did Gabriella know about what her daughter, Laura, had done, was an unasked question.

Karina nodded, still playing with fire, staring at it mesmerised.

"She came to talk with your mum and Tomasz, and showed me some simple tricks, like how to heat up water without fire or electricity. Or how to clean snow so it's safe to drink. She also helped Mum grow vegetables in the kitchen fast. She tried to catch Damian but he's still avoiding her."

"How did your mum react to all of it?"

Rafi and Damian had told me about it but I still couldn't imagine how Aunt Eliza would react to this much magic.

"With what's happening outside, it would be hard not to believe in magic. But then Gabriella showed up and was straight-up, oh, so here's yet another alchemist and, can you believe that Mum wasn't even surprised? She asked Gabriella to show her magic and had so much enthusiasm. For days, I'd catch her staring at plants, urging them to grow faster, even though that's not how you do it, trying to heat up water or mix up potions. Gabriella and Mum are basically best friends now."

"I can imagine," I said, wishing I could have seen it myself. "For so long, it was just Gabriella and—" I swallowed. I still couldn't say Laura's name. "Just the two of them, the only alchemists in the city, and then she meets my dad and then, suddenly, Damian grows stronger thanks to our bond and all the magic in the air and then there's you and your mum and Rafi…"

"Speaking of," said Karina, finally tearing her gaze away from the candle. There was a mischievous smile on her face. "Rafi has the biggest crush on a certain witch who has been spending a lot of time with us. They're inseparable."

"I noticed," I said. "But he's hiding it well, or, I guess, better than he usually does." Which didn't mean much, since Rafi didn't believe in subtlety and would spam his crushes with specially-prepared Spotify playlists, baked goods, usually baked by me, and book recommendations. "Which is probably smart unless he wants to get his heart broken."

Karina shrugged. "It's the end of the world. We don't have time for lifelong relationships, either way."

An idea sprouted in my head.

"When I gave Damian my magic, we could feel the bond between us. Would you like to try?"

Karina nodded and we held hands. The magic on my skin had quieted since she'd entered the room but I still had more than enough to push into her. I waited a moment then pushed more magic but nothing happened. There was no sparkle of magic.

"I guess my demon eats it all," said Karina with a sad smile.

I sighed, my heart aching.

"I need to get Artur out."

"What's stopping you?"

"I need to be able to walk without losing my breath for more than a hundred metres. And I need to talk to my mum. She wants me to learn to control my magic, too, but we all know that's impossible, and besides…she's my mum. I can't use magic around her."

Karina bent over and dug in her backpack for a bit. Soon, she retrieved a big glass bottle filled with familiar amber liquid glistening in the candlelight.

"Damian made it for you. Don't drink it all, just a mouthful twice a day, but it will help you regain your energy faster. And about your mum…I know it's crazy weird. But she's our best chance now. She's *Artur*'s best chance. And I'm here, so you won't have to face her alone."

EIGHT

MUM SAT IN THE LIVING ROOM BY THE FIREPLACE. JUST like the other rooms I'd seen in the house, it was spacious and old, but well-maintained. The wallpapers were darker green than in my bedroom, peeling off near the ceiling, the curtains white and furniture sparse and made of dark, old wood. There was a cabinet full of dusty dishes with hand-painted edges and two bookcases filled to the brims with books, some stacked on top of each other and another bursting with alchemist potions. There was also an old, dark red, saggy sofa and two matching armchairs. Had Igor furnished the place himself or had he got it like that?

Mum sat cross-legged on a worn carpet by the fireplace, wearing an oversize jumper, a notebook and pen in front of her. There were so many un-Mum things about her—I'd never seen her sit on the floor and she rarely wrote by hand, preferring her tablet. But I guessed that wouldn't work anymore. Or maybe the "sorceress her" disliked technology the way she used to hate magic when she hadn't remembered it.

She was writing but lifted her head when Karina and I entered the room. Karina sat in one of the armchairs but I remained standing, hovering near her, counting on her to take in any magic that might try to slip from me.

"How can we kill the basilisk?" I asked. I didn't want to beat around the bush and give the conversation a chance to escalate again.

"The way the kids did it in the legend of the basilisk of Warsaw," said Mum, her tone even and calm.

"With a mirror."

Mum nodded. "That's the safest way."

I crossed my arms. That was what I would have done, too. When in doubt, consult your local legends. And I'd studied this one in primary school.

I wandered off to the bookcase and browsed the titles. The crackling fireplace gave just enough light for me to see the spines, some of which looked like grimoires much like those that Zuzanna had had me leaf through, but there were also tomes of legends from various parts of Poland and the eastern neighbours as well as atlases, lots of nonfiction about herbs, plants, rocks, and stars, and a random Dan Brown novel pushed between *The Witcher* saga. The rain pattered softly on the window ledges and it would have been a wonderful setting to curl up with a book, if there hadn't been an angry red gash tearing the sky apart and one of my bondmates hadn't been turned to stone.

The Witcher was one of many things I had to read in a torchlight under my duvet because Mum hadn't approved of me reading anything containing magic or, horror of horrors, Slavic demons.

Hysterical laughter bubbled up inside me, but I bit my cheek.

"Was this place always supposed to be a hideout?" I asked.

"Yes," said Mum. "Igor bought it in secret from his family and we put in our best spells to keep it protected."

"But he was still killed."

Mum was silent for a long couple of moments. When she finally spoke, her words were quiet and she fixed her gaze on the fire.

"This place has always been meant for you. The four of you."

I realized too late that bringing up my biological father might not have been the smartest idea. Like my dad, Mum probably hadn't had a chance to mourn Igor.

"Damian prepared me a strengthening potion," I said, trying to get us back on track. "What else do we need? Do we have any way to distract the Children of Weles? Should we try the sleeping potion again?"

"That's a big problem," said Mum. "I don't think it will work the second time. They'll be more careful now. That's why it would be ideal if you could learn to control your channelling powers. A combination of Paulina's ability to mask the magical footprints and Artur's invisibility could get you anywhere you wanted."

I shook my head. "These aren't my powers to control. I can take magic and abilities from others, but I can't control it consciously. Sometimes it rushes to save me but it's a big risk. And it gets even more out of control in the tunnels."

"If you got some practice—" started Mum but I interrupted her:

"We don't have time! We've been out of time for too long! Maybe if I hadn't had to hide and suppress my powers all my life, maybe if they hadn't been blocked and hurt me for over seventeen years, if I had a safe environment to learn about them, it would be different. But I didn't and we don't have time to make up for all of it now, not if we want to have any chance of fixing the broken sky."

Mum stared into the fireplace again but I couldn't look at her after my outburst. Karina raised an eyebrow at me, and I dropped my gaze to the floor.

"You're right," said Mum after a long while, still staring at the fireplace. "We need to think of another way to get there undetected or some very good distraction for the Children of Weles. And we need to do it fast."

I didn't get much rest that night either, consumed by remorse. Karina slept by my side while I stared at the dark ceiling faintly illuminated by the red light. The light streamed through the patterned curtains, painting the ceiling in shapes of oak leaves. It reminded me of when I'd collected Tomasz's devil bargain and how Karina and Artur and Damian had saved me, and how we'd woken up from the magical sleep under a huge oak tree, finally feeling like the Circle of Four.

That had been the night when Arrow had hatched from the egg given to me by Węgliszek. And now I didn't know if I'd ever see Arrow again.

I was failing all of them, and I was taking it out on my mum. And it wasn't her fault she'd lost all her memory of magic to a devil all these years ago. Or maybe it was? She'd accepted the deal, after all.

I finally fell into a shallow, uneasy sleep, curled into Karina and woke up before sunrise, my stomach growling. Hoping that Mum wasn't up yet, I left my cousin sleeping and tiptoed across the cold corridor and to the kitchen.

I wasn't in luck. Mum sat at the kitchen table with a mug of tea but she wasn't alone—opposite her sat Tomasz.

"Wiktoria," he said, turning to face me. "I'm glad you got out."

"Damian and Rafi got me out," I said. It wasn't my own skill or luck. "And Artur is still there."

The hypnotist wore a warm brown jumper and a pair of jeans. I supposed it was impossible to iron his usual shirts without electricity or a domowik. There was a hint of dark stubble on his cheeks.

Mum didn't acknowledge me but she rose to prepare me a cup of tea.

"I can help you free him," said Tomasz. "It's not perfect, but my hypnosis should be enough to get us out of there in case things go wrong. And I might be able to fool the shadows, but I can't promise that."

"That would be perfect," I said, surprised. "Do we need to prepare anything else?"

"I already have the mirrors. Take the strengthening potion with you and we can go today," said Mum.

She poured boiling water into a mug and handed it to me. She wasn't using as much magic as before.

"Wiki," she said, her brown eyes in the same shade as mine gazing at me sadly. "I can't make up for the time we've lost and the harm I've done. But I hope that together we can build something new."

We walked towards the old market square in silence. The sun was up but only the bravest, brightest rays made it through the thick layer of rainclouds and they were outshone by the red gash in the sky. We passed a few people rushing from place to place, looking at their feet, trying to avoid trouble.

We crossed a street which usually bustled with traffic. Many buses came that way, along with countless cars driving from the old town or crossing the city. But today the street was empty, save for a military car driving slowly, two soldiers looking out from the windows, patrolling the street.

"Keep your eyes down," murmured Mum.

We kept a steady pace as we entered the old town but

then a voice shouted from behind us:

"Hey!"

I jumped and twisted around. Two soldiers marched fast towards us, rifles slung over their shoulders. My knees trembled even though soldiers were much better news than the Children of Weles.

"Show me your IDs," said one of the soldiers.

Mum and Tomasz took out their ID cards but I didn't have any documents on me. I wasn't eighteen yet so I didn't have an ID card.

"ID, please," said the soldier, their eyes drilling into me.

"She's my daughter," said Mum. "She's seventeen, she doesn't have an ID yet."

"A school ID, then."

I didn't have that, either. Well, I did, somewhere at the bottom of the wardrobe in my room that I hadn't been to in weeks. Which, as far as I knew, might have been plundered five times over by the Children of Weles or desperate neighbours searching for food.

"This one should work," said Tomasz, his voice honey-sweet, showing the soldiers once again his ID. But I knew he was using hypnosis to make the soldiers let us be.

I held my breath but then a soldier nodded and waved us off. Mum grasped my elbow as we hurried to the closest tenement. The door flung open as we approached and Tomasz made a disapproving sound, but Mum only threw him an annoyed glance over her shoulder. We walked inside and the door closed itself quietly behind us, sealing us in darkness.

I swallowed hard and retrieved the mirrors from my pockets. I squeezed them, trying to ground myself. There was a hiss and I backtracked so fast I collided with a wall but it was only my mum lighting a candle. She waved at us to follow her down the steps. I took a deep breath, squeezed the mirrors harder, and walked after her.

Damian's potion kept my pace steady as we descended into the tunnels, our steps almost deafening in the quiet stairwell. The wood creaked and groaned under our footsteps, making my stomach knot with nerves. I tried to keep my breaths even but the sheer thought of going back to the tunnels was paralysing. Mum walked in front of me, a single candle levitating in front of her, and Tomasz was right behind my back.

Magic pressed on me from all sides, making my hands shake and nausea rise in my throat. I tried to breathe. I needed a clear head if we were going to face the basilisk.

Tomasz put his hand on my shoulder and I let my magic flow into him. I'd asked him about it before we'd left, and he'd agreed without question. I counted it as a small victory and hoped it hadn't exhausted all my luck for that day. But fate owed me big time and it was time it started paying up.

Rafi and Damian had been able to map out the part of the tunnels where the Children of Weles had secluded the basilisk and kept all its victims. Mum and Tomasz had decided it was safer to stay underground for as long as possible. We didn't want more trouble with the soldiers.

"Mirrors at the ready," said Mum after some more steps and Tomasz took his hand away from my shoulder.

Mum opened her backpack and more mirrors flew out, two of them big enough to be bathroom mirrors, followed by a number of smaller ones. They hung in front of us, blocking the view.

"I was aiming for a full mirror shield, but couldn't find enough mirrors," she said.

"That's impressive," said Tomasz.

"Thanks."

We walked on, Tomasz murmuring under his breath. I couldn't distinguish the words but I could feel their magic, and I suspected he was willing the shadows not to see us. I didn't think we'd have to wait long to find out if it worked. Surely, Klara would be happy to capture the three of us.

Mum stopped and I bumped into her. I closed my eyes but, when I didn't hear the characteristic clicking of the basilisk's claws on the stone, I dared to peek between Mum's mirrors and I froze.

There was a collection of stone figures in front of us. Gray and human-size, some of them taller than me, most frozen mid-scream, their hands raised. My hands shook as I noticed familiar faces. Dawid and Darek, their fingers touching, Sandra and Julia, among a dozen others. Beata, Artur's mum, was a surprise—then again, maybe she shouldn't have been. She'd supported the Guardians, which was why she'd attacked me after the barriers between the realms had collapsed. She'd thought I'd killed Zuzanna.

Artur's dad, Mariusz, was nearby, too. And there, near the front, was Artur himself.

My heart stuttered and I walked towards him but magic forced me back behind Mum.

"No," she said. "Don't do anything rash. The basilisk must be nearby."

Silence stretched and my heart ached as I stared at Artur's statue. Unlike most of the others, he didn't wear his sorcerer's cloak, but regular winter clothes, the clothes I'd seen him in last, including the rip in his jeans at his knee. His hands were outstretched, his head half-turned, as if he'd tried to protect himself from the basilisk. Had they got him here right after we'd talked, right after Klara's shadows had dragged us apart? Or had he been forced to see my mock fealty first, maybe they'd even shown him the crystal they'd prepared for me?

Anger rose in my veins. Klara and the Children of Weles would pay for that.

The magic of the tunnels clung to my skin like a hot and clammy blanket. Nausea rose in my throat as my own magic rushed to meet its friend. I fisted my hands, trying to stop them from shaking.

Claws clicked on the stone and Mum's mirrors closed together, blocking my view of Artur.

"Close your eyes," whispered Mum.

A second later, a powerful cock-a-doodle-doo tore down the tunnel and I shivered. I looked at the stones below our feet, my hands with my mirrors raised high.

The basilisk ran at us, its heavy steps thundering down the tunnel, but it came to an abrupt stop. My skin vibrated with magic and I dared a glance. Mum thrust out her hand and the demon stumbled back, clucking. Mum's mirrors flew higher and I squeezed my eyes shut. Claws scratched the stone and a horrible roar made shivers run down my spine and reverberated down the tunnel, amplifying over and over. I peeked again and saw a pair of huge chicken's feet, easily the length of my arm, and feathered legs just before they turned into stone and then crumpled to ash.

I was shaking. If the Children of Weles hadn't known about us yet, now they surely would come to investigate the ruckus. The tunnels' magic burned my skin and I couldn't contain it anymore. Stones groaned as magic rushed out of me with powerful force.

"Wiki—" started Mum but whatever she was about to say next, was lost as the stones overhead thundered to the ground.

Mum thrust out her hands, her face contorting with effort to stop the stones from burying us. Mirrors fell to the ground, shattering. Tomasz grabbed my hand and flinched as my magic flooded into him. The magic and the tunnels kept on pushing at me and I trembled.

I'd always suspected that one day I'd make the tunnels collapse.

"Tomek," said Mum, her voice strained, her arms trembling.

"Stop," tried Tomasz but my magic was stronger than his hypnosis.

Smaller stones rained around us. Tomasz tore off his amulet and hung it in front of my face. His eyes were begging. He swayed the pendant and I looked at it, letting his hypnosis take its hold of me and the magic on my skin quiet.

"Now," said Tomasz and Mum moved a step back towards us, then moved her hands down.

With a deafening bang, the stone tunnel behind us collapsed. The tunnel shook but the stones jumped away from the force field that Mum had created around us. For a few moments, I stood frozen still.

The Children of Weles must have heard us now.

Ahead of us, the stone statues were still unmoving. Cold shiver ran down my spine. Gods, what if I had made the tunnel collapse on them?

Shaking, I walked over to Artur and stared at the terror in his unseeing eyes, at his mouth half-open in a scream. Could he see me or was he unaware of what was going on?

Why was he still turned to stone?

Steps echoed down the tunnel and Tomasz and Mum moved forward, blocking me and the stone statues from view.

"Stop right there," said Tomasz, his voice making the hair on the back of my neck stand.

The steps halted but then the tiniest voice said, "I can help."

Tomasz and Mum exchanged glances but didn't say anything.

"Killing the basilisk isn't enough," said the familiar voice. Laura. "They need to see the daylight. It's one variation of the legend, one where the basilisk isn't defeated by kids, but by a tailor. After killing the basilisk with a reflection of its murderous gaze, he smashes the mirror so it can reflect the sunrays getting to the cellar through the small window."

I closed my fists to stop my hands from shaking. We weren't in a cellar under a Warsaw tenement but in the tunnels under city. There were no windows nearby.

Though, if Tomasz hadn't stopped my magic, maybe I would have created a crack in the ceiling. Hysterical laughter bubbled up my throat but I swallowed it.

"So, you came to gloat at our stupidity?" I asked.

"I caught sunrays into a spelled bottle. I was waiting for the right moment to use it, to free them."

"I don't believe you," I said.

I used to trust Laura so blindly, to believe that she'd always had our back. And that ended with a broken sky, myself chained to a torturous crystal of her device, and half of the local magic-users turned to stone.

I couldn't stop my shaking anymore. The rest of the Children of Weles were going to find us any moment and I'd be back in that cell, used as a magical conduit, while they torture or kill Mum and Tomasz.

"Put the bottle down and back away," said Tomasz. "Stay ten steps down the tunnel and don't move."

When Laura's steps echoed down the corridor, Mum nodded at Tomasz and he walked to retrieve the bottle. Mum must have been shielding us with a force field.

"We can't use that," I protested, my squeaky voice

betraying my nerves. "As far as we know, the moment we open the bottle everything explodes or we fall asleep and the Children of Weles find us."

"I know I messed up," said Laura. "But I promise I want to help them. No one was ever supposed to get hurt, much less turned into stone. But you have to hurry before the others get here."

"It's our only option," said Mum.

"You're telekinetic!" I protested. How couldn't she see that trusting Laura was the last thing we should do?

"Yes, and stone statues weigh a ton, there are too many of them and we're away from all the stairs leading outside. My magic is exhausted after stopping the ceiling from collapsing on our heads. I can't risk crumbling any of the stones or worse, dropping them, and hurting or killing someone."

I bit my lip. I hadn't thought that far.

"I promise I want to help," said Laura.

I shook my head but Mum nodded at Tomasz and he opened the bottle. I held my breath as bright light streamed from the bottle. I shielded my eyes with my arm until the light subsided. I blinked rapidly and when my vision cleared, the statues were warming up from the greyish stone colour to different shades of human skin.

Artur swayed on his feet and I put my arm around him, his weight nearly bringing both of us crushing to the dusty stone floor. But I held on, keeping both of us upright. A sparkle of magic slowly appeared between the two of us and I clung to it.

"Get him out. Get yourselves out of here before your magic gets even more uncontrollable. We'll take care of the rest," said Mum.

Her words stung but she was right. Besides, I didn't want to be there with Laura, waiting for the Children of Weles to recapture us. I took out Damian's strengthening potion from my backpack and brought the bottle to Artur's lips. His head lolled but I got him to drink a little and his weight on me lessened. I handed the bottle with the potion to Mum so she could start distributing it around and pulled Artur down the tunnels. I probed a couple of doors until I found an entrance to a staircase.

"Can you climb the stairs?" I asked.

Artur's eyes were still misted over and I didn't get a response, but it wasn't like we had any alternatives. I kept my arm around him as we made our way up the stairs, magic growing stronger between us. I couldn't relish it, not yet, not when all my brainpower was focused on getting us out of the tunnels and as far away from the Children of Weles as we could get. I pushed the wooden door at the top of the stairs open and froze.

In front of me was a long hall, with polished floors—was it *marble?*—and walls made of glistening white stone and tall, arched windows, through which red light seeped in. The ceiling rose high above us with a painting depicting a battle on it.

Wherever we were, it wasn't one of the tenements in the city centre.

NINE

I WAS READY TO BACK UP, GO BACK TO THE TUNNELS, and try to find another way back through there, but Artur leaned on me more heavily, and I got him into the corridor before we could tumble down the stairs. The moment I shut the door, it disappeared behind us.

A shiver ran down my spine and I grasped Artur tighter. I glanced at him but his eyes were unfocused, his eyelids drooped low. I looked to the sides, trying to decide which way to go, but the hall seemed endless in both directions, all marble bathed in the red light, ending in shadows.

We were stuck. We were lost.

Focus, I chided myself, taking a deep breath.

I needed to make a simple decision: left or right.

I dragged Artur to the right, our pace slow and awkward, our steps echoing loudly in the empty hall. My muscles screamed and sweat trickled down my neck. Thick magic coated my skin, so strong it almost obscured the reawakening bond between Artur and me. Through the windows, I spotted the three granaries standing by the river, which confused me further. Where were we? And did it matter, when the only important thing was to get out of there as fast as possible?

At the end of the corridor, there were double gold doors, engraved with complicated symbols, easily twice as tall as me. I glanced behind my back, but the shadows were swallowing the corridor behind us. My stomach squeezed, my lungs constricting, making it hard to breathe. Was it all Klara's doing?

I couldn't let her catch us.

Not again.

I pushed the door, but it was so heavy it barely moved. The shadows were fast approaching so I shifted my weight around Artur and leaned on the door, propping it open with my shoulder.

We stumbled into a grand room, so big I couldn't see the walls, only endless marble floor. The ceiling was high, high above us. It was almost like a grand, but empty, cathedral, lit up by the eerie red light.

My legs shook. I tried to stop the heavy door with my foot, but it slammed closed with a thud and disappeared, leaving us in this endless room.

It couldn't be real. Was it a dream? A vision? Had the basilisk got to us and I'd been turned to stone and now dreamt of weird, impossible things?

I let out a shaky sigh, adjusted my grip on Artur and led us further inside the room. The floor and the ceiling were brilliant white, reflecting the red light, and with no point of reference, I was unable to say if we were even walking in a straight line. We could either keep moving and hope it got us somewhere or collapse and cry.

The second option sounded more and more tempting.

Magic prickled my neck, biting like a wasp, and I winced. It wanted me to look behind, but I wasn't ready to see the room swallowed by shadows or something even more nightmarish between us. I pressed on until I couldn't ignore the feeling anymore and glanced over my shoulder.

A startled gasp broke from my throat and I put myself between Artur, who swayed on his feet, and the new threat.

There was a familiar figure behind us, dressed in a suit, with sleek, brushed back honey-blonde hair and a goatee. His legs ended with hooves and a tail flicked back and forth behind him.

"Welcome to my humble abode," said Węgliszek.

"What did you do? Where are we?" I demanded, even though my heart was racing and hands shaking. Were we really in a devil's home? How did we get here? How screwed were we now that the devil wasn't inside a summoning circle?

"Such ungrateful visitors," said the devil, looking at his sharp claws. "And you walked in here on your own, without asking permission."

"Where are we," I repeated through gritted teeth.

"Should we make it more interesting? I could ask a

question myself for every question you do. Or take the answer directly from your head. Maybe I could take a memory. And maybe a year of your life. Ah, the options are endless."

I held on to Artur to hide how much my hands were shaking. I didn't trust myself to speak so I kept my mouth shut. I wanted to run, but my legs could barely hold me up and Artur wasn't in a state to run. I didn't want to put my back to the devil, either. Besides, where would we go? The room was endless.

The devil's lips slowly stretched in a smile.

"I take care of this city now," said Węgliszek. "As I used to, before your ancestors drove me out. And I don't like sharing power."

"We need to be going," I said, grasping Artur's arm tight.

"If you require safe passage and exit, that will necessitate a bargain."

"No, we're just going to leave," I said with more confidence than I felt.

The devil bared its sharp teeth.

"There is no way to leave this place without my help. You'll walk on forever until you collapse and beg for my help. Maybe I should let you do that. I'd enjoy watching you grovel."

I glanced at Artur, but if he was aware of what went on around him, it didn't look like he could communicate it.

I thought about Mum, Tomasz, and all these people down in the tunnels. What if they chose the closest door as well and ended up here?

"Safe passage and exit not only for the two of us but also my mum, Tomasz, and all the people who'd been recently turned to stone."

"So be it. In return I'll be able to use his eyes whenever it pleases me." The devil pointed a long black claw at Artur.

My fingers dug into Artur's shoulders.

"What do you mean by 'use?'" I asked. "It needs to be more specific. And what is the time restraint?"

And how could I ever make such a decision for Artur? It wasn't my decision to make, and he wasn't in a state to consent to anything.

"I will be able to see through his eyes, see whatever he sees. It won't hurt. He won't even be aware I'm there. And I'll have this power until spring equinox."

"Yes," whispered Artur.

My head snapped towards him, my hand shooting up to cover his mouth.

Węgliszek grinned.

"No," I said, shaking my head. "He doesn't know what he's saying. He isn't in his right mind."

The devil raised an eyebrow in an elegant arc.

"A deal is a deal."

"No," I said, my voice louder.

"No? You'd resign from getting safe passage, from saving not only yourselves but your mother and countless other sorcerers?"

I shut my eyes. It was an impossible choice. I needed to protect Artur but there were others to think about. What if the Children of Weles had already caught up to Mum and Tomasz?

Węgliszek leaned closer, his brown eyes bearing into mine like he was trying to look into my soul. Maybe he could. What did he see in there?

The devil extended a finger and touched my cheek with his claw, and I forced myself to stay still. He didn't scratch, just moved it gently up towards my temple, my magic pushing on me so suddenly I couldn't contain it. It flew out of me in a powerful gust but nothing happened. All three of us were still standing there.

"What will it be? Do we have a deal?"

"Yes," repeated Artur, his lips moving against my hand.

The devil grinned. There was a flash of brilliant light, and I shut my eyes. When I opened it again, the hall around us had disappeared, and Artur and I were standing on wet grass in front of a small stone house I'd never seen before.

ᛏᛖᚾ

ARTUR LEANED HEAVIER ON ME AS WE STOOD IN WET, melting snow. My knees buckled as I struggled to keep us upright. I was shaking, and I didn't know if it was from exhaustion or fear. We were on a street I didn't recognize, lined with one-family houses on both sides, red light streaming through the crack in the sky. Dogs barked, the only sound breaking the silence. The air smelled strongly of burning plastic and my eyes stung.

Where had the devil sent us? How stupid had I been not to specify it?

"Do you know where we are?" I whispered.

Just as I expected, there was no response.

The barking grew louder. We needed to move, but between the wet snow drenching my hair and leaking down my face and Artur's weight around my shoulders, I wanted nothing more than to collapse. I had no idea where to go—again.

Before I could muster energy, the door to the house opened and a dog launched itself towards us, barking. I gasped before I realized it was a beagle I'd seen before.

"Ciri?" I asked as the dog started jumping at Artur and me, yipping happily. I offered her my free hand and she licked it but didn't give up jumping, trying to reach Artur. To my surprise, he offered her his hand, too.

Hope flickered in my chest. Maybe he'd be okay.

"Wiktoria?" asked a voice from the doorway. "Artur?"

I lifted my head and noticed an older sorceress wrapped in a long, knitted cardigan. Artur's grandma. There was another dog by her side, with brown, shaggy-looking fur. It wagged its tail, its tongue lolling out of its mouth.

"Come inside, quickly," she whispered, stepping aside. "Ciri, shush. Come here."

I adjusted my grip around Artur's back and walked towards the house, Ciri dancing around our legs. Artur's grandma noticed my struggle because she hurried to our side and swung Artur's other arm over her shoulders, taking most of his weight.

"Magic," she said. "Telekinesis is useful, even if other sorcerers tend to dismiss it."

Artur had said something similar when we first met. Maybe he'd learned it from his grandma.

She locked the door behind us and led us to a kitchen, a small, warm room lit up by several candles. We sat Artur on a chair at the table. To my relief, he remained sitting. Ciri followed us and started nudging his legs with her head until he scratched her ears.

There were footsteps and soon we were joined by Artur's grandpa.

"What happened?" he asked, looking at the two of us. "You got out?"

I opened my mouth, but I was at a loss for words. Instead, I nodded. I leaned on Artur's chair, still shaking all over.

"Sit," said Artur's grandma. "I'll make some tea and reheat you some soup. You must be starving."

I sat heavily on the chair next to Artur. I tried to tell my muscles to relax and, when I was hugging a hot cup of tea and the air started smelling like vegetable soup, slowly, slowly, my shoulders dropped and the tension in my neck lessened.

My eyes didn't leave Artur. He was still pale like death and, while he was scratching Ciri, his eyes looked absent and a little wild. He didn't touch his tea.

Artur? I tried to call him telepathically but received no response, even though I could feel our bond. But his side felt utterly blank and my stomach sank.

Soon, two bowls of hot soup appeared in front of us, together with half a loaf of still-warm bread. I dug in, cherishing the potatoes and carrots along with the soft bread with its crunchy crust. It was such a nice change to have a warm soup after all the meals relying heavily on grains.

I didn't know what the correct etiquette was for when

a devil dumps you at your partner-in-crime's grandparents' doorstep during the end of the world, so I was grateful to have my mouth full and to not have to worry about whether I should say something, attempt small talk or explanations, or whether it was more polite to sit silently.

Artur ate a few spoons of soup, which I counted as a win.

"Artur's been turned to stone by a basilisk," I said, when I'd cleared the last of my soup with a chunk of bread.

"We know," said his grandma. "We were at your fealty."

My insides froze over with fear. Artur's grandparents had been there and they'd escaped being turned to stone. Were they with the Children of Weles? Gods, what if the soup or the tea was poisoned? I was feeling queasy but maybe it was nerves and—

"Wiktoria," said Artur's grandpa. "I'd never condone having anyone turned to stone, much less family. And nobody's magic should be taken and used against their will."

Artur's grandma nodded in agreement.

"How did you get out?" she asked. "Did you kill the basilisk?"

"Yes. Well, my mum did, but yes. I left with Artur while Mum and Tomasz stayed to help everyone else. We'd ended up in this weird palace and Węgliszek was there, and he'd sent us here. He was supposed to help everyone else, too."

I knew the story sounded improbable even by demonic apocalypse standards but Artur's grandparents took it all in stride.

"You're safe here," said Artur's grandma. "At least for now. I'll try to get in touch with Tomasz and you should get some rest."

I glanced at Artur, who was looking at the table with unseeing eyes. It was as if an invisible hand squeezed my throat and I could barely hold myself together. But I took in a breath, then another, keeping the tears at bay.

"He'll be okay," said Artur's grandpa, his voice gentle. "He just needs time to readjust to the world of the living."

We slept in a little room at the end of a narrow corridor. There was a small sofa bed squeezed between a few bookcases double-stacked with books, so Artur and I were cuddled close together. I was glad his grandparents hadn't tried to offer me separate accommodations because there was no way I was leaving Artur's side.

"We're alive," I whispered as a charm, or maybe I was trying to convince myself it was true. "We're here and we're alive."

Magic hummed between us, warm and comforting, but Artur's end of the bond still felt like a void. I tried to reach out to him telepathically a few more times but didn't get a response. Neither did my spoken words. In the end, I gave up, surrendering to my aching muscles and let the sleep claim me, hoping that maybe we'd see each other in dreams, that even though I couldn't remember them, they would help Artur.

But after I'd woken up from a restless sleep, Artur still didn't show many signs of life, his end of the bond weighing more and more heavily on me. He lay on his back, staring at the ceiling, his hand stroking Ciri who lay on his other side.

Eventually, hunger got me out of the room. The house smelled like yeast dough and my mouth watered as I made my way down a dark, narrow hall.

Artur's grandma was in the kitchen, standing over an old oven.

"Good morning," I said.

"Good morning," she responded with a warm smile. "I'm making a drożdżówka, it's almost ready. It's Artur's favourite."

I swallowed.

"He's still not well."

"He needs time," said his grandma, repeating her husband's earlier words. "And a good, warm meal, something sweet, and loving family are the best cure for what he's going through."

I wanted to demand how she knew what he was going through, how she knew how to help someone who'd been turned to stone, but I bit my tongue. I needed to stop antagonizing people, especially those who gave me shelter and food.

Artur's grandma put on an oven mitten and took out the cake. She cut two thick slices and prepared some herbal tea.

"Try to convince him to come here," she said.

So I left to get Artur. When I opened the door to our room, the weight of his emotions slammed into me. I hadn't known nothingness had a weight to it but it was like a heavy ballast, pulling me down.

I took a deep breath and sat at the edge of the sofa bed.

"Your grandma made a drożdżówka," I said. "She'd like you to come. And I don't want to disappoint her, she's been nice to me."

No response.

I reached out and took Artur's hand, magic sparkling between us.

"Come," I said, pulling him gently.

And, to my surprise, he moved. Artur got up, his movements sluggish and a little off-balance, but he followed me to the kitchen, his hand in mine. The plates of cake and tea were waiting for us.

"You aren't supposed to eat it hot, but I know that's how you like it best," said his grandma.

I sat at the table and Artur followed. We ate the cake and drank our tea, the hot cake burning my tongue but all the sugar, the soft dough and the crumble was so good I could cry.

"I remember your mum," said Artur's grandma, and I looked up at her surprised. "Oh yes, Oleńka. I used to babysit her. I helped her out with her telekinesis when she was little. I was friends with your grandparents, too, before they moved to the seaside. I'm sorry I didn't remember that before."

For a moment, my mind spun with all the information, with the possibility of all the alternative lives I could have led, all the what ifs, but I didn't let myself dwell on it.

"There's nothing to be sorry about," I said. "That was part of the bargain my parents had made with the devil, that everyone would forget my mum's name, herself included. That she'd forget her magic."

There was a knock on the door and I stiffened.

"It's just a neighbour," said Artur's grandma but I didn't relax.

She stood up from the table and retrieved a large supermarket bag from the cupboard. It was filled with a hearty part of the cake and fresh vegetables—some, like potatoes, carrots, or white radish could have been stored over winter, but I doubted the same was true for tomatoes, cucumbers, and kale.

Artur's grandma carried the bag to the door and I listened in, ready to run. But after a short, whispered conversation I couldn't follow, she returned to the kitchen and sat back at the table.

"Tadeusz has plant magic," she said, referring to Artur's grandpa. "It's always made our lives so much easier and we're trying to share as much with the neighbours as possible."

"They know you're sorcerers?"

"Oh yes. Though they still find it difficult to imagine that Tadek is the plant magician, they think it would suit me better for some reason." She gave me a mischievous smile.

By the time we'd finished our cake, Artur's exhaustion had worn me out so much I could barely remain sitting. His grandma sent us off to bed.

"I'll wake you up for dinner," she said.

So I lay in bed curled next to Artur, hoping that the magic flowing between us could help him. After we'd rescued him from the kidnapping ruse by the Children of Weles, Artur had been exhausted but not nearly as numb. He had been more anxious and I couldn't help him because with our bond making us feel each other's emotions, we had been making ourselves only more miserable. But as destructive and overwhelming anxiety was, at least it felt like *something*. Now, in a rare moment when I snapped out of the tangle of our bond, I was terrified of how numb Artur felt—terrified for him.

Terrified for us.

I hoped maybe this time our bond could be more help than hindrance, with how warm and safe it felt, like a warm blanket and a mug of hot chocolate on a cold winter day. But Artur barely moved and, while he seemed aware of what was going on around him, he didn't respond to words or touch.

His grandma kept preparing nice food and in other circumstances it would have been a long-awaited holiday. But my heart was heavy and my mind and body exhausted, and I spent most of the time worrying about Artur, with flashes of bigger panic that we were losing time as the world was falling apart.

Until early next afternoon, when Artur's grandma knocked on the door and said:

"Artur, your parents are here."

ELEVEN

Panic jolted me out of the numbness, flooding my system and leaving me breathless, my heart pounding. I looked at the window and the red light streaming through it and considered running. Not far, just outside to wait it out. Artur would be fine with his parents, but I doubted the same was true for me. The thought of seeing his mum again made me nauseous.

Artur's fingers wrapped around my hand. I looked at him surprised, still struggling to breathe. With his other hand he cupped my face, his fingers skimming up my cheek. Our bond roared stronger, and I realized he was collecting the magic that started escaping me.

"Stay here," he said, his voice barely a whisper.

His eyes were pale blue, almost colourless, not a spark of magic in them. But he'd said something. He'd touched me and he'd spoken, and through panic I felt a slice of hope.

I didn't know if he meant stay here as in not run away or stay here as in don't go face his parents. In either case, it seemed wrong to let him go on his own. He was still recovering. And I knew I'd have to face his parents at some point.

"You aren't well, either," Artur whispered, his voice so sad and sincere that tears flooded my eyes.

I squeezed his fingers one more time before releasing him. But when he got off the sofa bed and opened the door, I heard more familiar voices carrying down the hallway. *Raised* voices. Mum, *my* mum, and then Tomasz.

I scrambled out of bed so fast that my head spun and I nearly lost my balance. My heart kept trying to break free from my chest as I followed Artur down the hallway, the shouts growing louder and my stomach knotting more with every step. It felt as if we were little kids spying on adults. The kitchen filled with screaming adults was the last place either of us wanted to be, but whatever was going on was on us to stop.

From a corner of my eye, I thought I saw a shadow move, and I jumped and collided with Artur. I tried to calm myself down, knowing it was just nerves. Artur squeezed my hand and I clung on to him and to his newly rediscovered sparkle of life.

"How dare you!" shouted Artur's mum, Beata, her voice carrying through the closed doors.

"How dare I?" shouted back my mum. "I should have left you in those tunnels."

There were some more quiet, unintelligible words and then:

"You're in *my* family home!" screamed Beata. "You're a guest here, and instead you attack me in a sacred space."

"Really? Do you want me to remind you where you've attacked my daughter? Because that was *her* family home, *her* safe space. And you breached that and left her vulnerable to the enemy!"

I had no idea how my mum knew about it. Who'd been there? Beata and her friend. Filip, afterwards. But somehow, between ambushing me in the Guardian's flat and Filip finding me there, the Children of Weles got to Beata.

"She murdered *two* of our Guardians!"

Artur turned around to face me, his head tilted. We hadn't had a chance to catch up, though our bond usually did that for us. He must have known I'd been hurt, but I didn't know how much Artur knew about what had happened to me after we'd destroyed the barrier between the realms. I still didn't know what had happened to him.

But my thoughts were racing and my chest squeezing tight and I wasn't able to tell a coherent story now.

The sky broke and I ran, and there was the latawiec, and soldiers, and the sky was broken, and everything was a mess, and your mum searched my mind, until she knew we were bonded. Because whatever hurts me, hurts you.

"You keep throwing senseless accusations around!" shouted Mum, and I flinched.

There were footsteps and the door swung open. Artur and I jumped back. Artur's dad, Mariusz, looked out at us.

"Don't just stand here. Come in."

He enclosed Artur in a long embrace and nodded at me, which was more acknowledgement than I'd expected, then gestured at us to walk into the kitchen. I didn't like the way he guarded the door and at first my legs refused to move, but I forced myself to step inside. My and Artur's mums were facing each other in the middle of the room. Tomasz stood to the side, close to Artur's grandma who was hovering near the oven. Artur's grandpa was watching the scene unfold from his seat at the head of the table.

"Oh, thank gods," said Mum, spotting me. She moved as if to hug me then stopped herself, and I was grateful but also hated that her restraint made me calmer. "We were so worried."

Beata walked over to us and hugged Artur, avoiding my gaze. I guess it was progress from scowling at me.

Artur was quick to step away from the embrace.

"What did you do?" he asked, his tone just as quiet as when he'd addressed me in our room, but even more sorrowful.

Beata's eyes didn't leave his face, her hand smoothing her son's cheek.

"I didn't know," she said. "You should have told me."

Artur shook his head and took one more step back.

"I would never hurt you," said Beata.

"You shouldn't be apologizing to me."

Beata's eyes skirted towards me, but she didn't meet my eyes. I was trying to make myself as small as possible in the corner of the crowded kitchen, wilting under all the adults' gazes, wanting nothing more than to channel Artur's power and turn invisible. I was exhausted, standing only thanks to the adrenaline flooding my body, my heart pumping the blood way too fast.

Then, with a force of a speeding truck it hit me that if not for me, we wouldn't be in this situation. I was this weird sorceress-Guardian hybrid, I was the executor of the curse to destroy the Guardian system, I had too much power to control, I was Artur's bondmate, and the sky was broken because of me. And everyone in this room had every right to hate me.

The cupboards shook and Artur squeezed my hand, taking in my magic before it could wreak havoc around. And I felt even worse because he was barely standing, but he felt responsible for protecting me. Because I couldn't even control my powers and he needed to step in before I hurt someone.

"You can't even look at her," said Mum. "Well done, you bullied a teenage girl."

"Ola," said Tomasz, a gentle warning in his tone.

"Bullied?" said Beata, turning around to face my mum. "Do you realize what your daughter has done? Ah no, I forgot, you've been conveniently absent *for nearly two decades.*"

Mum took a step towards Beata but Tomasz grabbed her arm, holding her back.

"Stop," I said. "It's pointless. It doesn't matter now. We need to save the world."

I caught Tomasz's eye and he seemed to understand what I didn't want to say out loud. We needed to reunite with Karina and Damian. We needed our Circle of Four to be back together.

"Agreed," Tomasz said. "Let's go home."

"And just who gave you the authority to—"

Something ice-cold wrapped around my ankle and I shrieked, cutting off Beata. I knew the icy touch of the shadows too well, felt its phantom on my skin during the long hours when I couldn't sleep. But now it was all too real.

I fell to the floor, my hip colliding painfully with the floor. I kicked and struggled, even though the shadows were incorporeal and there was nothing to hit. Magic rushed out of me and furniture slammed against the walls with a bang, but my magic couldn't touch the shadows. Undeterred, they dragged me towards the shadowed corner.

Then, the kitchen filled with bright, white light. I put a hand over my eyes. The icy grip around my ankle dissolved as the shadows disappeared. And then Artur's arms were around me, pulling me to my feet, holding me close against him.

"It's okay, little fox," Artur whispered into my ear. "I have you."

The light dimmed just enough so I could open my eyes, spots dancing in my vision. I clung to Artur trembling, my heart hammering, my breath coming out in short gasps.

"We need to get out of here," said my mum and for once I agreed with her.

"Take the car. I'll strengthen the household protections here and join you later," said Tomasz. "Mariusz, will you help me?"

We streamed out of the kitchen to put on our shoes and jackets.

"I'm sorry for everything," I said to Artur's grandma. "Especially for putting you in danger."

She'd welcomed us, *me*, into her home, offered food and safety and I'd exposed her to Klara and the Children of Weles.

Artur's grandma put her hands over mine.

"There's nothing you have to be sorry about. Go, now, and stay safe. Let us know if we can help somehow. And don't worry, I'll talk some sense into my daughter. I brought her up better than that."

TWELVE

On the way back to our hideout, my heart kept racing, my mind a whirl. Artur's grandma had given us bags filled with fresh vegetables to take with us. I sat with Artur on the back seat, cuddled close together, as Mum drove us back to the city. She didn't attempt small talk, which I was grateful for. As we drove through the darkness, the feeling of nothingness spread through my body and this time I embraced it. I knew it was a trap, I knew we had important things to do, but I didn't fight it. When we got back, Mum offered us food, but I shook my head and took Artur to my room, where we hid under the patchwork quilt.

In the middle of the night, I startled awake. I must have rolled over in my sleep because I was at the edge of the mattress. But Artur had moved as well, spooning me, his arm wrapped around me, his leg between mine, holding me close to him. His face was burrowed in the crook of my neck, his breath warm on me.

"Artur?" I whispered.

I held my breath, but there was no response. His breathing was deep and slow, our bond quiet and it seemed like he was asleep. I relaxed into his embrace and let the sleep reclaim me.

But in the morning, everything was back to the new normal. Artur moved only to block out the light from his eyes and responded in monosyllables. There was a horrifying thought jumping around my head—Artur's parents also had been turned to stone and they seemed much more alive than Artur.

Why wasn't he getting better?

Damian stopped by in the afternoon with more strengthening potion but it didn't bring any results. Neither did anything else that Damian came up with—not potions, not herbs, not smudging, not crystals. Whatever Artur was dealing with, it looked like he needed to get through it on his own, without magical help.

"I know it's difficult, but give him time," said Tomasz when I bumped into him in the kitchen. "Artur's mental health wasn't great even before, and it looks like yesterday he pushed himself too far. He needs more time to heal."

Maybe Artur's grandma had been right. Maybe good food and family love was the best cure. Sadly, our food was much plainer than what his grandparents had been able to conjure up and our Circle of Four was the closest equivalent to family we could offer at the moment.

The next time I went into the kitchen, Damian was there, nursing a cup of tea, a pile of books next to him. It wasn't surprising that I kept meeting people there thanks to the huge coal oven; it was by far the warmest room in the freezing cold house.

Damian looked up when I entered, his eyes scanning me up and down.

"Give me some of your magic," he said.

His words made me realize that I couldn't feel the bond between us anymore. It must have faded as he'd spent my magic.

I put my hands behind my back and shook my head.

"You don't want to feel that," I said, my voice croaky with disuse.

"I think right now both of you could really use someone trying to live their life and feeling things."

"We'll drag you down."

Damian huffed out an exasperated breath.

"Just give me a chance, I can't watch you in this state. Let me try and help. Or at least take pity on me, it's cold in here and I miss alchemy. Your choice."

We had a little staring contest but I lost, too exhausted to argue or even maintain eye contact. I reached out and grabbed Damian's hand. As I pushed magic into him, the bond slowly came to life between us with a warm flicker of magic. Slowly, I became aware of Damian's reverence at the magic filling him up. Unlike Artur and me, Damian had grown up without magic flowing in his veins, able only to convert it from plants and crystals into other forms, and didn't take it for granted. To feel him cherish magic flooding into his body made my heart happy.

I was even happier he trusted me to feel his feelings at all.

Damian had been right—I needed to feel something, too, to feel something good.

"Stay," he said, holding on to my hand. "Just for a bit. Feel something good. Maybe that's what Artur needs, to remember reasons to live."

"I'm so tired," I said, and I meant it. My muscles felt heavy and speaking was a chore. I wanted to lay in the darkness.

"You can sit here. Have some food, have some tea."

I looked over my shoulder, towards the room where Artur was still lying in the bed, unmoving. The bond felt like a void on that side, a black abyss pulling me in. But now, there was another side to lean on. And, while Damian was far from cheerful, at least he was feeling something.

"I can eat," I agreed.

There was a pot full of kasza with forest mushrooms on the stove, and I helped myself to a bowl. I sat heavily at the table, opposite Damian, who pretended to read the book in front of him but kept glancing at me. But as I chewed, the meal reminded me more and more of the tunnels, of the Children of Weles, of the ice-cold grip of the shadows on me, of all the power I wasn't using to try to save the world, that I couldn't even use to help Artur.

Nausea rose in my throat, and I pushed the bowl away and stood up.

"You have to eat," said Damian, abandoning all pretence of reading.

I shook my head. "I can't."

"If you can't get out of bed, at least you need to eat," he insisted.

"I'm sorry," I whispered and left the kitchen.

Hours later, the door to the room creaked open and soon Karina's arms closed around me.

"Come," she said, trying to pull me off the bed.

"I don't want to move," I protested, holding on to the quilt.

"Don't make me bring reinforcements."

"Why? Just let me lie here."

"Just for a bit. You need a change of scenery. Then you can come back here and sleep through the end of the world."

I knew it was something I was supposed to care about, but I was too exhausted.

"Go," said Damian, appearing in the doorway. "Just for an hour or so. I'll stay with Artur."

I let Karina drag me off the bed and out of the room. I tripped, my legs unused to movement, but she held me steady, and got me across the hallway to the kitchen. Rafi was already there, standing by the stove. He didn't say anything, just pushed a warm mug into my hands. I breathed in the smell of coffee and hugged the cup close to me, so as not spill it with my shaking hands. I couldn't remember the last time I'd had coffee.

"We have more surprises," he said, setting a bowl of strawberries in front of me.

"How?" I asked, staring at the fruit. It was freezing outside.

"Dawid and Darek came by to thank you for un-stoning them."

I took a strawberry into my hand and turned it around with my fingers.

"So they're okay," I said, torn between happiness that they were doing well and the sinking feeling because it meant what was happening to Artur wasn't normal.

"Yes," said Karina gently. "And Artur will be, too, he just needs more time. And I think it could help him if you took care of yourself. Drink coffee, eat strawberries, try to remember something good about life."

"But—"

I couldn't. How could I try to make myself feel good when Artur was barely showing any signs of life? It wasn't fair to him.

"No excuses," said Rafi, his voice stern.

"If Artur can feel what you feel, wouldn't you want him to feel something good?" asked Karina.

"Just eat this strawberry," said Rafi.

I would have rolled my eyes at the two of them staring at me intently but that required too much energy. Instead,

I bit into the strawberry, its juicy sweetness bursting in my mouth, for a second almost making me believe that it was summer, that it was warm, that days weren't endless greyness and darkness, lit up by the eerie red light.

"See?" said Rafi, watching my expression. "Strawberries are pure happy magic. Damian didn't believe me but now I have proof."

We sat by the coal oven, enjoying the warmth, and I let my cousins jump around me and talk my ears off. They seemed intent on bringing up any happy memory they could think of, but seeing the two of them cooperating like that and so worried about me only made me feel worse.

I just wanted to lie in darkness and disappear. I didn't have the energy to talk to Kari and Rafi, I didn't have the energy to pretend whatever they were doing was working, I didn't have the energy to feel. I just wanted to sleep.

Karina sensed it first. The flicker in her eyes dimmed and she smiled at me sadly. Rafi's chatter took a bit more to die off.

"One more strawberry?" he offered, but I shook my head.

"I'm sorry," I said. "I can't. But thank you for trying."

I shuffled back to my room. Damian was sitting by the desk, but I noticed him only when the floorboards creaked as he rose to his feet. He touched my elbow and left the room without a word. I hid in the warm space under covers next to Artur. A few minutes later Artur moved closer to me, his face nestling in the crook of my neck, his breaths deep and even. But I couldn't sleep as I stared into the ceiling and the shapes drawn by the red light falling in from the outside.

The door creaked open and I looked up. Damian walked towards the bed. Without a word, he lay down on the other side of Artur and put his arm around him, his hand grazing my stomach. We held on to Artur, shielding him from the world, magic humming between us.

I woke up to my insides being squeezed by sadness and guilt. I sat up so suddenly my head spun. The space between Damian and me was empty. I looked around the room panicked, but Artur was nowhere to be seen. My heart drummed as I tore off the covers and raced to the door, following our bond.

What if Baba Jaga had gotten to him, too?

Artur wasn't in the kitchen and the door to the bathroom was ajar. The house was quiet save for the ticking of a cuckoo's clock. My hands shook as I approached the backdoor. It was unlocked.

Slowly, I pushed the door open.

Cold air sneaked under my t-shirt, numbing my skin. Reluctantly, I took a few steps back and pulled on the first jacket and pair of shoes I could find. I stepped outside, tripping in the too-big shoes—they were probably Rafi's—blinking against the stinging cold wind, trying to see in the darkness, trying to ignore the faint red light coming from the gash in the sky and the way it set my sixth sense on edge.

There was a dark shape lying on the ground and my heart stuttered. For a second, I froze, staring at the shadowed, human-shaped thing, faintly illuminated by the red light. The world stilled as I stood blinking, unable to move. Then I ran towards it and fell to my knees on the ground.

"Hey," Artur whispered, pulling himself up on his elbows.

"Oh my gods, don't you dare scare me like that again," I whispered back. I grasped his jacket, my hands shaking, eyes blurry.

"It's okay," Artur said, pulling me against him. He brushed my hair with his fingers. "It's okay, little fox."

But I was still so chocked with his emotions I could hardly breathe.

"No, it's not," I said.

"No," he agreed, shaking his head.

A tear escaped his eye, and then he started crying. I pulled him into a hug as sobs shook his body, my eyes watering in response. The reality around us blurred as I saw Artur with the Children of Weles—but not the way they'd parted, but the way they used to be a few weeks ago. Artur helping Klara make up protections in the tunnels so that no one could find them uninvited. Them discussing how to get as many magic-users on the Children of Weles' side as possible. All the while, the overwhelming feeling of guilt threatened to drag me down.

You didn't know, I said, holding him firmly against me. *You wanted to save magic. You wanted to help people.*

"You didn't work with them," said Artur, his words choked.

"No. Instead I worked with Zuzanna, supporting the system we're trying to destroy. I thought that it was different because I was half-sorceress, that I wasn't taking other's magic. But now we know that I'm using the magic of the people around me, I don't have abilities of my own."

"You were trying to save us."

"So were you."

It took a long moment for Artur's sobs to subside. He pulled me down to the ground and his emotions quieted. Guilt and sadness were still there but they weren't quite so overwhelming anymore. He played with my hair as we looked up at the sky above us and the glaring, long wound in it.

Aren't there any demons out here? I asked telepathically.

"Yes, there are," Artur whispered. "But there are some powerful protections around this place. And…I just needed to be outside. Feel the magic in the earth."

I squeezed his arm, trying to offer reassurance. But the hole in the sky was a glaring, as in literally a glowing-red reminder of how much we'd screwed up. A big, dark shape flew far overhead. A latawiec? Something else? It wasn't dragon-shaped, and I was losing hope we'd get to see Arrow again.

Leaves rustled and I twisted around, ready to run or fight, but the dark shape behind the fence simply walked by, never looking in our direction.

I let Artur draw me back to him, the bond humming between us. The protections held. Maybe we could be safe here for a little while.

We lay cuddled and watched in silence as unknown demons made their way around, walking, crawling, and flying, treating this world as their own. The reddish light made it all the more surreal.

How on Earth could we fix it?

A shudder tore through me and Artur held me closer, drawing shapes on my back with his fingers. I looked up at him. Maybe it was enough of a miracle for tonight. He'd gotten up, gotten himself outside, done something good for himself. We'd exchanged a few words and now he was holding me.

Maybe just the fact that he'd gotten himself out of the deep well of despair and nothingness, even just for a little bit, was the biggest miracle of all. Maybe patching up the sky would be nowhere near as hard. Maybe the most difficult part was over.

"We're here," I whispered, even if everything around looked like a bizarre dream, a bit of a nightmare.

"We're alive," Artur whispered back.

THIRTEEN

EARLY NEXT AFTERNOON, THE CIRCLE OF FOUR MET in the kitchen. We hadn't planned on it but, somehow—magically—the four of us appeared in the kitchen within minutes of each other, preparing coffee and slicing domowik's freshly-baked bread for a late breakfast. I was enraptured by the way we fit in together, the way we anticipated each other's moves. Artur passed Damian the bread half a second before he reached for it, I opened the jar of coffee just as Karina lifted the kettle. The kitchen wasn't big but we sensed each other's steps, aware of the space we took and we worked together seamlessly. Warm magic sparkled in the air and for a few moments I was able to forget about the red light streaming in through the window.

Then my mum joined us and, unwillingly, my internal walls rose again, everything around me taking on an extra weight. The red light streaming through the window. The Guardian's cloak, bunched up at the bottom of my backpack. All the reasons why Mum had decided to have me in the first place, a half-sorceress half-Guardian hybrid.

"So," I said, sitting at the dinner table and clutching my mug of coffee like the most prized possession. It sort of was. It was my second cup in weeks. "We need to talk about the hole in the sky and how to fix it."

I held the coffee close to my face and breathed in, enjoying the smell. It almost settled the nausea rising in my throat. Almost.

"Are we sure we want to fix it?" asked Artur. He sat by my side, so close that our hands were almost brushing. He was pale, but he seemed more alive than I'd seen him in a long time. His hair was still damp from his bath and he'd shaved, looking almost like his normal self.

"Artur might have a point," said Damian. "Do we want to restore the world to the way it was? Or do we accept that maybe this is the way the world had always been meant to be, with all the worlds intermingling?"

"You can't leave it like that," said Mum. "I agree, the previous system was no good and we don't want it back. But it's not all or nothing. And the longer we stay like that, the less chance we have of getting fully back to Jawia."

"What was your original plan?" I said, my eyes darting up to look at Mum before returning to my coffee mug. "You had a plan, right? You knew that the four of us were coming, that we'd change the magical world."

Mum nodded.

"We hoped to destroy the Guardian's system forever, to save the magic from disappearing. That's why we were with the Children of Weles at first. But when we'd learned about how the gods will return when the Guardians disappear, we thought you'd have the magic to change everything without paying such a high price. Especially you, Wiki, being half-sorceress, half-Guardian…we hoped you could ease the transition. We got the Twardowski's scriptures and we know that if the four of you perform the ritual to destroy them, the memory of Guardian's magic will be erased and magical balance will be restored."

We were silent for a little bit. I didn't raise my eyes from my coffee mug, unable to look at the others. My hands were placed firmly around it, and it took everything in me to keep them from shaking.

Back in the tunnels, Klara had said something very similar to me.

Artur put his hand on my knee, our bond sparkling to life, warmth flowing between us.

"Well, that won't work now, will it?" asked Damian. He stretched his legs under the table until his socked foot touched mine, more warm magic surrounding me. "Nyja already found their way here and that was before the sky broke. Sure, they wore a human skin and got here with a devil's help, but I dare say no god stepped in our world for a few centuries. As you said, we aren't properly in Jawia anymore, we're stuck somewhere in between, moving further and further away from the human realm. We're playing a completely different game. And we all know what happened when they tried to swear Wiki in as a Guardian."

"Before the Children of Weles got to me, I had another Baba Jaga dream," I said. "It told me about this special cloth it weaved from my dreams, a cloth that could patch up the sky. And it also told me that I passed the first trial."

"A trial?" asked Artur.

"It's a common motif in the Eastern Slavic folktales," said Mum. "A Baba Jaga challenges someone to three trials. Some believe it used to be an actual adulthood ritual, possibly when a person first got their period. That's why later the story said that Baby Jagi eat children—they were responsible for the adulthood rituals."

"I didn't agree to enter any trials," I said.

"I don't think it's something you can choose to or not to do."

I crossed my arms. Not having a choice seemed to be a common motif in *my* life.

"You passed the second trial when we were in the summerhouse," said Damian. "Most of it is over. It could all be done soon."

"We agree we want to destroy the Guardian's system, right?" asked Karina, speaking up for the first time. All of us nodded. "Well, from what I understand we can't leave this area at all, since we aren't properly in Jawia anymore. Or maybe because the Guardians cut us off. Either way, patching up the sky seems to be the only way to move forward. Then we can decide how to move on without destroying the world again."

I met Damian's gaze across the table, then Artur's. Slowly, we nodded.

"So we're just going to wait around for the Baba Jaga to show up, so I can pass the final trial?" I asked.

"It's almost winter solstice," said Mum. "We'll prepare for celebrations, We'll strengthen you up. Maybe," her eyes bore down on mine, "get you to train. And hopefully the Baba Jaga will show up sooner rather than later."

After days spent lying in bed, waiting around shouldn't have been so hard but it was. I wasn't in top shape but restless energy built up inside me and I paced the house, unable to stay anywhere for too long. Damian tried to interest me in a vanishing spell he was working on, but I didn't have enough focus to sit with him for longer than a few minutes at a time. I got Rafi to train with me, but my muscles were weak and he'd brought me down to the floor five times in four minutes, which wasn't great for raising morale. Karina was working with crystals, sitting by the fire in the living room and shaping them wIth magic into fantastical forms, then trying to spell them for good luck and protection with Damian and Rafi's help. But as beautiful as it was to watch the stones light up with magic and morph and shape into leaves and animals, I couldn't help her with it.

I stayed close to Artur, our hands constantly brushing, our shoulders close together, cuddling, enjoying the warmth of our bond. I could sense that staying up was exhausting him, but he was resolute to keep up with the rest of us. So we stayed close to the rest of the Circle of Four, playing cards by the fire. Mum had given up on trying to keep us away from each other and I revelled in the closeness we shared. Artur kept taking in every bit of magic that escaped me and used it to cast wondrous illusions around us, filled with multiple moons, eternal sunsets, and warm air. They were short lived and less detailed than I was used to, but I appreciated every second that we didn't have to see the red light streaming in through the frosted window. In between these moments, we filled each other in about everything that had happened while we'd been apart.

"Has anyone ever tried to interact with your illusions?" asked Damian.

"I don't think so?" answered Artur. "It's still new I can share them with others, not only Wiki."

"Can I try? Dream something up."

Swirls of orange twirled in front of us, forming a little fox. The cub looked around and spotted its fluffy tail. It spun around, chasing it, until it fell over. It lay on its back, staring up at Damian.

Damian held up a hand above the fox cub and snow flurries appeared in the air, descending towards the animal. The fox raised up on its hind legs, trying to catch the snowflakes. It stuck out its tongue. When a snowflake landed on it, warmth spread up Artur's body, not unlike the sparkle of the bond when we touched.

"Oh."

Artur looked at the fox cub wide-eyed, his cheeks flushed. Damian extended his hand and the fox touched it with its nose. Even though Damian was good at masking his emotions, the rush of magic took him by surprise. He grinned, stroking the fox's ears, magic sparkling, his eyes gold.

"I'm going to try it in your dreams, too," said Damian as the fox vanished.

"Wait, you…you were really there?"

Damian raised an eyebrow. "Why, do you dream about me often?"

"No, no, that's not what I mean." Artur's cheeks reddened more. "It's just that Wiki doesn't remember her dreams so even though I know the bond does it…I sort of forgot? If that makes sense?"

"I guess we'll have to make it unforgettable." Damian scrunched up his nose. "No, that sounded bad. Forget I said anything. I'm high on magic and shouldn't talk."

Artur stared at Damian for a couple more moments, flustered. I bit back a smile.

It was good Rafi wasn't in the room to witness it.

"Close your eyes," I said later than evening, when Artur and I wandered back to the kitchen.

Artur did as I asked. Carefully, making sure my mental barriers were strong and our bond betrayed nothing, I opened the window and retrieved a strawberry from the bowl.

"You're not going to shove snow under my jumper, right?" asked Artur, shivering as cold wind whipped through the kitchen.

"It's good to hear how much you trust me," I said, rolling my eyes as I closed the window. "Open your mouth."

The surprise and delight in Artur's face when he bit into the strawberry made my heart warm. When he opened his eyes, they were green, the colour of a summer meadow.

"How?" he asked.

"It was a thank-you gift from Dawid. For saving him and Darek from the basilisk."

Warm, warm feelings filled our bond like first spring days, and I found myself smiling.

"Thank you," said Artur, brushing my hair back behind my ear. His hand lingered there, his fingertips skimming my scalp, making me tingle all over. I leaned into his touch.

"I know it's a big deal for me to share food, but even I can make an exception every once in a while."

Now a ghost of smile played on Artur's lips, too. His eyes flickered with different shades of blues and greens, a sight I'd missed more than I'd realized.

With a start, I realized this moment was perfect. I didn't want to lean in and kiss him. I didn't want to rip off his clothes. I wasn't waiting for a love confession. What we had was perfect for me.

My heart stuttered, waiting for something to ruin it all.

"Not just for the strawberry," Artur said, his fingers brushing through my hair, his eyes fixed on mine. "Though, yes, I realize getting you to share food, and especially sharing off-season fruit at the end of the world is a big deal. I mean thank you for staying with me, for not abandoning me in this void. It wasn't the best choice for you, but I'm not sure I could have made it through without you. So, thank you."

"You're my partner-in-crime," I whispered. "We're in it together."

Warmth flooded between us, magic tingling and jumping everywhere we touched. We stared into each other's eyes, relishing this connection, wishing this moment to stretch forever. Artur's emotions for me used to terrify me but now I knew who we were for one another, what we wanted from our relationship, and I trusted him to respect my boundaries.

The door to the kitchen opened, and I stepped away from Artur's embrace. Mum walked into the kitchen, her eyes resting on us.

"I promised Damian to help him with the vanishing spell," said Artur, looking between my mum and me.

His words didn't register as a lie, but I knew his promise wasn't time sensitive. I narrowed my eyes at him.

Traitor, I said through the bond, but he squeezed my hand and left Mum and me alone in the kitchen.

I leaned on the counter, drumming my fingers on its surface as Mum walked to the kettle to boil water. I counted my breaths, promising myself that once I got to ten, I could make an excuse and leave, too.

Before I had a chance to do that, Mum cleared her throat and handed me a blue box. I stared at it appalled.

"You don't want to get pregnant right now," she said.

"It's not like that," I protested.

"It's better to be prepared."

In general, I agreed with that principle. But I couldn't even begin to describe how the very sight of the condom box made it hard to breathe, the weight of the world's expectations crushing into me. It didn't matter that I trusted Artur, that I knew he wasn't interested in me sexually, it didn't matter that I was comfortable with him and magic felt nice. Panic squeezed my lungs, filling my insides with ice.

But I knew Mum meant well so I closed my fingers around the box and nodded. My legs kept me rooted in place. I didn't know what to say. I couldn't come out as anything because I still had no idea how I felt about people. And maybe it wasn't the time for that conversation.

As Zuzanna had told me, it wasn't smart to have life-altering conversations without a clear exit strategy. And we were stuck in this house as the world outside ended.

Mum made two cups of tea and left the kitchen without another word. I took a deep breath and followed her out, my hand clasped around the condom box.

Just as I closed the door to the kitchen behind me, I bumped into Damian. Of course he wasn't working with Artur on any spells. I pressed the condom box into his hand and he stared at me with his eyebrows raised.

"I don't need it, and I don't want it," I said, my voice

drawn tight. "I'm not saying you have to use it, just take it out of my sight."

Damian put the condom box in the back pocket of his jeans. He looked me up and down, no doubt trying to unravel my tangled emotions.

"You know Artur is the last person who'd push you into something like that, right?" he asked. "I mean, not only he's unlikely to because he's ace but more importantly, he doesn't seem like an abusive bastard."

"I know," I said.

My hands were shaking and I folded them on my chest. Damian stared at me.

"I don't like it when people make assumptions about us," I said. "He's my person, but that doesn't mean I like it when people call us boyfriend and girlfriend or push condoms at me."

"You're shaking," said Damian and I wrapped my arms tighter around myself, willing them to relax.

"Does it matter? It's the end of the world, we have bigger things to worry about. And the problem is solved for now."

Damian shrugged.

"Suit yourself."

He pushed past me, but guilt gnawed at me, and I caught his arm.

"Hey," I said. "I'm sorry. And thank you for caring."

"It's all good," Damian said. "I don't think I'm in a position to be frustrated with people for being cagey and biting when someone prods at their internalized issues."

The door across the corridor opened and Artur joined us.

"What's wrong?" he asked, looking between Damian and I.

"It's nothing," I said automatically, and Artur flinched.

"Why are you lying?" His voice was soft, not insulted but worried.

It made me feel even worse. Here I was overreacting and he was all caring and understanding to me as always. Panic squeezed the air out of my lungs and I struggled to get a breath in, my heart hammering in my chest.

"Hey," said Artur. "Please tell me what you need."

I shook my head, my eyes wet with tears. *I don't know*, I said telepathically.

"Ok, how about a hug? Can I hug you?"

I nodded and Artur closed his arms around me, pulling me against his chest. I still struggled to draw a breath but the warmth of our bond lessened the pressure in my chest a little bit. Oh gods, how stupid was I, blowing things out of proportion, panicking over nothing?

"Damian, can you make some tea?" asked Artur, holding me close.

Damian disappeared in the kitchen, but he left the door open, hovering nearby.

"I'm sorry," I said, sniffling.

"I am sorry. I shouldn't have left you alone with your mum, it was a stupid idea. You have nothing to be sorry about," said Artur, tracing patterns on my back with his fingers.

"But I do," I insisted, feeling horrible with how easily he could comfort me and how badly I was repaying it.

"Okay. Do you want to tell me about it?"

I didn't respond straightaway, clinging to his jumper and letting our bond calm me.

"My mum gave me condoms. And I might have overreacted a little."

Artur just continued stroking my back.

"We can make balloons out of them," he said so seriously that a surprised laugh escaped my throat. "Or sell them in exchange for a lot of food, I imagine there might be a deficit. Maybe we could get a cake."

"I already gave them to Damian. I couldn't even look at them."

Artur was quiet for a couple of moments. He leaned his head over mine, his cheek resting on the crown of my head.

"I still don't understand what you think you should be apologizing for," he said.

"I shouldn't have overreacted like that! I trust you, I know you'd never push me into anything I wouldn't want and here I am having a breakdown in a hallway just because my mum cares about my health and safety."

"Well, seeing how I punched Tomasz when he gave me condoms, I don't think I'm in a position to judge. And I don't think you're overreacting. You're feeling what you need to feel and your emotions are yours. It's good you're letting it out instead of keeping it all in. And I'm glad you trust me enough to tell me all of this. Besides, I know you don't like when people make assumptions about who we are to each other. Of course you'd be upset if your mum pushed condoms at you. And I'm sorry that people see a boy and a girl and think they will instantly have sex and fall in love with each other. Does anyone actually do that?"

"I think they do. But I don't think our relationship is any weaker without these components. I mean, I would slay more basilisks for you, no questions asked."

"QPR," said Damian and I spun around to face him. He stood behind me, holding out a mug of hot tea towards me.

"What?" I asked, accepting the mug.

"Queer-platonic relationship. A close, committed relationship that's not romantic in nature. Just people being close in whatever way works for them, outside of the regular scripts written by the society."

Now that he said it, I'd seen this term on Tumblr. I hadn't paid much attention to it before, but now I liked it. It seemed right.

"I like it," said Artur.

"Really?" I asked surprised. "I thought you weren't sure about the romantic attraction thing."

"It's not about me, it's about us. And you strongly implied that romance makes you uncomfortable. If it was essential to me, I would tell you. But we discussed what we want our relationship to be like and I think queer-platonic describes it well."

I bit back a smile, trying to keep my expression serious.

"Would you be my queer-platonic partner?" I asked Artur.

"I would have hoped I already was? But, yes, of course."

We smiled at each other.

"By the way, now I understand why you constantly touch," said Damian.

"We don't," I said.

"Um, you really do. But now that I can feel the bond, I get it. The sensual attraction is off the charts, magic calling to magic. Maybe you don't realize you do it, but I understand why you're always close together."

FOURTEEN

The Baba Jaga didn't visit me in my dreams that night, or the next. During the last night before the winter solstice, I got another unexpected visitor. A hand closed around my arm, and I snapped out of a dream. I sat up, magic blasting out, throwing the hand off me and rattling the furniture.

"It's just me," said Rafi, throwing his hands up in a gesture of surrender. I pressed my hands to my chest as if it could slow my racing heart. "Come, I could use your help."

"What happened?" asked Artur, his voice raspy.

"Nothing," said Rafi. "But you can come, too."

Artur and I exchanged a look. I grabbed Damian's jumper from the chair, and we followed Rafi to the kitchen. Karina was already there, snuggled in an oversized hoodie, her hair pulled into a bun on top of her head. The place was lit up with a bunch of flickering candles and smelled like poppyseed from the kutia standing in a pot in the corner.

"What's happening?" I asked.

"We need to bake a cake," said Rafi, bouncing on the balls of his feet. "It's Damian's birthday tomorrow."

Karina looked at Rafi and smirked at me.

"We trust you most to bake an edible cake without a recipe and with what we have," she said.

"Okay," I said. "What do we have?"

It turned out we had quite a bit. There was flour, sugar, oil, and cocoa, and a box of oat drink that looked like it'd been through a lot but was still whole and before its best by date. Soon, the kitchen filled with the smell of chocolate cake. We crowded around the old coal oven, taking in its heat but also keeping a keen eye on the cake—none of us had ever used an oven like that and we didn't want the cake to burn.

In the end, the edges were a little blackened and it baked unevenly but it smelled like chocolate heaven.

It took everything in us to not eat it there and then but we put it aside and returned to bed. But I couldn't fall back asleep. I lay awake staring at the ceiling, trying to clear my mind.

"Are you awake?" Artur whispered.

"Yeah."

"Okay. Because I was thinking that there's one thing we haven't discussed when it comes to our relationship," said Artur, his voice uncertain.

"It's about Damian, isn't it?" I asked.

"Well, yes." Artur dared a glance at me, but then he looked back up at the ceiling. "But I think it's generally something we should discuss."

"It doesn't have to be just the two of us. To be fair, between our bond and the nature of our relationship, it would be hard for it to be. I mean, since sex is off the table and it's not a romantic relationship either, we basically rely on emotional intimacy and certain level of commitment, right? But that's what we expect from the whole Circle of Four as well."

"Physical closeness, too. That's a big part of what's so special with you, I like when you're close. I like cuddling with you, I like sleeping together, I like holding your hand. Yes, magic pushes all of us together but also, it's special with you. Damian calls it sensual attraction. Craving non-sexual physical closeness."

I squeezed Artur's hand. "But it's not just about me, is it?"

Artur shook his head.

"Well, yes and no. It's mostly our thing. But, as you said, because our relationship defies the traditional understanding, the boundaries aren't clear. In books and films, relationships revolve around sex, maybe kissing, that's what makes them special. But we don't do that and there are no clear rules for queer-platonic relationships."

"That's why I like it, we can make it whatever works for us. And it doesn't have to automatically come as the

most important relationship in our lives. That would be…
suffocating."

"I think that's part of what didn't work out with me
and Klaudia. I liked the dating part, but I had too many
important people in my life. I didn't want to sacrifice my
friendship with Simon or my relationship to the magical
community because I was dating someone and I was
expected to put everything aside for her. That's also why I
like what we have together. All of us."

"Me too. And I don't think we should close ourselves
off from an opportunity to explore it more. If you want to
deepen your relationship with Damian, you should talk to
him about it. Just, maybe, I'd keep it hushed from Rafi, at
least for now."

Artur ran his hand through his hair.

"It's not like anything happened. And I'm not saying
anything will. I just wanted to check if it could even be a
possibility. I don't even know how it could work, I mean,
between me being ace and him being aro, we sort of cancel
each other out? But also, in a weird way, we don't?"

"Talk to him, if you want to. As I said, I don't have
anything against it. I'm glad you want to have more close
people in your life. But I want us to be open about it. I don't
need to know the details, but I don't want you to shut me out.
I want to know how you feel, the good, the bad and the ugly."

"Of course."

"And…is it too much if I'd like to discuss anything major
first? Like, if you met someone else you might be interested

in, I'd like to know about it. Or, I don't know, if you start considering moving to Poznań or moving in together. I'd like to discuss things like these first. Am I stepping out of the line?"

Artur shook his head.

"No. It makes perfect sense. Of course, I'd tell you so we can talk about it first. What we have is important to me. *You* are important to me. And I don't expect that to change."

On the morning of the winter solstice, Mum was in the kitchen with Tomasz, tying together a bunch of dry grass with a red ribbon. I stared at them uncomprehending from the kitchen doorway. Surely, if they wanted a celebratory decoration, they could have picked a spruce from the garden.

"Diduch," said Artur. "We always have one for Szczodre Gody, too. Well, it's usually wheat, not wild grass, the last ceremonial bunch of wheat cut during the harvest, one that's carried around during the Święto Plonów. But you make do with what you have."

"Do you still get the ceremonial wheat from the Guardian?" asked Mum and Artur nodded. "I remember Stanisław brought it to your parents when you were born. I'm glad they kept up the tradition, you're the child of Święto Plonów. Now, get yourself some coffee and you can start rolling out the dumpling dough."

"We'll have dumplings?" I asked, lightening up.

Mum smiled at me from across the kitchen. "Of course.

You can't have a winter solstice without mushroom dumplings. Though, I'm afraid we'll have to do without sauerkraut."

It didn't matter—the prospect of the evening feast, of *dumplings*, filled us with energy and we rolled out the dough and started making the dumplings. Mum was humming *Gdy Się Chrystus Rodzi* under her breath as she prepared the wild mushroom soup—a very Christian and very un-solstice song. It had been her favourite Christmas carol before she'd regained her memory and for a few moments, in the kitchen filled with the smell of mushrooms, I could pretend that we were still fine, that the sky hadn't cracked open. But the red light streaming in through the window was impossible to ignore, and I knew the only reason we had so many dried mushrooms and poppyseeds, essential winter solstice ingredients, was the domowik—mushrooms and poppyseeds were for celebrating the dead relatives so of course he'd made sure we had plenty of them.

Artur grimaced, massaging his temple. I looked up, feeling his pain.

"Your eyes?" I asked. They'd been bothering him for the past couple of days, his head hurting from straining his eyes, but the sharp pain was new.

"Yeah. I've been without my lenses for too long. But I'll be fine."

I looked at him for a little longer, already making plans on how we could get his spare glasses from his parents. If his eyes hurt from just looking around the house, I imagined that once we'd ventured outside it would only get worse.

But there was another fear gnawing on my insides.

What if it's Węgliszek? I asked telepathically.

Artur shrugged, and I didn't need to be able to read his mind to understand his look. There was nothing we could do about it.

Soon, we were joined by Karina and Rafi, speeding-up our dumpling-making process. However, in the crowded kitchen we were still missing one person.

"Where's the birthday boy?" I asked.

"He says that it's a family holiday and doesn't want to impose," said Rafi, rolling his eyes.

"He already imposed." Karina huffed out a frustrated breath. "Thanks to him I got hardly any sleep. So he better gets his ass here and appreciate our efforts. I'll get him."

She brushed her floury hands on her jeans and left the warm kitchen. Before I could gather up the next circle of dumpling dough, there was a loud thud upstairs, then an unnatural, high-pitched sound, followed by a scream. Through the bond I felt a sharp sting of panic.

"Damian!" I shouted, abandoning the dumplings. "Kari!"

"No, you're not," said Mum, blocking my way to the door. She glanced at Artur. "The two of you are staying here. Tomasz will be with you. I'll go help them."

Before I could protest, Mum was out of the kitchen and running up the stairs. More thuds sounded upstairs but no more screams. Every fibre in me was begging me to follow her.

"It's for your safety," said Tomasz and I scoffed. "Like it

or not, you're the Circle of Four. There's a reason why your mum didn't want you in one place but we hoped this house was safe."

There was no such thing as a safe place, I wanted to say, but I bit my tongue.

Artur put his hand on my shoulder. The same restless energy was rushing through his body, urging him to act. While the panic on Damian's end of the bond diminished, replaced with pure adrenaline, I needed to know what was going on. Had Klara or her Children of Weles somehow got in here? Had she tried to smuggle him through the shadows?

I moved away from the shadowed corners of the kitchen. Artur raised his hands, flooding the kitchen with light, illuminating every nook and cranny. I sent him a grateful smile.

"Do you think it's a demon?" asked Rafi.

He was answered by more thuds upstairs, followed by a loud crash. I flinched and fisted my hands. I knew Mum was right. But also if anything happened to Damian or Kari, it was all over.

It took a few more minutes which stretched into eternity before the door to the kitchen opened. I jumped, but it was just Mum walking in, followed by Damian and Karina. Damian's dark hair was rumpled all over but it might have been from sleep.

"Gumiennik," said Mum. "A nuisance but it didn't cause too much harm. I got him outside. I'm more worried about how it got in here."

"It's the solstice. The barriers between the realms are at their weakest and all magic feels different," said Damian but his voice lacked conviction.

"We need to strengthen the protections," said Mum, nodding at Tomasz.

"I'll help," said Damian, shuffling out of kitchen after them.

Karina stood unmoving, hugging herself. Once their footsteps died, she finally spoke:

"Upstairs feels like magic. Strong, wild magic. I've only felt something like that a few times before." She stared me right in the eyes. "When we summoned the devil and when Nyja appeared in the old market square."

Our moods were dampened but not much happened until sunset, when we had our solstice meal. As the sun disappeared beyond the horizon, we were joined by Aunt Eliza and, soon afterwards, Gabriella—Damian's and Laura's Mum.

The moment the door opened revealing the alchemist, Damian's side of the bond filled with anger and pain. He pushed it away almost immediately, blocking out Artur and me, but the short insight was enough for us to gather close around him.

"Happy birthday," Gabriella said, trying to catch her son's eyes.

"Why are you here?" Damian asked, anger plain in his voice.

He rose to his feet, his arms crossed on his chest, reminding me of the first times we'd met. I hadn't realized how much he'd let his shields down around us until that moment.

"It's solstice," said my mum. "It's the time for community. For family."

Damian's scowl made it clear what he thought about that.

"And we really need allies right now," said Tomasz, embracing Gabriella.

We crowded in extra chairs around the kitchen table and squeezed close together, making sure to leave an empty chair for a dead relative. We were a strange group and seeing my family mix with the magical world had never seemed as weird as in that moment. The feeling was amplified once Mum sang in Latin, leading the solstice chant. Tomasz was the next to join, followed by Gabriella and Artur. More than half of us sat in silence, myself included.

Great job bonding the community, Mum.

I grabbed Damian's hand under the table. He glowered at me, but his expression relaxed as the warmth of our bond spread between us. He squeezed my hand, taking in my magic.

Artur's words faltered and he grabbed my other hand before finishing off the chant.

"I guess I should have taught you the words beforehand," said my mum, scratching the side of her head. "I thought Zuzanna would have…"

"I don't think she'd anticipated that either of us would stay alive this long," I said.

My heart pained as I thought of Zuzanna and Aysun. Where were they now? Were they still alive? Had we broken the Kromer's curse or was it just a temporary fix?

"I know the words, but in Polish," murmured Damian.

We shared kołacz and ate wild mushroom soup, dumplings, and kutia, the best meal I had in a while. Aunt Eliza had made us each a motanka—a simple, handmade doll, which she'd tried to spell for protection. After we were done and moved to the living room, the warmth and full stomachs making us sleepy, Rafi caught my eye. He glanced at Damian, then at me again. I grinned at him and Rafi left the room, a mischievous smile on his face.

"Tell me you didn't..." started Damian just as Rafi returned with a cake.

Damian groaned and Rafi's smile widened before he broke into the song. I joined in, lacing my arm through Damian's. Soon, everyone was singing. Through Damian's embarrassment, I sensed two different emotions. Joy. And a small seed of hope.

We shared the cake and sat around the fire deep into the night, drinking mulled wine and talking about the end of the world and our future plans. I was half asleep, filled with more warmth and joy than I had in ages, when a feeling of unease settled in my stomach.

Something was off.

A chill ran down my spine, strange magic prickling my

skin. Artur looked at me, his eyes widening.

"Wiki—" he started but he was cut off as magic burst out from me.

With a crush, all the furniture was thrown against the wall. Someone shouted but it all felt like coming from behind a thick wall. My limbs didn't feel like mine, strong, wild magic burning my skin.

Karina got to me first, taking my arm, taking in my magic, but my arm pushed her away against my will.

"STOP!" Tomasz's voice boomed across the room and my body froze.

My muscles struggled against his magic, but Tomasz was strong. And then the weird magic left me and I stopped struggling. I waited a few heartbeats to make sure the foreign presence had left.

"It's okay," I whispered, my voice trembling. "It's gone."

Tomasz's magic released me, and I wrapped my arms around myself. Karina touched my arm again, and Artur sat on my other side, hugging me.

"The devil has her blood," said Damian, confirming my suspicions.

"We should be safe here," said my mum.

Before anyone had a chance to say anything else, there was a powerful groan. White light lit up the room, so blinding that I put up my arm to protect my eyes. For a second, I thought that maybe it was Artur, but before I could ask, the ground shook and trembled. If I hadn't been already sitting on the floor, I would have fallen.

Artur and Karina reached for my hands at the same time. I caught Damian's eyes and I knew we were all thinking the same thing.

The last time the world had shaken and the sky had been blinding like that, the god Nyja had come to Earth.

FIFTEEN

As soon as the ground stabilized, Tomasz and Gabriella were on their feet, ready to strengthen the household protections. But then the room was flooded with the familiar warmth of sorcerer magic. Furniture banged against the wall again and books fell from the shelves. Tomasz lost his footing and tumbled to the ground.

Artur pulled on my magic, but it wasn't me.

"It's not me," I said out loud, doubting my own words. Because when hadn't a telekinetic burst been my fault?

But this time I had a grasp on my magic and with Artur and Karina holding onto me, grounding my magic, I wouldn't lose control. It wasn't the devil, either.

It wasn't me.

Artur understood it first. He looked at my mum in terror, and I followed his gaze just as another wave of magic escaped her, the power pushing against us like a forceful wind. More books tumbled to the ground.

"What are you doing?" asked Tomasz, his eyes on me.

"It's not me," I repeated, dread squeezing my stomach, struggling against the push of magic to remain standing.

Tomasz followed my gaze to my mum. Her eyes were wide open, her face pale, hair flying around her head as if electrified.

"I don't know what's happening," she gasped. "I can't control it."

The furniture rattled against the walls again.

Outside, bright light flashed again and I squeezed my eyes shut, the magic's push unrelenting, threatening to force me to the ground. Was my mum's loss of control related to what was happening outside?

"Stop," said Tomasz, his bewitched word prickling my skin.

Mum's telekinetic push halted. But so did everything else. I couldn't move even my smallest finger. I couldn't swallow. I couldn't *breathe*—

Panic squeezed my lungs, blood in my veins turning cold. I wanted to scream but couldn't open my mouth. I fought against the magic, but I couldn't even blink. A glance around the room told me that everyone was frozen in place.

"No," said Tomasz, fright slipping into his words. "Not like that. You can move, you can *breathe,* just don't use your magic."

My muscles slumped and I took in a deep breath, my heart racing in my chest. But my relief was short lived as my body stopped mid breath, unable to move again.

Because Tomasz didn't need to talk to use hypnosis. He hadn't spoken when we'd first met and he'd grown stronger since, as we all had.

"What are you doing?" asked Karina. She stared at us in terror, seemingly unaffected by Tomasz's magic.

Tomasz didn't respond, looking around the room with his eyes wide, his hands trembling.

Karina grabbed my shoulders, trying to shake me out of the spell but it didn't work, my body limp in her hands. And I still couldn't breathe, and I was running out of air, and—

Karina let go of me as suddenly as she'd grabbed me and sprinted out of the room. Her steps thudded on the hardwood floor and doors slammed in the distance.

Were we all going to die here?

No. I'd channelled Tomasz's magic in the past. Maybe I could do it again, maybe I could break this spell, but my mind was too foggy and the room in front of my eyes began to blur—

Karina ran back into the room and pushed something into Tomasz's hand.

"Drink," she ordered.

Just as spots started dancing in front of my eyes, my lungs began to work again. I doubled-over, drinking in the air greedily, shaking all over. But then a telekinetic push made me lose my balance and I tumbled to the floor next to Artur.

"What is happening?" he asked, struggling to push himself up.

As if in answer, a lightning struck outside.

Karina walked over to my mum and handed her a bottle filled with familiar yellow potion.

"Drink," she repeated.

Mum obediently took the rue potion and drank it. Moments later, the telekinetic push stopped. Slowly, I sat up, trembling all over. I reached for Artur and squeezed his hand.

"I'm not going to jinx it, but it's one of the most magical nights of the year and the thunder might mean something we'd rather avoid," said Damian.

We exchanged gloomy glances. We expected the gods to be angry that they had been forgotten. Maybe it wasn't them but…

A thunder growled outside.

"I'm sorry," gasped Mum. Her hands were shaking. "I don't know what happened. I suddenly lost all control."

"So did I," said Tomasz. He regained his composure but his face was still pale.

"We can't risk this happening again," said Gabriella. "You need to keep taking the rue extract until we find out what happened and how to stop it. Did anyone else feel their magic slip?"

I glanced around the room, but nobody spoke up.

Why was it just Mum and Tomasz? What made them different from the other magic-users in the room? They were sorcerers, but so was Artur and his magic was stable.

"It can't be a coincidence it happened on the solstice, just after the Earth shook," repeated Damian.

"We need to patch up the hole in the sky," said Artur.

I nodded

"I need to finish the Baba Jaga's third trial."

"Well, then I guess you need to get some sleep," said Damian. "But first we need to redo the protections around this place."

"How do we know it won't backfire?" asked Artur.

"We don't," said Damian. "But does your magic feel off? Mine neither. And we can't stay here unprotected, especially on a night like this."

"Maybe Artur isn't wrong," said Gabriella. "And you aren't either. But sorcerer magic works differently from alchemists…or witches. We transform things that already exist, draw power from nature, rather than from our bodies. It's safer and more reliable, and we can't risk more things going wrong now."

Damian frowned at his mum but after a moment he nodded.

"Fine. We have more than enough of us to step up the protections around this place, fast. Rafi? Eliza?"

Rafi's face lit up and he got up to his feet to join Damian. He looked at Aunt Eliza and the four of them left the room.

"You're resistant to my hypnosis," said Tomasz, looking at Karina. He still looked pale and wide eyed, clearly shaken by what had happened.

She shrugged. "There must be some perks to demonic possession."

But she didn't follow the rest of the alchemists. I tilted my head, looking at her questioningly.

"My magic doesn't feel stable at all," she said, her voice low. "The demon is restless."

"I think we should stay close together tonight."

So Karina, Artur, and I piled up pillows and blankets by the fire and lay together, trying to ignore the trembling earth. My skin was tingling with magic, my veins filled with adrenaline. The last thing I felt like was sleeping.

Other than hoping it'd appear in my dreams, I didn't know how else to find the Baba Jaga. I wanted to help but I knew that the best help I could offer was sleeping.

It was even harder because of Damian. He hadn't come back after he'd left to fix the protections. Rafi had disappeared as well, something I'd been trying not to think about. Damian was pretty good at shielding his emotions from us but, every once in a while, a strong emotion would come through. And that night he was distressed—angry and scared, and hopeless.

Do you think something happened? I asked Artur telepathically.

He shrugged, not wanting to wake up Karina who'd dozed off a while ago. I understood him perfectly, though. Between it being Damian's birthday, his mum showing up, and then a potential divine visit, there were enough triggers to throw anyone off balance.

Damian's distress increased and I was ready to damn it all to hell and go find him when the door opened and he tiptoed into the room. Artur and I made space for him between us and Damian hesitated for only a heartbeat before taking the spot. He didn't complain as we hugged him, letting the warmth of our bond settle his emotions.

Just like when we'd woken up on the forest floor, the next morning I felt more rested and without any pain I'd expect after spending a night on the floor. I was squeezed between Damian and Karina, magic filling my body with tingly warmth, our bond strong. For a moment, I just lay there, startled by how much I treasured this casual, platonic closeness.

Then I was startled even more as the ground shook. It was a minor tremor, nothing like last night, but it was a harsh reminder of what was going on. The sky was so dark it didn't look like day at all, wind howled against the windows, the wood groaning. The red light outside flashed with renewed vigour, cutting through the dark clouds and illuminating them.

It didn't make me want to leave our warm nest. And I probably shouldn't have, since my dreams didn't bring me any closer to the Baba Jaga.

But I needed to pee and once I was done, everyone was up and getting ready for breakfast.

Artur looked at me questioningly and I could only shake

my head. It was frustrating, how much everything depended on a dream visit from a demon-goddess who was taking its time. Was Baba Jaga playing with us?

Damian seemed better this morning, though it was hard to say as he was shielding his emotions again. I tried to read his face, but he was avoiding my eyes. I decided to give him time, at least until we finished breakfast.

"Did you sleep well?" asked Rafi as we entered the kitchen. There was something off about his tone, he was a bit too perky, even for himself. Mum, Tomasz and Aunt Eliza sat at the table, looking like they hadn't gotten a lot of sleep.

Rafi was answered by sleepy groans.

"No talking before coffee," said Karina.

"The best I can do is tea," said Rafi, pouring hot water into four mugs. "No dream visits from demons?" he asked, handing me a mug.

I shook my head and blew into the hot mug of tea. Guilt gnawed at my insides—I shouldn't be up, I should be trying to connect to the Baba Jaga. To find out about my last trial.

Damian was the last but as he neared Rafi, my cousin splashed the cup of tea over his head. Damian stood shell-shocked as Rafi stomped out of the room. Damian looked after him then at his soaking wet jumper. He brushed his dripping hair out of his face and, without a glance at the rest of us, left the room, too.

Mum was observing it all with her eyebrows raised. Aunt Eliza shook her head. Artur and I exchanged a glance and I followed Damian who had locked himself in the bathroom.

I leaned against the wall, arms crossed on my chest, waiting for him to come out. It took a couple of long moments for him to open the door. He'd taken off his jumper and wore only a white t-shirt, goosebumps raising on his arms.

"What did you do," I asked, my tone flat.

"Nothing," Damian responded but through his usual wall of leave-me-the-fuck-alone annoyance, I sensed a sad note.

I stared at him hard.

"Didn't look like nothing to me."

"I swear that nothing happened."

His words didn't register as a lie, but it explained nothing.

"Then why did Rafi pour the tea over your head?"

Damian was quiet for a few heartbeats. "Because nothing happened?" he tried but when I let out a frustrated sigh, he continued. "He wanted things to happen, Wiki. And I told him that I don't feel about him this way and that it could make things very complicated. I guess it still did."

I sighed again but my anger subsided. Yeah, he'd still hurt Rafi but it sounded like he'd done the right thing. His last night's distress was suddenly making more sense.

Still, I was confused.

"But…you are attracted to him," I said, even though it wasn't necessarily the conversation I wanted to have about my own cousin.

"Not in the way he wants," said Damian, his gaze fixed at the wall in front of us. He squeezed his fists so hard his knuckles turned white. "He's cute but we both know he doesn't want casual sex. And I…I didn't want to ruin it. We're a good team, he's fun to be around. But I didn't want to make it look like I could give him something more."

"Not 'more,'" I said, my tone gentle. "Something different. Romantic relationships aren't automatically superior to other kinds of relationships. And friendship isn't anything worse."

There was a moment of silence. Wind howled against the windows, shaking them, a flurry of snowflakes obscuring the outside world.

"I didn't want to hurt him," Damian's voice came out hoarse. "If I hadn't cared about hurting him, I wouldn't have said no."

"Did you try telling him that?"

"Yes. It went about as well as you've seen."

I waited for a second, Damian's emotions hitting me hard now. I came here with all intentions of protecting Rafi and murdering Damian, but now my heart ached for Damian.

"Can I hug you?"

Damian hesitated for a moment, his posture stiffening, his mental walls coming up. But then he nodded and I closed my arms around him. He rested his forehead on my shoulder, magic humming softly between us.

"Why does it have to be so hard?" he asked after a few moments. "I thought we were friends. Why people can't understand that sex doesn't always have to come with romance? Even if they accept it doesn't have to be present at first, they see it as an inevitability. If you can't fall in love, if you don't want romance, you're the villain or there must be something seriously wrong with you, because romance is always portrayed as the ultimate good, the superpower that destroys all evil, the fucking proof of humanity. People can understand not wanting sex, but romance? Hah."

The door to the kitchen opened and Damian drew back so quickly he almost fell over, his mental shields up. But it was just Artur, and Damian relaxed a tiniest bit.

"You know, I've been told that I give the best hugs," Artur said, looking between the two of us.

"He does," I agreed.

"You don't even know what it's about," said Damian, crossing his arms on his chest.

Artur held his gaze steady.

"You can tell me if you want. But I can feel that you're upset and hugs usually help at least a little."

"Hugs give you oxytocin. And I should check on Rafi," I said and Damian jerked his head up to look at me, his panic slashing through me. "I understand I shouldn't tell him anything."

"Please, don't."

"I won't," I promise.

I climbed the stairs and walked down the narrow corridor to the room Rafi often shared with Damian. I knocked and a muffled sound told me to come in.

The room was just big enough for two single beds lined up against the opposite walls and a wardrobe. The wallpaper was mustard yellow with a delicate floral pattern. Rafi was lying on one of the beds, his face buried in the pillow.

"Are you okay?" I asked, leaning on the wall.

"Nooo," said Rafi, stretching out the sound for emphasis. "I know that men are horrible. But I don't understand how I could have been so wrong about him. I can't believe I'm going to say that but I should have listened to Kari, she got it right straightaway. Freaking Angsty Asshole."

"So, what actually happened?"

"I've been deceeeiveeed. We were getting along so well, we spent so much time together in the past weeks, we definitely had some chemistry going on, and I'd catch him *staring* all the time. But then he flat-out rejects me because, apparently, he already knows it wouldn't work. You don't stare at someone like that and then give them the cold shoulder. You just don't."

"I think you might be a little unfair."

Rafi raised his head from the pillow, and I flinched under his stare.

"Unfair? You saw the way he looks at me. It's not in my head. But I guess with your bond it makes sense you'd side with him."

"I'm not siding with anyone."

"Doesn't look like it." Rafi's head dropped to his pillow again, then he jerked it up again. "You can feel his emotions, can't you? You could have given me some heads up."

"He's good at shielding his emotions. But I think you

should talk once you both have calmed down."

"Wow," Rafi murmured into his pillow.

I sighed and patted his back.

"I'm sorry he rejected you," I said. "It sucks and you have every right to feel like shit. But I don't think he wanted to hurt you."

"Ugh."

I kneeled next to the bed and laid my cheek on Rafi's back, hugging him.

"How do you know he was flirting and not just being nice?" I asked.

"That's the most aro thing you've ever said. You can just tell these things."

"Can you, though? Because there must have been some miscommunication. Isn't the difference between flirting and kindness or romance and friendship all about the intention behind it? And how can you know the intention unless you've discussed it?"

"I hate you. Let me wallow in misery."

I didn't move, pressing my cheek to his back. We stayed like that for a few moments, until the Earth rocked again. The sky growled, thunder rippling through the broken red sky and I shivered. We huddled together, waiting for the Earth to quiet again.

Rafi moved his head to look at me:

"As much as I appreciate your company, I'd like it all to stop even more. Are we going to wait around forever until Baba Jaga decides to speak to you?"

"No," I said, suddenly much more aware of the red light streaming in through the window. "I need to try again."

I found Gabriella in the kitchen, leafing through a thick book with my mum and Tomasz.

"I want to try a sleeping potion," I said. "But something mild that wouldn't knock me out for a day."

"I have something that could work," said Gabriella and I followed her to the corridor. "I'm glad you and Damian are getting close. He really needs people he can rely on."

I offered her a tight-lipped smile. Getting closer to Damian made me feel awkward about my connection to his mother. I knew the strain in their relationship didn't have to influence ours, but it was an elephant in the room.

"But I have another child I have to think about," she added.

I took a step back, panic clawing at my throat. Across the corridor, by the front door, shadows stirred, and I screamed, scrambling away. Gabriella whipped around, while I rushed into my room.

It was supposed to be a safe place. Safe. Far away from Klara's moving shadows.

But after yesterday it was clear that it wasn't.

Artur and Damian were sitting on the bed, but they scrambled to their feet when I opened the door. Before I could even open my mouth, white light shone across the room, blinding me. I shielded my eyes with my arm, while Artur pulled me into an embrace.

"Was it supposed to be an exchange?" I asked, trembling all over.

"What?" asked Artur.

"What?" repeated Gabriella.

"I should have known better than to trust any of you. Of course, you'd sell me to them in exchange for Laura."

Why wouldn't she choose her own daughter over me? It made perfect sense. Yes, Gabriella was one of my closest allies in the magical community but she'd backstabbed me before. Like when she'd concocted the poison that Zuzanna's father had used on me and refused to give me an antidote. Or after the funeral, when Artur had been kidnapped and together with Tomasz she'd forced me to drink the sleeping potion, to keep me from going after him.

"What?" repeated Artur, his tone harsher this time.

"Wiktoria, no," said Gabriella, her tone insistent. The bright light still filled the room so I couldn't see her. "I'd never do that. And it wasn't Klara, it was you channelling her shadow-walking ability. The shadows retreated when you panicked. Do you think Klara would have done that?"

"The shadows retreated because Artur flooded them with light."

But I didn't know what to believe anymore.

Artur's fingers bit into my back in a silent question.

I don't know, I said telepathically. *I don't know. It's your call.*

After a few more seconds, the light around us dimmed, but Artur's arms around me remained strong, tethering me to him. It took me a few long moments of blinking to see the corridor again.

"Why would Wiki think you'd do something like this?" asked Damian, his arms crossed across his chest. He was wearing Artur's hoodie, which hung loosely on him.

"Because you said you have another child you have to think about, too," I said, addressing Gabriella.

Hesitantly, I freed myself from Artur's embrace, but I held on to his hand. Klara had once said that she didn't have the magic to pull both of us through the shadows, but I didn't know how it had changed now that everyone had grown in power.

"Yes," said Gabriella. "But not because I'd sell you in exchange for her. But because you asked me for a favour and I'd like to ask you for a favour back. We need to free Laura from the Children of Weles."

I closed my eyes, but not only because colourful specks still kept filling it and I needed to clear my vision. No, I also needed to gather my thoughts.

"And if I don't agree?" I asked, playing for time. "You won't give me the sleeping potion? I can sleep on my own. Or ask Damian to prepare it for me. You know it doesn't all depend on you, right?"

"I'd still give it to you," said Gabriella. "But please consider helping Laura. She's your friend, isn't she? You don't abandon friends in need."

I needed to find a way to convey the truth to Gabriella without sounding too emotional.

"Laura chose to be with them," I said, fighting to keep my voice even. "She gave us the wrong ritual on purpose, without telling us what it would do. Because of her we've torn the sky apart. That's why all of this is happening now. All in a bid to get Weles back. Not to mention designing this horrible crystal device—"

I cut off, unable to continue. My skin tingled at the memory of the magic flowing from the tunnels, through me, into the crystal. But Artur squeezed my hand and another, comforting sort of magic rushed through me.

"She enabled the Children of Weles to torture Wiki for days," said Damian. "Why would you think she wants to be rescued?"

"She helped you free the people turned to stone by the basilisk, didn't she?" asked Gabriella. I nodded. "And do you think the Children of Weles would have been happy about it? You know best what they're capable of. And she, unlike you, wasn't necessary for them."

I swallowed hard. Gabriella was right. If the Children of Weles had found out about what Laura had done, as they'd probably had, she would have been in serious trouble.

"And you know what really happened last night," continued Gabriella. "You know that some god returned to Jawia. And whether it was Weles or not, I don't want my daughter anywhere close to gods. Nothing good can happen when forgotten gods return to the mortal realm."

I fixed my eyes on the ground, unable to look at the alchemist anymore.

"She's your sister," she looked at Damian, then turned her gaze to Artur. "And she's as good as yours, too. And how can we pretend to be any better than the Children of Weles if we leave close ones behind in time of need? How can we hope for any sort of better future?"

Through the bond, I could feel Artur agreed with me about what we needed to do. But Damian's mental shields were impenetrable and his face unreadable, so I didn't know what he felt.

"You know what you're asking of us, right?" he asked. "We are the only people who can fix this mess. Only we can patch up the sky. And we have the best shot at finishing the Guardian system once and for all. None of that happens if the Children of Weles catch us. This city will be stuck in this limbo until it's destroyed by gods or demons, and then, who knows, maybe the rest of the world will follow."

"It's your decision," said Gabriella. "But you also have the most magic at your disposal. If anyone can pull it off, it's you."

I looked at Artur. His face openly showed his feelings, his eyes swimming with sorrow. Laura had been in his life as long as he could remember. They'd grown up together, as close as siblings, the two children in our magical community closest in age. And siblings squabbled and fought and hurt each other, but they didn't leave each other behind. He didn't need convincing.

Damian's face was harder to read, his stare still hard, his arms crossed. But I knew that most of the time he only pretended to be all tough and unfeeling, it was a mask he used to shelter himself from the world. And even if Damian and Laura didn't seem the closest when I'd seen them together, he still had a bit of an older brother's protective gene. He hadn't let his roommate give her alcohol.

I couldn't make the decision for him, but my heart was set.

"Okay," I said. "I'll do it."

SIXTEEN

DAMIAN AND I SNEAKED OUT OF THE SAFE HOUSE. After a long discussion, we'd decided that Artur should stay. My mum was right to an extent. While keeping the four of us apart wasn't a great idea, all of us walking into the Children of Weles' lair was plain stupid. And Artur was still recovering, while Damian was glad to put some distance between himself and the safe house—and, I suspected, Rafi.

We'd decided against telling my mum about the plan for now. Gabriella and Artur would cover for us and only alert Mum and Tomasz if we weren't back by sundown.

The streets were blanketed by snow and lit up by the eerie red light. Dark clouds covered the sky, making it seem like it was dark even in the middle of the day.

"This is a horrible idea," Damian said as we walked down the stairs towards the old town.

He was right. I wished we could ask Mum or Tomasz for help but they'd never let us go. Besides, they were under the influence of the rue potion, their magic blocked. But Gabriella was right as well. If we wanted things to get better, we had to act better ourselves. And freeing Laura was the first right step. No matter what she's done, she was Damian's sister and our friend. She'd saved us many times before, she'd help us free Artur and the others, and, even if she'd designed the crystal that the Children of the Weles had used to torture me, I didn't want the Children of Weles to hurt her.

We had powerful magic. We were here to change the world. What good was it for if we wouldn't use it to save a friend?

"What if she doesn't want to be freed?" asked Damian.

"We'll worry about it when it comes to it." I squinted, looking ahead. "What happened there?"

In the distance, an entire district had been turned to rubble.

"I'm not sure I want to know," said Damian.

We reached a bigger road, and I pulled on Damian's sleeve, forcing him to stop. I remembered my encounter with the military too well, and this time we didn't have Tomasz to mind-trick anyone for us. Before leaving, we'd tried Damian's invisibility potion but we didn't know how long it would hold.

We surveyed the street, but there were no cars. The snow was undisturbed, not even footsteps crisscrossed it.

I looked at Damian and we ran. We sprinted across the street and towards the old market square. This time we didn't descend to the tunnels early, the Children of Weles had too much power there. We had to stay out in the open.

The old market square was desolate. The tenements blanketed in perfectly white snow could have looked like a Christmas postcard if it weren't for the horrible red light distorting the view. And there, behind them, rose a big building made of red stone, with four towers.

I'd never seen it before, but I immediately knew what it was. Węgliszek's castle. Of course the devil would rebuild a historical castle as its lair.

Blinding light flashed and a powerful thunder roared across the sky, rocking the earth beneath our feet. I stumbled and fell into the snow. My ears were ringing and I blinked furiously, trying to regain my sight. I tried to push myself up, but another thunder rumbled and the earth shook again. Magic in the air was suffocating, muting everything else, including our Circle of Four bond.

I reached out blindly until I found Damian's hand. He squeezed it and only then did I realize I was shaking. Leaning on each other, we managed to get up to our feet. It took a few more moments until I could see again. Smoke was rising in the distance.

Damian said something but I shook my head. My ears

were ringing too badly to hear him. He frowned and pulled me down the back street. Soon, we entered a low tenement through the back door. It looked like the inhabitants had attempted to barricade it with wood and furniture but the door had been forced open, splinters of wood thrown all over the concrete floor, an old chest of drawers lying on its back further along the corridor.

"This is where we spied on the Children of Weles, to find out what happened to you," Damian said, leading me towards the stairs to the basement. His words were muted, but at least this time I could hear him.

My stomach knotted itself into a tight ball as we slowly made our way down. Nausea rose in my throat and magic prickled my skin, and I struggled to keep both down. I grasped Damian's arm, my fingers digging into his jacket, as he pushed the wooden door at the bottom of the steps.

Damian looked in both directions before stepping into the tunnels. I followed.

Fire shot up behind us, bright hot. I jumped away, swearing. Along the corridor, shadows scuttled away.

We needed to get out. Now.

"Fuck," murmured Damian.

Magic burned hotter between us as he faced the flames. He brought his hands together, but the only sign that anything was happening was the flow of magic between us. Damian kept on swearing under his breath as he coaxed water to rise between the old, broken pieces of stone, but the fire was unmoved.

I froze. I needed to be out of here. Out. Back in the safe house, back in the safety of the Circle of Four.

"Let's find another door," said Damian.

I nodded, fear choking my throat too hard for me to speak. We got to the next door, but it was locked. Same as the next, and the door on the opposite wall, too. The third door opened to a small room. My heart pounded hard as we tried door after door but we didn't have time to keep on searching forever. We needed to get out.

Steps echoed down the tunnel. I clutched Damian's hand and we ran into the darkness. Soon heavier, louder thuds shook the corridor. I glanced over my shoulder but I didn't see anything in the dark. I tripped on an uneven stone and fell, bringing Damian down with me.

He swore as we struggled back to our feet. My knees hurt from the impact, warm blood streaming down my leg as I ran my hands alongside the wall until I found the next door but, of course, it was locked. Damian pulled on my sleeve, and we ran on. I winced at the pain in my knee, but the thudding sound was growing louder and acted as an excellent motivator to run.

Soon, the tunnel grew lighter, even though there was no visible source of light. We didn't have time to question it. We ran until the walls around us weren't made of centuries old stone anymore but white marble, illuminated by sconces.

Oh no.

"The devil lives here," I said through my gnashed teeth.

But we didn't stop running.

"I'd rather take my chances with the devil," said Damian, echoing my sentiment.

The thudding grew quieter until the only sound in the tunnels were our own steps and rushed breaths. The corridor ended with a tall gold door. We stopped in front of it, fighting to even our breaths.

"We shouldn't go in," I said. "We can't risk being forced to bargain away anything more."

"We need to find Laura and run."

Before we could decide on our next move, the thudding started again and I jumped while my heart tried hard to escape my chest. I didn't believe my eyes at first—a stone statue was running towards us. Damian grabbed my sleeve again and nodded towards the door. I swallowed hard but I helped him push it open.

Just like I'd expected, the door disappeared as soon as we'd closed it. In front of us there were white marble stairs. We glanced at each other but it wasn't like we had any real choice other than to climb them.

As soon as our feet touched the first step, the floor behind us disintegrated into black void. I screamed, my voice echoing around a hundredfold. Damian clutched my arm, his fingers digging into my flesh.

What would happen if we fell? Was the void a nothingness? Would we keep on falling forever? Would we get to Nawia? Or was it only Węgliszek's mind trick?

I didn't want to find out.

We took another step and the stair below disintegrated as well. I swallowed hard and tried not to look behind as we climbed up.

I'd remembered Darek talking about a sorceress who had an affinity for rocks and now started controlling stone statues as well. Was that what had chased us down in the tunnels? Had it really been a statue?

The stairs went on and on and my legs ached, my hurt knee screaming in protest. But we were too scared of the stairs disintegrating beneath our feet to stop and rest. After a small eternity, another gold door gleamed overhead. We pushed through it and all but collapsed on the marble floor beneath.

The gold door disappeared behind us, leaving us in a large, blinding white corridor with tall windows. The eerie red light shone through, flashing alongside the corridor and glimmering in the river visible behind the window.

This time, the choice was easy. To our left, there was only black void. The corridor ran to the right with the huge, double gold door gleaming in the distance.

I sighed.

"I guess the devil has his plans."

We set off towards the next gold door. It was clearly a trap but it seemed like a better choice than trying to find out what would happen if we stepped into the black void.

Damian and I had to lean on the heavy door to push it open. Inside was the familiar big marble room where Artur and I had encountered Węgliszek. However, this time the room didn't seem endless. It was huge but we could see the other end of it, also adorned with a double gold doors. They were open, people streaming through. A small crowd of people walked towards a large wooden throne at the centre of the room. Some people kneeled in front of it, others left offerings. Money. Jars of honey or pickled cucumbers. Clothes. Books. Jewelery.

Damian looked at me questioningly, and I shrugged. Slowly, we joined the crowd. A middle-aged person approached the throne, kneeling before it. The throne was simple, more of a large wooden chair. Węgliszek sat or rather half-lay comfortably on top of it in his usual suit, one leg thrown over the side of the throne, his tail curled around the armrest. He twirled his goatee around his finger, looking at the person kneeling in front of him. Damian squeezed my arm in anticipation.

"I don't have anything left, kind lord," said the person petitioning the devil. "Please, I need food and my wife needs medicine. She's diabetic, we can't go on like that."

"You shall receive all you need," said the devil. "You'll be taken care of. Since you have nothing else to trade, all I'll take is a favour, to be called on anytime. Do you accept?"

"Yes, kind lord. Thank you. Thank you so, so much."

"Go home to your wife. You won't need for anything else."

The person scrambled to their feet, bowing once more as they made their way to the large gold doors. My throat squeezed as I expected something horrible to happen but the person left the room unscathed.

For now. Goodness knew what favour Węgliszek would request of them in the future.

Węgliszek stood up from his throne and walked to the side. There was a circle drawn with chalk there. The devil stomped its hooved feet and fire shot up around it. People gasped and a few screams broke out as another demon appeared in the circle.

It was a tall, human-looking figure, easily two metres tall and with massive muscles shown off by a linen tunic it wore. It had light hair, brushed back as if by the wind and dark blue eyes, like a stormy sky.

"Why was there a tornado in my territory, płanetniku?" asked Węgliszek, his voice chilling. "I thought we had a bargain."

Was that what had happened to the part of the city we'd seen from the stairs? A tornado?

"The bargain had been broken," said the płanetnik. "We don't owe you anything."

"Is that what you think? I call in the old favour. You will keep my city safe. No tornadoes, no destructive winds or storms."

"There are other players in the game now."

"You will do your job. You don't want to find out what happens otherwise."

The devil stomped again, and the płanetnik disappeared. A few people clapped and the devil grinned and bowed as he made his way back to his throne.

"Ah, but I see familiar faces in the crowd," said the devil, his dark eyes piercing mine. "Come forward, sorceress, witch. Don't be shy now."

We stepped closer, stopping next to a line of kneeling people. Some had their heads bowed, others stared at Węgliszek. Some of their faces were pleading, others were filled with adoration.

"What do you want of us?" I asked. I didn't have patience for games.

The devil smiled.

"You think I'm a mere demon, but I used to be so much more than that. Look at all these humans." Węgliszek moved his arm towards the people kneeling in front of him. "They know the truth. They sense my power. They know I can protect them, like I used to protect this city for centuries, long before the Guardians came to be. And I do protect those who show me respect."

I couldn't chance a glance at Damian, I didn't dare to tear my eyes away from Węgliszek. But I wanted to know what Damian thought, if he knew what Węgliszek meant. It wasn't a mere demon? Because devils were more powerful demons or because they weren't demons at all? But that would mean…

"You used to be a god," said Damian, his grip on my elbow strengthening.

Of course. There was no such thing as good and evil in the pre-Christian beliefs, and the devil was pure Christian imaginary. And wasn't that the case for all the gods who wouldn't be forgotten? Their memory was turned into demons instead—or, if they were lucky, another kind of Virgin Mary. The more powerful the demon, the bigger the chance that humans used to worship it once upon a time. And devils were among the most powerful of them all.

It made all the sense in the world that they'd used to be gods.

"Yes. And I appreciate everything you've done to help me regain my power, to rebuild my kingdom. But, of course, you'll understand I can't let you continue on your quest. I apologize, but I can't let you fix the hole in the sky. I can't let you take my kingdom away from me again."

"We're working to destroy the Guardian system," I said, my heart beating fast in my throat. "It won't be the same as it used to be."

"I'm not stupid, sorceress. I know why it's you and not someone else trying to achieve this, just like I knew why your parents summoned me."

"You promised you wouldn't directly hurt us. You can't break our pact."

"I promised I wouldn't do that until the winter solstice. And I didn't. And please, don't get me wrong. I don't wish you harm. I'd truly regret hurting you. But if I have to stop you, I will. As an act of goodwill, I'll even give you a head start."

The devil's eyes bore into mine.

"Wait," I said. My heart pounded in my chest as I scrambled for the right words. I didn't like talking to a devil without preparation, without a script to follow, but we were already in a dire situation. How much worse could it get?

"We're trying to rescue another magic-user. She helped us break the sky, she helped you regain your power. She worships gods, and she will likely try to stop us, much like you do. But she needs our help now. We are the only people who can save her."

The devil stared at us with an amused smile. He was silent for too long, giving my mind a lot of freedom to come up with all the ways he could torture or end us. The river was just outside the castle, perfect for drowning. He could probably ask any of the people in the crowd to hurt us in exchange for food or protection. He had pacts with demons. The possibilities were endless.

"Fine," said Węgliszek after a long while. "Rescue Laura the Alchemist. We will have plenty of time for our games afterwards."

Light burst out around us and the castle faded away.

SEVENTEEN

I BLINKED AS SPLASHES OF COLOUR DANCED IN FRONT of my eyes. I was cold but not freezing cold, which meant that wherever the devil had sent us was indoors. As my vision cleared, I spotted a familiar, messy living room with a tall balcony door overlooking the old market square.

We were in the Guardian's flat, in the tall white tenement.

"Great," said Damian, taking in the mess around us.

Footsteps sounded in the corridor and I clutched Damian's hand, magic tickling my skin. I let it flood me, ready to push the assailant away.

But it wasn't Filip or Klara who appeared in the corridor, only a petite girl with long hair that was a frizzy mess and which likely hadn't seen any flowers in weeks. She was wrapped in a black cloak with a blue mark that was probably supposed to be her usual flame symbol stitched unevenly on her breast.

"Damian?" asked Laura. "Wiki? What are you doing here?"

"That makes our job easier," said Damian. "We're leaving and you're coming with us."

"You can't be here," said Laura. "This is really bad."

"Is anyone else here?" I asked, scanning the room.

Was there any point in asking her that? Would she answer truthfully?

Laura shook her head.

"Of course not," snorted Damian. "Because she's not here under duress. Does it look like a dungeon to you? It's probably all one big trap. Let's get out of here."

Damian pushed past Laura towards the front door. Laura tried to catch her brother's arm, but he pulled himself away.

"It's a horrible idea," she said.

"The door isn't even locked," said Damian, throwing it open. "Let's get out of here."

"No, wait!" shouted Laura, but he didn't listen.

Shadows reached for Damian the second he stepped outside of the flat. He screamed as the shadows dragged him to the floor and towards the stairs.

"Damian!" I shouted, reaching for him.

"Wiki, don't!"

Laura snatched my arm, keeping me away from the door. I tried to push her away, but she held on to me fiercely. Magic lashed out of me, but Laura didn't let go.

"They will get to you, too!"

"We need to save him!"

"Yes! Yes, we do. But you won't do that, if they capture you, too."

It took a moment for her words to sink in. Damian's panic made my body shake, but I stopped struggling. Laura was right. The last thing I wanted was to be recaptured by the Children of Weles.

Or was it already too late?

Laura clung to my arm, keeping me still. Panic clawed at my throat as I stared at her. As I thought of everything she'd done.

"Please let me go," I said, my voice smaller than I would have liked.

Laura released my arm and I stepped back, hugging myself.

"You came for me," she said, her voice uncertain.

I nodded.

"If you don't want or need to be rescued, tell me now. I'll get Damian, and we'll be on our way."

Laura bit her lip. "I could use a hand getting out of here. And then we can free Damian together."

I nodded and turned to face the door. Clearly, leaving this way wasn't the best option. And the Children of Weles must have known I was here by now. Would they wait for me to go after Damian or would they try to apprehend me before? How much time did we have?

"How can we get out?"

"If I knew, I wouldn't be here. The good news is that the others can't get in here. The tenement wouldn't let them inside. But they are keeping an eye on the staircase. How did *you* get here?"

"The local devil teleported us in. Well, I guess he isn't really a devil but never mind. He seemed amused at the idea that we want to free you."

"You bargained with a devil to get me out?"

"No. The Children of Weles chased us to his castle so we didn't have a choice but to join his court."

"I'm sorry," Laura said.

I nodded. I acknowledged her words but I wasn't ready for this conversation. Besides, we had more pressing issues at hand.

"Let's find out if the tenement still responds to me," I said. "Then we can free Damian and get the hell out of here."

I kneeled on the floor and put my hands on the old wood. I stroked it with my fingers, trying to unravel the tenement's magic from the hole in the sky. The warmth reached back to me, running up my body, wrapping me in a hug.

"No foreign magic can infect our ancestral home," said a low, croaky voice behind my back.

I turned around to look at the domowik.

"But it does," I said. "How do I get rid of it?"

"Ask your ancestors for protection. Rebuild the spells protecting your home."

I nodded and got myself up to my feet. I headed for the kitchen. If there was one magical thing I knew how to do, it was the protective spells, Zuzanna had made sure of it.

I hoped her ingredient stash was still here.

"I used some of the herbs and moon water, trying to create a potion that would help me get out of here," said Laura, who followed me to the kitchen.

I looked through the herbs, and there was still more than enough to make a smudge stick. I considered making a second one for Laura but I suspected blood was important for this sort of familial magic. And currently Laura didn't feel like family at all.

"Wait," said Laura. "Are you sure you can trust your magic?"

"What do you mean?"

The last thing I needed was to doubt my magic now.

"Hasn't it been more unpredictable since the winter solstice?"

"No," I said, narrowing my eyes. "Why would it be?"

"Because the gods are back. And Weles punished the magic-users who forgot about him. So if your magic doesn't feel more unpredictable than usual…that means you have the divine favour."

"Great," I said. I didn't know what else I could say. It was a lot of life-changing information at the time when I needed to clear my mind. "Finally some good news."

I took a deep breath, trying to calm my mind. I bound a bunch of thyme and pansy with a red string, whispering a spell under my breath three times over. I lit up the smudge stick and walked around, smoking the room, whispering the same spell under my breath. The tenement's magic grew stronger, embracing me as I moved around, wishing all the evil away. I threw salt into all the corners, renewing this most basic of protections. Then I put away the smudge stick into a clay dish, grabbed a piece of spelled chalk and kneeled on the floor. I drew a circle around myself, decorating it with the protective symbols that I'd drawn for Zuzanna so many times that I could see them inscribed on my eyelids when I closed my eyes. I put my hands on the floor one more time, urging the tenement's magic to the surface.

Warmth flooded me and I flinched as magic rushed from the air, through me, to the floor, and the other way round. It reminded me too much of being the Children of Weles' magical energy conduit, chained to the crystal that Laura had designed for them.

I didn't want to remind her that I had a lot of magic and maybe it really was best used for rebuilding the protections around the city.

But I didn't have time for doubts and hesitations. I was doing it for Damian. And for Laura. And for myself. I was going to get us out of here and back to safety.

So, I let the magic flow through me. When my mind calmed, I realized it wasn't like in the tunnels. This magic knew me, cherished me, recognized me as its own. It didn't hurt me, it enveloped me in its warmth and caressed my arms and neck. For better or worse, the Guardian's blood ran through me and the tenement knew it and welcomed me home.

I reached out with my mind and felt the magic flowing through the old floors, thick walls, and high-carved ceilings. I let it fill the air and chase the shadows away from the corners. It flooded down the windows like a waterfall and spilled under the doors. It rushed down the stairs, swirling around the handrail with craved żmije, reinvigorating the old wood with its energy, chatting with the stone making up the walls. Slowly, steadily, magic flooded the entire tenement, crept into every nook and corner, closing it from the others' magic and reclaiming it for me. For us.

I opened my eyes and blinked a few times, trying to reorient myself. I was in the kitchen in the Guardian's flat, where Aysun had fed me French toast after I'd run away from Mum's attempts to cure my magic, where Damian had made me hot chocolate the morning after Aysun and Zuzanna had escaped from the city, where we'd sat with my dad as he remembered bits and pieces of his magical life.

I had a bondmate to rescue.

I grabbed the smudge stick that was still smoking in the clay dish and got up to my feet. Laura stood a respectful distance away, her gaze uncertain.

"Let's find Damian," I said.

We walked out of the Guardian's flat and nothing happened. The wooden floor groaned under our footsteps but shadows didn't snatch us. Only the tenement's magic was there now, sneaking up my back, under my jumper, gently encouraging me on.

We climbed down the steps illuminated by the red light. The shadows were long and dark but they didn't move. I held the smudge stick in front of me, chanting the spell under my breath. I followed the pull of the bond between the two of us. I couldn't pinpoint his exact location, but I knew we were drawing close.

I pushed open the back door to the Clavichord Café. Foreign magic momentarily slammed into me and a cold shiver ran down my spine. But the shadows didn't move. I smudged the door, whispering the spell three times over, and stepped inside. The café was a mess, full of broken glass and splintered wood. Armchairs were thrown over, the cushions ripped open, feathers littering the floor. Only the piano in the corner looked untouched. Red light streamed in through the dusty windows, making the room look as if it had been splattered with blood.

A sole chair stood upright in the middle of the café. A figure sat slumped on it, shadows binding him tight.

"Damian," I whispered.

He didn't react and cold dread flooded my veins.

Laura walked past me towards her brother. She didn't hesitate next to Klara's shadows, just reached over them to Damian's neck, checking his pulse. We were silent for a tense few moments.

"He's just unconscious," said Laura. "I don't have any

potion that could help him. And we can't risk going down to the tunnels, to the ritual room."

I pulled at the shadows binding Damian. They were ice cold and surprisingly solid, like a thick black rope. They didn't budge as I tried to pull them away or break them.

"Light," I said. "We need light. You don't happen to have any more bottled light, do you?"

Laura shook her head. I looked around the room but it wasn't like we would find a magical potion that would help us in this mess.

"Please, pre-Mother," whispered Laura, and I stiffened. Was there another god around that I should be worried about?

I couldn't let her distract me. I closed my eyes, concentrating on our bond. Damian was right here, and I could feel the magic between us clearly. But when I focused, I could feel my bond with Artur just as strongly. I pulled on it, trying to channel his magic. I'd never consciously borrowed another sorcerer's gift. I could barely use telekinesis.

But now seemed like a great time for it to work.

I concentrated on the magic between Artur and me, and the feeling of warmth and closeness. I thought about how his magic felt on my skin, tingling and familiar.

When I opened my eyes, a small ball of light appeared between my hands.

I stared at it open-mouthed. I'd done it. I'd channelled Artur's magic on my command.

The shadows moved, sneaking around Damian's throat. Laura screamed and clawed at the shadows as Damian's body jumped and flailed. Panic flooded my body and the ball of light almost disappeared, but I focused on our bond again, forcing it to grow. Guided by instinct, I moved the light towards the shadows and pushed it into them. With a blinding burst of light, the shadows disappeared and Damian slumped forward. Laura and I caught him, holding him to the chair.

His eyes slowly opened and he groaned.

"Oh good," I said. "I was scared I'd have to find some poor prince to wake you up with a kiss."

"Ugh," said Damian, leaning against the back of the chair. "No non-consensual kisses."

"Fair. Now, are you ready to get back to the safe house?"

EIGHTEEN

Despite my worries, the Children of Weles didn't catch us, Węgliszek didn't go after us, the ground didn't open up, blood didn't start pouring from the sky. We left the tenement, made it across the old town, and started climbing the stairs leading to the safe house. Damian was a bit unsteady on his feet, but he had a strengthening potion in his pocket, which gave him enough energy to climb the stairs from the old town to the safe house.

Thunder growled again, and I flinched but this time a lightning didn't strike. I looked over my shoulder where the smoke still billowed towards the sky. Heavy clouds hung ominously overhead. Hopefully, we'd be home before the skies opened.

Ha. As if it hadn't been already open, with the red light blasting through.

"Are we sure we want to bring her back here?" asked Damian, without sparing his sister a glance.

No. No, I wasn't sure about it at all. But we couldn't leave Laura on the street, either.

"The Children of Weles are after her. She needs a safe place to stay as much as we do," I said.

"I was thinking about this divine favour," said Laura, ignoring our conversation. "And it makes a lot of sense that Weles would look kindly upon you. After all, he's the god of magic. And you've been chosen by magic itself as the Circle of Four. But what if it wasn't magic but a god?"

Damian and I exchanged glances. He didn't seem any more comfortable with this idea than me. We walked the last bit in silence. When we reached the safe house, I reached out my hand to Laura, and she grasped it. The building was an ugly concrete brick, with scratched walls and an overgrown garden—though, to be fair, all flora was overgrown since the barriers between the realms had broken—but it was as close to a home as we got these days.

When I opened the door, we were greeted by raised voices.

"Why would you even suggest that?" said Mum, her raised voice carrying through the open kitchen door.

She was shouting at Gabriella, who stood with her arms crossed by the table. Tomasz was by Mum's side. Artur, Karina, and Rafi were there, too, hiding by the wall.

All their heads snapped up towards us when we walked into the house.

"Hi," I said.

Gabriella brushed past my mum and enveloped Laura in a hug.

"Of all the irresponsible things to do, Wiki, do you have a death wish?" asked Mum, striding towards us. "How many times do I have to stress how essential it is that you stay alive?"

"We got Laura out," I said, stepping aside to try to move the spotlight onto her. That was the least she owed me. "You're welcome."

"You could have been captured! They could have killed or tortured you. You're back only by some stroke of luck."

"No. We're back because we have a lot of powerful magic at our disposal. And we have the duty to use it well. If we want to change the magical world, change the way our society is structured, we have to do better than our predecessors. And freeing a friend from captivity seems like a good start."

I turned around to face Gabriella.

"Can I have the sleeping potion now? I still need to pass the Baba Jaga's third trial."

Gabriella nodded and retrieved a small glass bottle from her coat's pocket.

"Thank you," she said squeezing my hand. I couldn't meet her eyes. "Take just a sip."

I nodded and went to my room, followed closely by the rest of the Circle of Four. When we were safely crowded inside, Artur hugged me—or more like crushed me against him. The magic between us was urgent, jumping around, as if trying to make sure that I was back and whole, that we were together again. Damian tried to walk past us but Artur extended his arm to pull him into the hug, too.

"I was scared for you," Artur said. "I could feel your panic so many times. I'm glad you made it back in one piece."

"It was close," I admitted. "We met the devil again. He said that it's past the winter solstice now and if we try to fix the hole in the sky, he'll stop us."

"Great," said Karina. "Just what we needed. Another obstacle to our already impossible mission."

"Well, good news is that Laura thinks we might have a god looking after us," I said and quickly filled the rest of them in about the chosen-by-Weles theory.

"Honestly, that sounds like at least semi-good news and at this stage, I'll accept any good news," said Karina.

"Let's start with the Baba Jaga's trial," said Damian.

"You know the sleeping potion might not work, right?" I asked. "It's just a gamble."

"We deserve something to go right just once."

Artur sat on the bed and patted the mattress next to him. When I joined him, Damian extended his hand towards me and I gave him the potion. He opened it and sniffed the contents.

"Poppyseeds, of course," he murmured, then continued louder. "Sit comfortably, it will knock you out fast. You just need a tiny sip."

I pulled myself up on the bed. When I was ready, Damian brought the bottle to my lips. Almost as soon as the first drop hit my tongue, my eyes began to close. Artur caught me before I fell and the last thing I was aware of was the tingle of magic between us as he lowered me gently to the mattress.

When I opened my eyes, I stood in front of a house with a chicken's leg.

It doesn't look like the Baba Jaga's hut I visited but I immediately know it's one. It's like in every fairy tale I heard—a simple, wooden house with a steep, thatched roof, supported by a gigantic chicken's leg, taller than I am, with claws the size of my arms but considerably thicker. It's standing on a meadow blanketed in snow. Pine trees with snow-capped tips sway gently in the distance.

The scene is flooded in the same eerie red light I'm used to by now, but the sky is the familiar cracked egg of my dreams.

I walk towards the house on the chicken's leg. My feet are bare and the snow is cold but it doesn't hurt. The red Guardian's cloak is wrapped around me, its magic keeping me warm, but the mere sight of it makes me shiver.

I stop in front of the claws and look up. The house is above my head, dancing on the snowy meadow. For a second, I wonder how I'll get there but then, with a loud crack, not unlike a sound of a bone snapping, the leg bends until the house is on the ground level. I knock on the door and it springs open.

"Come in, come in, Sorceress," says the Baba Jaga.

This time, I don't hesitate. I'm here for a reason and I step in. The moment the doors close behind me, the house lifts up. I brace myself for the dancing but the house feels stable.

Inside, there's a peculiar tea party going on. The Baba Jaga is standing by the table, leaning heavily on its stick with a carved żmij's head at the end. By its side, seated comfortably with his long, hoofed legs stretched out in front of him and crossed at the ankles, is Węgliszek. There's a steaming cup in front of him.

Shit.

"Sorceress," he says, nodding his head at me and tipping an imaginary hat.

I nod back and the devil-god grins at me, his eyes flashing red. The tail is swishing behind him like a whip.

The Baba Jaga clucks its tongue, calling my attention.

"Sit and have some tea with us," says the Baba Jaga.

"I'd rather not," I reply, standing by the door. "You know why I'm here and it's not for tea."

The Baba Jaga's walking stick moves fast but I jump out of its way just in time. Węgliszek laughs and the Baba Jaga murmurs under its nose.

"No manners," says the Baba Jaga.

"I came for my final task," I say.

The scene darkens. I blink but it's not my eyes—the light around me disappears, shadows devouring us. I scramble back then remind myself that it's just a dream. I force myself to stand still, heart drumming hard in my chest as darkness falls around us until all I can see the red criss-cross pattern of the light shining through the broken egg of the sky and two dark shadows of the

Baba Jaga and the devil. They look grotesque now, lengthened. Pointed horns grow out of Węgliszek's head and the head of the żmij on the Baba Jaga's walking stick expands, its jaws spreading wide.

"I could trap you here forever," says the Baba Jaga. "I could make you my servant. Someone to cook my food, to peel the sacrificial meat off the bones for me. I'm far from powerless but with you around…oh, sorceress, we could rule over all the worlds."

I squeeze my fists, nails biting into my flesh. It's just a dream. It's just a dream.

"You need me for something else," I say with more conviction than I feel.

"Do I, now? And what are you willing to risk to find out?"

What did Węgliszek tell it? What did he convince it to do? He promised to hunt us down but does he have power over the Baba Jaga? Which of the demon-gods is more powerful?

Silence stretches between us, broken only by an occasional groan of the hut and my wildly beating heart. Neither of the demons is breathing.

"There's one last thing I need from you," says the Baba Jaga. "You'll get me a feather from a firebird's tail."

The Baba Jaga stomps its cane hard on the floor and the dream vanishes.

It was difficult to wake up, sleep clinging to me like toffee of a particularly chewy krówka. My eyelids were heavy, my muscles weak, but I fought through the remnants of the dream.

Firebird. How on Earth was I going to find a firebird?

A scream made me sit up fast, heart racing in my chest. My head spun as I scanned the room. It was filled with bright light, coming from Artur who sat next to me. Damian stood by the door, his eyes closed as he whispered. Karina was on my other side, her hand on my shoulder, her eyes turned towards the door.

A scream shook the house again. Footsteps thundered on the floor.

"What—" I asked, unable to finish the thought.

"The Children of Weles are here," whispered Karina.

NINETEEN

I RAN FOR THE DOOR, KARINA AND ARTUR AT MY heels. Damian held up his index finger, still singing a protective spell under his breath, and we stopped. Outside, more heavy steps pounded. The door was ajar and I could see Klara, Filip, and Paulina in the hallway. My mum stood in the kitchen door, Tomasz behind her. Shadows were wrapped around their arms and legs, holding them in place. It didn't seem like they could see us.

Damian was squeezing the sleeping potion in his hand.

"Do the magic," I hissed but Damian shook his head and held the index finger in front of my face.

My body was begging me to push him to the side, to do something. What was he waiting for? For Klara to storm in, for her shadows to capture us?

"You're making it too easy," said Klara. "We knew your

magic would be out of control, we knew our god would punish you for turning your back on him, but I'd never hoped you'd be stupid enough to drink rue with gods and demons on your doorstep."

I bit my lip. Artur caught my hand.

A movement caught my eyes. The door to the living room was open and Rafi, Laura, and Gabriella were inside. Rafi stood by the shelf filled with the potions. Damian caught his gaze and shook his head but, with a cat-like grin, Rafi pushed the first bottle to the floor. There was a hiss and a small bang and Klara and Filip jumped, looking around.

"You—" started Klara but, before she could finish, Damian broke the bottle with the sleeping potion, vaporized it, and sent the cloud over the Children of Weles.

The cloud iced over and fell to the floor, shattering.

"Ah, there you are," said Filip, turning to face us.

I felt cold all over. Was it his magic or my body's reaction to his presence? I didn't know. Power rushed to my skin, ready to protect me, but I pushed it down. It was too unpredictable and we were in close quarters.

Damian grabbed my hand, magic warming my body. Shadows stirred but Artur's light kept them at bay. Shadows raced across the room until they got to my mum, wrapping around her. She screamed.

Across the room, Laura grabbed a potion bottle and threw it into the fireplace. There was a powerful bang, and the room shook and filled with smoke.

"Run!" someone shouted. Mum.

But Gabriella had been right. What good was our magic if we couldn't use it to save our family and friends?

If only I knew what to do.

It turned out, I didn't have to. When the smoke cleared, Filip and Klara stood in the middle of the room, frozen in place.

I glanced at Laura, but her eyes were wide. Gabriella looked just as surprised. Rafi shook his head.

"Don't you dare touch my family," said Karina, her voice so icy that I shivered.

Her eyes were demonic white.

Artur put his arm around her and, after a few moments, Karina's eyes changed back to brown.

"Alchemists can also play with ice," she said.

It took a moment for everyone to realize what had happened. Mum rubbed her wrists and I could almost feel the phantom iciness of the shadow-touch.

"We'll take it from here. But you need to get out."

We'd all been packed and ready to go, so all we needed to do was to grab our things. Mum gave us some extra food, water, and potential offerings to any demons we could encounter—poppyseeds and nuts, since our options were limited. Damian filled his backpack with potions and crystals.

"You're not leaving me behind," said Rafi, appearing in the hallway where Karina, Artur, and Damian were triple-checking if we were ready to leave the safe house.

Damian stiffened but even he didn't protest when Rafi pulled on his winter boots and heaved a backpack of his own.

While we prepared, Tomasz and Gabriella forced sleeping potion down Klara's, Filip's and Paulina's throats and then, just to be extra safe, rue potion as well. It wouldn't last forever but it would buy them time to figure out their next move.

We said our goodbyes and set off down the dark streets, illuminated only by the red light shining through the crack in the sky. We walked alongside the main roads but we had Artur to keep us invisible. Every time a military car drove by I flinched, but Artur's illusion held. They couldn't see us. I felt his headache settle in as he tried to keep track of our surroundings, straining his eyes without his contacts.

"I need a feather from a firebird's tail," I said as we walked.

"Of course, you do," Damian murmured.

"That's very on the nose, isn't it," said Artur. "Don't Baba Jaga usually lead people to firebirds instead the other way round?"

"I'm sure there's one around, there are all sorts of demons out there," said Damian. "The fun part will be finding it before the Children of Weles or the military hunt us down. I hope you don't have a deadline."

"I don't," I said. "And I saw a firebird. When we did the ritual and the sky broke, the firebird flew through the crack in the sky. Arrow went after it—it *flew*!—and they fought each other. That was the last time I saw Arrow."

I did a double take as a military car drove by us again. I couldn't be certain as they all looked the same, but I could swear it was driving in circles, following us.

"I don't think it's looking for us," said Artur, responding to my thoughts.

"They're probably just making rounds as usual," said Karina. "Looking for anyone who's breaking the curfew."

"Or anyone they could steal food from," added Rafi.

We turned to take a shortcut between residential buildings and for a moment I could breathe more easily, away from the military car's headlights. All the windows were dark, not even a flicker of a candle in sight. Were the flats abandoned? Or were the people inside hiding?

"The firebird should be on top of the tree of life, right?" said Artur. "The oak connecting the worlds? Nesting in the highest branches?"

"Where do we find it?" I asked.

"Well, I'm not a specialist on magical oak trees but I'd bet good money on the tree growing where you'd paid Tomasz's debt to the devil," said Karina. "And where we'd tried to bring your mum's memory back."

Now that she'd mentioned it, it sounded obvious.

"It's worth trying," said Damian. "It's not like we have any other idea where to look."

"Let's do it, then," said Karina. "I mean, we can't keep walking without direction. I hope you remember where you left the car, that freaking meadow is far away."

At the street corner, we came face to face with four

soldiers, their torches shining straight at us, rifles slung over their shoulders. I clamped a hand over my mouth as they came from around the corner, almost walking into us. I moved to the side at the last possible moment, pulling Karina with me. They walked right in front of us and I held my breath, lest they could hear me, heart hammering in my chest.

Anxiety spiked through me—Artur's? Damian's?—before a couple of things happened simultaneously. Rafi pushed me to the ground at the same time as Damian dove for Karina. Her scream caught in her throat as we came tumbling down in a pile of limbs, the force of impact knocking the breath out of me. My mind was shouting at me to run, run, run, but I was pressed against the snowy ground by Rafi, or maybe it was Karina, and then there was a shout and a heavy thud and the breath was knocked out of me, again, only, no, it wasn't me, and sympathetic pain shot through me.

"Show yourselves!" barked one of the soldiers. All their torches and rifles were now trained on us.

We were still invisible.

But our footprints in the snow weren't.

I tried to push the heavy weight off me but it wouldn't bulge. Artur, the last one of us still standing, was bent in half, holding on to his stomach, but his illusion over us held. Magic burned my skin and I let it out, trying to push the soldiers away. Rafi clung to me, keeping me down, but the soldiers stumbled back. A shot fired and someone screamed, and, gods, please, don't let Rafi get shot for me again. And then I saw us—*us*, myself included—scrambling up and running. The soldiers turned to follow and I stared. But it wasn't an out-of-body experience, only Artur's illusion. Then the weight pinning me down disappeared and hands were pulling me up to my feet.

"Behind you!" shouted a soldier and another shot flew dangerously close to me.

The soldiers realized they had been deceived and they rushed back towards us.

"Run," said Rafi, pushing me the way we came from.

I grabbed Artur's hand, making sure that this time he was with us, and pulled him along, Karina on our heels. But when I looked back, Rafi and Damian were sprinting in the other direction, now out of range of Artur's invisibility spell and fully visible to the soldiers.

I didn't have time to worry about it as the soldiers split up, two of them chasing us, the other two following Rafi and Damian.

"Halt!" shouted one of the soldiers.

We sprinted across the snowy grass, slaloming between the carpet-beater structures, recycling bins, and a rusty set of swings, but the soldiers were catching up quickly to us and I was already out of breath.

We can't outrun them, I said telepathically to Artur.

The moment I said it, there was a roar and I looked up just in time to see a big, winged demon diving at us. A griffon, with a powerful body of a lion, larger than me, and wings of an eagle. Artur grabbed my hand, urging me not to stop.

"It's an illusion," he said, his words barely audible over the shot of the rifle tearing through the night.

I caught Karina's hand, partly to make sure she was still with us and partly to reassure her. I wasn't sure if she'd heard Artur.

We ran around a residential building, ignoring the soldiers' screams. Artur halted, gesturing for us to move towards low shrubs growing by the wall. We crouched behind the bushes and Artur's magic erased our traces in the snow. As we heard the steps of the oncoming soldiers, I saw the three of us sprinting across the yard. I held my breath as the soldiers followed the illusion.

"While we are here," said Artur. "Would you mind if we took a short detour?"

Artur pushed open the door to a nearby building. He hesitated, then took off his shoes. I quickly realized why—the concrete steps were hard to climb without our steps echoing, and we wanted to be as discrete as possible. Though, if anyone was inside the building, they'd probably watched our clash with the soldiers.

We climbed the dark stairwell to the second floor, and Artur knocked on the last door to the right. Even though his knock was soft, it echoed down the corridor and I flinched, my muscles stiffening. I clung to Karina and she squeezed me back. We were far enough into apocalypse to stop hiding our fear and need for support.

There was a loud scraping as the door opened, revealing a tall boy with a mass of brown curls on his head—normally jumping with every move, now frizzy and matted with grease. He stared at us for a moment, then gestured for us to get in. He locked the door behind him and pushed a dresser against it.

He pulled Artur into a hug.

"Now," said Simon after a few long moments. "I believe you might have a story or two to tell about the mess happening outside."

"Yes," agreed Artur. "But first we need to strengthen the protections around this place. It's not safe at all, not for the end of the world scenario."

He pulled out a pouch of salt and chalk from his pocket, while I retrieved a smudge stick made of thyme and lavender. With Karina's help, the three of us got to work, putting salt in every corner, placing protective sigils at all windows and doors, and smudging the flat, all the while singing and chanting. Simon's family had put up blankets and cardboard boxes over the windows, blocking out the view and the crack in the sky, so the only light came from a few tealights. As we worked, Simon's parents appeared to greet Artur and watch our progress from safe distance. It was cold inside and they were bundled up in thick jumpers and blankets.

Being open about my magic might have been the hardest thing I'd done in the past weeks. Not running away from demons, not surviving in the tunnels with the Children of Weles, not even sharing Artur's numbness after we'd rescued him. No, there was something vulnerable about trusting that piece of myself I'd been trained to hide with virtual strangers, people who, as far as I knew, didn't have magic themselves. Opening myself up to potential scorn or attack, knowing they could judge me by something I couldn't change about myself. Something that, until recently, I'd used to hate.

Artur brushed my hand. He mouthed *thank you,* and I gave him a small smile.

Then Artur started explaining the end of the world. He didn't go into too much detail, and he didn't betray how crucial a piece we were, just filled in the gaps in what was becoming more and more obvious to everyone in the city. Magic was real, demons were everywhere, and, as far as we knew, we weren't fully in Jawia anymore.

As he talked, I focused on the bond, on my connection to Damian. I couldn't sense his location, could barely feel him at all.

Safe, I tried to communicate. *We're safe, we're safe.*

There was a bit of telepathy, but I focused on passing on the emotions. Damian couldn't read my mind before but it was worth a try.

Safe, safe, safe.

Just when I was about to give up, the same feeling appeared on Daman's side of the bond. It was vague, as if trying to get through a dense, heavy barrier, but it was unmistakably Damian.

Safe. Anxious, safe.

I clung to our thread of connection. We would find Damian and Rafi. We'd soon be together again, ready to find the firebird.

"There isn't much I can do yet," said Karina bringing me back to reality. "But I can heat up water for you, if you want to? A pot, if you have some food you could boil, tea, a bathtub, anything like that?"

Karina followed Simon's dad to the kitchen when we heard loud noise on the stairs.

"Open up!" shouted someone a floor below.

"The soldiers are making rounds again," said Simon.

"Make sure the food is hidden," said his mum.

Artur squeezed my hand, and we exchanged a look. My heart was racing. It was our fault; the soldiers were looking for us. We were trying to help but we only brought trouble with us.

"We need to hide," I said.

"Let's go to the balcony," said Artur. "I'll make us invisible."

Karina joined us and we sneaked outside. Simon shut the door behind us, and we hunched down and cuddled close together, flinching as the stomping of the heavy military boots grew louder.

There was a bang at the door followed by a rough, "Open up!" I leaned more heavily on Artur as the soldiers stormed inside Simon's flat. Boots stomped loudly, furniture screeching on the floor, doors banging. I was shaking. Artur wrapped his arm around me, and I pressed my face into his chest, willing the world around us to disappear, or at least hoping for our bond to calm me enough so that my heart would stay put in my chest.

The door to the balcony flew open and we froze, holding our breaths. A soldier pointed a rifle directly at Karina's head.

TWENTY

TIME SLOWED DOWN. MAGIC RUSHED OUT OF ME IN a powerful blast, throwing the soldier against the doorframe. The rifle shot. Heavy boots thundered on the floor and I pushed my magic out, keeping Karina, Artur, and myself inside a force field and hoping it would withstand a bullet.

We needed to get out of here. But we couldn't leave Simon and his family to the soldiers' wrath.

Another soldier rushed to the balcony, and Karina stood up to face them. Artur grabbed her hand, but she slapped it away.

"Leave," Karina said staring at the soldiers. Her voice was so cold that the hair on the back of my neck stood. "Leave and don't come back. Forget you've seen us."

For a second, the soldiers stood frozen. Then they walked back to the flat, Karina following. Artur and I scrambled to our feet and rushed after them. The soldiers walked slowly past Simon and his family through to the front door and closed it behind them. We stood waiting until their footsteps died off.

"What happened?" asked Simon.

"I thought we were invisible," said Artur softly, his voice filled with dread. "I'm so sorry."

Karina waved it off but when she looked at us, her eyes were demon white.

"Maybe you're just tired. You've been using a lot of magic this past hour." She shrugged then turned to Simon. "I'll help you with that water."

He stared at her for a moment, his mouth hanging open. He shook his head and tried to smile, but it looked forced.

"Can you use snow as well?" he asked. "We gather it up and let it melt. It probably has demonic cooties but desperate times and all that."

"Sure, it's also water. I can even clean it for you."

Karina helped with what she could while Artur and I double-checked the protections. When everything was as ready as possible, Artur and Simon exchanged another long hug, then Simon squeezed Karina and me.

"I'm sorry we couldn't help more," I said.

I wished more than ever that I could channel other sorcerers' magic at will, that I could channel Dawid or Tadeusz and grow food for anyone who needed it—which was likely a vast majority of the city. But that would be fine if I had time and magic to create huge communal gardens around the city.

But I didn't.

"Keep my boy out of trouble, okay?" Simon asked.

I gave him a weak smile. "I'll try."

We made our way downstairs, cautious not to make any noise. At the bottom of the stairs, we put on our shoes and went out into the darkness.

"We're invisible, I hope, and this time I'll know to mask our footsteps, too," said Artur. "Let's find Damian and Rafi and get to this freaking car."

"Do you know how to find them?" I asked.

"Yes," said Artur. When I looked at him in surprise, he pulled up his sleeve, revealing a red thread woven around his wrist three times over, with a black stone resting against his pulse. "Damian gave it to me. I guess you used similar magic before to find me."

We followed Artur between the residential buildings, flinching at every noise. In the distance, loud footsteps marched in the snow—most likely the soldiers.

Artur opened a door to one of the buildings. I hesitated, scared of being ambushed again, but I followed him inside. We descended to the basement, our steps echoing in the total darkness.

"It's us," said Artur as we neared the bottom of the stairs, his voice low.

"Do you have to sneak? I could have hurt you," said Rafi.

I pulled him into an embrace, then hugged Damian, too.

"Are you okay?" I asked.

"As okay as anyone can be under such circumstances," said Damian, lightning up a small flame in his hands. "What happened to your eyes?"

Everyone turned to Karina. Her eyes were still white.

"The soldiers found us," she said. "I made them leave."

Rafi stifled a burst of joyless laughter with a gloved hand.

"This is going great, isn't it? We made it, what, half a kilometre from the safe house?"

I shivered. How had the soldiers found us? It couldn't have been an accident.

Artur hugged me to his side, and I leaned into him, trembling. Gods, we'd been so stupid, so, so stupid to think we could ever escape this city.

"We just need to make it to the car," said Karina.

Our second attempt at leaving the city started better. Artur remembered to mask our footprints and I couldn't stop marvelling at how much power he had now. I gave Damian more of my magic, terrified of losing our bond in case we got separated again. We walked along the main road, but the streets were desolate now. The only sign of life was an odd demon crossing the sky or rustling in the bushes every once in a while, and they left us alone.

All the while, Karina's eyes remained white.

We weren't far from where we'd left the car when there was lightning striking in the distance, soon followed by thunder.

"A lightning storm at the end of December?" asked Rafi, doubtfully.

I doubted it, too, but I didn't want to voice my worries. I didn't know if mentioning gods out loud caught their attention. We walked on, casting wary glances at the sky.

Then the silence was broken by a loud boom. Explosion tore through the night, distant, but not distant enough. We cuddled closer together, staring at the horizon, as if we could see anything in the darkness.

"Please tell me that wasn't the old dynamite factory," said Rafi.

"Haven't they turned it into a museum?"

"Only parts of it. Most is still military area."

Karina was the first to move. Only she wasn't walking towards the car anymore, but towards the explosion.

"I don't think that's a great idea," I said, but she didn't respond.

"Kari?" asked Rafi, but even her nickname didn't irritate her enough to react.

We ran to catch up with her.

"This isn't funny," said Rafi.

I caught my cousin's arm and she didn't react at first. Only when I tried to keep her in place, did she shake me off. She walked on without a second glance at us. When Rafi tried to stop her, she pushed him away like an annoying fly.

Damian and Artur caught up with us but neither of them was able to stop Karina from walking towards the explosion.

"I have a sleeping potion," said Damian, taking off his backpack, and searching through it, while trying to keep up with us. "I don't think she's aware of what's happening."

Magic crackled on Karina's skin, shocking me, but I didn't draw back.

Damian retrieved a small bottle from his backpack filled with familiar dark blue liquid and unscrewed it. Rafi and I stood by Karina's sides, trying to stop her at least for a moment. At Damian's sign, we moved simultaneously, holding her in place while Damian put the glass to her lips. He poured a little potion into her mouth and, to my surprise, Karina swallowed it without a fight. But, instead of falling lifelessly to the ground like I had after drinking the poppyseed potion, she pushed Rafi and me away with surprising strength and kept walking.

We followed her, expecting her to drop to the ground at any moment, but it didn't happen. Karina walked on in a fast, steady pace. Why was she walking towards the explosion? And how could we stop her?

"I don't like this at all," said Damian.

"What's gotten into her?" asked Rafi.

"I have a theory, but you don't want me to jinx it," said Damian. "Because we know for a fact that a certain god is back."

Sharp anxiety spiked through the bond, freezing my veins, and I rotated around to Artur. He stood a dozen of steps behind.

Artur? I asked telepathically, but before he could respond, there was a scream, and more terror filled my bond.

I twisted around just in time to see Damian fall to the snow, followed by Rafi.

Heart pounded in my throat and magic warmed my skin, ready to strike, as I looked around, trying to identify the threat. Artur was still rooted in spot, unmoving. No, not just unmoving.

Frozen.

Metres away, Rafi and Damian were held to the ground by the shadows.

Karina was far ahead, still moving towards the explosion, unresponsive to anything around her. Shadows reached for her, but she stepped right through them. At least that was a blessing. All four of us getting ambushed together was my mum's worst fear come true.

"Show yourself!" I shouted, magic crackling at my fingertips.

I didn't feel brave, especially not if I was to face the Children of Weles again. But anything, even confrontation was better than this anticipation, waiting for them to strike, and seeing my friends immobilized, helpless, vulnerable.

Ice encased my feet and magic rushed out of me but it didn't help. Ice kept climbing up my legs at an agonizingly slow pace. Filip was toying with me.

Anger rushed through me and I relished it. Anger was so much better than fear. I let my magic out fully. But it did nothing against the ice, and it didn't hit any target. Of course it didn't, I still had no control over magic and I'd ignored all my mum's suggestions that I should train.

Was the moral of the story to listen to your parents, no matter how certain you are that you know better?

"Look at that," said Klara's voice from the shadows. "Our little bird thought she'd escaped but she got caught again. And she brought us a treat."

"Stop hiding!" I shouted, more magic lashing out from me.

I kept hoping to channel Artur's light ability. I'd done it before. If I could light up the shadows, if I could free Damian and Rafi, maybe even melt the ice…

"You aren't in position to give orders here," said Filip.

I still couldn't see them. The shadows must have been hiding them. They wanted to scare me, but the joke was on them because I didn't have any more fear left in me.

"Are you certain?" I asked.

"Let's see," said Klara. "We have three and soon four people you keep dear trapped, at our mercy. And you yourself are frozen in spot, and your magic is as useless as ever."

"And at least two of them are useless to us. So, dear Guardian. What will be your justice tonight? Which one of your friends survives this evening?"

TWENTY ONE

I KEPT PUSHING OUT MAGIC, HOPING FOR SOMETHING useful to happen. But apparently, I'd used up all my luck for the day. My legs were frozen, limiting my movements, but my torso was still free. I could still do something.

"I know you have a sweet spot for our dear Artur," said Klara.

One of her shadows rose from the ground and its long hands reached towards Artur. Frozen as he was, Artur couldn't even flinch as the shadow drew its finger along his jaw. He was trapped, just as he'd been when the basilisk had turned him to stone. Defenceless, at Klara's mercy.

Rage gnawed at my insides.

"And I promised to keep the sorcerers safe. So, you can choose to spare him. Or, you can choose to cut your losses first."

Behind me, Damian shouted, and I twisted my head around, heart hammering in my chest. More magic escaped me as the shadows holding Damian extended their fingers to his neck.

"Or maybe it will be the witch?" asked Klara. "Does he have a chance of surviving tonight? Or are the odds against him?"

"Fuck off," said Damian, and the shadows squeezed his throat. I flinched as sympathetic pain choked me.

I needed to do something. And I needed to do it fast.

"And then there's the alchemist. Honestly, also not the best choice, because I'd love to play with your magical bond. But, who's to discard a childhood friend, a boy who's like a brother to you? Might be as good an incentive as anyone else."

"An incentive for *what*?" I asked, my words coming out harsh.

"To come back, of course. To do your sacred duty as our Guardian and keep protecting your sorcerers. A duty which you've so easily shrugged off the first chance you got. And, dear Guardian, your magic is the only reason you're alive."

I focused on my legs, willing the ice to break. I'd thawed myself before, and I was clearly distressed enough for magic to help me. Then why wasn't it working?

I should have listened to my mum. I should have trained.

"How did you find us?" I asked, playing for time. "Through the shadows?"

"I'm not revealing all my cards, Guardian. Now, it's time to make your choice. Who will die first?"

I didn't respond. There was no way I was going to respond to that question.

I needed a miracle.

"Why do you need me? Your god is back. What could you possibly want from me?"

Tearing pain bit into my arm—no, not *my* arm—and I screamed before I could stop myself. My scream was drowned by Damian's, but it wasn't him being hurt either. I twisted my neck and saw a shadow perched over Artur's arm, grinning a grotesque smile full of sharp, needle-like teeth. Artur's jacket was torn at his shoulder, blood soaking the material.

And. Artur. Couldn't. Even. React.

"Your bond truly is marvellous, isn't it?" asked Klara. "I'm sure we can provide you enough incentive to do your job. But the real question is, is it strong enough to kill the rest of you, if one of you dies?"

"You wouldn't risk that," said Damian.

"Are you sure?" asked Klara.

She finally stepped from the shadows, but she looked like one of them, her sorcerer cape blending her right in. She leaned over Damian, and I trembled, willing my legs to move, my magic to work.

Please, please, please let us all walk out of here.

If anyone died here, I wouldn't survive it, and it wouldn't be the magical bond's fault.

A knife gleamed in Klara's hand, and I screamed as magic rushed out of me. With a powerful push of magic, Klara fell to her back, shadows catching her, the knife falling from her hand. I caught it with my telekinesis, but the shadows ripped it from my grasp and handed it back to Klara.

"Impressive," said Filip. He was way too close to my ear, and I flinched as his breath tickled my cheek. "Let's see if it was just luck or if you can repeat it. But let's make it a little harder for you."

His ice-cold fingers touched my neck and magic exploded out of me, throwing him off before he could grasp me. The ice melted off my legs and I ran to Artur. If I could unfreeze him as well, he could fend off the shadows.

But before I could get to him, the shadows caught me in their cold arms, stalling me in place.

"You don't want to miss the spectacle," said Klara as the shadows pushed me around to face her, Rafi, and Damian. "I guess you've made your choice clear."

Slowly, oh so slowly, she drew the knife across Rafi's cheek. I screamed again and this time the magic inside me felt like liquid fire. The shadows around me disappeared as if burned as I raced towards Klara with the speed I didn't know I had and tackled her to the ground. The shadows reached their icy fingers towards me but they couldn't touch me.

"You will leave us alone," I said, looking into Klara's dark eyes, my voice sounding foreign to me, deep and cold.

There was another explosion and the ground shook under us and my head jerked up involuntarily, the fire inside me reacting to it, pulling me towards it.

"Weles," whispered Klara.

I could barely hear her, my magic sizzling and dulling my senses. And then I understood what had happened. This was my bond with Karina. Our bond had finally come to life in all its fiery glory.

"He isn't alone," said Filip, as a lightning struck over the city.

"There must always be balance," said Klara, still lying in the snow, splayed under me.

I stared down at her and she flinched. Did my eyes look wholly white now?

"Sleep," I said in the same foreign, deep voice as before.

Klara went slack under me. Rafi and Damian moved, sitting up in snow. I pushed myself up and walked up to face Filip. He stared at me with a smirk on his face, but he paled when he looked at me.

"You're nothing to me," I said, the fire in my veins roaring. "The lowest sort of human scum. Sleep."

Filip fell to the snow, and I looked around. The explosion site was still calling to me, the fire inside me roaring, but I stared at my companions instead. Artur leaned forward and placed his hands on his knees as if he'd run a marathon, his body trembling. Damian frantically searched through his backpack until he retrieved a small jar filled with a green substance. He opened it and, with a questioning look at Rafi, spread a bit of the mixture on his cheek. Then Damian rose to his feet and walked towards me.

"Wiki," he said, squeezing my hand, grounding me.

The bond between us sparkled and the fire in me died down. I exhaled.

"I'm okay," I said.

"You have to stop saying it, it's a stupid lie," he said but he walked over to Artur. He put more of the green mixture on his shoulder, and Artur hissed in pain.

I flinched, but I forced myself to move.

"Are you okay?" I asked, helping Rafi to his feet.

"I hate to admit it, but Damian's is right, it's a stupid question," he said.

Damian took Artur's hands in his, warming him up with his magic. When he was done, I walked over to them, and pulled Artur into my arms.

"I'm sorry," I whispered, clasping my hands around his back.

I'm sorry, I'm sorry, I'm sorry. I'm sorry you had to go through it again. I'm sorry if it was even worse this time.

"It's not your fault," said Artur, his voice choked. "You saved us."

I wasn't fast enough. I shouldn't have left you behind. It's my fault, we shouldn't all be in the same place, I should have trained, I should be able to control my magic by now, I-

"Wiki." Artur squeezed my shoulder. "You've done enough. You've done more than enough. We're alive. We're here."

"We're queer," added Damian.

Artur and I stared at him in silence, then a surprised laughter broke from Artur's lips.

"What?" asked Damian. "That's how the catchphrase goes."

And it was a perfect addition that warmed my heart.

"I'm sorry to ruin the moment but Kari is far ahead of us, still heading towards the explosion," said Rafi.

I sighed.

Shit.

TWENTY TWO

WE'D LEFT THE CITY BEHIND AND RAN THROUGH THE forest. Soon barbed wire and signs "Military Property, Entrance Strictly Prohibited" appeared on both sides. But the fence was largely obscured by the plants climbing all over it—I would have bet anything that they hadn't been there before the sky had cracked open.

Well, "ran" was maybe a bit of a stretch. We walked fast through the snow, following Karina's footsteps, and occasionally breaking into a jog only to slow down to catch our breath soon afterwards. Rafi, who was in the best shape among us by a long shot, was restless with our sluggishness, eager to catch up with Karina, but he didn't leave us behind.

"You said you have a theory about Karina," I said.

"Yes," said Damian. "And Klara confirmed it. The Children of Weles were pretty sure that the explosion was related to Weles. And Karina is part-demon now. I mean, sure, we all are, but only by a fraction while her demonic part has been very real since her possession. And Weles rules over Nawia and all the demons. It looks like he's calling her."

"So you're saying that we'll have to face a god or two to break her free?" I asked.

"We'll see."

We walked on, the backpacks on our shoulders getting heavier and heavier, but now my mind was distracted, running through all the possible scenarios of what lay ahead.

Unfortunately, I had no experience in breaching military areas or apprehending gods.

"Do you think Mum and Tomasz are okay?" I asked. "If Klara and Filip got out…"

"I don't think they planned to keep them imprisoned," said Artur.

"No," said Damian. "Not while their magic is cursed by Weles. They knew they wouldn't manage to keep them. They probably won themselves enough time to move somewhere else. Or redo protections around the safe house."

I hoped they were right but the gnawing feeling in my stomach wouldn't stop.

Then, with a powerful roar, the ground trembled under our feet and I almost lost my balance. I grabbed Artur's arm instinctively. We held each other up as the world shook.

"Look," said Rafi, pointing to the sky.

I squinted, trying to see what he was showing me. There, on the background of the tear between the worlds, a lone figure crossed the sky. It had powerful, crow-like black-and-red wings, glistening in the red light streaming from another world. It also wore a pair of jeans and a light jumper.

"Is it Aysun?" I asked.

"Looks like it," agreed Damian.

"Would a Slavic god have control over a non-Slavic demon?"

"I don't know. But I also don't think that the old beliefs were strict on any sort of binaries."

"A lot of groups embraced newcomers and opening up to their way of understanding and celebrating the world. So, I'd imagine that the old gods would welcome any foreign demons as their own. But I guess we're about to see."

The shaking stopped and we walked on. It was a weird feeling, as if I were a bit drunk, my body not fully under my control, my legs jelly-like. As we rounded a corner, shouts broke the silence, followed by shooting.

We froze. Artur was keeping us invisible, so it probably wasn't necessary, but it'd been a long evening and it was better to be safe than sorry. I squeezed his hand.

I'm not leaving you behind this time, I told him telepathically. *I have your back.*

As the soldiers' shouts and shooting faded, we moved on down the snowy road. Soon, Karina's footsteps veered off road and towards the barbed fence separating us from the military area. The steps continued in the snow on the other side.

We exchanged looks.

"I'll help you up," said Rafi, putting his hands together.

Artur went first. I took out the Guardian's cloak from my backpack and we put it over the barbed wire, hoping its magic would protect us. Rafi hoisted Artur up and he made it over the fence onto the other side. My magic prickled at the ready, and I hoped this time it would work if needed and save us from hurting ourselves on the barbed wire.

Rafi helped me up next, then Damian. When we were safely on the other side, Rafi agilely climbed the fence and pushed himself over the barbed wire as if it were nothing. He took off the Guardian's cloak and handed it back to me. I was tempted to leave it there, but it would attract unwanted attention. Besides, it might still be useful.

We walked between the dense, tall trees. The shadows devoured everything almost immediately and not even the red light made it through to the ground.

"Can you mask torchlight as well?" I asked Artur once it became obvious that we couldn't see the trees in front of us, much less Karina's footsteps.

"I can try," he said. "But either way, we don't have a choice."

I pulled out a torch from my pocket and blinked at the sudden brightness. Once our eyes adjusted, we followed Karina's footsteps again. The further we got between the trees, the stronger the magic prickled my skin. Soon, it was almost suffocating. It was in the earth and the snow covering it, in the trees, in the sky. Magic permeated all the elements, all the world around us. Everything around us *was* magic.

I remembered the note written by the alchemist Regina, back from when the Guardian system had been designed. She'd written Magic with a capital "M", and I could understand why.

We pressed on and on, the forest stretching forever as we made our way through the snow.

We kept on following the footsteps until the forest opened into a meadow. The red light streaming from the crack between the worlds reflected from the snow. That combined with the omnipresent, powerful magic, made hair on the back of my neck stand.

I clicked off the torch as we hesitated at the edge of the forest, unsure about leaving the cover of the trees. But the steps continued down that path, so we trudged on.

Another explosion rocked the world and I caught Artur's arm, keeping him close, making sure he was still there. Shouts carried from the distance, followed by a powerful roar. Everything in me screamed to run, to hide, but we stayed rooted as a dark shape rose to the sky. A big demon, at least twice taller than me and with powerful wings, flew through the sky, the red light making its green scales gleam. There was a rider on its back, a dark shape with two horns on its head.

"Arrow," I said, my voice blending in with the boys'.

We shared a quick glance and Artur squeezed my hand as we watched the demon cross the sky and disappear on the horizon.

Arrow was *alive.* Relief flushed through me, a weight I hadn't realized I'd been carrying around removed from my shoulders.

I could worry about the rider on its back once we found Karina.

As we walked on through the meadow, I heard a soft cry. It sounded almost like a baby crying but what would a baby do in a place like that? Goosebumps spread up my arms and I shivered.

"We need to check it out," said Rafi. "What if someone needs help?"

"Why would anyone be here?" countered Damian. "It's most likely a trap."

"You're heartless," said Rafi, stalking towards the crying.

"Rafi, don't!" I said, but he didn't listen.

I ran after him, even though my sixth sense screamed it was a bad idea. Whatever was out there, I couldn't let Rafi face it alone. The wailing sounded miserable and what if Rafi was right? Maybe it was a little puppy or a baby. It wasn't a stretch to imagine someone in need of help during a demonic apocalypse.

Really, how could I have been so self-absorbed, so focused on our mission to even consider just passing by? Wasn't the whole thing my fault? It was us who'd cracked the sky open and it was my existence, the curse that had been placed upon my blood family that had caused it all. Generations upon generations of the Guardians abusing the natural magical order until we came to the breaking point. And how many people were paying the price for it? How many people were torn apart by demons or starving in their homes or robbed by a mob or the soldiers? And here I would have almost passed another one without a second glance?

And what about those who were supposedly dearest to me? Karina was somewhere out there, in a demonic trance, probably in danger. Artur had spent weeks turned into stone because he'd dared try to help me. Rafi had barely healed from the shot wound before I'd thrust him into this new reality. I kept ignoring my mum, even though I'd fought so hard to break the devil's hold on her. And I didn't even know if Zuzanna was still alive, or had my existence killed her, too. How could I even sleep at night?

More anxiety and despair flooded me. What was I even doing here? I had nothing to contribute, only some tricks that wouldn't save us from demons, wouldn't patch up the hole in the sky. I was probably already dooming us because I couldn't see well enough to create a convincing illusion. If anyone attacked us, if we encountered a demon or a god, we were done for. I'd failed us over and over, trusted the wrong people, always blindsided, never able to fight back. I'd put so much time and energy into helping people who'd hurt us. I'd tried to get more people on their side. Everyone around was smarter, funnier, stronger. I had nothing to contribute. It was supposed to be my world, I was supposed to know how it worked, but here I was stumbling around in the dark. Anyone could do better and they were doing better. It was only a matter of time before they realized how much better off they were without me. And where would I be then?

—Unwanted. Destroying the group dynamics. Always creating tensions, unable to make friends, unable to make any sort of connections, unable to even pretend to be likeable. Always ruining everything. Useless, utterly useless. My magic only worked if I was around them, leeching their power. And even then, what use was it, really? They'd been right not wanting me around, I'd never be a part of the sorcerers' world. All I was good for was disappointing people who dared trust me, who tried to like me. Creating divisions, stirring senseless drama because I couldn't to fit in—

Sharp pain blossomed on my cheek and I gasped. But the feelings were stronger than the physical pain and, gods, how could I stand anymore, how could I go on, what was the point—

"It's not real!" a shout broke through my mind fog.

There were hands on my shoulders, shaking me and I opened my eyes. I focused on the fingers squeezing my arms, on the pain in my cheek, on the coldness of the snow under my knees, trying to ground myself.

"What?" I asked, my voice hoarse as if I'd been screaming.

Where was up and where was down? Where were we? What was going on?

"It was a demon," said Rafi, his grasp on me strengthening. "You were right, okay? I shouldn't have gone there; it was a demon."

He pulled me into a tight hug. I was kneeling in the snow, my jeans soaked. I was trembling but whether it was the cold or the emotional hangover was hard to say. Rafi was trembling, too, clinging on to me for a couple of long moments.

He helped me up to my feet and led me back to the rest of the group. We didn't say anything, I just put my arms around Artur and Damian and we stood there for a few long moments, squeezing each other close, letting our bond warm us while we found our way to ourselves.

"I think it was a lelek," said Rafi. "The demon-bird that flies around, foreshadowing bad events, and feeding off negative energy. I've read about it in one of the demonologies at the hideout."

We hadn't figured it out there and then, but it had been the fears that Węgliszek had lifted from us as a part of our bargain playing in front of our eyes. Ours shown to us by a demon-bird, Karina's coming painfully true.

But then, my brain was too fried to think. I couldn't rest yet, but I let myself hold on to Artur and Damian, for a moment, two more, to revel in the soothing warmth of our bond just for a bit longer. To ground myself but also to be reminded that the amplified fears were just that and I wasn't alone. To let myself be held, to acknowledge our hurt, our vulnerabilities, and know that despite everything I still had people around me, holding on for dear life, their fingers digging into my back.

I reluctantly pulled away from the group hug.

"Well, I hope it's gone now," I said. "It got what it came for. I dare say we have enough negative energy combined to feed it for weeks."

"And I really don't need a bird to bring to my attention that something bad might happen while we're trespassing military grounds during a demonic apocalypse," said Damian.

His voice was stern and cold, but I wasn't fooled. I'd felt his feelings clear like a summer day. I still felt the aftereffect now, his anxieties echoing in my brain as we struggled to get back to reality, to focus on our mission.

Walking was a chore. Damian had dried my jeans with his magic so at least I wasn't wet, but my brain felt like it'd been pushed through a meat grinder and I still wasn't fully aware of my body. Every step felt weird, off.

At the edge of the meadow, a figure stood still, waiting for us.

TWENTY THREE

"It's too much to hope that it's Karina, right?" said Rafi.

We stood still, recognizing the familiar light hair and a goatee of the figure in front of us. Even in military fatigues instead of his suit, I'd never not recognize Węgliszek.

My brain couldn't process what was happening, too exhausted after the lelek bringing up all our insecurities. I was so tired of being constantly on edge, constantly in danger.

"LIE DOWN AND DON'T MOVE!" yelled a voice behind my back.

I jumped, my heart and stomach coming up to my throat and I was suddenly aware that I could still, in fact, feel things. And not just me, our bond was now cold with fear. We were surrounded by soldiers.

Węgliszek disappeared inside the forest with a smirk.

Rough hands manhandled me to the ground, spluttering snow that smashed into my face, my arms wrestled back. My magic didn't like it one bit. It rushed out of me, throwing the soldier away. More shouts and shooting followed but I managed to keep up a force field around Artur, Rafi, Damian, and me.

I scrambled up to kneeling, jerking my head around. At least a dozen soldiers surrounded us, their rifles pointed at us. Not only pointed—with a horrible, ear-splitting sound, they *fired* and I forced myself to watch, to see how it would end, magic flushing my skin

Bullets stopped metres from us, and fell to the ground.

If my magic wavered, we were dead.

I swallowed, my hands shaking. I took a deep breath, gathering all the strength I had, pulling on our bond, and pushed out my magic with all my might. The soldiers flew back screaming and landed in the snow a few meters back. Another shot sounded and I didn't need to tell the boys to run. We sprinted towards the treeline as a screeching sound tore through the night. Suddenly, the sky above us was filled with demons, mostly bird-like monsters that dove towards the soldiers.

"It's an illusion," said Artur. The sympathetic headache from his pain blossomed behind my eyes. "To buy us time."

But not all the soldiers were deceived. Two were already chasing us, and they weren't a couple of exhausted, terrified teenagers but professionals trained for running in difficult conditions. Their torchlights bounced in time with their steps, the only thing breaking the darkness of the forest. Until there was a flash of fire and a tree fell right behind us but the soldiers ran *through* it, as if they knew it was an illusion. The distance between us was closing fast and I was already out of breath and I'd known that my inability to run would get me killed—

Something hard slammed into my back and I fell to the ground with a scream. I landed hard on my stomach, my hands digging into the snow and catching my weight, saving my face from crashing into the frozen ground.

"Witch," spat a soldier, disgust plain in his voice.

There was a metallic clink of a rifle being reloaded and I balled up, shielding my head, breath catching in my throat. But instead of a shot, there was a shout and the sound of a body falling to the ground. Then Artur was pulling me up to my feet and we ran, ran, ran, heart hammering in my chest, my lungs struggling to catch enough air.

We were going to die in this forest.

We'd faced so many demons, we'd fought other magic users, and we would die at the hands of very human soldiers.

The trees grew sparser and a flash of the red light streamed between the branches, illuminating an old brick building. It had no door or windows, just gaping holes in the walls.

"We'll entrap ourselves," whispered Rafi, as we made for the door.

"We can protect ourselves better with walls around us," said Artur.

We walked in, trying to keep our steps soft so that the echo wouldn't carry. The building was empty inside, just naked concrete all around. We stood in a main corridor, surrounded by darkness broken only by the red light. Long shadows ran alongside the walls and I shivered.

We're invisible, right? I asked Artur telepathically, my heart trying to escape my ribcage.

Artur nodded. "Yes. And our footsteps in the snow are masked, too. I learnt my lesson. But…I don't know. It's easier in the darkness but I don't see that well so it's difficult to create a convincing illusion."

And it wouldn't stop Klara. She could find us through the shadows, especially when Artur bent the light to keep us invisible. And now, after I'd left her and Filip asleep in the snow, they had more reason than ever to try to find us. Were they awake yet? Would they freeze outside or would their magical cloaks keep them warm enough?

We walked into the second room on the left—just another empty concrete box with wind blowing in snow flurries through the hole where the window was supposed to be—and momentarily started our work. Rafi took out salt from his pocket and Artur handed me a piece of chalk. I broke it in half and handed a piece to Damian. Quickly, we drew a circle around us and scribbled protective symbols along the circumference, singing spells under our breaths, while Rafi reinforced the circle with salt. We were invisible and this should make us additionally undetectable and protected.

We were drawing the last symbols when loud stomps sounded inside the building. I finished the sigils and drew closer to the boys. We stayed close together, our backs and elbows brushing. When the torchlight skirted around the room, I flinched, but the soldiers didn't see us. They walked on and my shoulders relaxed the tiniest bit.

"They must be here," said one of the soldiers as they moved along the corridor. "I can see that they're inside this building."

"They're probably using mind magic."

We exchanged glances. What did it mean that the soldier could *see* we were here? Was Artur right, was his illusion imprecise because he couldn't see well?

Rafi pulled on my sleeve and pointed his head towards the window. I hesitated, unwilling to leave the place that we'd just made remotely safe, when the soldiers stormed into the room opposite ours, throwing their rifles wildly around, as if trying to hit an invisible target.

We followed Rafi to the window and climbed outside.

"They're escaping!" shouted the same soldier who had claimed they could see us.

We ran back to the forest. It seemed that while the soldiers knew we were escaping, they didn't know which way we took, which bought us time. Which was good, because we couldn't run in total darkness—even walking was difficult when at every step we could collide with a tree. My feet kept finding more and more roots under the snow and I face-planted more than once.

Torchlight broke through the darkness and I shivered. Not again. I was so tired, we couldn't go on like this.

"This way!" shouted the soldier and their steps grew louder.

It couldn't have been a lucky guess.

But before I could focus on that thought, wild magic seized my limbs and I came to a stop. The world was veiled from me, as if a thick fog separated us, and my limbs felt weirdly light. My feet spun me around against my will, magic sparkling on my skin.

The moment I'd dreaded since the solstice, and more so since I'd seen Węgliszek at the edge of the forest had come.

My mouth opened and a scream escaped my throat.

Artur got to me first, his hands clamping around my mouth, but magic pushed him off me. But before I could scream again, hands seized me from behind, bringing me to the ground. Magic lashed out from me and my legs kicked and arms flung around, trying to get Rafi off me, but he knew my magic better than anyone else, even when it was controlled by a devil. He clung onto me as I thrashed around, one hand firmly against my mouth. I tried to regain control of my body but I couldn't, I couldn't, and I didn't want to fight Rafi, and then more arms were on me as Artur and Damian helped hold me down and drink up my magic, and I couldn't stand it, I couldn't even control my body, and the soldiers were getting closer, and I couldn't breathe—

"We're close," said a soldier mere metres from us.

Another scream built up in my throat, but Rafi muffled it well, his hand pressing into my teeth, bruising my lips.

The devil was going to get us killed.

I was going to get us killed.

Magic burst out of me again but the boys drank it all up. My muscles thrashed, but not even the devil could shake off the three boys holding on to me for dear life.

Not that it needed to. The soldiers' steps crunched in the snow as they approached us. But then, impossibly, they walked past us as the devil possessing me screamed and flailed for their attention.

Artur, Rafi, and Damian held strong, holding me down, not letting the devil win. They didn't let go when the magic on my skin quieted, waiting, making sure I was truly myself. Only then did they help me up to a sitting position and I was in a group hug again. I let them hold me as I trembled.

"This can't keep happening," whispered Damian. "As long as the devil has your blood, we're ten steps behind."

"I'm sorry," I said as Artur pulled me up to my feet. The trees were a little sparser here, enough for the red light to flood in so that I could distinguish the shapes of the forest around us.

"It's not your fault," he said firmly.

But then we heard the snow crunching again as the soldiers ran towards us again.

And I realized my blood wasn't the only thing Węgliszek had gotten.

Don't panic, I told Artur telepathically.

I caught his arms and I spun him around, once, twice, and then I covered his eyes with my hands.

It was a wild guess but we couldn't keep on running forever. Especially not if our enemy could follow us so closely.

The soldiers' steps faltered. We were careful not to make any sounds, not to crunch the snow. Artur held on to my arms and I made sure his eyes were covered. The torchlight skirted among the trees as the soldiers scanned the forest and I held my breath, hoping I was right.

"This way," said the soldier, his voice harsh. But their steps retreated and soon I could take a first full breath in a while.

We waited a couple of long moments, until the only sounds in the forest were the creaking of the branches under the snow and our breaths.

"The devil can see through Artur's eyes," I whispered. "That was his bargain to get us out of the castle. And it looks like he might use soldiers to get rid of us. I don't know how they know what the devil sees but that's the least of our worries right now."

"The devil said it's a god," said Damian. "Isn't it ironic that your parents summoned and bargained with a god to stop the gods from coming back? And then we've done the same. Of course, it would backfire. Our ignorance of our own history is hunting us."

Of course. Now it all seemed like a divine punishment for trying to stop the gods—Węgliszek included—from coming back. Mum forgetting about her magic. Dad scared of any mention of magic. Igor killed. It was a miracle I was alive and that was probably only thanks to Baba Jaga—oh look, another goddess. Or maybe Laura was right and it was Weles looking after me. But now, here we were, in a military area, surrounded by soldiers. Karina was missing and Węgliszek was using Artur's eyes to track us.

My heart squeezed as I helped Artur tie his scarf around his eyes. We wouldn't get far like that.

The bigger problem was that, in all the running around, we'd lost Karina's footprints.

TWENTY FOUR

WE STOOD IN THE DARKNESS, COLD NUMBING OUR limbs. What were we going to do? How could we find Kari?

"Do we have anything that belongs to Karina?" I whispered.

There was a moment of silence. Why hadn't we exchanged belongings before leaving home?

"I don't know if that helps, but I have something *from* her," said Damian.

He unzipped his jacket and pushed something cold into my hand. I clutched it in my hand, feeling its smooth and intricately-shaped surface in my hand. An amulet, a thin piece of stone in some unusual shape hanging from a piece of string.

My bond to Damian sparkled. But as I kept squeezing, focusing on Karina, a wilder, stronger energy pulled me in the direction we'd come from.

"I think I can find her," I said.

"I'll go with you," said Rafi.

I reached out to touch Damian's hand. Thanks to our bond, I was aware of where he was, even if I couldn't see anything.

"Will you stay with Artur?" I asked. Then I reached out my other hand to Artur. "Is that okay?"

"Yes," said the boys in unison, their voices blending together.

Rafi was harder to find in the darkness but after a few attempts I managed to catch his arm.

"Let's go," I said.

We walked for a long time. Making it out of the forest, back towards the building took us a lot of time, as we stumbled in the dark, holding on to each other. We passed the building where we'd hidden and followed a snowed-in road. It was easier to find our way around there as thanks to the crack in the sky we could see something.

I was acutely aware that we were no longer invisible and everyone could see our footprints, but I tried not to think about it. Instead, I focused on the stone in my hand and my bond with Karina.

Now that there was some light, I could see the crystal in more detail. It was white, almost transparent and carved into an oak leaf. The details were incredible, down to the tiny nerves.

After some minutes of walking through the snow, I heard noise in the distance. Rafi pulled me between the trees and we did our best to obscure our footsteps but if anyone looked too closely, we were toast.

A car rolled past us, driving in the direction we were walking, and we hid ourselves in the shrubs, hoping that it was too dark for the soldiers to see us. When the sound of the car's engine died in the distance we pressed on between the trees, still wary of the noise ahead of us. There were caws and squeaks, intertwined with shouts and an occasional shot.

We rounded a corner and in the darkness we could make out a group of people standing close to a building similar to the one where we'd hidden. No, not only people—many of them were definitely demons. The people wore military fatigues and screamed orders that the demons, unsurprisingly, didn't follow.

"Stand down!" a soldier screamed as a furry demon approached them on all fours.

When the demon didn't stop, the soldier opened fire. The demon roared and charged harder, undeterred by the rain of bullets, until it reached the soldier and tackled them to the ground. The soldier screamed as the demon ripped the rifle from their hands and threw it into the forest but, as far as I could see, it didn't actually hurt the soldier.

Rafi and I exchanged a glance. We needed to find Karina. And the stone kept pulling me in the direction of the commotion.

Slowly, we made our way towards the commotion, trying to stay as quiet as possible. Something brushed my calves from behind and I barely choked back the scream as I twisted around. There was a cat-like figure behind me, the size of a lynx. Its eyes were red and gleamed as the demon looked up at me and brushed against my calves again in a cat-like manner.

I looked at Rafi, hoping he knew what demon it was and how to appease it. And maybe he did, because he reached for his backpack and soon he extended a hand with a piece of cheese towards the demon.

"I'm afraid I don't have anything more like cat food," he whispered, crouching down.

The demon sniffed the cheese then gently took it out of Rafi's hand with its long, long teeth. As it chewed, it purred.

"Can I stroke you?" asked Rafi.

The demon didn't respond and I was about to slap Rafi's hand, but he touched the demon's head before I could do that. The demon purred louder as Rafi scratched it behind the ears.

"You're a cute friend," he announced, and I pulled on his other hand.

I spotted Karina in the crowd.

She looked the most human in the demonic crowd, her jeans soaked through and clinging to her legs, her long, dark hair in complete disarray, her steps somehow heavier as if she was bound to the Earth more than the demons around her. But when I caught sight of her face, her eyes flashed white.

Just then, the soldiers opened fire again, and I flinched. The demons pressed on but Karina was towards the back of the group, maybe less bloodthirsty than the others or maybe more aware of the limitations of her human body. Whatever the reason was, that was our chance.

Rafi and I ran, using the commotion as a cover. We caught Karina and pulled her back, ignoring her kicking and thrashing. We didn't get far, just a bit inside the woods, trying to put any distance between us and the demons and soldiers. Some heads turned towards us, but the soldiers were too busy trying to save themselves. When we were between the trees again, Rafi knocked the legs from under Karina. They fell to the ground, him pinning her under him. He threw me a bag of salt from his pocket, struggling to keep Karina down.

"Draw," he said and I didn't need to be told twice.

I drew the protective circle around us in the snow and reinforced it with salt. I placed a few crucial symbols and pushed my magic out, grateful that it was listening to me for once, keeping us inside a forcefield.

Karina thrashed under Rafi, kicking and biting, and he struggled to keep her down—especially since the kicks from her Docs really hurt. The demon had made her stronger which wasn't helping our situation.

"You aren't a demon," I said, forcefully, focusing on our bond. "Well, okay, you're part demon but that's not all you are. You're our family. You hate maths and you've always been top of your class in Polish, even if you don't like it, either, and, for some inexplicable reason, you love raisins in your cheesecake. You love them so much that, when we were kids, you'd steal the raisins I'd pull out from my cheesecake. You love summer, and sea, and dancing, and cheesy romance novels, the more predictable the better, because you prefer familiar plots and happy endings. You cut my hair for me and before magic decided to come and ruin everything one more time, you dyed my hair and it turned orange, even though it was supposed to be strawberry blonde. You're so many things, and if demon is one of them, then who cares, but don't pretend you don't know us. We're your family."

As I talked, the bond between us changed. The magic on Karina's end no longer felt so strong and wild—it diminished to just a flicker but now that I knew it was there, I could feel it. She stopped struggling and she lay limply under Rafi, her eyes closed. I was about to check if she'd passed out when she opened her eyes. They were brown once again.

"Weles is really back," Karina whispered, her voice equal parts fear and awe.

TWENTY FIVE

"THAT WAS THE WORST FEELING IN THE WORLD," SAID Karina as we made our way back through the forest. Her voice was barely louder than a whisper and, in the distance, we could still hear demons' screeches and gunfire. "And there are a lot of contenders for that title. But just…being there but also not really? Having zero control over my body, over my thoughts? And hearing this voice inside my head, calling me to him. I wasn't myself. I was *his*. And whatever he'd like me to do, I would have done it, no questions asked."

Karina shuddered, and I squeezed her hand. She didn't pull back.

"These demons out there are still under his control. He's angry with the military because they'd captured Arrow."

"Wait a moment," I said. "Weles, the ruler of Nawia, the god of magic, came here for *Arrow*? Our Arrow?"

I thought back to the figure we saw riding Arrow across the sky. Had it been Weles? I couldn't see it clearly but the thought of a god riding a dragon who nestled in the nook of my neck and slept so many nights between Artur and me was disconcerting.

Then again, the same dragon had flown off to fight the firebird when the sky had cracked. We'd suspected all along that Arrow might be a żmij, that it might even be an incarnation of Weles himself. It shouldn't come as a surprise.

Sending an army of demons to help free Arrow bought Weles some points.

"They flew away together," said Karina, confirming my suspicions.

I thought back to the soldiers and all the demons surrounding them. If that's what Weles had brought to them for imprisoning Arrow, what would he do to the rest of us, all the people who'd forgotten all about his existence? He was already punishing the sorcerers, but would he go after non-magic-users as well?

The return journey went faster and soon we were back in the complete darkness of the forest, using Damian's amulet to lead us back to the boys. Without it, they would have been impossible to find as they were still invisible. Once Artur let us under the spell, I saw that Damian had melted off a patch of snow and they were sitting in the grass, leaning against a tree, a small blue fire dancing between them and bringing warmth. Artur's eyes were still covered by the scarf.

"You're alive," said Artur, hugging Karina. Damian joined in the group hug.

"Okay, the gang is back together," said Rafi. "Now, onto Wiwi's mission. The feather from the firebird's tail."

Artur pulled back from the hug.

"I can't go with you," he said. "If the devil can see where we are through my eyes, it won't stop chasing us. And I won't get far like that. We'll never make it there."

Something heavy settled in my chest, and I blinked. I knew he was right but I wasn't ready to separate. I put my arms around his neck, closing him in an embrace, and clung on.

"We need the feather from the firebird's tail," said Damian after a couple of moments, and I hesitantly drew back.

"Wait." Artur caught my hand, anxiety shooting through him. "Wiki, would you…would you exchange amulets with me? I know I can find you either way but…"

I squeezed his hand.

"Yes."

I reached to my neck and unclasped my mum's amulet. I hadn't given it back to her. Had Gabriella made her a new one?

I put the amulet around Artur's neck, and he hung his around mine. Somehow, the amulet with the little black bird—an actual blackbird, as I knew now—fit better. Now that I was more confident in our relationship, in who we were to one another, I no longer minded that among the magic-users the gesture often replaced engagement. Because it didn't matter what it meant to others, it mattered what it meant to us. And it had always been about keeping each other safe.

"I'll stay with Artur," said Karina, once the exchange was done.

"You're a driver," I protested. "The two of you are our only two drivers."

Karina shook her head. "I shouldn't go with you. You saw what just happened here. And it's likely that Weles and Arrow flew to fight the firebird again, so if you find it, they'll be nearby. As long as that demon's in me, I can't—"

Her voice broke and I hugged her. Of course, she shouldn't have to suffer through Weles controlling her again.

We needed to free her of the demon once and for all.

"It's okay," I whispered into her hair. "I understand."

"Go," Karina said. "Go and make it fast."

An hour later, Rafi, Damian, and I were passing the last cluster of buildings before the forest where we'd left the car. A shrill, screeching sound made me stop.

"We're walking towards the trouble again, aren't we?" asked Damian half a second before I started towards the sound.

In the parking lot there was a person waving a long stick at an owl flying around their head. And it wasn't just any random person.

"Ada?" I asked, recognizing my classmate and deskmate.

"Ugh, fucking strzyga!" she shouted as the bird dove

under her stick. "Hi, Wiki. Rafał. What are you doing here? And who's that?"

She flung the stick around, pointing it at Damian. He flinched back.

"Damian," I said. "He's a friend."

"How do you know it's a strzyga and not just an owl?" asked Rafi.

"Because that fucking owl keeps flying into my room every night and sucking the blood out of my sister. It's too powerful in its regular form so I'm trying to hunt it now because no one sucks anyone without their explicit permission."

With that, she flung the stick but the owl avoided it again. Ada pressed on, undeterred. Damn, my former deskmate was slaying the apocalypse. If more people were like her, maybe I didn't have to worry about the population of this city.

"I thought you were sick," said Ada. "Well, at least I thought so the first week you were gone. Now I suspect you're somehow related to this," she waved her hand around at the broken sky.

I exchanged a look with the boys. That was a frighteningly good guess.

"Why would you think so?" I asked.

"Because things started getting weird with the creepy guy stalking you and it got worse when you disappeared. And no one ever questioned why you were gone. And now you're here, on a casual evening apocalyptic stroll, I assume, not surprised about the strzyga at all."

She raised her eyebrow at me.

"It's a fairly good guess," I admitted reluctantly. "We're trying to fix it now. Do you need help with the strzyga?"

"No," said Ada, attacking the bird with the stick. "It went after my family so I will be the one to kill it."

"You won't do it with a stick," said Damian.

"No shit. But I can't exactly burn it while it's flying. And I'm not a Witcher who would spend an entire night with this creature to kill it."

Rafi laughed. "I think Ada will be just fine."

She grinned in response. "As always. It was nice seeing you. Good luck with whatever secret mission you're on."

We walked back towards the forest and finally made it back to the car. It was snowed in and we'd almost missed it, but at least the forest hadn't eaten it. Damian melted the snow with his magic. Rafi got behind the wheel and we slowly drove through the snow.

The heating was on and I was starting to get sleepy, the exhaustion of the past hours slamming into me with a force of a jackhammer. The tension in the car was palatable. I'd pushed Damian and Rafi's fight away from my mind but now that we were in a car together and in no imminent danger, it was impossible to ignore the charged silence.

"Hazelnuts?" I offered, taking out a handful from a pouch in my backpack.

"Yes," the boys said at the same time.

Rafi glared at Damian in the rearview mirror and the silence became even more weighted. I ignored them and handed some nuts to Rafi, who, after all, was the driver, and then to Damian.

The radio in the car was dead and I wondered what time it was. It felt like the middle of the night and keeping my eyes open was a hustle, but winter nights dragged on forever.

The drive was slow, as Rafi tried to manoeuvre through the snow, but the car was a simple sedan and we didn't even have wheel chains. To make matters worse, as we got further away from the city, the snow started falling, soon turning into a full-on blizzard.

Rafi stopped the car.

"I don't see anything," he said. "And we're running out of petrol. It's pointless, we'll crash if we go on. We need to stop. I don't think it's passing soon so we might as well get some sleep."

We didn't argue. Rafi got out of the car and brought a blanket from the trunk, while Damian and I set up protections, strong wind blowing snow into our faces and blinding us. It took us no more than a few minutes, but we came back to the car covered in snow from head to toe and shivering.

Damian held out his hands and the car filled with warmth, the snow evaporating, our clothes drying. I was becoming a greater and greater fan of alchemy with every second.

"We have only one blanket," Rafi said.

"I have the Guardian's cloak," I said. "But I'd rather not wear it."

In the end, Rafi kept the blanket, Damian got the cloak, and I got the jackets from both boys. We made ourselves as comfy as possible, lowering the seats while Damian took the backseat. Damian made a small blue fire, the same sort he used in the forest for himself and Artur, and closed it in a jar. He placed it on the console between all of us and soon the car filled with pleasant warmth. The vicious wind outside rocked the car every once in a while, howling. I closed my eyes and let the exhaustion pull me under…and I dreamt.

TWENTY SIX

It isn't like the Baba Jaga's dreams. Everything around me is less concrete, less sharp, more, well, dream like. I see myself from a third person's perspective, standing in the clearing in the forest where I collected Tomasz's debt to Węgliszek. I'm not sure how I know it as the scene lacks details, but I'm deeply aware of where I am—standing in front of the enormous oak tree that looks even larger than I remember, its tallest branches disappearing in the clouds. Behind me, there are two powerful figures fighting. I'm not surprised by that, as if I'm expecting them. They are both human like but one of them has bull horns on his head.

Weles.

Which means that the light-haired being he is fighting should be Perun.

They hold swords and spar across the meadow, the blades clicking and clanking, both of them too quick to injure another.

272

The horned god is facing me, but he doesn't pay attention to me. Instead, he draws the other god back, away from the oak tree.

My dream self catches the lowest branch. Apparently, in the dreams I have more upper body strength than I do in reality because I make it look easy-peasy. I climb, and climb, and climb, never once stopping to catch my breath, until I see a tell-tale glimmer of a fire-like feathers far above me, on top of the tree.

When I woke up, the world outside was white. It was impossible to say if it was still snowing as the car windows were covered in a thick layer of snow. The wind had died down, and I took it as an encouraging sign.

Had I had my first true dream? Had the Baba Jaga given me my dreams back? The dreams sent to me by the demon had been different, sharper, full of crucial details, so it couldn't have been one of them. What did it mean? Was the Baba Jaga gone?

No. It couldn't have been a real dream. I must have had it for a reason. There were enough supernatural forces at play—if not the Baba Jaga, then some other demon or god must have sent it to me.

Rafi was still asleep, snoring softly on the driver's seat, but Damian was awake, sitting on the backseat with his arms crossed and staring at the window gloomily. When he noticed I was awake, he pulled out some bread and a jar of jam from his backpack and passed it to me.

We ate in silence, washing our meagre meal down with water. If everything went well, I'd have the feather from the firebird's tail soon, I'd give it back to the Baba Jaga, and we'd be able to fix the hole in the sky. Then I'd eat all the pizza and hot chocolate I could get. And coffee. So much coffee.

Rafi woke up soon afterwards and we shared our sad meal with him.

"Let's see what it looks like outside," he said when we were done. "Oh, and Merry Christmas."

I jolted, realizing that it was Christmas Eve. With a bit of luck, maybe we could have a proper celebration tonight.

I didn't want to leave the warmth, but I knew Rafi was right. The sooner we were on the road, the better. We were still maybe an hour's drive away from the meadow, likely more, considering the snail pace we'd set last night.

I pushed the door open, or rather tried, because it wouldn't bulge. Rafi struggled as well. Damian was the first to manage to open the door and I strongly suspected magic. Snow fell inside and a freezing gust of wind made me shiver. Damian got out and from the outside he opened the other doors. Soon, we were standing in the snow that reached our knees. I looked up and down the road that now looked like a river of snow, cutting a line between tall, tall trees. The sky was covered in dark clouds, so dense that the red light barely cut through.

"That's not optimal," I said.

"We can't drive in that," said Rafi. "We couldn't even open the door."

"It looks like it might storm again," said Damian, looking up at the sky. "You said that we're running out of petrol. Let's start with that and see how it goes."

He took out an empty canister from the trunk and filled it with snow, then added contents of a prepared vial into it—some crystals and herbs. He looked expectantly at Rafi.

"Will you help me?" he asked, an uncertain tone to his words.

"It's a part of the mission," scoffed Rafi.

He crouched next to Damian and the boys put their hands on the canister. They sang softly, letting their magic do the work. Soon, the air stank of petrol.

"Wait—" I said, fear gripping my insides, but I was too late. The tank exploded with a powerful bang, throwing both boys away into snow.

"Shit, are you okay?" I asked, pulling Rafi up.

He looked dazed, but he nodded and I went to Damian. He'd pulled himself up to sitting, his eyes big. There was a smudge of dark soot on his cheek.

"Alchemist power was reliable," he said.

"It's still magic. And we know that Weles was furious with the soldiers for capturing Arrow."

We shared a look. Would the city still stand before we got the firebird's feather?

The car wasn't going anywhere now. It was tempting to bunker up inside and wait for the spring to come, but we had a mission and the faster we accomplished it, the faster we could be in warmth and safety.

We set down the road, our pace sluggish in the high snow. Snowflakes sprinkled around us gently, but it was nothing close to the blizzard last night. I didn't want to think about how far we had to go to reach the oak tree.

What if it was all for nothing? What if the firebird wasn't even there?

No. I didn't believe that. The dream couldn't have been a coincidence—I didn't have regular dreams; it must have been a vision.

A cawing sound broke the silence as a crow flew over us. But while I'd seen many demons around, I hadn't seen animals. I remembered the way Lila, Rafi and Karina's cat, reacted to Karina after she'd been possessed. Was it possible that all animals were scared of demons, and they were hiding?

More crows appeared and soon they surrounded us, cawing. We drew closer together.

"I don't think they're the firebird's pals, are they?" asked Rafi.

"No," I said, digging through my backpack. "It's a latawiec. Kneel down and show respect."

But before I could do that, Damian pulled me to his side.

"Keep Rafi back," Damian said under his breath. "Do whatever it takes and run the moment it's safe."

I opened my mouth to protest, but Damian cut me off.

"Trust me, I can handle a latawiec."

He kneeled and I followed suit, back to digging through my backpack. This time I didn't have any poppy seed cake to offer. I took out a handful of nuts and brought it up over my head in an offering.

The birds descended towards my hands, and I flinched. Damian put his arm over my head and the other one over his, shielding us from the birds. Hard, pointy beaks attacked my hands, pinching and tearing into my flesh as they took the nuts. What if I was wrong? What if it wasn't a latawiec but another demon?

But then, with a powerful whoosh of wind, bare, human-like feet appeared in the snow in front of me. A tall, slender, and half-naked figure stood so close we almost touched. I didn't know if it was the same latawiec I'd met before, but it looked identical, with shoulder-length brown hair, a striking face with high cheekbones, and black eyes framed by long eyelashes. Black feathers covered its torso and genitalia and ran up its arms which extended into wings.

"Sorceress," said the latawiec in its whispery voice. "We meet again. And you brought friends."

The demon looked over our group. Before it could get a good look at Rafi, Damian stood up, standing eye to eye with the latawiec and taking its attention off the rest of us. The demon tilted its head and looked at Damian. Even though the latawiec towered over him, Damian straightened up, looking at the demon calmly as it brought a long claw to his cheek. Damian's emotions slammed into me, and I was glad I was already kneeling. Warmth spread over my body, focusing on my lower belly, making me feel flushed and uncomfortable. It was just a phantom of what Damian was feeling but it was a proper woah moment—was that how the sex demon was supposed to make me feel? No wonder it had been surprised by me the first time it'd hunted me down.

"Brave witch," said the latawiec, stroking Damian's cheek, its voice as light as a summer breeze.

The demon left its claw on Damian's cheek and warmth flooded into my face—even though *I* didn't feel warm at all, quite the opposite. I shivered. The latawiec sniffed the air and it took everything in me not to cower.

But I couldn't cower and protect Rafi at the same time. And when I dared a glance at my cousin, his lips were slightly open and his eyes glazed over, trained on the latawiec.

Shit. Shit, shit, shit.

I took Rafi's hand and squeezed, hoping to ground him.

Damian shifted closer to the latawiec, bringing the demon's attention back to himself.

"What a wonderful group you've brought me, sorceress," said the latawiec, its black piercing eyes fixed on Damian.

"You can have me and only me," said Damian.

"No," said Rafi, his voice rough. I put my hand over his mouth, shielding him from the demon before he could say anything else.

"See?" said the latawiec. "We could have so much fun together…"

The demon looked longingly at Rafi and me.

"Only me," said Damian, stepping closer to the demon. "I stay. They go."

The demon moved around him to stand in front of me. I rose to my trembling feet, trying to keep Rafi shielded. Because Damian was right, and he was the person who needed the most protection right now.

"Wiki, stay down," growled Damian.

The latawiec drew its claw along my jaw, and I couldn't suppress a shiver.

"There's magic between you," said the latawiec, tilting its head. "Interesting."

Rafi stood up behind me, too, and the latawiec turned its head towards him. I did the only thing I could think of—I tackled Rafi to the ground. He landed on his stomach in the snow with me on top of him. Rafi threw me off easily, but I clung to his arm. His eyes were still glossy and dazed, his attention fully on the latawiec.

"It's either me or no one," said Damian, catching the latawiec's arm.

The latawiec's eyes flashed red. It rose its other arm, spreading it into a wing, and with one powerful move, the snow around them whirled, blinding me for a moment. I blinked, trying to clear my vision, but the latawiec and Damian disappeared.

They. Disappeared.

Rafi was still fighting me, so I smashed a handful of snow into his face.

"What the—" Rafi spluttered, pushing me away. He wiped the snow of his face.

I put my hand on his back, keeping him down.

"Promise me you're thinking clearly," I said. "Promise me you won't chase after a sex demon. Or I won't hesitate to smash more snow into your face."

"Unnecessarily cruel," growled Rafi but his eyes looked clearer. Still, I stared hard at him until he sighed. "I'm fine. Let me go before my clothes get completely drenched."

We got to our feet. I was still trembling, looking around for any sign of the latawiec and Damian, but the magic must have taken them far. I couldn't feel our bond, either.

I couldn't believe what Damian had done.

TWENTY SEVEN

"Wow. Just wow," raged Rafi, kicking his way through the snow. "Even a demon is better than me? I mean, I understand that it's a crazy hot demon, some serious Howl vibes, but, come on. You'd think that being human would win me some extra points."

I decided not to respond. We trudged down the road until our legs started sinking in snow up to the knees, our pace slowing and slowing. My thighs were screaming for a break. It was useless. We wouldn't make it to the oak tree before spring.

"We need to go between the trees," I said. "There's less snow there."

"I hate snow," said Rafi, which saddened me more than the rest of his rant. Just a few short weeks before, Rafi had still loved snow more than anyone else I knew. But the apocalyptic winter was overwhelming, and I shared his sentiment.

As we plodded on through the snow, my mind drifted away. I dwelled on our encounter with the latawiec, on the echo of Damian's feelings. The low burning in my stomach, desire filling my veins…had anyone ever made me feel that way? And what of all the other demons I'd encountered that were supposed to drive people crazy with lust or fall madly in love? I'd met the latawiec before and felt nothing like that—even it noticed the change, now that I could feel a shadow of Damian's feelings. I'd encountered the rusałka a few times and still lived to tell the tale. And then there was the time when Artur and I met the wiła—it was the only sex demon that had managed to bewitch me, if only for a few moments. I'd longed for it to touch me and, in that moment, I hadn't seen the world beyond it. It'd managed to entrance Artur, too. I remembered him saying that he'd never felt anything like that before, how confused he'd been. I'd told him it was a lust spell but now I had to wonder if that had been the right description. Yes, it was still the most passion I'd ever felt from his side of the bond but it hadn't been the same pure heat that Damian had felt around the latawiec, the "I want to rip off your clothes immediately" energy that was foreign to me. Did it have to do with the specificity of the demons? Or was it something fundamental about our nature?

I wished for the internet to work again, to be able to search for others who had similar questions, to read about other's experiences. To find some reassurance that my questions weren't purposeless.

Rafi and I took a lunch break. We stood by the tree, sharing bread and cheese, jam and nuts.

"I feel like a fantasy character on a quest," said Rafi, leaning back against the tree. "I only need a handsome royal who needs help in leading a rebellion and overthrowing an evil king, and we'll fall in epic love along the way."

"Do you realize you're enough on your own? You're a whole person. Not everything in your life must lead to an epic romance, not every person you meet must be a love interest."

"Of course I'm enough on my own." Rafi tore off a piece of bread with more force than necessary. "But that doesn't mean I don't want to be someone's person. You know, the first person they think about when they wake up and the person they message when they see something funny because they want to share it with you."

"You don't need epic romance for that. Friends can be that. Family. There are so many amazing ways to relate to people in your life who can be that for you."

"Wiwi, you're saying that because you already have that. You have your Circle of Four, you are surrounded by people who'd kill for you. I'm just a fifth wheel, a set of muscles."

Rafi avoided my eyes. Was that how he thought we thought of him?

"No one thinks about you like that." I squeezed his arm. "I'd kill for you. It was you who triggered the magic back when the Children of Weles had found us. It happened when Klara threatened you with the knife. Not Artur, not Damian. You. Thanks to you I could feel my bond with Karina and save us. Whether you like it or not, you're an important part of this team."

We finished our meal in silence, packed our sad provisions, and walked on through the forest. Rafi had managed to distract me, but now I was worrying about Damian again. I still couldn't feel our bond. What if he'd been too cocky? The latawiec was a powerful demon; it could have hurt him.

Would I know if Damian was hurt? Would I feel it if the worst came to be?

The sky was darkening fast—which wasn't hard with all the clouds. Soon, it was as dark as if it were night and the red light barely broke through the clouds.

"Wiki!" a familiar voice shouted and I swirled around.

Damian stood a dozen or so metres behind us, surrounded by crows. I ran to him and hugged him. He looked whole, he felt whole, and magic sparkled at our touch. But he kept his emotions firmly shut from me.

"Done playing around with your sex demon?" asked Rafi, crossing his arms on his chest.

It took everything in me to not run back to him and punch him.

Damian sighed.

"Yes, latawce are one of many, many sex demons in the Slavic mythology. And, like with many, though not all of them, it isn't the sex part that kills you. It's them making you fall in love with them and lose your mind from loneliness when they abandon you."

"And?"

"*And*, you wear your heart on your sleeve, Rafi! It would have killed you. Not instantly, but in a torturously slow way, playing you all along, just the way it loves to."

"So you're pretending to be a hero when you just wanted to fuck a hot demon."

"And if that were the case, so what?"

Rafi and Damian's eyes locked in a staring contest. I knew what Damian was doing, his posture all stiff, his jaw locked. He was retreating into his snarly, cagy mask to protect his real self. Meanwhile, Rafi's hands were shaking. I bit my lip, wishing him not to crumble down.

"Rafi, the demon would have killed you," I said. "It would affect you more than anyone else here."

But Rafi wasn't listening to me. He was staring at Damian's neck, where red scratches were visible under his scarf. Claw marks. Damian readjusted the scarf and Rafi swirled on his heel and stomped onwards.

"I'm immune to it," shouted Damian, starting after him, but Rafi didn't react.

I ran forwards to catch up with Rafi. It was hard as his legs were longer than mine and I had to jog to keep up with his fast pace. It was hard to jog in the deep snow, and after almost two days for hiking my legs were screaming for a break.

"Rafi, you're the one who reminded me that sex and romance don't always come hand in hand. Maybe it's time I reminded you, too."

Rafi walked a couple more steps then he slowed down and came to a stop. He turned around and I followed suit. Damian wasn't trying to keep up with us, staying a dozen metres away, the crows still flying around his head.

Rafi opened his mouth and then closed it.

"I won't take that moment away from you," he finally said, his eyes locked on Damian's. "But if you want to tell me something, now seems like a good time."

For a moment, we stood silently, snow falling softly around us. In the end, Damian walked forward until he stood in front of Rafi, tilting his head up to look him in the eye.

"I'm demiromantic," he said. Everything about him, from his stiff posture to his cold gaze screamed a challenge, "just dare to deny me" sort of message. He'd blocked me out, so I didn't know how he truly felt but I'd had some insight during our own conversation. "The latawiec wouldn't be able to kill me, because it wouldn't be able to make me fall in love with it. Even demons can't make you feel something that is against your nature."

There was a moment of silence, broken only by the cawing of the crows.

"That makes a lot of sense," said Rafi. Then he raised his eyebrow, a shadow of smile on his mouth. "Demi, but not aro-aro, huh? I can work with that."

"It means aro-aro unless specific conditions are met," said Damian flatly. "Close emotional bond or whatever. Years of friendship. Magic. Okay, not literally, magic doesn't change that for me. It happened only once so don't hold your breath."

Rafi's smile grew.

"I *knew* it. You do like me."

"I want to be your friend," said Damian.

It seemed to me that these words coming from Damian were as important or maybe more so than a declaration of undying love.

"But I mean a *friend*," stressed Damian before Rafi could say anything. "If you keep hoping that it will become a romance, it won't work."

There was a moment of silence as the boys stared silently at each other.

"Friends," said Rafi tasting the word. "I guess I can do that."

Damian's posture relaxed a tiniest bit as he turned to me.

"Wiki, I arranged for a ride for you," Damian said, nodding towards the birds swarming around his head. "The meadow is still too far away; it will take us days to get there on foot in this snow. And, if the firebird isn't there, the latawiec will bring you back here so we can come up with a new plan."

I hugged him again. Damian still didn't let me in, keeping his emotions to himself, but I showered him with my worry for him, for what he'd done for us and whether he was really okay with it. For how he'd been practically forced to come out. And gratitude, deep gratitude because he'd been right, Rafi wouldn't have had survived the latawiec but neither would have I. Maybe the demon wouldn't have been able to kill me—that was up to debate—but I didn't think I could have taken it mentally.

"Thank you," I whispered.

Damian squeezed me in response, holding on for a few long moments, his face buried in my shoulder. I'd wondered about how he'd told me to take Rafi and run but maybe what he'd needed in that moment was to be rescued, too.

And I hadn't even tried. I'd let him sacrifice himself.

"You will be okay, right?" he asked.

"Our friend doesn't affect me if our bond isn't there to muddle my feelings, if that's what you mean." I hesitated, unsure if I should voice my concern but decided to go for it. "Will you be okay?"

Damian squeezed me harder, his fingers digging into my back, and didn't respond for a couple of moments.

"I'll survive," he said but his voice was hoarse. "Now go. You have a firebird to find."

TWENTY EIGHT

THE LATAWIEC AND I TORE ACROSS THE SKY. THE demon kept the winds warm, shielding me from the snow. Why didn't the latawiec use the same magic it'd used to whisk Damian away? Was it because that passage didn't lead to anywhere in this realm? Or maybe the demon simply enjoyed me clinging to it for dear life?

I hoped Damian was okay. I hoped Rafi would put aside their differences and take care of him in a way that he wouldn't realize he's being taken care of.

By the time the latawiec started descending, my arms were shaking from holding on to the demon with all I had. The demon flew slowly, manoeuvring between the trees, before bringing us to ground. We weren't at the meadow but when I was about to open my mouth and ask about it, powerful magic slammed into me with so much force

I almost fell down. The magic on my skin prickled in response, warming me up.

As a confirmation of my darkest thoughts, a thunder growled.

"I can't take you any further," said the latawiec. "You'll find what you're searching for in the tallest branches of the tree."

I wanted to ask if it couldn't fly me there if the bird was up in the sky, but I bit my tongue. It wouldn't be smart to press my luck. The latawiec had already shown me much more kindness than expected.

"Thank you, oh great latawcu," I said, bowing my head.

The latawiec brought its claw to my cheek, stroking it. Then, as it turned to fly off, I blurted out:

"Will Damian be okay?"

The latawiec looked at me over its shoulder, its head rotating full one-hundred-eighty degrees, way more flexible than it should be, more bird like than human.

"I can't force humans to do anything they don't want to do. But not everyone can withstand the toll of their desires bared to them."

I wasn't reassured but I had more questions. It was stupid but it was a once-in-a-lifetime chance.

"What would have happened if I'd gone with you?" I asked.

"Would you have?" asked the latawiec, tilting its head all the way to its shoulder. That made it look even more like a bird. "You had three chances, sorceress. You never acted on them."

Then, with one powerful move of its black wings, the latawiec flew back to the sky.

Against my better judgement, I walked towards the magic blasting from between the trees. The forest grew sparser, the trees lower, soon opening into the clearing.

Just like in my dream, in the middle of the clearing grew a gigantic oak tree. It was grander than when I'd last been here, so tall I couldn't see its peak. Its branches were naked, not even snow touching them. Heavy storm clouds hung low over the meadow and a thunder growled again as I stood in the shadows, observing the scene unfolding in front of me.

Also like in my dream, there were two gods on the meadow. Perun wore a light linen robe and trousers, tied in the middle with a handwoven belt—an outfit that wouldn't have been out of place in Biskupin or some other outdoor museum displaying life before Christianity. His cheeks were sun-kissed—I imagined they always were, since no one had seen the sun for a while—and had a long, reddish-blond braided beard. The air around him sparkled with pure energy. Weles was an optical opposite of his brother. He wore a similar outfit, only in black, his dark hair and beard were similarly long and also braided. His skin was so pale it was almost translucent.

It was like in the stories I'd found in the Guardian's collection after learning that the gods might come back.

Perun and Weles were two sides of the same coin, powerful god-brothers who'd shaped the world hand in hand. Perun, the god of the skies and Weles, the god of the underground, of the arcane. They'd been in conflict since the beginning of the world, but neither was truly good or evil, because the pre-Christian beliefs didn't have such dualities. Beings—human, divine, or demonic—just *were*, each bound to their fate, each with a role to play in this world.

The two differences between the gods were the bullhorns growing from Weles' head and the fact that he was sitting astride a żmij.

Not just any żmij. Arrow. Arrow was here.

And it was huge. It'd been weeks since I'd last seen it, but the demon was easily five metres long and its wings spread probably as wide. It had massive claws, emerald green scales glistening in the red light, and golden eyes, just as I'd remembered, just way, way bigger. It'd also grown a pair of horns, easily as long as my arm.

Would Arrow recognize me? A part of me hoped it would, but a more sensible part wished not to attract its attention.

As I watched, Arrow and Weles flew closer to Perun, taunting him, then flew up, staying just out of reach. The gods didn't carry swords like in my dream. They didn't have to. Weles had Arrow and Perun…

The skies thundered as a lightning struck just next to the żmij. The earth shook and Arrow roared, but Perun didn't even flinch. Instead, more energy sparkled around him and another lightning struck. Now the sky's roars were almost on par with Arrow's growls and I shivered, part from fear, part from cold, and part from the sheer amount of pure magic that filled the air. Magic was so thick that I could hardly breathe, but I forced myself to close my eyes and focus on my mission.

The oak tree grew in the middle of the meadow and the gods were in my way.

What if the firebird wasn't there? I took the presence of the gods as an encouraging sign. If Arrow was with Weles, the firebird must be close to Perun, too. The whole scene looked like my dream so it couldn't be a coincidence.

The gods kept on fighting, the magic sparkling wilder, lightnings striking faster, Arrow's roars growing louder. The gods were evenly matched and it didn't look like they were going to stop anytime soon—if the myths were right, they'd been fighting since before the world had been created. It had been their competition, them trying to outdo each other, which had created our world in the first place. And while they were distracted for sure, hoping that they wouldn't notice someone trying to climb the oak tree was a stretch.

With a screech, Arrow dove to the ground and Perun moved back just in time. The żmij flew closer to the forest across the meadow and Perun followed, the air around him sparkling. Slowly, the way to the tree opened up ahead of me. A path of gold sparkles appeared in the snow, showing me the way. It might have been a trap, but I couldn't wait for a better opportunity.

I ran across the meadow towards the oak tree.

The snow was deep and my movements weren't as fast as I would have liked. My thighs screamed in protest as I pounded on, icy air freezing my throat. Magic stuck to my skin like particularly annoying glitter, making my cheeks itch and coaxing my own power to the surface. I clung to my magic with all I had, held it close to my chest. If there had ever been a bad time for my magic to slip, it was when two gods warred metres away.

Just as I reached the oak tree, I could have sworn that Weles looked me right in the eye, but he continued fighting with the other god without any acknowledgement.

I didn't dwell on it. I had more immediate problems, like how on Earth would I climb a tree. Sure, I'd used to climb trees with Rafi and Kari when we were kids but they were of the garden plum tree variety, not gigantic oaks that connected the worlds.

It wasn't a regular tree at all. It radiated pure magic and warmth. Its magic felt different to the gods'—it was less wild, more rooted, and much more powerful. Now that I stood in the oak tree's shadow, I couldn't sense the gods at all.

I decided to take it one branch at the time. The biggest problem was getting on the tree in the first place. The lowest branches were out of my reach, so I looked at the trunk. It was wide, so wide that three people could easily sit against it and not be visible from the other side. I made sure that the tree stood between the gods and me, took off my gloves and put them in my pocket, reached for a knob in the trunk, put my foot on another one, and lifted myself up. I held my breath for a second, thinking I'd fall but the bark was strong, so I put my other foot higher up. In few more steps, I'd made it to the first branches.

Now, I only had to climb, oh, a kilometre or so more.

It went slowly and I flinched every time a thunder rolled. Climbing a tree during a thunderstorm was a horrible idea. Sure, Perun was focusing his lightning bolts on Weles and Arrow, but if he'd noticed me, I'd be an easy target.

Then I misjudged my strength and my hand slid down the bark, tearing my skin. Pain shot down my arm. My stomach raised to my throat as I fell, swallowing a scream. My butt collided painfully with the nearest branch and I clung to it, afraid to move even a tiniest bit.

I looked down. The earth was now at least twenty metres below. If I fell, only magic could save me.

I hugged the branch, my body shaking. I decided to rest and retrieved a water bottle from my backpack to take a few sips. I had a long, long way to go and my arm muscles had already joined my legs in screaming for mercy.

Another roar from Arrow prompted me to go on. I pushed myself up and up, my arms and legs burning, my hands scratching against the hard bark. The magic of the tree kept getting stronger or maybe I was getting more in tune with it and soon it was almost scalding me. I ignored my body's protests. I was on a quest. I needed the feather from the firebird's tail. I needed to finish the Baba Jaga's trials to mend the crack in the sky. Our world quite literally depended on that.

I took more breaks on the way to drink some water and give my trembling muscles a chance to rest. I didn't look down anymore—I wasn't afraid of heights, but I didn't want to dwell on how easy it would be for me to slip and fall and crack my skull open under the oak tree.

It felt like hours passed and the air around me grew colder. Snow started falling around but it didn't fall near the trunk of tree, the warmth of its magic keeping it away. But I still couldn't see the top of the tree. My arms shook so much that I struggled to lift them. Would that be it? The end, the quest failed because the reluctant heroine didn't have enough upper body strength to pull herself up the tree?

And then there was a roar, a thunder, and the lightning struck right next to me, making all the hair in my body stand. With a crack, the branch that I was standing on broke—and I fell.

TWENTY NINE

I SCREAMED. I WAS AIRBORNE, PLUNGING TOWARDS the ground, unable to draw in a breath. Wind whipped around me and I closed my eyes. Just when I'd lost all hope, my body connected with something hard. It wasn't a branch—it was warm and it was *moving*. I barely had time to twist around and wrap my hands around Arrow's neck as it skyrocketed towards the sky.

Lightning flew around us and Arrow manoeuvred back and forth, ditching them in a wild dance that made me nauseous. Freezing cold air and snow slashed against my face and I struggled to see. Down on the meadow, Weles stood by Perun, so far below that they looked like ants. Perun ignored his brother altogether, focused on trying to strike us. Arrow screeched and roared as it danced across the sky, flying higher and higher towards the clouds.

When I was sure that I'd throw up any second, I noticed a flash of fire in the oak tree. The firebird screeched, its shrill voice drilling into my brain, as Arrow flew straight at it. The firebird rose from its nest in the topmost branches and dove towards us. It was much smaller than Arrow now, and I'd admired the demon's courage. The favourite bird of the gods or not, it looked like a Chihuahua going after a German shepherd.

It was a full-blown thunderstorm now, the lightning striking one after another, aiming at us as Arrow attacked the firebird. The demons shrieked and roared, their wings beating against each other while I gripped Arrow's neck with all I had. The firebird was so close that it nearly set my jacket on fire, but it flew out of my range before I could reach for its tail. And then Arrow dove again and I had to clutch it tightly while my stomach made an effort to escape through my throat.

The firebird flew at us, and I reached for its tail but it just scratched my arm, ripping my jacket. The next lightning flew so close to us that it left my skin feeling all dry and sensitive, like it'd felt after days of magical exertion when the Children of Weles had kept me imprisoned. Arrow roared and I clung to it as it cannonballed to the ground before abruptly turning up again.

My stomach rioted, and I was so focused on not throwing up that I almost missed my chance. The firebird was left behind, but Arrow brought me close to its nest. Inside, a long, red and orange feather gleamed as if it were on fire. I took it, then quickly stuffed it inside my backpack. The firebird was already flying at us shrieking violently and I flinched.

But then the firebird stopped mid-air. It looked around and made a little circle in the sky, before disappearing in its nest. For a few moments there was silence. Not even a thunder sounded and my ears drummed, my senses confused after listening to the gods' fight for hours. My body tensed as I waited for something to happen. I wasn't disappointed. A powerful wind came in, shaking the trees. I hugged Arrow close as it dove towards the ground. Down below, Perun and Weles disappeared in the forest, almost as if running away, and dread settled in my stomach. The wind sped up and a blizzard started, snow blasting from all around. I trembled as ice flew at me, getting under my clothes and soaking me to the bone. When a few moments later Arrow landed on the ground, the world around was white, the snow making it impossible to see more than a few paces away.

Legs shaking, I stood on the ground and made my way towards Arrow's head.

"I missed you, my dragon baby," I said, stroking Arrow's nose. The żmij was an effective protection from the blizzard, shielding me from the worst wind. "I'm glad you're okay. Thank you for helping me."

Just like when it was just a baby, Arrow headbutted my hand. It misjudged its strength and pain shoot up my arm as my hand was slapped away. I rotated my wrist, making sure I was okay, and scratched Arrow's nose some more. The żmij leaned into my touch, closing its eyes in pleasure. But then a shudder tore through it. Arrow stepped back, lifting its head, as if listening. Then, with one more blink of its big, golden eyes at me, it flew into the forest.

Snow slammed into me with renewed vigour, wind whipping against me so strongly I nearly lost my balance. My face was numb with cold, my body shivering. I hid behind the oak tree, trying to use it as a shield but the snow now came from all directions.

Before I could decide if I should run for the forest, a new figure appeared in the snow. I squinted but at first all I could make out was the long black hair and a flower wreath on top of it. For a moment I thought it might be Laura, but the figure was taller than the alchemist and its magic felt like Weles' or Perun's. As it approached, I noticed that the new god wore a long, white dress—a bride's dress, cut in an old-fashioned way with lots of lace and layers. They had a string of red coral beads hanging from their neck.

I stood rooted, shielding myself against the tree as the goddess approached. Their magic brushed against my skin and went deeper, touching my heart and mind. I shivered but I decided that running was the worst option. Instead, I fell to my knees in front of a goddess that made both Perun and Weles flee.

And then, suddenly, it clicked. I knew who it was. It was perhaps the best remembered Slavic god in general, the goddess of winter or, as some claimed, of the whole seasonal cycle. The goddess we made ritual of dolls of and burned or drowned them on the first day of spring—my birthday.

Marzanna.

Just like Weles, she was a goddess of magic. But when I browsed the Guardian's collection, it seemed to me that while Weles took care of divinations, prophetic dreams, and powers that corresponded to the sorcerers', Marzanna was more of a mother of witchcraft and alchemy—powers that came from nature, not from demons. But that had been just one Guardian's opinion and the Slavic gods didn't seem to have such clearly divided roles—it all depended on where you were and whom you asked.

The goddess reached her hand towards me. I hesitated for a moment before grasping it. Icy cold pierced through me but I didn't pull back. Snow whirled all around me and the world turned white. Wind whooshed fast, slashing against me and I squeezed my eyes shut. When it quieted, I dared to peek. We weren't on a meadow anymore, but in a forest, next to a wooden hut. Marzanna released my hand then drew her hand through my hair, her gesture gentle and maternal. Then, with one more whoosh of the wind, the goddess disappeared.

I looked around. Was it the Baba Jaga's hut? In the darkness it looked similar and hope bubbled inside me. It could all be over now. I'd give the demon the feather, I'd get the dream cloth and patch up the sky. By morning, the crack in the sky could be a half-forgotten nightmare.

Then a familiar figure came out of a forest. Her long blonde hair was braided, a knitted hat on her head, and a large scarf wrapped around her shoulders. She was carrying a pile of wood in her hands. She stood still when she saw me, the wood nearly falling to the ground.

"Wiktoria?" asked Zuzanna.

"Merry Christmas?" I responded with a question.

TH1RTY

It wasn't the Baba Jaga's hut. The wooden cottage consisted of only one room with a small kitchenette in a corner, a wooden table, a fireplace, and a narrow bed squeezed in the corner. The place might have been an abandoned hunting cottage or, indeed, an old Baba Jaga's hut. But right now, it was Zuzanna and Aysun's home.

It didn't seem like a bad way to spend the end of the world, stuck with your girlfriend in a cottage in the middle of the forest. The place was well-protected and so far they hadn't been visited by demons, the Children of Weles, or gods. I spent the first hour or so explaining how I'd ended up there—and everything that had happened since Zuzanna had cut her ties to the family and passed me the Guardian's ring.

I was so relieved she was alive I could have cried. And maybe I had. Maybe when I'd seen Zuzanna and Aysun alive and safe, happy in their little hut in the forest, I'd started sobbing so badly that Zuzanna had thought I was hurt.

"I'm just so glad you're alive," I managed to say, though, judging by Zuzanna's stare, maybe it'd come out as gibberish.

Aysun kept topping up my tea mug and made sure that the fireplace that I sat by didn't stop crackling merrily. She'd found me bread and blackberry jam and I ate my fill. By the time I was done with the story, my eyes were closing and it took a lot of effort not to fall asleep there and then. But I had more urgent matters at hand. I could fix the world and then I would be able to sleep forever.

"I need to get to the Baba Jaga," I said. "Only...I don't know how to find it."

And I had no energy to wander aimlessly around the forest. I wasn't sure if I had enough energy to even get up from my warm seat by the fireplace.

"If you need to see the Baba Jaga, you'll always find it," said Zuzanna. "Just follow a forest path. If you encounter any black cats, ravens, or owls, you might want to follow them, too."

I took a deep breath. If I remained in front of the fireplace any longer, I'd fall asleep. I needed to move and finish all of it.

With effort, I pushed myself up to my feet, wincing as my muscles protested at the move.

"Thank you for the meal," I said.

I put on my coat and shoes and hoisted the backpack over my shoulder, squirming under its weight. I turned back in the doorway, looking at Zuzanna and Aysun.

"I'm so glad you're okay," I said and stepped outside into the forest.

It was dawn and the forest was filled with noises—branches crunching under the snow, wind roaring between the trees, demons giggling in the shadows, an occasional bird screeching in the sky. It was counterintuitive. Winter was for rest and regeneration, for feasting with the ancestors and divination. It was a quiet time, the time of death and deep sleep. But the ever-present magic had changed everything.

The trees grew dense and tall here and the snow was thick, so I didn't bother looking for a path. I picked a direction at random and walked between the trees. I was too exhausted to worry about anything else than having enough energy to make it to the Baba Jaga and back. Every muscle in my body hurt and my head throbbed, and I just wanted to be done with everything. I definitely didn't want to have to trudge through heavy snow.

I walked for a long time. So long that I started to worry that I'd never find the Baba Jaga or that the gods would find me first, and that they wouldn't be as kind as Marzanna had been. But then a cottage appeared illuminated by the red light. It wasn't the same hut as the first time when I'd visited the Baba Jaga, the one that had burned. There was another, smaller wooden house beside the main one. No chicken leg to be seen, either.

I approached the door and knocked.

"Come in, come in, sorceress," said the Baba Jaga.

I didn't have to be told twice. I walked in, the door so low that I had to duck to fit through it. The inside of the hut also looked different than the first time when I'd visited the Baba Jaga or the hut that I'd seen in my dreams. It reminded me more of Zuzanna and Aysun's cottage, only with dried herbs hanging from the low wooden ceiling and a stool in front of the fireplace with a huge cauldron inside. Just like the previous times, there was no bed.

"I brought you the feather from the firebird's tail," I said, extending the feather towards the Baba Jaga.

The demon didn't take it from me and something inside me started to crumble. What had I done wrong now? Was it another one of the demon's games? Come to think of that, why would the Baba Jaga give me a way to fix the crack in the sky in the first place? Wouldn't most of demons, not to mention demons that ranked equal with gods, prefer the doors between Jawia and Nawia to remain open? Was it some weird, twisted trap, a merry goose chase to keep us occupied, lowering our chances of actually fixing the problem?

"Put the feather on the table and come," said the Baba Jaga at last.

I did as it said and followed the demon outside. We headed towards the second, smaller house.

"Bring wood," said the Baba Jaga, pointing to a pile next to the house.

I gathered an armful of wood and followed the demon inside, praying that I wasn't preparing kindling for the demon to bake and eat me. But inside the small house was a sauna—or, maybe more accurately, a banya, with wooden benches, an oven with stones on top of it, and more herbs hanging from the ceiling. The Baba Jaga instructed me to put the wood inside a small oven—which was way too small to fit me inside—and lit the fire.

"Undress," the demon said.

"What?" I asked, taken aback.

"You're in a banya. How do you want to clean yourself when you're wearing clothes?"

"I came for the cloth you've woven from my dreams. I brought you the firebird's feather. I completed my trials."

"You will complete your trials when I say they're completed. You completed the final task but your journey isn't over yet. Now, undress."

Undressing in front of the demon was the last thing I wanted to do but I obeyed. Thankfully, the Baba Jaga stepped out of the banya, giving me some privacy. I looked down at my pale, bruised body. My hands were scratched raw and I'd lost weight in the past weeks. My muscles were so tired that they shook just from standing so I cautiously sat on a wooden bench, wrapping my arms around myself. The room was cold but the heat was slowly starting to drift from the oven.

The Baba Jaga returned a few long minutes later, carrying a cup of steaming tea and handed it to me.

"Drink."

"No, thank you," I said. I wasn't stupid enough to accept a drink from a demon.

"Fine," said the Baba Jaga. "It's your choice. Apparently, you aren't in such a great hurry after all. If you don't drink the tea, we can't go on."

I took the cup from the demon and drank half of the contents in one go, burning my tongue. I discerned the taste of wild strawberries and honey.

The Baba Jaga clucked its tongue.

"You're supposed to enjoy it. Sip it slowly, let the steam warm your face."

I stopped myself from rolling my eyes. Instead, I took a cautious sip and let it roll over my burned tongue. The honey was sweet and the wild strawberries reminded me of summer and of the long, long days spent searching in the forest with Rafi and Kari for the little red berries. No matter how much Aunt Eliza tried, she could never get them to grow in the garden or in a pot and you couldn't buy them in store. The only way to get the wild strawberries was to look in the forest at the beginning of summer and it made them so much more precious.

When I was done, the Baba Jaga took the empty cup from me. The banya was getting warmer now and sweat was beginning to pearl up on my forehead.

"Lie on your stomach," the demon said.

Reluctantly, I followed the demon's orders. The demon walked across the room and back towards me. Then there was a whooshing sound and I cried out as something whipped against my back.

"Calm down, it's part of the banya ritual," said the Baba Jaga, bringing up the willow branches again.

Now that I knew what was coming, the branches didn't feel so hard. It wasn't pleasant but it didn't really hurt, either. After a couple more smashes, the Baba Jaga put the willow branches back against the opposite wall. A small demon appeared by the oven and poured some water over the heated stones and steam filled the room. It looked similar to domowik, like a tiny human with a long beard and birch leaves tangled in its hair.

"Let the banya warm and cleanse you," said the Baba Jaga. "Once you're ready, there's a barrel of water outside. Dunk yourself in it, then come back to my hut."

And so I lay in the Baba Jaga's banya while the world outside kept on ending. While the heat felt oppressive at first, after some minutes the warmth loosened my muscles and I felt more relaxed than I had in a while. It was okay to take this moment for myself. Unless I was missing the point, it was a part of my trial and if I didn't follow along, I wouldn't be able to do anything about the end of the world.

The little demon poured more water over the stones and they hissed, steam rising around. The warmth calmed my mind, quieted my thoughts. Magic stilled under my skin, letting it rest from the constant buzz. My muscles stopped aching and I felt almost rested.

After some more minutes, I opened the door. Cold wind snapped against me as I quickly crossed the distance to the barrel by the side of the building. It was just big enough for me to fit in and, before I could think about it, I climbed inside the freezing cold water, then immediately jumped out. I returned to the banya only to notice that the Baba Jaga had taken away my clothes, leaving only the Guardian's cloak behind. With a sigh, I dried myself, wrapped the cloak around me and wandered back to the Baba Jaga's hut, snow crunching under my bare feet.

Inside, the Baba Jaga led me to the fireplace and sat me on the stool. It put another cup of tea in my hands and brushed my hair while I slowly sipped it, looking at the crackling fire, my heart lighter than it'd been in days.

"You've completed your trials," said the demon. "You proved the strength of your mind when another sorceress combed through your worst memories and fears. You proved the strength of your heart when you didn't destroy the basilisks' eggs. And you proved the strength of your body when you retrieved the feather from the firebird's tail."

The demon braided my hair while I finished the tea. I didn't move when it was done, squeezing the cup to my chest.

"You're ready to go on now." The Baba Jaga handed me my pile of clothes. On top of it lay a long piece of black material, shimmering like a sky full of stars. It didn't look nearly long enough to fix the broken sky.

"You'll take your Circle of Four and the cloth to the gates to Nawia. You'll take it between the four of you and wish for the crack to be mended."

"Why do you want it to be mended?" I asked.

"Baba Jagi have always helped humans, even after you'd forgotten about that, reimagining us into evil witches who eat your children. And I prefer being one of the few beings who can easily move between the worlds. Now, sleep."

THIRTY ONE

I WOKE UP IN FRONT OF A ROARING FIRE, THE MAGICAL cloth wrapped around me like a blanket. At first, I thought I was still at the Baba Jaga's but then I heard hushed voices. I was back in Zuzanna and Aysun's hut. And my hosts weren't alone.

"Mum?" I asked, surprised.

I sat up, brushing the sleep from my eyes. Why did I keep ending up with Zuzanna? And how was my mum here?

Mum stood with Zuzanna and Aysun in the kitchenette, talking quietly. The room smelled like cookies.

"What are you doing here?" I asked. "How did you get here?"

"Your dragon brought me here," she answered.

"I think Arrow might be a żmij," I said. "Seeing how much Weles did to free him from the military and how they rode together to face off against Perun."

Mum just looked at me.

"It's been an eventful couple of days," I said. I stretched out my arms and, to my surprise, nothing hurt. Huh. Apparently, the Baba Jaga's little spa treatment had worked. "I passed the final trial and I have the magical cloth. We can patch up the sky now, I only need the rest of the Circle of Four."

Why did Arrow bring Mum and not Karina, Artur, and Damian? Where were they? Did they find safety? They weren't in immediate danger but the bond between us felt stretched, as if there was a long distance between us, and muted by all the wild magic around.

"No," said Mum, shaking her head. "It doesn't make sense. As long as the devil has your blood, it will be able to rip the barrier between the words again. We need to get your blood back first."

"Oh yes," I said. "Let's just go and take it, then. I'm sure it will be easy."

Why did she have to come up with additional tasks for me? Why couldn't all of it just end? I'd just finished the Baba Jaga's trials, everything was supposed to go back to normal now.

But then it hit me that repairing the barrier between the realms would be just the beginning. That had never been my purpose. My existence was supposed to guarantee that the barrier would survive, that we'd get rid of the Guardians without the risk of gods coming back. Only we'd ruined everything and everything we'd done in the past weeks would only get us back to square one. The real work would start afterwards.

"I'm afraid that no one is going anywhere," said Zuzanna. "The storm has been going on for a few hours now."

Only then did I notice that the cottage was groaning in the wind howling outside. The windows were whitened out by snow.

"Would you like some breakfast?" offered Aysun.

We had cookies and coffee for breakfast, which almost made up for the fact that the world was still broken. After the banya and a good sleep and now coffee and sugar, I should have been the happiest in a long time. Instead, my heart was heavy with what Mum had said.

Because she was right. There was no point trying to patch up the sky as long as Węgliszek had my blood. Was there a chance he'd hidden it in his castle? Or had he learnt from his mistakes after the Children of Weles had broken his bargain figurines in the tunnels?

"If I find and take back my blood from Węgliszek, wouldn't that break the pact?" I asked. "Are we going to just sacrifice Tomasz and whoever else the devil decides has to pay?"

"I talked about it with Tomasz," said Mum. "As everything with devils, it's all about the wording. The devil got his payment, but it was never promised that he'll get to keep it."

It reminded me that my mum had personal experience with devils. That I'd wanted to hear the whole story for so long but I hadn't had a chance. That I'd been avoiding Mum since she'd got her memory back and turned into a complete stranger. But now we were snowed in the middle of the forest and it was high time to hear it all.

I looked Mum in the eye.

"Would you tell me the story of how you made the pact with the devil?"

Mum whipped her head to look at me, her eyes widening. I opened my mouth to take my words back but then I bit my tongue. I wanted to hear the full story. I needed to hear it. And, at this point, I deserved the truth.

After a few moments, Mum nodded.

"Nineteen years ago, Igor, Adrian, and I tried to break the Guardian's curse. It wasn't something we'd planned on doing in the beginning. We'd worked with the Children of Weles for a few years and even Igor agreed that his father deserved to be cursed. But then Adrian started training with alchemists in Gdańsk and one of them had a copy of the diaries of the alchemist who'd created the Guardians' rings, Regina. Adrian read them as a part of his training, to understand his history and heritage, but instead of reaffirming him in how overthrowing the Guardians was the right thing to do, he found out the price we'd have to pay once the Guardians are gone. About the vengeance that the gods and demons might seek on humans after the barrier between the realms collapses. We started probing the

Children of Weles about that, not outright saying what we knew, but wondering out loud if there might be some serious consequences if the Guardians were removed suddenly. And then we found out that their goal was to seek favour of Weles himself, for bringing him back to our world. That was when we knew we needed to break the curse.

It wasn't an easy decision. We'd been planning for so long to overthrow the Guardians and now we were supposed to save them? None of us wanted it. But then Gabriella gave birth on Szczodre Gody and we found out that Eliza was pregnant and would give birth around Noc Kupały. That seemed like a sign enough when Beata got pregnant, too, after years of trying. It looked like magic had a plan, that we'd once again see a Circle of Four. And we knew that Igor's child would complete that circle. And, sure, that child would make the curse come true. But what if we broke the curse before? A child that was half-sorcerer, half-Guardian would still wreak havoc in the magical world, especially as a part of the Circle of Four.

We researched it, looked everywhere we could but we kept coming back to the same conclusion. The only way to break the curse would be to get our hands on the Twardowski's scriptures. They were our only hope. We knew there was a ritual inside, which, when performed by representatives of different sorts of magic, could break the curse *and* end the Guardians, too. The problem was that no one knew where the Twardowski's scriptures were. Igor knew that they'd been stolen from the Assembly centuries ago, not long after the Guardians had first appeared. Since then, no one had heard about them and it looked like the devil might have destroyed them. There were rumours of the copies, though no one knew where they were. We thought we might wait, maybe we had time, maybe the Circle of Four would get things done, but then the Assembly caught a Child of Weles and suddenly there were suspicions that it might be a bigger movement. And then some suspicion fell on Igor and we knew we needed to act before it was too late. It wouldn't have been the first time that the Guardians had turned on their own and we couldn't risk that.

We summoned the devil and asked him for the copy of the Twardowski's scriptures. And he brought it to us but we soon found out that he was very unhappy about it and told the Assembly that the three of us had the scriptures and we were plotting to overthrow them. Meanwhile, the scriptures were useless to us. There was no way to break the curse without overthrowing the Guardians and we couldn't risk the vengeance of gods and demons. We wanted to preserve the magical balance, not to doom humanity. We thought of hiding the scriptures, saving them for the four of you, so you could use it once you were older. But the bargain with the devil was kicking in and it was getting harder and harder. I kept forgetting about magic, Adrian was scared of it. He kept trying new potions and crystals to buy us time but it wasn't enough. And then, one day, the Assembly discovered where we were."

Mum's voice broke and she looked into the fire, tears swimming in her eyes. I sat stiffly at the edge of the chair, listening, enraptured in her story. After a few moments, Mum cleared her throat and continued.

"Adrian and I escaped only because of Igor. He'd sacrificed himself so we could run. The Assembly tried and murdered him for conspiring to sacrifice Jawia to demons. They also stole back the Twardowski's scriptures. Meanwhile, the Children of Weles took in Adrian and me, they kept an eye on me while I was pregnant. They blocked your magic once you were born to keep you safe. It was difficult, as I kept forgetting about magic, but they knew the potion that Adrian had used to keep parts of my memory and they reproduced it for me. After you were born, we decided to stop with the potion, and I forgot all about magic. Until the four of you brought my memory back."

We were silent for a few moments.

"You loved them," I said. "Both of them."

I'd been pretty certain of it ever since seeing my dad's reaction to seeing my mum's letter. Even more so after seeing the memory from rusałka. It hadn't been a love triangle, at least not the toxic kind, and it hadn't been purely a business transaction to create a sorcerer-Guardian hybrid. The three of them had loved each other.

"Yes," said Mum. She brushed out tears from her eyes with the top of her palm.

"I'm sorry" didn't seem like a good enough reaction to the whole story. "I'm glad" seemed even worse, even though it was true. It was such a relief to hear it spoken out loud, to know that once upon a time three people wished for me to come to life, even if they'd placed a lot of expectations on me, too.

Instead, I put my hand on top of my mum's and I squeezed her hand. It was the most physical contact we'd shared in ages but I wanted her to know how much it meant to finally hear the whole story, spoken in her own words.

Mum looked up at me.

"You need to get your blood back from the devil. Then you'll patch up the sky, get the Twardowski's scriptures, and finish the Guardian's system once and for all."

Her words were like a splash of cold water. They shouldn't have hurt. I knew I had things to do, I'd literally just heard the story of how I was here only because my parents couldn't get some things done on their own. But my heart still ached.

I wanted to reconnect with her. I wanted her to at least pretend I was more than just a pawn in a game too big for me. I wanted my mum back.

I retreated my hand and squeezed my knees under the table.

"We just need to find out where the blood is stored," I said, trying to keep my voice steady.

"Well," said Zuzanna. "You could ask for divine inspiration. And I happen to know that a god of knowledge and prophetic dreams has been hanging around this forest."

I'd never been religious and meeting the gods hadn't changed it. But here I was, shovelling away the snow, my arms burning. According to my mum and Zuzanna, I couldn't just ask a god for a favour without paying the price. Prayers required sacrifice and sacrifice had to be something that would cost me and benefit the community. Throwing a feast was traditional but wasn't an option. I didn't have any food apart from a handful of nuts in my backpack. Donating blood or volunteering wouldn't work either, seeing how it was the apocalypse and we were stuck in the woods. And my "community" was currently limited to Mum, Zuzanna and Aysun, since we had no way of leaving the middle of the forest. So I found myself in deep snow, creating a tunnel out of the cottage and into the woods, trying to clear my mind of all thoughts but asking Weles to kindly tell me where Węgliszek stored my blood.

I tried not to let my doubts get in the way, not to think how Weles might decide to use the blood himself. But then, hadn't he helped me at the oak tree? Now, knowing he was the god of prophetic dreams, it made sense I'd dreamed about the tree. And Weles had seen me at the meadow and he'd distracted Perun to give me a chance. More, he'd let Arrow save me when I'd fallen. Maybe Laura had been right about the divine favour. Maybe I could use it again.

I stumbled inside the house exhausted. The cottage smelled like potatoes and when I sat by the fireplace to warm up my frozen hands, Zuzanna brought me a plate filled with baked potatoes.

"How do you have all this food?" I asked, devouring the contents of the plate. "How did you end up here?"

"We flew here," she said, looking into the fire. "Aysun

got us as far as she could and when she was running out of energy, we found this cottage. It was probably magic. There was a well-stocked cellar and a stash of wood for the fireplace. No one ever came by and it's such a remote location with no roads leading here. We walked in the forest but we've never managed to hit any road."

"Maybe it's an abandoned Baba Jaga's hut," I said, voicing the thought I had when Marzanna had first brought me here.

Zuzanna smiled.

"Oh, Aysun would love that."

She repeated what I'd said in German and Aysun grinned.

"Dream come true," she said in English. "Even better than a cat café slash bookstore that the Clavichord Café had always had the potential to become."

"We were very lucky," said Zuzanna.

I couldn't get over how different Zuzanna seemed now. So much more peaceful, so much more at ease. It was weird to see her just sit and look at the fire instead of rushing from place to place, browsing grimoires, and frantically trying new rituals to protect the city. The dark bags under her eyes weren't quite gone but she looked more rested than I'd ever seen her. As far as the demonic apocalypse went, she'd drawn the long straw.

"Do you think that in the outside world they'd notice this area is gone?" I asked. "Is there like a black hole on the map or did everyone forget we'd ever existed? Do you think NATO is cordoning off this area now? And, was this area cordoned off as an off shoot of the sky cracking or did someone on the outside do it?"

What about Dad? Did he go work in Bergen as usual? Had he forgotten that Mum and I even existed? I knew how magic could alter memories, but the thought stung.

"I think it was the Assembly," said Zuzanna. "I might have given them the idea with my protection spell but they'd probably redone it after your ritual. I don't see any reason why the gods or demons would want to cordon off this area. If anything, I suspect they'd prefer to spread all over the place, which is probably what the Assembly would assume as well."

"So when we fix the hole in the sky, they'll be waiting," I said.

"It might not be the worst thing," said Zuzanna. "Isn't your plan still to get to the Assembly? That might be your chance."

I didn't want to think about it now. There were so many things to consider, so many things I'd disregarded and they were coming to haunt me now.

Anxiety started building up in my stomach and I squeezed the little black bird amulet under my jumper. Magic sparkled stronger around me and for a moment it felt as if Artur were sitting just next to me.

Are you okay? I asked telepathically into the void. It was a rhetorical question—even if Artur could hear me over the great distance, he wouldn't be able to answer.

So when I heard his voice in my head I jumped and would have fallen over if I hadn't been sitting on the floor.

As okay as anyone can be at the end of the world, said Artur's voice in my head.

Either I fell from the oak tree and bumped my head or I can hear you, I responded, grasping the amulet tighter in my hand.

The first option seemed more likely. Everything that had happened afterwards, with Arrow catching me and Marzanna, and the Baba Jaga, and Zuzanna and Aysun, and Mum seemed like a fever dream. Or a side effect of a concussion.

Wait, really? You can hear me? I'm not just responding into nothingness?

Do you normally respond to voices in your head?

Yes. Especially yours. But I never managed to have a conversation with you before.

My heart squeezed. More than anything, I wished Artur was here now. I wanted to snuggle next to him, by the crackling fire, and let our bond settle my worries. I wanted to make sure personally that he was still in one piece.

Do you think it's because the magic is so crazy right now? I felt a sparkle of stronger magic when I squeezed your amulet.

I'm squeezing yours now, too. I felt your anxiety and hoped you were okay.

I smiled, looking into the fireplace.

I'm okay. I got the firebird's feather and the Baba Jaga gave me the cloth. We can patch up the sky. And I found Zuzanna and Aysun. I'm with them and my mum now; Arrow brought her here. Only…it doesn't make much sense to fix the sky when the devil still has my blood.

Yeah. I was wondering about it ever since we realized he can see through my eyes.

Are you somewhere safe?

Yes. Karina and I made it back to the safe house. We strengthened the protections so hopefully they'll hold up.

We talked for a while longer, sharing our thoughts until we fell asleep. Even though we were kilometres apart, it felt as if Artur were there, whispering into my ear, and the dark forest seemed a little less scary, the reality a little less overwhelming. It wasn't the same as cuddling together, but it was a decent replacement.

It's dark, completely dark, but it's been weeks since the electricity stopped working and I'm more used to the total darkness now. The darkness isn't quiet, either, whispering and giggling, and moving around. But it's a noise made of whispers, everything is hushed, as if I have cotton stuffed into my ears.

There's a flicker of light in the distance and I break the first rule of walking alone in the dark—don't follow the moving light. But I know it's a dream and I feel safe, despite what the Baba Jaga told me in a dream before. How I could get trapped in it.

I follow the light until the darkness becomes a little less encompassing. A dim red glow appears in the distance, and soon I stumble to the edge of water. Across it, far ahead, the sky is broken in half, red light streaming through it. And then I recognize what's on the opposite bank, the beach, the familiar forest, and the river itself. And I know where I am.

I'm in Nawia.

THIRTY TWO

I WASN'T SURPRISED TO SEE ARROW OUTSIDE THE NEXT day. The dragon slept curled in the tunnel I'd made in snow, its nostrils expanding and narrowing as it breathed, tendrils of vapour rising in the cold, melting the snow around its head.

Could it breathe fire now?

"You should go," said Mum. She must have seen the surprise in my face because she continued. "I'll stay here for a bit. Zuzanna and I have lots to discuss."

Right. I guess Mum had been sleeping with Zuzanna's dead brother. She'd loved him. They were family, bonded through me.

So I said my goodbyes, filled my backpack with cookies from Aysun, and went to stroke Arrow's nose.

"Hi, big dragon," I said, running my hand up and down

its nose. Not long ago I could scratch it there with a finger, now its nose easily fit my whole hand.

Arrow slowly opened its golden eyes and stared at me for a moment. It bumped my hand gently, way lighter than the last time, as if it'd learnt about its strength and didn't want to hurt me.

"Shall we go?" I asked, climbing onto the dragon's back.

I barely had time to hug Arrow's neck before it waved its long wings once, twice, and we were off, flying with the wind. I'd learnt from my previous experience and put on the Guardian's cloak this time. It wasn't the best camouflage but it kept me warm. Besides, it wasn't like I was inconspicuous flying on a dragon.

I was *flying* on a *dragon.* Despite everything that had happened in the past weeks it was still mind-blowing to think about it.

We raced across the sky, over the never-ending frozen forest. I closed my eyes against the icy wind and focused on clinging to Arrow and not letting go. I trusted that the demon would take me where I was supposed to be.

I wasn't surprised when we landed on the beach I'd seen in my dream. I squeezed Artur's amulet in my hand.

Meet me at the summerhouse, I passed through the bond.

I walked through the snowy forest. Arrow had taken off, maybe, hopefully, to help Artur and Karina. Because without Arrow, it would take them hours to get here. And, if Artur was still blindfolded so Węgliszek couldn't find them, maybe even days.

I hoped they'd have a way of contacting Damian. I didn't know where he and Rafi had ended up. I could feel Damian through our bond, which was growing weaker as the time passed, but I couldn't pass him telepathic messages.

When I got to the summerhouse, the door was unlocked. Magic prickled my skin, ready to protect me. Did someone break in? Were they looking for food?

But inside I saw Damian and Rafi. They both looked tired, pale, with bags under their eyes. There was dark stubble on Damian's cheeks and his jumper hung on him even looser than usual. Rafi's dark hair was messy probably for the first time in his life.

I ran forward and hugged them and didn't let go for a long moment.

"You're okay," I said, relief flooding me.

"Did you get the feather?" asked Rafi.

"Yes. And I exchanged it for the cloth to patch up the sky. Artur and Karina are on the way. However, before we fix the sky, I need to take one more detour. Just a tiny one. To Nawia."

I told them about the bargain with the devil and the dream I'd had.

"Wasn't Nawia supposed to be in the roots of the oak tree?" asked Rafi.

"Yes," said Damian. "But to get there, you need to cross the river. Space and time don't make much sense when magic is concerned. They're human concepts, ways of trying to make sense of the world. Oh, and some say that the entrance is guarded by a żmij."

There was nothing left to do, but wait. We ate Aysun's cookies and drank mint tea, made with fresh leaves from the garden. Because apparently even the apocalypse couldn't stop peppermint from growing like crazy and taking over half of Aunt Eliza's flower patches.

We played UNO and talked about nothing, the boys clearly sensing my need for distraction. When the sky started darkening, Rafi went outside to cut more wood for the fireplace.

"Are you okay?" I asked Damian.

Damian shrugged. His eyes were on the cards he was shuffling in his laps.

"Is anyone okay these days? I'm over this whole demonic apocalypse thing."

"You and Rafi seem to be getting along better now."

"Not like we have much choice, being stuck in the forest together during the end of days. But talking things out helped." He raised his eyes to look at me. "Are you okay?"

"As okay as I can be, I guess. Just having a full-blown identity crisis during the apocalypse." I looked into the fire and snorted. "Why do demons always make me question everything? The latawiec said that we've met three times and I never once reacted to it like, well, you or Rafi did. And I could *feel* your reaction to it, and I don't think I've ever felt anything even close to that and...I don't know."

"Well." Damian kept on shuffling the cards. "If it makes you feel better, no human ever made me feel the way the latawiec did, either."

"But you've felt similarly about humans before."

"I mean, yes, I'm definitely not ace. So yes, it's similar, but not as intense. Sex demons got their name somewhere."

"What if a sex demon doesn't work on me?"

Damian pointed his finger at me. "I hear what you're doing, and I'm not going to fall for it. Your identity is yours to figure out. I'm not going to assign any labels to you."

I sighed.

"I just want to know for sure. I don't want to pick one label and change my mind afterwards."

"Why not? Your understanding of yourself can change with time, it's normal. Besides, these words, aro or ace, they are umbrella terms, you know. You don't need to know exactly how you feel or where you belong on the spectrum to use them. And they encompass lots of different experiences. See what you're comfortable with, what makes more sense to you. And it's okay if it takes time. Sexuality is complex and that's before we start untangling romantic and tertiary attractions. If you want to talk about it, I'm here. But I won't pick labels for you."

I picked at the sleeves of my jumper, unsure what to say.

"I'm going to be brutally honest," said Damian.

"That's not a question."

"No, it's a warning. Because I think you know, Wiki. You know but you're scared. And there's nothing wrong with being scared but maybe between running from one life-threatening situation to another you might want to consider *why* you're scared."

Rafi opened the door and a strong gust of wind got inside, making the cards fly away. We collected them as Rafi stomped his boots to shake off the snow and created a little pile of wood to dry by the fireplace.

"UNO?" asked Damian once he had all the cards back in his lap.

Before we could respond, I heard Artur's voice over our bond:

We're on the beach.

Damian, Rafi, and I made our way through the forest to the beach. Karina and Artur were there, together with Arrow. Artur's eyes were still tied over with a scarf. I hugged them both.

"I knew it was vital to teach Arrow to fly," said Rafi, stroking the dragon's nose. Arrow headbutted him and Rafi laughed.

"I'm going with you," said Karina.

"I don't think it's a great idea. I don't think anyone should go to Nawia. I don't think I should be going there. And that's why I need you here, to be my tether."

"Artur and Damian will be our tethers. You're not going alone. Besides, I'm hoping to leave my demonic part where it belongs."

I opened my mouth, then closed it. I couldn't argue with that. The banishing spell hadn't helped, no one knew how to help Karina. At that point, a trip to Nawia sounded like a sensible solution. Since we had to go there either way, it only seemed right that we'd help Karina, too.

I looked at Damian and Artur, but they didn't protest. Rafi looked uncomfortable but he didn't say anything.

"Give me your hand," said Damian.

I extended my hand palm up towards him and his lips quirked up a tiniest bit. I raised my eyebrow in a silent question.

"You trust me," he said softly.

"Of course, I do."

Gold speckled in Damian's eyes as his emotions hit me with full force. Bewilderment. Fear. He wasn't used to people trusting him and if they did, he disappointed them fast. He wasn't used to people staying by his side, wanting to be around him.

I squeezed his hand.

Damian lowered his eyes and took out a long piece of red string from his pocket. He wrapped it around my wrist three times, chanting softly under his breath, then tied a triple knot, making sure it held. Once it was done, he prepared an identical talisman for Karina.

"Thank you," I said. "Then the only question is, how do we get across the river? It's too cold to swim, the river is half-frozen. And then there's this barrier."

"I think Arrow will fly us," replied Karina.

Arrow raised its head in recognition, blinking its golden eyes at us.

That was going way faster than I'd anticipated. But then, what had I hoped for? Time to kill, more days spent wondering about our next move while we were only with one foot in Jawia? So many people suffered since the sky had broken. We needed to fix our mistake.

"Right," I said. "Okay. Well, then, I have the magical cloth here. I think you should take it for now."

I handed it to Artur. He took the black, shimmering cloth from me, then pulled me into a hug. He clung to me, his cheek pressed to the side of my face. Our bond sparkled stronger, magic jumping between us, tying us closer together. His emotions slammed into me with unexpected force. There was mostly anxiety but also lots of warmth and tenderness, soft feelings that squeezed something in my chest. Things that used to scare me and which I hadn't felt from him for a while, not in such force.

Are you…were you quieting your emotions so as not upset me? I asked telepathically and the feelings momentarily dampened. *Don't. Please don't. You won't upset me. What would be the point of this relationship if you couldn't be yourself around me?*

His feelings didn't scare me anymore. I wasn't trying to play them down, to focus on anything else. Quite the opposite. I wanted to cocoon myself in them and never leave this warmth and safety.

Soon, I promised myself. Soon everything would be okay, and we'd have all the time in the world to sit and enjoy our bond.

But first, I needed to go to Nawia.

I'll break your bargain, too, I promised.

Artur's fingers dug into my back, and he held on to me for two more shuddering breaths. Then he stepped back.

"Come back to us when you're done," he said.

We flew on Arrow, because what's a better way to get to Nawia than on the back of żmij? Well, probably getting there after living a long and fulfilling life in Jawia, to rest before flying as a bird to Wyraj, and from there to be reborn back in Jawia. Not that I would know.

I held on to Arrow, and Karina clung to me. The żmij flew just above the water until, suddenly, without a warning, it dove. My scream was bit off as we fell into the river. But instead of submerging into icy cold water, we emerged in a world exactly like ours, just without the red crack in the sky. I took in a hesitant breath but while the air seemed denser, heavier, harder to breathe in, it was enough to fill my lungs.

We were officially in Nawia.

The sky above us sparkled with hundreds of stars and the riverbank ahead of us was filled with pine trees, just as crazily tall and thick as in our world now. The river was wider, too, its flat surface shimmering with the reflected stars. Arrow glided so low over it that it stirred the surface with a tip of its wing. I held my breath, worried that a rusałka or a topielec would snatch it and drag us under, but nothing happened.

I'd expected darkness, screams, gnarled, naked trees, maybe some torture devices, but that had been the imaginary of Christian hell. And Nawia wasn't hell, it was afterlife. Even the red light that had been illuminating our world wasn't here. Whatever it was, maybe a wound in the sky or a physical manifestation of magical imbalance, it wasn't from Nawia.

Nawia was still, silent, and stunning.

We landed softly on the riverbank. The message was clear, that was as far as Arrow could take us. While it would have been nice to be delivered straight to where Węgliszek stored my blood, I'd never expect that. I knew we'd have to earn it.

Besides, that wasn't the only reason we were there.

"Ready?" I asked my cousin.

Karina gave me a grim smile.

"Let's go," she said.

We hugged Arrow goodbye and we watched it dive back into the river. When the water stilled, Karina and I turned to face the forest.

And so I walked into Nawia hand in hand with my best friend.

THIRTY THREE

Nawia was magic materialized. Every tree around us, every stone and grain of sand was made of warm, pulsing magic, much like in Jawia they were made of atoms. I'd thought the magic in our world had been suffocating since we'd broken the sky, but that was nothing compared to Nawia. We didn't even breathe air, but magic. It was as if no other elements existed here.

As if to prove the point, the magic in me pushed to the surface but nothing happened as it broke free. Nothing flew away, no fire started, nothing froze. My magic simply joined the magic in the air, dancing happily around us like a warm summer breeze.

"If that's where our souls go after we die, does it mean we're also magic?" asked Karina. "What if everyone has a sparkle of magic inside them but only some find ways to use it?"

"Back in the day people believed that farmers and crafters had divine powers because they could transform things from one state to another. Seeds to plants, clay to bowls. Even cooking, especially baking bread was seen as a manifestation of the divine."

Karina and I walked into the forest. We didn't know where we were heading, just walked blindly between the trees. I hoped there would be some supernatural pull, some magical presence that we could navigate by, but everything got lost in the ever-present hum of magic.

We didn't walk long when the forest opened up into an endless grassland filled with cattle. The animals walked around, munching on the green grass. The sky above the meadow was lighter now, the deep purple blue of a long summer dusk, light enough to see without extra help. The air was warmer.

We'd left winter behind.

"I don't think we should walk there, in the open," said Karina.

I nodded my agreement and we followed the edge of the forest.

If I were a devil, where would I place my secret Nawia hangout? In the city, Węgliszek had rebuilt the castle but did he live in similar luxury in Nawia? Or was he able to build his little kingdom on Earth only because people remembered and praised his name?

"Do you have any ideas how to banish the demon from you?" I asked Karina. Maybe that could be our starting point instead.

"I hoped I would once we were here. Magic, or something." Karina looked at the horizon, a tiniest tremor to her voice. "But I still don't know how to do that."

By silent agreement, we walked further into the forest, trying not to crack too many branches and not to step on mushrooms. Apart from the cattle, we hadn't encountered any living creature in Nawia so far. Well, living was probably the wrong adjective. Maybe I needed to reassess every thought I'd brought from Jawia with me. I knew the myth about how birds were really departing human souls. I knew that still in some rural areas people believed that an odd ray of sunlight or a speck of dust could be a sign from their dead ancestors. I knew that in the old beliefs life was a cycle and once your soul had rested in Nawia, it would move on to Wyraj and then be breathed into another creature again.

So maybe everything in Nawia had a different shape. Maybe the cattle used to be people in Jawia. After all, everything here was made of the same magic. The fungi climbing up the tree was just as magical as the tree, as the soil we stepped on, even the broken branches. Everything was equally important, equally magic, a part of something bigger.

My thoughts drifted, magic lulling me into a sense of peace similar to the way I felt around Artur or Damian when I could feel our bond. Karina and I walked in silence until the wind carried the sound of singing and we followed. Soon, we reached a meadow filled with wildflowers in all colours carrying a sweet scent. A group of human-like demons danced around the meadow, jumping and singing, and twirling around. They wore long, airy dresses and trousers in earth colours that swirled in the air. Their hair was decorated with flower wreaths. Their voices were like the sweetest song, their movements mesmerizing. It was impossible to tear your eyes away from the scene.

"Dance with us!" said one demon and soon I was pulled into the dance.

The dancer was breathtakingly beautiful, with long, brown, wavy hair and unnaturally purple eyes. It was a wiła but it didn't matter, because we were dancing, twirling around the meadow. I saw Karina's dark hair swirling around her as she whirled around the meadow. A wiła placed a flower wreath on my cousin's head and then another wreath landed on mine.

Time ceased to exist. I felt lighter than air as dread and anxiety evaporated from my body replaced by joy, pure joy, that made my lips stretch in a smile and laughter bubble up my throat. I knew how to fight wiły, I could easily pull out a hair from their heads, but I didn't want it to be over. I wanted to cling on to this feeling, to feel happy and weightless forever.

We danced, jumped, and whirled around in joyful abandon. Wiły held my hands, twirling me around and passing me from one to another. We sang and clapped, and sang some more, dancing to the tune we created. My heart was bursting with happiness as we jumped around the meadow, dancing and laughing, magic sparkling on my skin.

"You should stop," said a wiła with dark blonde hair, gently putting hands on my shoulders. "Human legs aren't meant to dance for so long."

"Humans shouldn't have legs in this realm," said another wiła, with a crown made of poppies, stroking my hair. "You shouldn't have a body here at all."

"But don't worry, we won't tell."

I didn't want to stop dancing, but the wiły led me to the side of the meadow and lowered me to the ground. I felt distant throbbing in my legs, but it didn't feel real. The wiła with the poppy wreath stayed, playing with my hair, while yet another one handed me a clay bowl filled with water and I drank, only then realizing how parched I was.

"I recognize you," said the wiła who had brought me the bowl.

It had brown hair and a wreath made of wildflowers in all the colours of the rainbow. I didn't recognize it but all the wiły looked alike to me, with their striking, too perfect features and distinct eyes.

"I met your ancestor," the wiła continued and a ping of anxiety almost made it through my bubble of happiness. "I'm glad you danced with us. Humans, demons, and gods were created to exist side by side. We're nothing without each other."

"I'm sorry," I said.

The wiła walked closer to me and cupped my face, stroking my cheek while the other one continued playing with my hair.

"Most of us used to be human women once upon a time. Others thought we were too strong-minded, too wild, too confident. They didn't like that we knew what we wanted and that we weren't afraid to go after it. They were scared of our confidence, of our joy of life. So, they tore it away from us." The wiła's fingers paused on my cheek. "Each of us was murdered. That's how we became wiły."

"And now we can do what we love best for all eternity," said the wiła with a poppy crown.

"We can. But humans must remember that they create the demons they fear the most. You pretend that we aren't there, but it doesn't help anyone if you try to hide us away. As long as you keep us at bay, there won't be a magical balance in the world."

"Thank you for letting me dance with you," I said, something squeezing in my chest. "It was an honour."

The wiła with a colourful crown bowed its head in acknowledgement.

"Rest," said the other wiła, smoothing my hair one more time before standing up.

The demon and its friend walked back to join in the dance, singing, and clapping. I lay among the flowers, watching the wiły dance around me. Nearby, under a cherry tree, Karina was kissing a wiła. Far above, a thousand stars blinked at me from the sky. I tried to make out the constellations but they were nothing like in Jawia or maybe the world was swirling in front of my eyes. The stars formed the shapes of żmije and a hut on a chicken leg, and a bearded head with bull-like horns, and oak leaves scattered all around it. The earth drummed with magic, the air was filled with singing and joy.

Karina lay down in the grass next to me. Her cheeks were flushed.

"I think I might like girls," she said, a little breathlessly. "But, also, I'm not sure gender matters all that much to me. It's such a rare feeling when it happens, it's impossible to tell. How do people even figure out these things?"

"You're asking the wrong person." I rolled to the side to look at my cousin. "How was your first kiss?"

"Never thought it would be with a demon in Nawia." Karina was looking up at the sky, the stars reflecting in her eyes and twinkling at me. "It was better than expected. Not awkward, it just felt…right. Made me feel a lot of things. I'm glad it happened."

I squeezed her hand.

"Then I'm glad for you, too."

We looked up at the sky. I tried to count the oak leaves made of stars.

"Are you in love with him?" asked Karina.

"What?" I asked. I let go of her hand, taken aback.

"Are you in love with Artur?" she repeated calmly.

My mind reeled. I'd almost forgotten there was life outside of this meadow, a world outside of Nawia. It should have been a simple question, but it wasn't. I'd do anything for Artur. He was an important person in my life. I liked looking at him and being around him. He made me feel safe and calm. Was that what being in love meant?

I thought of all the warm and fuzzy feelings Artur held for me, the feelings that used to terrify me. Feelings that I couldn't match. The next words felt too horrible to say out loud. But why did they seem horrible? My feelings for Artur were strong, too. Different, but strong.

"No," I said. "I don't think I'm in love with him."

I opened my mouth to say more, to talk about how I'd save Artur from more basilisks if necessary, and claw my way out of Nawia to be by his side, and how he made me feel safe and accepted me wholly, just the way I was, and gave the best hugs…But I forced myself to swallow back the words. Karina knew all of it and I wouldn't ramble trying to justify how my feelings weren't any less strong just because they weren't romantic.

"And I don't like when people call us boyfriend and girlfriend," I said instead. "He's my queer-platonic partner."

"Yeah, Artur told me. He also told me he's ace."

I smiled at the thought of two of the most important people in my life growing closer.

"I like that I don't feel like I need to earn his companionship," I said. "That we can cuddle and comfort each other and just be without any additional pressure. I felt it at first. Well, part of it was the curiosity about our bond, the way it made us feel, but I think to some extent it was also about getting him to hang out with me. I wanted to be worth the trouble I cost him. I'm glad I no longer feel this way."

"It shouldn't feel like pressure. Some people actually crave these things. To kiss someone, to take off their clothes, feel their body under your fingers. It's not a chore."

I was quiet for a few moments.

Karina pointed to the demons who still danced around us.

"When you look at them, what do you feel?"

"Joy," I whisper. "There's so much happiness here, as if nothing bad could ever happen."

"But you do see that each of them is breathtakingly beautiful?"

"Yes. But so is the sky. It's such a beautiful place, filled with so much magic."

"You know they're sex demons, right?"

"Yes. Wiły."

Karina waved her hand. "I wanted that demon to kiss me, even though I knew it was a demon, even though I knew there's lots of magic in the air. It happened maybe twice before that I wanted to do something more than just stare at someone pretty. But now it felt right. And it was amazing."

"Wait, you haven't really wanted to act on those feelings before? How come I didn't know that?"

"Perhaps because I talk a lot about people I find pretty. And others add the rest in their head. Besides, I love reading romances, I love hearing people's love stories, so that's what people see."

My head spun, trying to process this new information.

"Was it that way with Simon, too? But you wanted me to introduce you when I started hanging out with Artur."

"He's one of the exceptions. But, Wiki, I've been talking to you about one, and only one guy for six years.

And I definitely had a chance to do something about it but I always preferred admiring from afar. My mental health is definitely at least partially to blame, but talking to Artur and comparing our experiences made me realize I'm probably somewhere on the ace spectrum."

"I guess that makes two of us."

"Yeah, no shit." I elbowed her, but Karina caught and squeezed my hand. "It's a very aspec Circle of Four."

TH1RTY FOUR

I WOKE UP FEELING HUNGOVER. MY HEAD POUNDED, my lips were parched, my mind slow to comprehend the world around me. My legs hurt as if I'd run a marathon without proper training, every muscle on fire. I shielded my eyes from the sun rising between the trees. I was lying on the meadow, curled into Karina's side, wildflowers growing all around us. There was no trace of the wiły.

With effort, I pushed myself up on my elbows, nausea rising in my throat. Dread returned with tripled power, my stomach coiling, my hands shaking. Gods, how long had we been here? How much time had we lost? How could we have been so stupid? We still had to banish the demon from Karina, we still had to find my blood, we still had to find our way back to Jawia…How were we going to do all of that?

Karina groaned. She rolled to her side, hugging her knees to her chest.

"Everything hurts," she moaned.

It took us a long time to collect ourselves enough to stand. Walking that morning was hell. My head was pounding, my muscles were screaming for rest, and I wanted to lie down and never get up. Karina didn't feel any better, occasionally stopping to lean on a tree and pressing her hand to her mouth as if she were about to throw up. But the constant drum of anxiety in my stomach made me keep going, even if we didn't know where we were going.

"I think it's an emotional hangover," said Karina, leaning on a thick oak tree. "You can't be so happy and carefree for so long, it's unnatural to humans."

"Living humans," I added.

We shared a look. Maybe Nawia was a lot more welcoming and less terrifying than we'd expected from a demon realm, but it wasn't a place meant for us.

We needed to banish Karina's demon, find my blood, and get back to Jawia.

We walked on with new resolve. The shadows around us grew longer and the sky above darker, even though the sun had just risen. Intellectually, I didn't expect the time in Nawia to make sense but a feeling of unease grew in my stomach. The wind picked up and the air seemed denser, like just before the storm. I looked up at the heavy clouds covering the sky and stumbled, barely catching my balance. Karina looked up at the sky as well and flinched, and swore.

She caught my hand and together we retreated deeper into the forest, hoping for the thick branches to shelter us from the sky.

The clouds above us had faces, ridden with deep wrinkles and twisted in angry grimaces. I'd seen a cloud like that before, once—it had been a wind demon, chmurnik. Artur had given it an offering of flour and it disappeared, but we didn't have any flour with us. And, somehow, I didn't think blowing a bit of flour into the wind would appease an entire demon army.

A thunder rumbled and Karina and I sped up, even though we didn't have any shelter to get to. We weren't meant to be in this realm to begin with, there was no safety for us here. Wind blew against us, roaring in my ears and soon the first drops of rain started falling.

Karina opened her mouth, saying something, but her words were lost in the howl of the wind.

"What?" I shouted back but Karina's grimace told me she couldn't hear me either.

She grabbed my hand, and we ran.

The rain pounded hard now, the skies above us opening. Magic around us strengthened, burning my skin as we sprinted, slipping on the wet moss and soil, tripping on the roots that seemed to pop up everywhere. Rain got into my eyes and I blinked hard, trying to see where we were going. Wind slammed against us, threatening to throw us over.

We passed a thick oak tree and I halted. I pulled Karina towards the powerful roots of the tree—there was enough space between them for the two of us to squeeze in, enough to offer us a basic shelter.

We sat shoulder to shoulder, shivering, as the rain pounded on. Wind chased between the trees, tearing off smaller branches, and I whispered to the oak tree a quiet thanks for protection.

"That was one hell of a hangover cure," said Karina.

I struggled to catch my breath. Wind howled and thunder rumbled again, so powerful that the ground seemed to shake.

"It feels like we're hobbits hiding from the Nazgul," I said.

"Please don't jinx it. We don't need any more enemies. Though, to be fair, if destroying the Guardian system thing had been about travelling across Europe to throw your Guardian's ring into Vesuvius, I wouldn't have anything against it."

"Now you're jinxing it. We don't need another side quest." A small smile fought its way to my face though. "I'm glad you're here with me."

"How else are you supposed to enter hell than hand in hand with your best friend and cousin?"

"Thank you." I squeezed Karina's hand. "I hope we banish your demon, find my blood, and get the hell out of here soon."

Even if the task seemed more impossible with each second.

"I'm terrified of this demon," whispered Karina. "Of how easily it can control me, how it can force me to do horrible things. I'm terrified that it's getting stronger, I—I'm scared one day it won't leave and I won't exist anymore."

"You're so much more than this demon. And you're so much stronger than it."

Karina didn't respond but she leaned her head on my shoulder. We sat huddled close as the wind roared and rain pounded on the ground. I played with Artur's amulet but I couldn't feel our connection across the realms, so I focused on the soft drum of magic between Karina and me. I looked at the forest in front of us, at the rain soaking the ground. Magic clung to my skin, warming me up…

…and then there are flowers in my hair, which is longer than I'm used to, falling down my shoulders and touching my breasts, and the light around me shines brighter, and there are purple crocuses growing by the river. The sky above is the light blue of an early spring.

"There you are," says Mum, putting her arm around me.

I startle—what is she doing here?—but then I relax into her hug.

"Are you ready?" she asks, looking me up and down. "You look beautiful."

I'm wearing a simple white dress reaching above my knee. My eyes widen, throat constricting. Is it a wedding dress? Please don't let it be a wedding dress. A cloak is thrown around my shoulders, black with red sleeves, keeping me warm in the chilly breeze.

"I'm ready," I say, my mouth forming words without my permission.

But it's not a lie. I feel ready and for a moment I'm torn between me who knows that something is wrong and me who understands what's going on.

Mum plants a kiss on my forehead, loops her arm through mine and leads me alongside the river. Singing and laughter sounds in the distance. Soon, we approach a fire burning by the river and a group of people clad mostly in black, with some blues and reds mixed in. The crowd parts as Mum and I approach and we walk between familiar faces, everyone smiling. Rafi stands by Karina, both dressed in dark blue cloaks. He extends his hand and I high five him, and there are laughs from the crowd.

At the back of the group, by the river, stands Zuzanna, dressed in a red Guardian's cloak. Mum escorts me to her and bows, while I kneel in front of Zuzanna.

"We gather here on this doubly-special day of spring equinox to celebrate my niece Wiktoria's coming of age. Before we start the equinox celebrations, let's proceed with zapleciny." Zuzanna holds out a wooden rattle and shakes it, making noise. "Ancestors, bless Wiktoria on this special day, at the beginning of her adult life. Sława Wam!"

Zuzanna removes the flower wreath from my hair and hands it to my mum. She brushes through my ash-blonde hair with her fingers and braids it around my head, into a crown, weaving in a red ribbon. She ties the ribbon around the end, securing the crown. Once she's done, she places the flower wreath on my head again.

"You're now officially a full-fledged member of our community," Zuzanna says, helping me to my feet and presenting me to the crowd.

People clap and cheer. Dad steps out from the crowd, wearing a dark blue cloak, and hugs me. He's joined by another man who looks vaguely familiar, with long dark hair pulled into a bun. But what gives him away is the red cloak—it's Igor, Zuzanna's brother and my biological father. He has her smile and hazel eyes. He gives me a long hug, and then follows a crowd of other magic-users, more and less familiar—Tomasz, Darek, Dawid, Julia, Laura, Artur, his parents, Stanisław, Sandra, Filip…The crowd is never-ending, everyone full of smiles and wishes of prosperity and health. My parents, all three of them, stand beside me while the crowd passes by.

When it feels like I've been hugged by every single member of the local magical community, my grandpa hosts up a large straw doll.

"Odejdź martwe, odejdź stare, my palimy ognie jare!" he intones, and we gather around the fire, singing along.

Normally, I'd stand at the front with the Guardian side of my family, but today I hang back. Karina loops her arm through mine and Laura takes the other one. We sing the song three times and then grandpa sets the straw doll on fire. The flames burst and he lifts it up and we all cheer, then follow him to the river. He throws the straw doll in. The water extinguishes the fire and the current carries the remnants away.

"The old year is officially over," said grandpa. "The cycle of nature starts anew and so do we."

We cheer and head back to the fire. There's a long wooden table heavy with food—lots of eggs, for new beginnings, breads, cakes, and first spring vegetables, radishes, chives, cress, and cucumbers, as well as bowls of pasta salads, platters of meats, and bowls of żurek.

"I have a gift for you," says Artur, appearing by my side.

"And you think that's enough to distract me from the food?"

"Well, I considered waiting until your non-magical birthday party, but gifts given on birthdays have special power."

Artur pulls out a roll of thick paper wrapped with a ribbon from his black cloak's pocket. I take it from him and untie the ribbon. It's a drawing of a girl who looks like a cartoon version of me riding a green dragon. The girl holds a bow and arrow in her hands as she flies over the sea. The sun is setting in the distance, painting the sky in shades of orange and yellow.

"It's perfect," I say, taking in every detail. And it's very detailed, every scale on the dragon gleaming, the sea coloured in hundreds of shades of blue. And the girl, she looks so much like me that I can't get over it, even though I've seen thousands of Artur's drawings.

"Thank you," I say, pulling Artur into a hug.

"So is our next event going to be a swaćba?" asks Danuta, Darek's mum, looking at the two of us.

I roll my eyes then share a smile with Artur. People never believe that childhood friends can just stay childhood friends, forever important but not in a romantic or sexual way. We stopped trying to correct the other magic-users ages ago, letting them make whatever assumptions they wanted. They were undeterred, even when Artur dated Simon. At this stage, it's an inside joke and we sometimes make bets about the number of subtle and less subtle pushes we'd receive at the next magical celebration.

We take plates from the long wooden table and load them with food. I pile up veggies on top of a freshly baked rye bread and dig in. But then something burns my collarbone and I gasp. For a second, the meadow around me blurs, the laughter fades. Instead, I see the outlines of tall, tall trees in the darkness.

Stay, *whispers a voice in my head.* Isn't it a better world?

I close my eyes and there's sunshine on my face again, and my lips are stretched in a smile, and I'm surrounded by people I love and who love me back. But then the burning sensation is back and I grasp the amulet on my chest. Only it shows a blackbird and it's not mine, it's Artur's, and it doesn't make any sense. Why would we exchange amulets? That would only give our community even more reasons to push us into each other's arms.

I look at the people around me and the feeling of wrongness returns. It's all a beautiful lie, concocted to make me stay.

Stay, *repeats the voice in my head but I squeeze the amulet harder.*

Artur gave the amulet to me, so we could find each other again. Because we aren't really on a Jare Gody celebration, I'm not eighteen yet, I might not survive until then, and I don't have a community like that. My hair is shorter and I'd never wear white.

Stay.

This meadow isn't real.

I'm with Karina in Nawia.

I opened my eyes. I was still huddled under the roots of the tree, though the rain had stopped. Moonlight streamed in-between the branches and Karina stared at me.

"You should have stayed asleep," said Karina. Only it wasn't her voice—it was deeper and colder. And her eyes were completely white.

THIRTY FIVE

Karina—the demon?—launched at me. I rolled away just in time, but I wasn't quick enough to stand before the demon was on me. It straddled my stomach, knocking the wind out of me, and its fingers pressed around my neck. I kicked and struggled, trying to get it off me. I couldn't let it kill me. Karina wouldn't survive knowing what the demon in her had done.

I gasped for breath, clawing at the demon's hands, but it was stronger than me. I kicked but I couldn't reach it. I tried to hit its ear but the demon was undeterred. My mind went foggy when I reached for my magic. And, for the first time in my life, it listened.

Magic leashed out of me, pushing the demon off my chest. I scrambled to my feet, hands pressing against my throat, gasping for breath. The demon fell on its back, but it was getting up again and I kept my magic close to my skin, ready to protect myself.

"Karina, please," I said, my voice more of a broken whisper. I winced at the pain every word caused. "You're more than this demon. It isn't everything you are and you hate—"

The demon pounced at me and I jumped back, magic tickling on my skin.

"—you hate when it takes over! You hate losing control. Don't let it win."

We moved as if in a weird, jerky dance, full of sudden jumps and retreats.

"You're my family," I continued, despite the pain in my throat. "You're my best friend and cousin, and bondmate, you're the person who followed me into Nawia. And I know it must be much harder to remember here but it's not the world where we belong. Our place isn't here, not yet. We belong in Jawia and we're going to get out, we're going to get the demon out of you, and we'll patch up the sky, and the horror of the past weeks will be just a strange dream."

The demon lunged at me, but my magic kept it at bay. I forced myself to stay still, keeping the demon just out of my reach with magic. I looked into the demon's white eyes, trying to see beyond that, to see the warm brown of Karina's eyes under the demon.

"You kissed a wiła and you liked it. You made Damian an amulet, you carved a white crystal into the most intricate oak leaf, and it led us to you the last time the demon inside you took over. You stayed back with Artur while Damian,

Rafi, and I searched for the firebird. I know the magic in this place can't make it any easier but you're human, as human as it gets, and you belong with us."

My little speech made no impression on the demon, which kept scratching at the invisible barrier that kept it away from me, its teeth bared.

"You're human," I repeated, more of a prayer.

But Karina's eyes remained demon white. My magic held steady but it couldn't help her. Unless…

"You're human," I said again, magic sparkling on my tongue. I'd never felt Tomasz's magic so strongly, I wasn't able to control my magic like that outside of Nawia. "You're human. Not a demon."

But the hypnosis didn't work, either. Of course, it didn't— Karina was the only one who had been unaffected by Tomasz's magic when the gods had come back at our solstice celebration. The demon kept scratching at the invisible force field around me, baring its teeth. My hands trembled but not with effort only with desperation. I needed to help Karina. I needed to free her from this demon once and for all.

A new pair of eyes flashed in the forest and I extended the protective bubble around me, marvelling at how easily the magic came to me. I was used to being surrounded by magic but not to be able to command it like that. Was it how Artur or even Damian felt, able to bend this powerful element to their will with no effort?

I glanced over my shoulder and saw a wolf emerging from between the trees. It was thin and grey but its eyes were pure gold. It looked straight at me and started circling around Karina and me. I considered extending the protection around her, too, trying to imagine how I could wrap my magic around both of us, while keeping the barrier between us, but the wolf didn't look ready to attack.

It paced around us, waiting for something.

"Are you a Leszy?" I asked the wolf circling us.

The wolf didn't respond, but my vision dimmed and instead I saw flashing images. Or rather the same image over and over.

Moon, moon, moon.

"A werewolf?" I guessed.

The wolf growled and the moon flashed in my head again. Not just full moon, but the moon in all its stages— moon eaten by *wolves,* as people had believed once upon a time. And we were in a forest, after dark, and even Artur remembered to thank the god of night if you left the forest after dark unscathed by demons or wolves.

The god of night. The god of wolves and night demons.

"You're Chors," I said and the wolf stood in place, a few steps away from me. "You can help Karina?"

The wolf stared me in the eyes. Next to him, the demon in Karina was still fighting, pushing at the magical shield around me.

"Please," I said, the sound coming out choked as desperation clawed at my throat. "Please, help her. Please take this demon out of her. You can do it, right? Call it back to yourself?"

Chors growled again. He didn't send me a vision this time, but magic sparkled stronger on my skin. At first, I thought it was a reaction to my proximity to the god. But magic kept biting my skin, so strong it almost burned.

Right. I couldn't possibly ask for so much without a payment.

Breath caught in my lungs.

"You want my magic?" I whispered.

The wolf kept on staring at me.

"You will free Karina from the demon, take it once and for all, in exchange for my magic?"

The wolf blinked.

Everything around us seemed to blur into the background. I swallowed, focusing on the tingle of magic on my skin, on the way it played with my hair, on how easy it was to bend to my will now. But things were different outside of Nawia.

I looked at Karina, at her white eyes, bared teeth with a bit of spit running down her chin, fingers bent and stiff, clawing at the force field between us, ready to close around my throat again.

It was no choice at all. I was always going to choose her.

"Yes," I said. "I agree. Let's do it."

The wolf walked towards me and nudged my side with its head. Before I could react, it bit my hand. I gnashed my teeth, biting back a scream. Warm blood trickled down my skin and little by little, the sparkle of magic on my skin died.

THIRTY SIX

THE MAGICAL SHIELD BETWEEN KARINA AND ME collapsed and Karina launched at me. But before she could reach me, she shrieked in a high-pitched tone that sounded nothing like her. The hair on the back of my neck stood.

Karina fell to the grass, the wolf staring down at her.

My hand pulsed with pain, blood trickling from the wound. My heart drummed in my chest but I forced myself to stay back, to trust the wolf, to trust that it was really a god, that it could help Karina.

Her eyes slowly changed from white to brown, her angry features first relaxing, then morphing into panic at the sight of the wolf. But Chors stepped away and, without a backward glance, disappeared between the trees.

"What was that?" asked Karina, her voice shaking. She pushed herself up on her elbows. "I remember hiding from the thunderstorm and then everything felt like a dream. But that wolf was real. And now I feel…"

She sat up, hands pressing against her chest and I held my breath. Please don't let the god have taken anything else than what was promised. Please let Karina be whole.

"The demon?" I guided her when she didn't continue.

Karina's eyes, brown and wide open, met mine. Not with fear but with surprise.

"Is it gone?" she whispered. "I can't feel it, but it can't be true."

I closed my eyes, whispering thanks to Chors under my breath.

"It was Chors. A god of night. He called the demon back."

"It's gone?" repeated Karina and I smiled at her.

But my cousin's face darkened when she saw the blood trickling down my hand.

"What did you do?" she asked.

"That was the payment for Chors calling the demon away."

"Your blood?" asked Karina. "You wouldn't pay with more blood when we're here to steal your blood back from a devil, right?"

I shook my head and swallowed, but it was hard with a knot growing in my throat. I still felt the magic in the air around me, but it didn't jump on my skin. And maybe a month or two ago I would have been happy to have my skin to myself, to be rid of magic. But I couldn't think about this loss just yet. We needed to move, we needed to go. We needed to get my blood, and leave this place, and patch up the hole in the sky.

"It wasn't my blood," I said. "And it doesn't matter now. You're free. We just need to find where the devil stores my blood and we can go back to Jawia. It can all be over soon."

Karina stood up, her eyes drilling into mine.

"Wiktoria Maria Potocka, what did you give to that god for extracting the demon from me?"

"My magic."

Karina stared at me in silent shock, her mouth open. But before she could say anything, her hands became transparent, the forest behind her showing through.

"Kari?" I asked.

I reached for my cousin, and she reached for me, but my hand went right through her. Our screams tore through the night, Karina's ending abruptly as she disappeared.

I stared into the empty forest, tears streaming down my cheeks.

Once again, I wandered through the forest without a clear destination in mind, but this time I was alone. Restless energy drummed inside me, pushing me on. I'd searched the area for any sign of Karina, but it looked like she'd really disappeared into thin air. But that explained nothing. Where was she? Was she still in Nawia or had it spit her out to Jawia? I hoped it was the latter, but what if she was still here? What if some demon or god had kidnapped her, what if it was torturing her?

I couldn't feel our bond. I couldn't track her.

So, once the initial shock had worn off, I walked on, hoping that by sheer luck or through some demonic powers I'd stumble upon my cousin or the place where the devil had hidden my blood. My legs ached but I walked on, counting my steps to keep my mind from spinning.

If I sat down, everything would catch up with me.

The wound on my hand was still bleeding, my palm throbbing with pain. I'd cleaned it with water, but I didn't have bandages or clean cloth to spare. It was yet another reason to get the hell out of Nawia as soon as possible.

But I needed to find Karina and the place where Węgliszek stored my blood.

Leaves rustled and before I could look over my shoulder, something hard slammed into my back and I fell to the ground. I cried out, trying to push the thing off me, tapping into my magic only it wasn't there.

It. Wasn't. There.

The demon licked the blood on my hand and I gnashed my teeth as I rolled and kicked and punched. It wasn't until last month that I started trusting and relying on magic, but I had seventeen years of experience in not using it. I wasn't going to start missing it now.

In the moonlight streaming in-between the tree branches I could make out a long furry shape and sharp gleaming teeth. I tried to shake it off, frantically thinking of a way to appease it. Even if it was after my blood, I didn't necessarily want to hurt it. Maybe there was something else I could offer instead. But I didn't even know what demon it was.

With my good hand, I pulled out Artur's amulet from under my clothes and pushed it into the demon's face. It fell back howling and ran off into the forest, yipping pitifully.

Maybe bleeding all over the demon realm wasn't the best way to go.

Using my pocketknife, I chopped off a piece of my scarf and wrapped it around my hand, hoping I wouldn't get an infection. Once the improvised bandage was tight around the wound, I resumed walking, the demon's howls replaying in my mind.

So many demons in the Slavic beliefs were born of traumas. So many restless human souls who couldn't or didn't want to stay in Nawia. Like rusałki trying to drown men because they'd hurt them when they were alive. Like wiły, who, when they were humans, scared people with their willpower and independence. And who knows what that poor beast had been.

There weren't good or bad demons. Demons just existed, like humans or gods. And my ancestors had destroyed the natural balance when they'd created the Guardian system. They'd imprisoned the demons here, in Nawia, forgetting they were a natural part of the magical balance.

I trembled, thinking of what awaited me if I ever got out of Nawia. We had to patch up the sky, but wouldn't we unleash something even more horrible over the entire country when we brought down the Guardian system?

I shook my head, forcing myself to walk on. I tried to count my steps but my mind kept wandering. It strayed to a sunny meadow from my dream. Vision? Alternative reality? I wasn't sure what had happened, only that it had been a story I wouldn't mind living through. Full of warmth and happiness and family, full of magic and community I was really a part of, that took me in as one of them.

And now that I'd given up my magic, it would never come true.

No. It never would have come true any way. It was an impossible dream, full of people who were dead, connections that had been severed before they could be formed.

But if I closed my eyes now…would the vision be back? Could I go back to this world, to this life that was never to be?

I winced in pain as the amulet scorched my collarbone again and I grasped it, ready to tear it off. It took all my willpower to let it go and I'd done it only because I didn't want to have my throat ripped open by another demon lured in by the smell of my blood.

Because even if staying in Nawia seemed more and more appealing with every moment, I was still human. Even if I didn't want to go back, even if I wanted to dance with wiły and dream of impossible lives.

What was waiting for me in Jawia apart from more challenges and pain?

How would we patch up the sky and destroy the

Twardowski's scriptures now that I didn't have magic?

I shook my head. I'd been standing still, staring into the dark forest ahead of me with unseeing eyes. I forced myself to take a step forward, then another.

A flickering ball of light appeared in front of me.

I shielded my eyes against the sudden burst of light. I was certain it was the same ball of light I'd seen in my dream, the same light that had led me to Nawia in the first place.

Yes, the dream had been sent by Weles. Yes, it was possible he would trick me, the ball of light could lead me to swamps or some ravenous demon with taste for human flesh. But I suspected that Weles had a lot to gain by us overthrowing the Guardian system. If Laura was right, he'd selected us for this task himself. And he likely knew we wouldn't do it until I'd collected my blood from Węgliszek.

It wasn't like I had any direction in mind either way. There wasn't much to lose.

I followed the ball of orange light between the trees, navigating between thick, thorny bushes which kept catching my clothes, branches snatching my hair and wrapping around my limbs. But I gently pulled them away and kept on walking.

I was covered in scratches when the orange light halted. I ran the last couple of steps, my heart hammering in my chest.

There, framed by thorny bushes, stood an iron cauldron filled with blood.

THIRTY SEVEN

THE CAULDRON COULD EASILY FIT A GROWN HUMAN OR two. It was impossible that all the blood inside was mine— I didn't have nearly enough blood inside my body to fill this cauldron. But that wasn't my main concern now. I looked at the glimmering blood, wondering what I was supposed to do with it. Spilling it sounded like a bad idea, but what other options were there? Could I steal the cauldron and carry it to Jawia? And then what?

A cold laughter broke through the night and I spun around, my heart hammering. Węgliszek stood metres away from me. He'd ditched his human suit in favour of a long, dark linen tunic spun with gold thread, his hooves standing bare in the ground. His face looked the same, with the honey blonde goatee, piercing eyes, and a smile which made me tremble but his head was now graced with a pair of black, pointed horns. He leaned against a tree, his arms folded, watching me.

"It's fascinating how magic always abandons humans," he said. "No matter how hard they try, they're unable to hold on to it."

I stood still, paralysed with fear. I'd faced many demons, I'd faced gods, but there was something about encountering a devil in Nawia that ignited a primal fear in me. I was unable to speak or move, willing to make myself as small and unobstructing as possible, so maybe the predator wouldn't notice me.

"Kneel and I might consider sparing you," said the devil, his power throwing me to my knees.

Ground bit into my legs, stinging, and I bit my lip, trying to keep my response to a minimum. I tried to contain my shaking, to not show the devil how greatly he affected me, as my mind raced, trying to find a way out.

"You thought you could steal what's rightfully mine?" asked Węgliszek, walking towards me and coming to stand so close that his hooves almost grazed my knees.

I didn't respond. Speaking up was the stupidest thing I could do. I had no prepared script for this encounter, and I didn't want to make any unwanted promises or bargains. And bargaining my way out seemed like the only possibility now. I had no magic and even in regular circumstances, it wouldn't have been enough to face a devil-god as powerful as Węgliszek. But I also had nothing left to bargain with and the last thing I wanted was to have another debt to a devil.

"Well, human? What shall it be? Will you plead for mercy?"

I bit my lip, trying to find a way out. Whatever was about to happen, I couldn't plead, couldn't give the devil an opening to ask for anything in return.

What could I do? Yes, I'd had a stupid thought to stay in Nawia but that was because of the dream I'd had. I wanted to live in that vision, not to become Węgliszek's slave, be skinned alive, or whatever else he'd planned for me.

I'd remembered the story Artur had told us when we'd found Węgliszek's figurines, about Apolonia Strychalska, who had been Węgliszek's lover or maybe a bewitched minion. She and her daughter had performed lots of horrible tasks for him until they'd managed to break the figurines that had kept them spellbound. But then Węgliszek had alerted the authorities and Apolonia and her daughter had been burned on stakes for witchcraft.

I didn't want to end up like them. But what could I do? How could I get out?

And what would happen if I didn't? Would my city remain halfway between Nawia and Jawia forever? Would people starve to death and demons take over? Would the Guardians rule for however long they had until magic disappeared from the world, probably within the next generation?

A small ball of orange light flickered over the cauldron.

I saw it with the corner of my eye, then quickly focused on the hooves of the devil pacing in front of me. I waited, muscles tensing. Then, when Węgliszek had his back to me for a second while he was turning around, I sprang up.

I jumped into the cauldron, blood splashing all around me. I anticipated the stink but it didn't smell of iron—it smelled of thyme and chalk, the smells I came to associate with magic. Magic sparkled all over my body and the devil screamed as I took a deep breath and submerged myself. Blood closed over my head. Magic—my magic—clung to me, tickling my skin, recognizing me, and I welcomed it back. As I floated in blood, a weight grew around my wrist, keeping me submerged. I didn't open my eyes but I used my injured hand to touch it and there, where Damian's red yarn had been knotted around my wrist for protection, now was a long, heavy chain.

I grasped it and stood up. I took in a breath and wiped the blood from my eyes and lips. Magic sparkled on my skin and with one precise blow, I threw Węgliszek to his knees. The devil opened his mouth, but I brought a finger to my lips. His eyes bulged as he opened and closed his mouth, unable to speak.

Keeping the devil in place with my magic, I wrapped the chain around his wrist and the other end around the nearby tree. Pure power filled my veins. The chain hissed, my knots searing together until the chain was a whole piece again.

"You won't be leaving Nawia anytime soon," I said.

I turned around and faced the cauldron. Magic drew me towards it. It was still filled with blood, probably of many other Węgliszek's victims. Now that my magic was back, I could sense a similar sort of repulsive, cold energy emanating from the cauldron as I had from the figurines in the tunnels.

I raised my hand and magic flew out of me and collided with the cauldron. It trembled and I pushed more magic out, until with a clink, the cauldron broke in half. Węgliszek shrieked, making the hair on the back of my neck stand, as the blood seeped into the moss underneath. The plants around sparkled with magic.

The world around me blurred. For a moment everything was dark, then I saw the face of a horned god and my magic pulsed harder, like calling to like. Weles looked me in the eye and held my gaze and suddenly I knew, I knew he was letting me leave his realm only because I was supposed to restore the magical balance between our realms. That had always been my purpose in life.

Then I saw Węgliszek again and froze, thinking something had gone wrong. But it was a vision of Weles handing a familiar purple egg to the devil—Arrow's egg. The god had ensured we'd get it. Arrow had always been meant to bring Karina and me to Nawia. And it still had a role to play.

When I blinked, I was on a river shore and the sky above me was torn in half.

The beach on the shore of Brda river, in Jawia, was dark and empty, lit up by the red light. The sand looked as if it was soaked with blood and I shivered. I'd forgotten how terrifying the view was.

The rush of power stopped. I was drenched to the bone, shivering in the wretched cold that stabbed right through my soaked clothes. The blood made my body sticky, hair clumped together and now freezing to my face. The air tasted weird, the oxygen too light in my lungs after breathing magic for so long, and my feet clung to earth more strongly, as if the gravity itself was different here. The only familiar thing was the omnipresent wild magic, though after Nawia it felt dull.

My muscles trembled in the cold and I forced myself to move. I'd hoped Artur, Damian, and Rafi would be waiting at the beach, but I'd spent days in Nawia, and I didn't know how the flow of time differed between the worlds.

And Karina. Where was Karina? Had she also returned to Jawia or was she stuck in another realm?

What if I'd been gone for human years?

I felt cold at the thought but I didn't let it settle. It was still winter. It would have been too much of a coincidence that I'd re-emerge during another winter. I couldn't have been away for that long.

Unless the winter never passed…

I took a step forward but stumbled. My knees shook but I forced myself to move, to relearn how to walk in this world. I tried to calm my spiralling thoughts as I climbed a sandy scarp and made my way into the dark forest. I pulled out a torch from my pocket, but the batteries had died. I clicked it on and off a few times, but it wouldn't work. My hand was shaking so badly I nearly dropped it, so I put it back in my pocket. I walked on in the darkness, navigating only by the red light streaming through the crack in the sky.

The bushes rustled and the snow crackled under demons' feet but I didn't pay it much mind. I'd just returned from the demons' realm.

The sounds of the forest were interrupted by heavier steps and familiar voices. I would have run towards them if I'd had any energy left. Artur was the first one to reach me, followed closely by Damian, and thankfully, Karina.

I wanted to run and hug her, but Damian stopped me in my tracks.

"Jesus fucking Christ," he murmured.

Right. I must have been quite a sight, drenched in blood.

"Please tell me it's not your blood," said Artur.

I tried to open my mouth to answer but my teeth were chattering too much, and I was scared I'd bite off my tongue. Damian closed the distance between us and took my hand and warmth spread through my body, my muscles relaxing.

"Thank you," I said once I trusted my body enough to speak. "And some of it is my blood. But I'm not bleeding. I just took a bath in the devil's cauldron to get it back. It broke, so I believe we're all free of our bargains now."

"You were gone for so long," said Artur.

"I'm sorry but I'm not going to hug you now," said Karina. She held the shimmering black magical cloth from the Baba Jaga.

"I wouldn't say no to a bath. But mostly, I think I just want to be done with it. Let's fix the sky."

We walked back to the beach. The Baba Jaga had been clear that we had to hold the ritual there.

"You're alive," I said to Karina. "I was so worried about you."

"I don't know what happened," she said. "I blinked and I was back in Jawia."

"It happened to me after I'd retrieved my blood, too."

"I guess your purpose in Nawia was fulfilled so you returned to our realm," said Artur. "I don't think the gods would like you to stay there indefinitely. You are still alive. The harmony between the realms must be preserved."

"Your magic is back," Damian said. "Last we heard, you were left alone in Nawia, magicless."

"I think I got it back with my blood. At least that's when I felt it. But I don't know how long it'll last."

We needed to hurry up and fix the sky in case it disappeared again.

"If it's all really Weles' plan, I don't think he would let another god take away your magic for long. Not if it's needed to accomplish our mission."

The forest opened into a clearing and we descended to the beach.

"What day is it?"

"Tenth of January," said Damian.

I closed my eyes for a moment. It was the new year. I'd lost over two weeks.

I forced myself to exhale. It could have been worse; it could have been more. I could have been gone for years. I could have been stuck in Nawia forever.

Artur squeezed my hand, the bond between us sparkling stronger than ever. I enjoyed this new power. Could I control it in Jawia, too?

"Where's Rafi?" I asked.

"You've been gone for a long time," said Artur. "Much longer than we anticipated. We didn't have much food so after a few days we decided it would be better if he gets back to the safe house. We were just considering a trip there ourselves, to stock up on more food, when you returned."

Guilt squeezed my chest. While I had been tempted to stay in Nawia forever, people in Jawia were starving, cut off from the rest of the word.

"Any idea how we're going to do it?" asked Karina as we climbed down to the beach, bringing me back to the present.

"We'll hold the material between us and wish the sky to be mended," I said.

Just like when I'd conducted a ritual with Artur here, when we'd unblocked my magic, we drew a circle in the sand, with one side touching the water. Artur found a stick and placed it in another side and Karina lit up the end with her lighter. Following Baba Jaga's instructions, we held the dream cloth between us.

I looked at my three companions: Karina, her hair a tangled mess, the blue tips washed out; Artur, his cheeks sunken, the bags under his eyes more pronounced in the eerie red light; and Damian, who looked even thinner and smaller than when we'd met, his dark hair long enough now to start curling. My heart squeezed, my throat closing up. The past weeks had taken their toll on all of us and I'd missed my friends, I'd missed our bond. I was so glad to be back together, magic flowing strong between us.

"We can be sappy later, after the sky is fixed," said Damian.

"You can hear my thoughts?" I asked surprised.

Damian shrugged.

"You left us for weeks with nothing better to do than experiment with our bond." Artur's cheeks reddened and Damian glared at him. I opened my mouth to speak but Damian beat me to it: "Focus, everyone. Five deep breaths, let's try to clear our minds."

It was easier than expected. I closed my eyes, focused on the magic between us, and breathed. The air was cold and crisp, the wind playing softly with the reeds. A demon cackled in the forest. A branch broke in the distance.

There was a powerful whoosh. I looked up but the sky was still torn, the red light as insistent as before. But now Arrow was flying towards us, its wings skimming the water. The żmij landed in the sand and we exchanged a glance then let go of the cloth and went to hug Arrow.

I looked into its golden eyes.

"When the sky is fixed," I whispered. "Will Arrow disappear as well?"

"Probably," said Artur.

Tears stung my eyes. I scratched the żmij's nose.

"Thank you for being the best baby dragon," I whispered. "Thank you for helping us over and over."

Arrow bumped my hand with its head and screeched, and I furiously wiped the tears from my eyes. We had a job to do, I couldn't get distracted.

Arrow screeched again and stomped towards the circle. The żmij couldn't breach the magical circle but it screeched again, pointing its head at the magical cloth within.

"You can fly high enough to patch up the sky," I said and the żmij blinked.

I looked at the rest of the Circle of Four. Karina shrugged; Artur looked contemplative.

"Worst case, Arrow will destroy the cloth or take it somewhere where we never find it again," said Damian.

I frowned. I loved Arrow, but it was a powerful demon which likely wouldn't be able to return to Jawia after the sky was patched. What could it gain from helping us now?

Arrow screeched again, stomping on the ground like a toddler throwing a tantrum.

Weles had said that Arrow still had a role to play.

"You will help us, right?" I asked, looking into the żmij's eyes. "You've only ever helped us. You'll fly the cloth high up and we'll complete the ritual down below and together we'll patch up the sky."

Arrow blinked.

"I love you, little dragon," I said, throwing my arms around the żmij's neck.

I took a few deep breaths, trying to collect myself. It needed to be done. We needed to fix the sky.

But, damn, that żmij had my heart.

After a few long moments, I pulled back and brushed back the tears from my cheeks. Artur touched my back and scratched Arrow's nose. Arrow bumped his hand in acknowledgement.

I looked at it for a moment more, tearing up again. Then I picked up the cloth and offered it to the żmij.

"Thank you for everything, baby dragon," I said as Arrow gently took it in its teeth.

Arrow brushed its head against each of us then beat its wings and tore up and up and up, towards the hole in the sky.

Damian and Karina took my hands, leading me back to the circle. We held hands, magic flowing between the four of us and into the world around us as Arrow's silhouette grew smaller and smaller in the sky until it disappeared. Slowly, without fanfare, the red gash in the sky closed and the night was dark again.

THIRTY EIGHT

The sky was filled with thousands of stars. The world was deathly still, dark and silent. A regular winter night like hundreds of others.

Arrow was gone.

Artur, Karina, Damian, and I held on to each other's hands. Magic between us stilled, tired from the excessive use. Would it come back to me at all?

I blinked, bringing myself back to reality. But nothing felt real. Not after Nawia, not after all this magic. It was so anticlimactic.

"I guess it's time for a bath then," I said.

"Not in the river," said Artur.

"Not in the river," I agreed.

We walked back to the summerhouse. The forest was silent now, the demons gone, the trees back to their usual size. Exhaustion was settling in my bones, my muscles aching. I wanted nothing more than to crash and sleep, but I was still covered in blood, my skin itchy. As Damian's magic was exhausted, I scrubbed off as much blood as I could with a cloth dunked in lukewarm water, warmed by the fireplace. Whether electricity was back, we couldn't tell—the summerhouse complex was always disconnected from power and water over winter.

Judging by the exhausted faces of my companions, it was a good thing. None of us was ready to deal with sudden changes yet. Squeezing four people semi-comfortably inside the tiny summerhouse was the only puzzle we were ready to solve before we fell asleep.

I was woken up by a loud, mechanical sound. I sat up, squeezing the duvet to my chest and looked around for the source of the noise, heart drumming in my chest. It took me a few moments to realize it was a helicopter.

"I guess it worked," said Artur, who was also awake now.

The whirring sound faded away, but all memory of sleep was gone.

It had worked.

We'd done it. We'd fixed the sky.

And now we only needed to get the Twardowski's scriptures from the Assembly and destroy them.

I almost wished for the sky to break again.

We had a simple breakfast of slightly stale bread made

by Damian some days before. There was nothing left to put on top of it, but it didn't matter. If we'd done everything right, soon we'd be able to go to any shop and buy all the food we wanted.

But none of us were in a hurry to leave. We knew it had to happen, but it would have been nice to remain in our bubble for a bit more. So we stayed in the summerhouse, behind the closed shutters, trying to ignore the incessant whirring of helicopters. Karina helped me wash the blood out of my hair the best we could in a lukewarm bucket of water and then we sat by the fireplace and played cards, pushing away our responsibilities, trying to convince ourselves that we deserved a morning off.

"I'm so glad you're back," said Artur, leaning his head on my arm.

The lack of the tingle of magic between us was disconcerting, but Artur didn't seem to mind. He was burrowed close to me like always, while I worried if my magic would return at all.

"I wouldn't have made it back without your amulet," I said, pressing my palm against where it lay under my jumper. "It reminded me that I had a life to get back to, people waiting for me."

As we kept playing Uno, all of us became twitchier. Our peace couldn't last forever, but we weren't ready to give it up. We didn't even have magic back.

"We should be at studniówka today," said Karina, her voice cracking a little.

"And fighting demons and saving the world is better alternative to dancing and drinking with your teachers?" I offered.

Karina stared at her cards.

"I was looking forward to dancing polonaise. You know, this grand moment at the beginning, when the orchestra starts playing and everyone in the final class starts this terribly old-fashioned dance? All perfectly rehearsed, everyone dressed in fancy dresses and suits. And, sure, in the grand scheme of things it's such a small thing, but did the magic have to take that from us as well?"

Artur stood up and extended his hand towards Karina.

"I don't have a suit," he said. "Or a dress. But I know the steps. Well, at least the major ones."

Karina stared at him for a moment.

"You're serious, aren't you?" she asked.

"I know it's not the same but I won't let magic take that moment from you."

Karina blinked, then let him pull her to her feet. Artur extended his forearm and Karina placed hers over his.

I intoned the first sounds of Ogiński's *Polonaise* and Damian joined in. We mimicked the musical background, getting really into imitating different instruments, as Artur and Karina marched in front of us, three short steps followed by a long one. Artur whispered something to Karina and she laughed. I couldn't stop a smile. After they finished the second circle, Damian nudged me in the ribs and we got up and created an arch with our hands, never stopping the musical background. With laughter, Artur and Karina dived under our joined hands.

Then, the sound of a car engine drowned out our laughter and humming.

We froze. There was only the tiniest tingle of magic on my skin, which minutes ago I would have welcomed with joy, but now it wouldn't be enough to fight someone off. What if the Children of Weles found us? What if it was the Assembly? We didn't have a plan yet, we didn't know what to do, and here we were wasting time on dancing…

We walked to the window and peeked in-between the window shutters. The world looked weird without the red light distorting it. Artur squeezed my hand as a familiar silver Skoda rolled to a stop outside the garden. It was followed by my mum's Opel. We quickly put on our clothes and went to meet them.

"You've done it," said Tomasz, getting out of the car. He'd grown a good few days' worth of dark stubble and a rumpled shirt peeked from under coat, which hung on him too loosely. "Did you manage to get your blood from the devil as well?"

I nodded. "And banish Karina's demon."

"That's some really impressive magic. You realigned the world again. Well done."

"It's a great start but there's still a lot to do and we don't have much time. You've been gone for so long," said Mum, getting out of the other car. She looked more put together than Tomasz, though there were bags under her eyes. She was wrapped in her sorcerer's cloak.

But I paid more attention to the passenger door which opened as well.

"Dad!" I exclaimed.

"The whole world is talking about a city disappearing off the map," he said, stepping out into the snow. "Did you think I'd just go to work as if nothing is happening?"

I ran up to him and hugged him. His arms closed around me, strong, and I hid my face in his chest. For a few moments everything was okay. Maybe the adults would take over now. Maybe they had everything worked out.

"You can't be found together," said Mum, and I reluctantly stepped away from Dad's embrace. "The Assembly is probably already in the city. Wiki, stay here, but the rest of you should go with Tomasz, he'll tell you the plan."

Artur, Damian, Karina, and I exchanged glances, but Mum was right. We couldn't be caught together.

It's just for now, I thought as we gathered for a group hug. *It's almost over.*

But my stomach squeezed with realization that we still needed to get the Twardowski's scriptures. We needed to destroy the Guardian system once and for all. And I doubted that the Assembly would make it easy.

We held on to each other for a few long moments. There was only the tiniest hint of magic between us, but I didn't want to let go. I wasn't ready, we'd just gotten back together. But we needed to end this nightmare once and for all.

We returned inside the summerhouse to take our things. There wasn't much to gather, mostly some of Damian's leftover alchemist supplies and some of Karina's newly-crafted amulets, shaped into improbable shapes.

Damian tore through his backpack before taking something out, hiding it in his closed fist.

"I have something for you," he said to Artur.

He opened his palm to reveal a glistening black ring.

"Oh," said Artur.

He stared at the ring then at me, his eyes wide.

"Well," I said mock-seriously. "I know we weren't super clear on boundaries, but engagement seems like something we maybe should have discussed beforehand."

I knew what I was looking at, but I couldn't miss an opportunity to mess with them. I needed to grab a chance to play around for a few more moments.

Both boys stared at me horrified. Artur's cheeks were burning.

"It's not—" Damian sputtered, at a loss of words. "That's not what it is!"

He looked panicked between Artur and me.

"I know. But the opportunity was too perfect to miss." I squeezed Artur's hand. "It's an ace ring."

"Made of black tourmaline," said Damian. "Just like the bracelet I gave you before. It's an extra protection from negative energy, for anxiety."

"Oh," repeated Artur. He looked between the two of us. "Thank you."

Artur took the ring and rolled it in his fingers.

"It goes on the middle finger of your right hand. The

left hand is for aro ring," said Damian, wiggling his fingers. "It's a reminder that your identity is valid. And that there's a whole community of people out there who'd recognize this symbol. Also, it's cool to flip people off with it."

Artur closed his arms around Damian, hugging him close.

"Thank you," he repeated softly.

The moment was interrupted by my mum, who appeared in the doorway.

"Tomasz is waiting," she said.

I followed Damian and Artur back to Tomasz's Skoda, where Karina already sat on the passenger seat.

"I'll see you soon," said Damian, getting in the backseat.

But Artur didn't move from my side.

"I'm not going anywhere," he said—the four most beautiful words.

Relief flooded me and I squeezed his hand to show my gratitude. It was hard enough saying bye to Karina and Damian. I was glad to have at least Artur by my side as we discussed the future plans.

Mum sighed. "Fine. The Assembly knows about you two either way. Come inside so we can discuss the plan."

Inside the summerhouse, Dad poured us huge cups of hot chocolate from a thermos and gave us sandwiches. Between the sweet taste of chocolate on my tongue and fresh cucumbers and tomatoes in the sandwich, for one second everything was perfect. I allowed myself to relax the tiniest bit. Mum had a plan. Sure, our relationship had been a bit patchy in the past weeks but she knew the situation better than anyone else. She would know what to do.

"We need to get the Twardowski's scriptures from the Assembly in Gdańsk and we need to ensure that our city doesn't fall apart while you're getting them," said Mum. She sat on the sofa while Artur and I took the floor, food spread out between us. Dad hovered nearby. "The Assembly is likely already trying to re-establish control over the city, looking for scapegoats. We can't let them hurt our community. But we also can't let the Children of Weles try to take over once the scriptures are destroyed. We don't know how many people would still back them but it's not a risk we can take. We need to ensure that the power will really go to the people and not just the select few. Thankfully, we have something that the Assembly wants."

Mum turned to look at me. Artur squeezed my hand, a shy sparkle of magic flowing between us, growing steadily stronger.

"You can't enter the Assembly without an invitation," she continued, her eyes drilling into mine. "Even Zuzanna has never been there, and she wouldn't be welcome now. But we know they want you, Wiki. They wanted you before the sky broke open, but now they will want to give you a proper trial, to make an example out of you. And that's your ticket inside. That's the easiest, fastest way to get there, one that will ensure that their wards won't hurt us as they would if we tried to break in. And there, at the centre of their great room, they keep the copy of the

Twardowski's scriptures. They will definitely take you there because that's where all the trials take place. You need to get the scriptures and then you get out using the magic inside them. You could probably also get out with a Guardian's ring."

"That's the worst plan I've ever heard," said Dad. He stood by the fireplace, his arms crossed on his chest.

"She needs to get inside the Assembly," said Mum. "She needs to get the Twardowski's scriptures."

The hot chocolate was suddenly tasteless. I put my mug down on the floor next to me. It all came down to this point. The very reason for my existence. I had always been supposed to be the means to an end, a weapon, a pawn in a much bigger game.

"Not like that," said Artur.

"I'm open to suggestions," said Mum, throwing her arms wide open. "Who has a better plan? Who has any plan whatsoever?"

Her raised voice made me hide further into the wall. I welcomed its cold. I needed to stay present. I couldn't let my emotions take over, I couldn't let my brain wander, I couldn't let myself think—

"Sara," said Dad, pleadingly.

"That's not my name," said Mum, throwing him a pointed look. "I discussed it with Zuzanna. It's the best shot we have, the best chance we have of you actually getting to the Assembly and keeping our city intact while you get the scriptures."

I drew my hands through my hair, scrubbing out leftover blood. It had faded back to its original mousy blond colour, grown coarse, and lost all its volume from constant cold and lack of conditioner. Which was a stupid thing to notice at a moment like this. I knew Mum was right. We were out of time. We needed to act now if we wanted to have a chance of getting it right.

As my fingernails dug into my scalp, I couldn't stop thinking about that stupid, stupid dream from Nawia. Zuzanna braiding my hair for my coming-of-age ceremony, Mum escorting me, proud and happy. Belonging among the sorcerers, among the Guardians, not as a pawn, not as a weapon, but as one of them.

But it wasn't true.

"Did Zuzanna also mention that she doesn't have the best track record of keeping Wiki alive?" asked Artur, his tone harsh.

I didn't want them to fight. There was nothing to fight about.

Mum was right.

"Yes," I said, my voice more decisive than I would have expected. "We need the Twardowski's scriptures. No, we don't have a better plan. So, let's get it over with."

There wasn't time to waste. As we readied to leave, Dad hugged me close, "You shouldn't be doing that," he said. "It shouldn't be on your shoulders."

I didn't respond. I didn't trust myself to speak up. If I did, I'd never go through with this plan.

"I love you," I said instead, and he squeezed me harder.

When it was Artur's turn, he didn't say anything. He held me close, the tingle of magic jumping between us strong enough now to provide warmth. But Artur's emotions were impenetrable.

I want to know what you feel, I said.

"No," murmured Artur into my hair. "I know you want to go through with this, and I won't be the one to stop you."

He released me and took off his grey hoodie. He handed it to me. It was surprisingly clean but then I guess they'd had a lot of time and alchemist power for magical laundry while they were waiting for me to get back from Nawia.

"Wear this. I don't trust them not to take the amulet, and I want you to have something that's mine in case something goes wrong and you need to find me."

"Thank you," I whispered, gladly trading a thin summer jumper I'd found to replace my blood-stained clothes for the hoodie. I put my own jacket on top of it.

Artur looked at me, his eyes glistening, and he pulled me into another quick hug.

"You aren't a weapon," he said, his fingers biting into my arms. "You aren't a pawn. You're *human*. And if things go badly, please get out of there, no matter whether you manage to get the scriptures or not. We can try to get them another time, but I doubt the gods will grant you another life."

I squeezed his hands.

"I'll meet you in Gdańsk," was all I trusted myself to say.

THIRTY NINE

I FOLLOWED MUM TO THE CAR. ARTUR AND DAD would have to wait for Tomasz to pick them up as we couldn't be caught together.

"You have to drink that," said Mum, passing me a small glass bottle.

"What is it?" I asked, though I was pretty sure I knew.

"Rue extract from Gabriella. We can't let the Assembly find you before we get to them."

I took a deep breath. The last time I'd had the rue extract, Filip had forced it down my throat to keep me from escaping the tunnels. But I knew Mum was right, so I lifted the bottle to my lips and downed it quickly. My throat closed and I gagged at the familiar taste and the memories it evoked. Almost immediately, the shy sparkle of magic in my veins died down.

Would it come back at all?

Mum started the car, her eyes trained on the road. We drove in silence. The moment we got to the main road, I was hit by how busy it was. Trucks and cars driving towards the city, carrying supplies, and lines of cars leaving the city, going anywhere, anywhere else. Mum shook her head impatiently and took us down smaller roads so we could get to the city as soon as possible. More and more it was starting to sink in that we'd done it. The world was as close to normal as it could get after the events of the past weeks. Even the trees were back to their regular size, the forest not nearly as terrifying as it used to be.

It was almost as if nothing had happened. Like it all had been a nightmare.

As my thoughts started to drift away, I put on the radio. I didn't expect it to work but it did.

"*...cold, so cold, worse than any winter I can recall. I'd never seen so much snow in this city. And one doesn't realize how much they rely on technology until it stops working. You can't cook, you can't heat up water, the lifts don't work, and in winter it gets dark early. Not that we got much sunlight at all, only this horrible red light.*"

"*Did you know where the light was coming from?*"

"*My dear, if you'd been there, if you'd lived through it, you would know there was nothing natural about it. It was magic.*"

"*There have also been reports of animals attacking people.*"

"*What animals? These were definitely not animals, they were demons. Magic...*"

"How are we going to move on now that everyone knows?" I asked as the person on the radio continued describing the demons they'd seen and heard of.

"They don't know yet. People in the city know, of course, but few others will believe them. Not if they haven't lived through it. They will study what had happened as an anomaly. But people will know once the scriptures are destroyed, once the world is back to the way it was before the Guardians took over."

"Will it be like it was here for the entire country?"

"No. What happened here was magical imbalance, a tear between Nawia and Jawia. When you destroy the scriptures in a correct way, the magical balance will be restored and the gods appeased. The Guardians' will lose their knowledge and power once and for all. And the rest of the magical community will be ready this time to set up the basic protections against the demons. But yes, the world will be different."

I brushed my hair with my fingers, trying to work out the tangles.

I hadn't asked Artur whether the sorcerers celebrated their coming-of-age the way I'd seen in the vision in Nawia. I opened my mouth to ask Mum, but I closed it. No. I didn't want to ask her about it, not now. Maybe when it was all over, when we got a chance to live as a real part of the magical community. It could be our first big event together, a reconciliation of sorts.

We left the forest behind but the traffic in the city was even worse and soon we were stuck. Mum drummed her fingers on the steering wheel and people on the radio continued recounting their experiences of when the city had been cut off. Apparently, it hadn't been cut off properly—people had managed to get out while the sky had been broken, telling crazy stories of weird red light shining from the sky and demons. It'd been only the magical community which had been truly stuck—though most others didn't dare attempting an escape, cut off from their cars and public transportation, in the intense cold and snow.

As a young woman started telling the story of her best friend torn apart by gryphons, Mum tried to turn off the radio, but I didn't let her. I needed to listen to the horrors shared by people. I needed to remember what would happen if the Children of Weles managed to stay in power. I needed to understand the extent of the atrocities that people had experienced. I played with Artur's amulet, rotating it in my hand, listening to their stories.

"Wiki," Mum said as we moved towards the old market square at snail's pace. "What Artur said—"

Before she could finish, someone yelled outside and then something crashed into our car's bonnet, cracking the windshield. Mum and I screamed, then Mum's magic pushed the thing away and it slammed into the car in front of us.

Mum swore. It was a giant stone eagle. I'd seen it before, perched on top of an old hotel on the main street. Was it a gargoyle? The thing moved again, flapping its gigantic stone arms but Mum kept it at bay.

"Jagoda," murmured Mum through gritted teeth.

Of course. The sorceress with affinity for rocks who'd chased Damian and me in the tunnels.

The stone eagle flew down, making a dent in the roof of a car in front of us. More screams followed and my hands shook. I couldn't do anything. My magic was blocked and I couldn't stop a piece of stone that easily weighed a ton with my bare hands.

"We need to get out of here," said Mum.

The window next to her broke and we screamed again. She redirected her magic to force the pieces of glass outside, but then the window next to me exploded as well. I leaned forward, shielding my head. Mum screamed again, and I didn't feel any glass fall on me so I dared to look up.

I momentarily wished I hadn't. I wished I'd stayed in the summerhouse, that I'd stayed in Nawia.

Filip stood outside, his bare hand pressed to my mum's neck. I unbuckled my seatbelt but before I could push him off, he clucked his tongue.

"I really wouldn't do that," he said, pointing with his head to the left.

There was another statue there, and I recognized it, too. It was one of the symbols of the city—a naked archer, who was now pointing her arrow at Mum.

I fell back into my seat. I looked at Mum, her eyes pleading as Filip finished freezing her. I couldn't decipher her expression, I couldn't even begin to guess what she was thinking, but there was one thing I could try.

I swung the door open and ran.

I got two whole steps before the stone eagle snatched me up in its claws, lifting me off the ground. A scream tore out from my throat. I tried to fight it, but punching a piece of stone was stupid.

"Good," said Filip, walking towards me. "Your magic is already bound. That makes my work so much easier."

The eagle lowered to the ground and I struggled harder to rip away from its grasp, but it brought no result. Filip climbed on top of the eagle and we rose to the sky.

I stopped struggling. While I was certain I didn't like whatever Filip had in store for me, I didn't fancy dropping down twenty metres onto concrete. Instead, I tried to grasp the eagle's claws with my hands, to give myself this extra protection as I swayed back and forth in its claws. But it was freezing cold, my fingers stiffened quickly, and my grasp kept slipping from the smooth stone.

People screamed and pointed as we flew.

"Smile for the cameras," shouted Filip over the wind. "You will be all over the news."

We flew in between colourful tenements and over the river. The eagle rose up when we got to the tall white tenement, then crashed through the balcony door into the Guardian's flat. I raised my hands to shield my face from flying pieces of glass, then curled up as the eagle dropped me to the floor. I cringed at the impact, but stopped myself from screaming. The eagle landed heavily next to me and moments later Filip grasped my jacket, wrenching me up.

"Let's go," he said, pushing me towards the door. "Let's not keep our esteemed guests waiting."

I expected the Assembly to meet us halfway, to try to stop Filip, but the staircase was quiet and empty as we walked downstairs, the wood creaking under each of our steps. What if Filip worked for the Assembly? What if he'd struck some deal with them? I guess at least I'd end up where I was supposed to be. But Mum might still be frozen in the car. What if Jagoda had hurt her? And what about the rest of her plan, what if Filip used me now to get more swing to the Children of Weles?

I tried to break free one more time, tearing from Filip's grasp but the moment I did, he pushed me forwards. My scream broke the silence as I fell headfirst down the stairs, taking the strength of the impact onto my arms.

Warmth tickled my skin as the tenement's magic reached for me, as if trying to protect me. But it felt off and it hadn't stopped Filip from entering the building.

Something was wrong. A lot of things were wrong.

"I just need you to be alive, I don't need you in one piece," said Filip, his voice low, as he once again grabbed a handful of my jacket and lifted me to my feet.

I trembled, grateful that nothing seemed to be broken as he led me down the last flight of stairs and kicked open the back door to the Clavichord Café.

Filip pulled my back close to his chest as we entered. I recoiled at the contact, but his grip was firm. The café was dimly lit and there were three people dressed in Guardian's red cloaks standing in the middle and at least a dozen more in sorcerer black, their hoods covering their faces.

"I found what you've been looking for," said Filip.

"Out of the goodness of your heart?" asked a voice I'd instantly recognized. Konrad Koniewski, the Guardian of Gdańsk. The one who'd been appointed a temporary Guardian to our city, when Zuzanna had been voted down from her role. The one whom the Children of Weles had managed to frame for many of their own crimes against our community.

I'd lost track of what was them and what was Konrad. And I didn't feel like finding out.

"Drop it, Guardian," said another Guardian I'd recognized. Guardian Skalski, whose first name I didn't know. He'd led the meeting against Zuzanna. "We did promise a reward for bringing the girl to us."

He nodded and two sorcerers stepped towards me. I squeezed my eyes, my muscles tensing in preparation, but Filip pulled me back a step.

"The reward first," he said.

"I don't think you're in position to negotiate," said Konrad.

"Oh, really?"

Filip shifted his grasp on me and something ice cold and sharp touched my throat. I stood frozen, my back as close to his chest as I could get, afraid to even breathe as my heart beat wildly in my chest.

"I can slice her throat before you can make your move,"

he warned. "And I think you want your Skybreaker in one piece."

Guardian Skalski sighed.

"Very well," he said, his tone bored. "What do you want as a reward?"

"The city stays in our control," said Filip.

"No. Guardian Koniewski will secure the city until we can appoint a new Guardian. But we can make you his assistant, and turn a blind eye to anything we might hear about your actions during the blockade."

When he finished speaking, I heard Filip's sharp inhale of breath as his hand was thrown to the side with a blast of powerful magic. The blade—a sharp piece of ice—fell from his grasp, shattering to a thousand pieces. Two sorcerers I didn't recognize approached us again, their hands clasping my shoulders. Even as my heart threatened to escape my chest, I let them lead me toward the centre of the room without a struggle. It would have been pointless.

"The girl's powers are blocked," said one of them.

"Perfect. Let's go," said Guardian Skalski.

I flinched as a hand touched my neck. Then the world whirled around me and I felt weightless for a moment before the world turned black.

ᚠᛟᚱᛏᛁ

Everything hurt. It wasn't anything new, but it wasn't possible to dismiss, either. My head pounded and my throat was parched. My arms, my legs, my stomach—every muscle in my body screamed. I wanted to fall back asleep, but dread closed around my throat and I sat up, my heart pounding, head spinning as I frantically tried to understand where I was.

It wasn't what I expected. Not a dungeon, not a car trunk, not a forest. No, I was in a small but comfortable room, with white brick walls, tall, tall ceiling, and a large window. It was dark outside, but enough artificial light streamed in for me to make out my surroundings. I lay on a soft, queen-sized bed, on top of the bedding but with a knitted grey blanket thrown over me. I was clutching it and I didn't let go as I scanned the rest of the room. Dark, hardwood floors, with a sheep's skin thrown in front of the bed in lieu of a carpet, and a dresser with a pitcher of water and a glass on top of it. There were also two pairs of dark, tall, wooden doors.

I swallowed hard and tried to forget about my parched throat as I slowly walked to the window. Someone had taken off my shoes and they lay side by side next to the bed. My heart didn't stop pounding as I looked through the window. Outside there was a river with a few old ships docked at the sides, which were there only for the tourist's sake—a "pirate ship," an old warship, and a ship that was now a hostel. People walked alongside the river, couples holding hands, parents pushing children's prams. I was four, maybe five floors above them. It couldn't have been late, even though I couldn't see any clock. Tenements rose on both sides of the river, narrow and tall, with pointy roofs, much like the Guardian's tenement.

I was in Gdańsk.

I was still wearing my clothes, the jacket with a rip in the shoulder included. My body was achy but didn't feel wrong or otherwise altered, which was the only bit of relief.

I couldn't feel magic on my skin.

The window didn't have a handle, so I walked across the room and tried the door. The first one was locked—I guessed it led outside. The second door revealed a small but tidy bathroom with a stack of towels and a collection of travel-sized cosmetics.

Everything in me screamed that it was wrong.

Yes, of course I'd expected to end up in a dungeon. I'd heard over and over about how the Assembly was after me, how they wanted to put me on trial. They'd murdered my father, they'd made my parents desperate enough to make a deal with a devil. Zuzanna hated them, the sorcerers hated them, we'd been working to undermine them for so long. They'd made a pact with the Children of Weles just to get to me.

Was it some sort of trap? I mean, yes, the Assembly was supposed to be one big trap, but so far it was nothing like what I'd expected.

I rummaged through the drawers, but they were empty. The pitcher on top of the dresser looked more and more enticing with every second, and I gave in to the thirst. I didn't trust the pitcher, but I gulped water from the tap until I couldn't drink anymore.

I paced the room, my stomach knotted, waiting for something to happen. My stomach growled in hunger, but the door didn't open. No strange magic washed over me. No one came to bring me more rue extract to keep my powers at bay.

Nothing happened.

After a while, I sat on bed, my legs screaming for a break. I'd slept through the day but it'd been a magical sleep and I was tired again.

Were they waiting for me to be exhausted until they came? To drag me off to a torture chamber or a trial?

I forced myself to stay up, to keep vigilant, but nothing

was happening. I found a newly packaged toothbrush and brushed my teeth, still waiting for the door to burst open at any moment. It didn't. My scalp itched and the promise of warm water and shampoo to finally get rid of the remaining dried blood in my hair once and for all was more and more tempting by the minute but I didn't give in. I didn't want the Guardians to come when I was in the shower.

I paced the room some more then sat on the bed until my eyes started dropping closed and my eyelids got too heavy to keep lifting. I fell asleep curled on top of the bedding.

I woke up to bright light streaming in through the window. The sky was crisp winter blue, the world outside frosty but not snowed over. Someone was jogging alongside the river, on the other side two older ladies walked slowly by. I dragged a hand over my face. My stomach rumbled with hunger, and I regretted not finishing the hot chocolate back at the summerhouse.

Was Mum okay? Had someone found her, helped her?

What were Artur, Karina, and Damian up to?

Had Konrad taken control over the city? Would anyone swear fealty to him? Would they be forced to?

Did the Assembly have enough power to force an entire city to submit to them?

There was still no magic on my skin and it began to feel weird. It's been hours, close to a day since I'd taken the rue extract. Assuming that I'd slept only a couple of hours, and not over a day. But in either case, it never lasted that long, four hours was the average. My magic should have been back by now, unless something else was binding it. Was it gone because I'd given it to Chors and the blood worked only for a limited time?

I paced the room again, wondering what was going on. Why had no one asked for me yet? Were they trying to starve me? Was that their plan, lock me away in this room and let me lose my mind thinking about why nothing was happening?

My hands were shaking, my fists pulling on the strings in Artur's hoodie when there was a knock on the door.

"Yes?" I asked, feeling ridiculous. I was a prisoner here. It wasn't up to me to open the door.

Fear chilled my heart and I released the strings of the hoodie. Slowly, the door unlocked and then opened.

"Miss Potocka," said Guardian Skalski. "We'd be honoured if you'd join us for breakfast."

I followed the Guardian down the corridor. The walls were the same white brick as in my room, the ceiling high overhead, so that our steps echoed loudly. It reminded me of Węgliszek's castle. Had the devil done it on purpose, creating his lair as a mirror of the Assembly?

As far as I could tell, there was no one else here, just Guardian Skalski and me. No sorcerers to keep him safe, no other Guardians to keep an eye on me and pass judgement.

"Lovely weather today," commented the Guardian, his tone politely neutral.

I didn't respond. I didn't know what I could say. Yes, the bright sunlight streamed in through the tall windows, the white walls almost shining. Yes, apart from my holiday in Nawia, it'd been forever since I'd seen sunlight. But also, I was shaking all over and my stomach was tied in knots, and I didn't trust myself to open my mouth without throwing up. Maybe it hadn't been so bad living under the broken red sky. Maybe I'd give a lot to go back in time a day or two, to be back in the summerhouse with the Circle of Four.

No. I couldn't think like that. I needed to focus on getting the Twardowski's scriptures so we could finish it once and for all.

But we didn't go to the great hall that my mum had described. Instead, we entered a bright room with a large wooden table that took up most of the space. There were enough chairs to seat twenty people but only four seats were set. Two Guardians sat at the table, both wearing their beet red cloaks just like Guardian Skalski did. I didn't know their names. And the table was covered in more food than I'd seen in weeks. Platters of fresh fruit cut into small, colourful pieces: fresh berries, apples, pears and bananas, peaches leaking juice. And then there were more plates filled with cheeses and meats, poached eggs, sliced tomatoes and cucumbers, lettuces and colourful bell peppers, baskets filled with breads and rolls, and pitchers of juice and tea. There was a huge French press filled with coffee, its aroma filling the air.

Guardian Skalski pulled out the chair closest to the window and gestured for me to sit. I hesitated for a moment but I couldn't think of anything I'd gain by disobeying so I sat on the chair. He took the spot opposite me.

"Beautiful weather," remarked one of the other Guardians, carefully inspecting a raspberry.

"Indeed," said the third one, spreading some butter on a roll. "Lovely sunshine on a crisp winter morning."

I sat at the edge of the chair, unsure what was going on and ready to pounce at any moment. Surely we weren't going to actually eat breakfast and discuss the weather?

"Please help yourself," said Guardian Skalski, gesturing to the food in front of me. "Would you like coffee or tea?"

I didn't move. My stomach hurt from hunger but I didn't want to get myself poisoned. Instead, I observed as Guardian Skalski piled up his plate with two rolls, two eggs, multiple slices of cheese and a little pyramid of fruit, my stomach growling at me to follow his lead.

The Guardians ignored me as they continued discussing the weather—the amount of clouds in the sky (none, as far as we could see), the temperature, the frost, the humidity. All in the same flat, polite tone which made me want to grab a knife off the table and throw it at someone.

Interesting that they trusted me to have a knife an arm's stretch away.

Trap, trap, trap, chanted my brain. I hoped it was Damian coming to my rescue again. But as the breakfast proceeded and nothing horrible happened—nothing happened at all—my muscles relaxed a bit and I sat more comfortably in the chair.

"It would be good for you to eat something, Miss Potocka," said Guardian Skalski. "You must be starving."

He was right. I was starving and it would have been stupid to bypass a feast like that. When had I last seen so much fresh produce? When had I last had a proper meal? Probably at the solstice.

I ate a couple of berries. They were perfectly ripe, like in the middle of summer, sweet and flavourful. Did the Assembly have magical greenhouses where it was summer all year round?

I waited a few moments but nothing happened. I didn't drop dead, nothing felt out of the ordinary. The Guardians paid me no mind and my stomach kept growling, so I filled up my plate properly this time, with bread and eggs and all kinds of cheeses and as many veggies as I could fit. The Guardian sitting to my right passed me the French press, the only acknowledgement I'd got from them, and I poured myself a cup full of coffee and a glass of orange juice.

I dug in and cherished every bite.

After breakfast, Guardian Skalski led me back to my room. I stared at the door as it locked behind me.

Why hadn't I tried to get out when I had a chance?

Why hadn't I used this knife?

Why hadn't I tried to get to the scriptures?

All I could do now was mentally kick myself as I paced around the room. My stomach was pleasantly full and I kept expecting some unknown poison to kick in. I'd seen what the Assembly had done to Magda, how the poison had slowly consumed her. I'd remembered what Stanisław had done to me with his poisoned cheesecake. Just because there wasn't an immediate effect didn't mean that the food had been safe to eat.

As the sun got low on the horizon, the door opened again and Guardian Skalski invited me to share lunch with the Guardians. We walked down the same way towards the dining room.

"Why?" I asked.

My voice, unused for a long time, came out louder than expected, carrying down the corridor. My heart drummed so loud that I thought Guardian Skalski could hear it, too.

"I'm afraid you'd have to be a little more precise," said the Guardian.

"Why are you pretending to be nice to me? We all know I'm here to face the trial."

"Nobody is pretending anything." Guardian Skalski's voice remained smooth and polite.

"You kidnapped me."

"We saved you from a group of sorcerer anarchists. You've been through a difficult time, Miss Potocka. We're glad to offer you a chance to recover."

We entered the dining room. This time there was only

one other Guardian there, a person who hadn't been there in the morning.

"What a lovely day we had," said Guardian Skalski.

"Indeed. Let's have some soup, shall we?"

Lunch went much like breakfast, only with even less talk. I guess there was nothing more to remark about the weather, especially as it got dark outside. We ate vegetable soup and fresh rolls, and Guardian Skalski locked me back in my room.

I had no idea what was going on. What game were the Guardians playing?

Or, plot twist. What if everyone had been lying to me all along, what if the Assembly wasn't the enemy at all?

No. It wasn't possible. It must have been some trap, some game I didn't understand yet.

I sat on my bed, wondering if they'd call me for supper, too.

And they did. This time it wasn't Guardian Skalski but a new, unfamiliar Guardian whom I hadn't seen before. There were two more Guardians in the dining room. Why weren't any of them back in their cities? It only made sense that they were waiting for my trial, but when was it going to happen?

I was eating my nice sandwich of fresh rye bread with lots of veggies when the Guardian across the table caught my eye and broke the silence:

"I wonder what your aunt told you about us?"

It took me a moment to realize that the Guardian didn't mean Aunt Eliza but Zuzanna. Zuzanna, who hated the Assembly. They hadn't seen her fit for the Guardian's position. They'd murdered her brother. She hated being tied to this system, to have her life depend so heavily on them.

"Not much," I said.

"I doubt she had many good things to say," said another Guardian.

"Poor Miss Kromer," agreed the third Guardian, taking a slow sip from a teacup.

"She's never even been here. Never got a chance. What a shame."

"You removed her from her post," I said.

I didn't want to keep on biting my tongue. I wanted something to happen and for anything to happen, I needed to be in the trial room, near the Twardowski's scriptures, and not dining with the Guardians.

I needed them to put me to trial even though that was the last thing I wanted.

"That's not the way I remember it."

"No, me neither. Miss Kromer accepted what's best for the well-being of the community."

Yeah, no, that didn't sound like Zuzanna. But the Guardians didn't know that I'd witnessed their last Assembly when they'd voted her out and chosen Konrad to step in.

We finished the meal in silence. One of the Guardians led me back to the room but I was over it. I knew the layout of the corridor well enough by now and I'd spotted stairs a few doors down from the dining room. I needed to find the scriptures.

Instead of following the Guardian, I took off running in the opposite direction. Fear squeezed my insides but the Guardian didn't chase me and soon I realized why.

There were no stairs. I halted just in time, catching myself before I fell. I could have sworn I'd seen the stairs but now there was only a stair-sized hole and a ten, maybe twenty-metre drop with more marble tiles at the bottom. I wouldn't have survived the fall.

The Guardian reached me at a leisurely pace. I closed my eyes, wishing to be taken to the trial. Maybe that was the push they'd needed.

"Let's get you to your room, shall we? I'm sure you could use some rest."

ᚠᛜᚱᛏᚤ ᛜᚾᛖ

FOR THE WHOLE NEXT DAY NOTHING HAPPENED. THE door didn't open. I didn't hear a single sound from the outside. I spent a restless day, pacing around the room, and later, when my energy was spent, staring through the window into the river outside.

Was this a punishment for attempting to escape?

Was the Assembly waiting for me to get desperate enough to force the window open and jump? To splatter my brains all over the pavement? That wouldn't have made for a great advertisement for the Assembly. Then again, they didn't need an advertisement. As long as we believed that their system was better than the alternative, they didn't need to be liked, they didn't even need to be good at their job.

The next morning the door to my room opened as if nothing had happened.

"Would you care to join us for breakfast, Miss Potocka?" asked Guardian Skalski.

And so we repeated the breakfast charade again, complete with the careful dissection of the weather—still sunny, a bit more cloudy, and cold. I focused on eating, happy to fill my stomach again.

"I wonder, can you channel the abilities of any sorcerer?" asked one of the three Guardians at the table and I froze, my fork mid-way to my mouth. "Does it depend on how much time you spent with them?"

"I don't know," I said, my heart in my throat.

I put the fork with eggs down on the plate. I couldn't tell them that I couldn't control my magic. They'd probably known it already, so many people had witnessed it and some of my major accidents had happened in Gdańsk. I'd set the fire at the airport. I'd caused an accident on the motorway. But I hadn't felt a single sparkle of magic on my skin ever since my mum had given me the rue potion.

What if it wasn't coming back? What if diving into Węgliszek's iron cauldron had been only a temporary fix?

But finally, finally we were getting to something I knew interested the Assembly a lot.

"You've never tested it?" pressed the Guardian.

Was that the part when we proceeded onto torture and dissecting my powers?

Guardian Skalski chuckled. "Don't scare our guest. She must think we're some monsters that will drag her to the dungeons and experiment on her."

He spread some butter on his piece of bread then leaned conspiringly over the table.

"We aren't sorcerer anarchists, Miss Potocka. Our job is to keep this world and its inhabitants safe."

"We're simply curious," added the other Guardian, biting into a piece of melon. "Rumour has it, you have some extraordinary power at your hands."

My muscles relaxed, a wave of relief sweeping through me. But it wasn't right. I didn't trust the Assembly. I didn't want to relax, I wanted to be on my guard.

I clenched my hand into a fist under the table, but it didn't take long for my fingers to unfold. I listened to the Guardians chat about the weather while I sipped my coffee and ate some more berries.

When I got back to my room, I lay on the bed, staring at the ceiling. The mattress was soft and the ceiling perfectly white, no crack or stain to be found. It seemed like no time had passed when Guardian Skalski came to collect me for late lunch. I went through the motions automatically. The reality felt muted, the stimuli coming in from a great distance. The sounds were hushed and hard to make out, our steps didn't even echo in the corridor, the low light streaming through the windows was less bright. I sat with the Guardians and ate a bowl of beetroot soup without really tasting it, not even hearing their conversation. Then I returned to my room and lay on the bed again.

It was a relief to stop my mind from spinning, to stop

the restless energy begging me to do something, to be able to relax, and not think about anything.

The door to my room opened soon afterwards.

"It's time," said Guardian Skalski.

The stairs were there this time, narrow and wooden, much like in our tenement. It didn't match the rest of the grand building at all. But the reality was blurred, shifting every time I blinked, so I didn't trust my eyes. Was the stair wooden? Or was it marble? We walked downstairs until we reached a large pair of doors with the words *Assembly Room* engraved into them. They opened into a gigantic white room that looked much like the corridors I was used to, with white stone walls and tall ceilings. I blinked at all the whiteness, trying to focus, but quickly let it go. Sixteen Guardians stood in the middle of the room, their red cloaks a stark contrast to the overwhelming whiteness. A nagging thought that I was forgetting something stabbed me, but I swatted it away like an annoying mosquito.

Guardian Skalski led me to stand in front of the Assembly and joined their ranks.

"Wiktoria Maria Potocka, the Assembly has decided to give you a chance to redeem yourself," he said. "Magic is too precious to be wasted and yours is truly unique. You will be able to work closely with the Assembly, repairing the evil that has befallen this world. We have much to fix after what the sorcerer anarchists have done to your poor city and we will need everyone who can prove they are dedicated to the cause."

I stood still, facing the Assembly straight-backed. My mind was pleasantly numb, as if the world was behind a thick veil. Guardian Skalski's words made sense. Of course, they'd want to patch up the world—I wanted to do that, too.

A scream tore through the building, and I flinched but the calmness quickly spread through my body again. My vision was blurry at the edges when two sorcerers dressed in black dragged a kicking and punching figure into the room. They slung her to her knees in front of the Assembly, keeping her down with magic.

I knew her. I recognized that mess of brown hair and pale, almost translucent skin.

Klara.

"What do we have here?" asked one of the Guardians.

It was as if I was watching the scene from a great distance. Everything was a bit muted, unreal, my brain slow to process what was happening. Klara spat on the floor then raised her head to throw a hateful glance at the Guardians towering over her.

"An unregistered sorceress," said Konrad, reading from a piece of paper. "Born in Gdańsk, a niece to a known traitor. Leader of an anarchist group, responsible for overthrowing one of the Guardians and tearing the barrier between the realms. Conspirator against the Assembly, attempting to destabilise our world. Openly attacked other sorcerers, engaging in torture and exposing them to demons. Her actions led to still uncounted deaths of members of our community and regular humans, currently estimated at seven hundred sixty."

"We haven't found a single redeeming quality about her," said another Guardian.

"It's against our duty to allow a person like that to roam the streets and endanger our world," said Guardian Skalski. "The sorceress has shown no remorse, no hope of changing her ways. It is a recommendation of the Assembly to execute her on spot. All in favour?"

All the Guardians raised their hands synchronously.

"Anyone against?"

No hands were raised.

Guardian Skalski approached me with a red cushion. In the middle of it lay a dagger.

"Miss Potocka, this is your chance to prove yourself to the Assembly. Kill the traitor and redeem yourself."

My hand reached for the dagger. I clasped my fingers around the handle and turned to face Klara. I flinched as a wave of terror struck me, but it was pushed back by the overpowering calmness. I walked towards Klara, my ears and brain filled with cotton. The blade in my hand flashed in the candlelight, blinding my eyes. I blinked.

I didn't want to feel calm.

It wasn't real, someone was messing up my emotions.

It wasn't real.

As the thought rooted in my brain, adrenaline flooded

my bloodstream, my muscles tense and ready to pounce, my brain sharp. The Guardians formed a semi-circle around Klara and me. She was on her knees, two sorcerers standing behind her, keeping her down, hoods obscuring their faces.

And there, behind us, on an old wooden table lay a heavy, leather-bound book.

The Twardowski's scriptures.

"Miss Potocka?" asked Guardian Skalski.

I took a step towards Klara, the dagger grasped tightly in my hand. Her eyes widened as she looked at me. She was shaking all over, nothing like her usual self.

I jumped towards the sorcerers behind Klara and my knee struck the first one between the legs. Magic blasted against me, but it was too late and my elbow connected the other sorcerer's stomach. There was a shout as they fell to the floor, but I sprinted towards the scriptures. I clasped the book to my chest just as Konrad got to me. I twisted around, freeing myself from his grasp and brought the knife to his throat. All the fight left him and he went limp, letting me use him as a shield.

"Let me and Klara go, and no one else will get hurt," I said.

What did my mum say? How was I supposed to get out?

"Now, let's take it easy, Miss Potocka," said Guardian Skalski. "No need to do anything rush."

I needed a Guardian's ring or to use the magic inside the scriptures. My magic was still blocked and I didn't exactly have time to leaf through the volume. And I didn't have a free hand to take Konrad's ring off.

Before I could come up with a plan, a cold hand touched my neck and the world went black.

ᚱORTY TᚹO

I WOKE UP FEELING NAUSEOUS, MY HEAD POUNDING. I needed to stop waking up feeling so miserable. My muscles ached and I shivered from cold. I was curled up on bare stone, its rough surface biting into my side. I forced myself to open my eyes and squinted, trying to make out my surroundings. It was dark, but there was enough light for me to see stone floor, walls and ceiling, and metal bars separating my cell from a wider stone corridor.

I'd finally gotten myself into the Assembly's dungeon.

I would have laughed if the situation hadn't been so dire. I had tried to go through with my mum's plan and failed miserably. How had I been supposed to escape a room with so many enemies and with my powers bound? Maybe if I'd known what the scriptures said, what magic they contained, but when was I supposed to study them?

I pulled myself up to a sitting position, wincing as every movement brought a wave of pain to my body. My muscles felt as if they were on fire and I grimaced with an effort to hold myself up.

Light reflected off something on my wrist and I looked down. Two thick, dark pieces of crystal encircled my wrists and for a moment I forgot how to breathe. The crystal looked like the one the Children of Weles had used to force the magic out of me and into the city defences.

I could have been wrong. It could have been just regular shackles that the Assembly used on their prisoners. But I didn't believe it.

It was the same crystal.

It didn't burn yet. I still couldn't feel my magic and it was a blessing. But I knew it was just a question of time.

My breaths came in fast and shallow now, leaving me gasping for air. I'd failed. I'd had one task, my whole reason for existence had come down to collecting and destroying the Twardowski's scriptures and I'd failed. I'd failed, I'd failed, I'd failed. I'd been so close but I hadn't been enough. Maybe if I hadn't wasted time attacking the sorcerers, maybe if I'd tried to convince them to help me, maybe if I'd been better prepared…but it didn't matter now. The Guardians would take over the control of our city, Konrad probably already had everyone in his claws. Maybe the Children of Weles would rebel, maybe Filip would replace Klara as a leader, but would that be any better for our magical community? They would be stuck with the Guardians until magic disappeared from these lands, from this world forever, sucked out by a broken system and human greed. We'd had a chance to restore the magical balance, to start to correct the crimes of our past, but I'd failed.

And now I'd spend my last hours here, in the darkness. The Assembly would experiment on my magic and once their curiosity was sated, they'd kill me.

Breathe, I told myself. *Breathe.*

But did it matter? I was never going to leave the Assembly building.

It was all going to end here.

I balled my trembling hands and pushed them into the sleeves of Artur's hoodie. At least I wasn't wearing the wretched Guardian's cloak.

Steps echoed down the corridor and I braced myself for what was to come. Three Guardians cloaked in red appeared in front of my cell, with two sorcerers in black cloaks following them.

"Look where you got yourself, stupid girl," said Guardian Skalski. "We tried to be nice to you, we gave you a chance, and you wasted it. Your life could have been so easy but you've chosen the difficult path."

I didn't acknowledge him.

Guardian Skalski came closer, his fingers touching the metal bars of my cell, his eyes drilling into mine.

"Apologise. Beg for forgiveness and we can still spare you."

As if. I looked away, fixing my gaze on the stone wall next to me.

The Guardian let out an audible sigh. Metal groaned and I shut my eyes as heavy boots stomped closer to me. Hands clasped around my arms and I flinched but pushed down the instinct to fight. The two sorcerers pulled me up to my feet, my sore muscles protesting at the movement, and then pulled my arms above my head. Before I could understand what was happening, they connected my wrists to the same dark crystal hanging from the low ceiling.

Panic squeezed my stomach and closed around my throat, like a hand squashing my windpipes, and I tried to pull on my hands but it was pointless. I was trapped. This damned crystal was here and the Guardians and sorcerers came to watch as I was about to relive my nightmare.

I pulled on my hands again, then one more time, but the bracelets held firm. My arms were already beginning to feel numb from being over my head. I tried to focus on breathing, but all I could think about was the dark crystal encircling my wrists. I flinched every time I thought I felt a sparkle of magic on my skin. Any moment now it would rush through me towards the crystal. Any moment now my skin would burn again. Any moment now I wouldn't be human anymore but a conduit for magical energy.

Unless my magic was really gone now.

The metal bars clang again and I stiffened, remembering my audience. The sorcerers left my cell and retreated to their positions at the sides of the three Guardians. I forced myself to breathe, to pretend to be calm. I didn't want to give them the satisfaction of seeing my panic.

"We have your community to thank for this idea," said Konrad. "It's a truly inspiring contraption. Granted, it was designed with your particular combination of sorcerer and Guardian power in mind and no one else would be able to use it to power the city defences. But it could have so many other uses, to harvest raw sorcerer power. But that's not what interests us now."

Magic tickled my skin, and I flinched. It intensified quickly, and I became more and more aware of how much magic these dungeons held. It slammed into me, warmth seeping through my skin into my bloodstream, and climbing up my arms towards the crystal shackles. I focused on breathing.

I wouldn't let them see me panic.

"Let's see how much of the Guardian's magic you really have. Let's see how well you could protect the city."

The crystal bracelets on my wrists grew burning hot as magic rushed out of me into the crystal, and I screamed.

I was bent forwards, letting my poor wrists take my weight. My skin felt fried, hot and sparkly with too much magic. I was still shackled to the ceiling and whenever the pressure on my hands grew too much, I'd try standing on my tiptoes to relieve them for a bit. But it never lasted, my muscles screaming in pain, my whole body shaking from magical exertion.

The Guardians stayed at first, looking at me like an animal in the zoo, whispering every once in a while. But they'd grown bored or maybe their curiosity had been satisfied and they wandered away after some time, leaving me shackled, my magic forced viciously out of me, the two sorcerers still guarding my cell.

"What did they offer you to make you serve them?" I asked, trying to distract myself.

The sorcerers remained silent, unmoved. Okay, the Assembly likely wasn't paying them.

"What did they threaten you with?" I tried again. "Would they hurt your families? Hurt you? What did they do? Why would you work for the Assembly?"

The sorcerers didn't acknowledge me.

Soon, I didn't have energy to speak. Artur's hoodie was drenched with sweat, hair clung to my face, my lips were parched, my skin flushed. I felt feverish and my stomach squeezed from hunger. Magic kept flowing through me with no respite.

I don't know how much time passed before the steps echoed down the stone corridor again. The Guardians appeared in front of my cell and I closed my eyes, unwilling to look at them. Having audience made the whole thing so much worse.

The bars to the cell opened and hands closed against my wrists. I winced at the pressure on my oversensitive skin. And, damnit all to hell, yes, I missed Filip's cold hands, and hated myself for it.

The chains released, and I collapsed to the floor, banging my knees painfully on the stone. It didn't matter. The stone was cold and brought at least some relief to my poor skin, even as magic still tickled my skin.

Magic still tickled my skin.

I forced it out with all my might. The two sorcerers were thrown against the wall and I kept them there as I struggled to get to my feet. My muscles wouldn't listen, but I didn't give up. It was my chance.

A burst of magic fought against mine, pushing strongly, but I kept my magic firm. Since Nawia, I finally knew what I was doing. Magic wasn't a useless burden anymore; it was a tool I could use to free myself.

If only my body would cooperate.

After a few attempts, I managed to push myself up to standing, my knees shaking violently. The three Guardians still stood outside the cell, looking at me like an interesting albeit unthreatening animal. I pushed my magic at them, but they didn't even flinch. Instead, the bars trembled and screeched a high metallic tone that made me wince.

A blast of magic pushed me back to the floor and I gritted my teeth. I pushed my magic out harder as I tried to get back up but the magic held me down, the floor shockingly cold in contrast with my burning skin.

Fine. I could do a contest of will. I'd grown up with two competitive cousins.

I kept a firm magical grip on the sorcerers as they fought me. It looked like only one of them was using their powers on me and I wondered why. Clearly one of them was telekinetic, but what was the other one's ability? Were they the one who'd made me lose consciousness with a single touch? Or were they able to block my powers?

"She's pretty entertaining, I'll give her that," said Konrad.

And just like that all fight left me. I cut off my power, letting the sorcerers go. I stayed lying on the cold floor. I just wanted to sleep. I definitely didn't want to entertain a bunch of old men.

Hands closed around my wrist and, to my shock, one of the crystal bracelets released. I sat up fast, my head swimming. One of the sorcerers left the cell and shut the bars behind them. The other one stayed and I looked up at them as they slowly clasped the bracelet around their wrist.

What the—

I gasped as a strange, unfamiliar magic flowed into me, making my skin burn with renewed vigour. What the fresh hell was this new form of torture?

"There's one part of your magic that is of particular interest to the Assemby," said Guardian Skalski. "You might remember us asking about your channelling abilities. You could have answered then but you've chosen to ignore us, so we had to find another way to satisfy our curiosity. It isn't a perfect experiment, but it should give us a clear idea of what is possible and, more importantly, how much control we could have over your powers."

More magic pushed at me and I fought against the instinct to fall back to the floor, to get closer to the cold stone as my skin burned. I forced myself to stay kneeling, my eyes locked on the other sorcerer.

Seriously, what did they threaten them with?

The magical pressure grew, and I couldn't hold the magic in anymore. I let it out, aiming for the sorcerer.

Only it wasn't a telekinetic blast but an arrow of pure fire that flew at them.

I screamed, horror closing around my throat. But the sorcerer caught the fire in their hands, shaped it into a small ball and then squashed it.

I hadn't hurt them. I hadn't burned them.

I trembled all over, more magic begging for release as I struggled to keep it in. Not fire. Anything but fire.

I glanced at the Guardians and noticed wide smiles on their faces. I looked away. I didn't want to see how I was living up to their expectations.

If they could use me as conduit for any power…I'd be a perfect weapon. The Assembly's dream. They wouldn't have to kill me, they'd use me for as long as they could.

"Mateusz," said Guardian Skalski.

The sorcerer—Mateusz—made fire appear out of nowhere and climb his arm. My magic pushed more and more and I squeezed my eyes as if that could help me keep it contained, but then it erupted, mimicking Mateusz. Fire climbed my arm, not burning, but the additional heat on my overstimulated skin was too painful to bear.

"Wonderful," said Guardian Skalski.

Mateusz extinguished the fire on his arm and raised his hands up. A fireball appeared between his palms, growing as he moved his arms apart.

My arms didn't move but magic fled from me, forming the fireball. I stared at it, terrified but transfixed, as it grew in a perfect imitation of Mateusz's fire.

"That's enough for now," said Guardian Skalski. "Oh, we will have so much use for this sort of power."

Mateusz took off his bracelet and reached for my arm. I threw one last, defiant blast of power at him and he stumbled, the crystal falling from his hand. He tried to catch it but it fell to the floor, shattering into pieces.

"Stupid girl," murmured Konrad.

Mateusz bent down to collect the pieces but I threw my power out again, forcing him back. The pieces of crystal scattered around. He threw me a furious look as he picked up the bigger pieces but I kept blasting my power out and out, interrupting him, until my power was suddenly cut off, the fire on my skin dying.

I almost sighed in relief but I didn't want the Guardians to know that this punishment was more of a reward to me.

Mateusz collected as many pieces of crystal as he could find before the other sorcerer let him out of the cell. Before closing it, he threw in a bottle of water and an energy bar. They clattered to the floor next to me.

"Get some rest," said Guardian Skalski. "I'd suggest using this time to think about your attitude. Trust me, cooperating will be much better for you."

FORTY THREE

I DOWNED A BOTTLE OF WATER, DEVOURED THE ENERGY bar and fell into a restless, feverish sleep. The stones bit painfully into my hypersensitive skin, each scratch reverberating through my entire body. When sleep abandoned me for good, I was still exhausted, so I lay on my side, trying not to move and wondering when the Guardians would be back.

I tried to break the bracelet that still encircled my wrist but I didn't have enough energy to slam it against the stone hard enough. Or maybe it was the fear of getting hurt even more that stopped me from using my full strength. I gritted my teeth as the crystal dug into my skin but it had to stay there for now.

Something glimmered on the ground. I moved my head a little to get a better look and hissed in pain as the skin on my neck burned.

It was a piece of broken crystal. No bigger than my pinkie's fingernail, but maybe large enough to be usable. I glanced at the corridor but I was alone. I gnashed my teeth as I extended my arm and grasped the piece of crystal. I put it in my hoodie's pocket.

Forever passed until the steps echoed down the corridor. I'd managed to drift off again, but the heavy stomping woke me up, my body already tensing and bracing for more abuse.

The three Guardians and two sorcerers appeared by the bars to my cell again.

"It's still not too late to beg for forgiveness," said Guardian Skalski.

There were few people who awoke such unabashed hatred in me. What sort of person gets off on making others powerless? On ripping away their dignity, their humanity?

I threw him a hateful look.

"So be it," he said.

The door to the cell opened and the sorcerers got in. I let them haul me to my feet and pull my right hand that still had the bracelet on to the ceiling and shackle it to the crystal construction.

"I guess we'll see if one bracelet works as well as two did," said Konrad.

Slowly, I became more aware of magic. I bit my lip to not scream as heat rose on my already irritated skin, magic tickling all over, exploding in millions of tiny electric charges. The pressure grew until a steady flow of warmth and electricity flew from all over my skin to the single shackle in the ceiling.

Just like the last time, the Guardians stayed for some time, watching me struggle and squirm, waiting for the screams to start. I closed my eyes so I wouldn't have to see them, trying to focus on breathing.

I wouldn't give them a show. Not this time.

My wrist burned, my insides on fire, and I gnashed my teeth but I couldn't stop the tears stinging my eyes. I would have wiped them with my free hand but I didn't want the draw the Guardians' attention. Maybe they hadn't noticed.

I wanted to disappear. I wanted to scratch off my skin. It was hard enough being degraded to an energy conduit, but it was much harder with an audience. Maybe the Children of Weles hadn't been so bad after all. Even Filip had never stayed to watch me suffer.

After an eternity, steps echoed down the corridor and I breathed more easily. I dared to open my eyes and noticed that the Guardians had left. The two sorcerers remained, like before. One of them stared at me wide-eyed. Good. It was good to know that they were terrified of what the Assembly could do.

"I will destroy the Assembly," I said. "That's why I'm here. And I can really do it. I'm not asking for your help, I know it's a huge risk. But next time I have a chance to get to the scriptures, just give me time."

They could tattle to the Guardians, but it wasn't like any of it was a secret. The Assembly must have noticed that the first thing I'd run for were the Twardowski's scriptures.

The sorcerers ignored me, which was for the best.

Headache was building just under my skull, my energy levels depleting quickly as magic streamed through me relentlessly, burning my skin. I tried to use my free hand to relieve the pressure on the arm stretched over my head but nothing was helping. It was impossible to get comfortable shackled to the ceiling and the free hand was throwing me off balance.

I closed my eyes and focused on not throwing up.

Hours seemed to pass before the Guardians returned. Just like the previous day, they made the sorcerers unshackle me, but today they didn't have the extra bracelet to play with my magic. I collapsed to the floor enjoying the coldness of the stones.

I knew what I had to do next. I opened my mouth but nothing came out. I couldn't force myself to speak.

"Anything to say?" asked Guardian Skalski.

No words came. I sat there numbly, staring at my knees, unable to speak. I knew I needed to make my move but I couldn't force myself to plead with them.

"Very well," said Guardian Skalski, the pleasure in his voice making the little hair on my neck rise. "You destroyed our bracelet so we had to come up with a new idea to test your magic. Let's see how fast you can channel others without that extra help."

The sorcerers left the cell and the bars clang shut. And then the room was on fire.

I screamed as the fire surrounded me, fast. It wasn't *real* fire, it wouldn't have spread on bare stone, but the oppressive heat felt real enough. Smoke rose fast and I put my trembling elbow against my mouth and nose, coughing. My eyes teared up as I forced myself to my feet, but there was nowhere to run, the fire was surrounding me fast, licking my feet.

I didn't want to give Guardians a show but I didn't want to die, either. Magic broke out of me, squashing the flames, forcing them into corners and then stifling them to nothing. It felt good to use the magic that had been rushing through me for hours. To take control.

Konrad clapped.

"Impressive," said Guardian Skalski.

"Burning witches is very 1600s," I said before I could bite my tongue. I erupted into another coughing fit, my lungs begging for fresh air.

"I see you still have fight in you. Which is fortunate because we have another guest here."

The Guardians parted, leaving the view of the corridor open for me to see. I blinked, trying to clear my teary vision as steps sounded on the corridor. I braced myself for a new magic to fight as two—no, three—figures approached. Two sorcerers clad in black cloaks with a slumped person in-between them, blonde hair stuck to their face.

My heart stopped.

No.

No, no, no, no, no.

"I'd heard stories about bonds like yours but I've never witnessed it," mused Guardian Skalski. "There are limitless possibilities. Tell me, is it true that you can feel what the other feels?"

"No. Please, don't do that. Not—"

Guardian Skalski raised a hand. Mateusz turned towards Artur and touched his arm. A scream rung down the corridor as Artur buckled. Piercing pain shot down my arm but I bit my lip to stop myself from reacting, staring terrified at the scene in front of me. Mateusz retreated his hand and Artur looked around, his eyes wide open. Then his eyes met mine.

"Wiki," he said.

One of the sorcerers holding Artur elbowed him in the stomach. I shouted as Artur bent over.

"Please," I said, hating myself for saying this word. "No more."

"What was that?" asked Guardian Skalski. "I didn't hear."

I gritted my teeth but I forced myself to speak louder.

"Please," I repeated, my voice cracking. "Please, just stop."

"Ah, Miss Potocka. But the fun is only beginning."

FORTY FOUR

They took Artur further down the corridor and locked him in another cell. I could feel his presence loud and clear through my bond, even if I couldn't see him.

I didn't sleep.

I sat on the cold stones hugging my knees to my chest, staring at the corridor. The two sorcerers who'd brought Artur remained to guard us. I could barely breathe, frozen with fear. Physical pain had been hard enough to bear. But this new torture, knowing that they had Artur, knowing they knew about our bond and would use it against us, was unbearable.

How on Earth were we going to get out?

Hours dragged endlessly as my mind spun and spun. I flinched at every small sound. One of the sorcerers guarding us picked up on it and started startling me on purpose—a loud stamp here, a clang against the bars there. I jumped every single time and was too jittery to be upset about it.

It took forever but at the same time no time at all for the Guardians to return.

"Please," I said upon seeing Guardian Skalski. "Please. I'll do anything, just let Artur go."

"You see, Miss Potocka, the problem is that we have a bit of a trust issue here. You've proven to be quite duplicitous. Your word isn't good enough."

"Please, don't."

Guardian Skalski waved a hand and the sorcerers moved down the corridor. I flattened myself against the bars, straining to see, but Artur's cell was out of my range of vision. Moments later a muffled shout carried down the corridor, together with a wave of pain. I squeezed the bars harder and closed my eyes. Another wave of sympathetic pain rolled over my body and I collapsed to the floor, tears running down my cheeks.

"Are you ready to cooperate now?" asked Guardian Skalski.

I wasn't dragged to the Assembly Room this time. Instead, Mateusz and another sorcerer led me a couple of cells down. They entered with me and locked the bars behind. In front of us, Klara lay curled on the floor, her hair messy and her clothes stained. She startled awake and sat up, her narrowed eyes trained on me.

A couple of moments later, another pair of sorcerers dragged Artur close enough so that he could have a good look at what was about to happen. His eyes were wide, face pale, and bottom lip split but I'd never been happier to see anyone else. He was standing on his own so they couldn't have hurt him as badly as I'd feared.

"The Assembly recognises your unique power and has decided to give you one more chance," said Guardian Skalski. "Wiktoria Maria Potocka, kill the traitor to prove your loyalty to the Assembly."

Mateusz handed me a dagger that I'd held before. I stared at it, frozen. I didn't want to use it against another sorceress and even if I did, I was still locked inside the cell. In my hoodie pocket, I had a shard of the bracelet, a shard that could hopefully allow me to channel someone else's powers without fail—but no matter whom I chose, the sorcerers and Guardians on the other side would have enough time to hurt Artur.

If I refused, the torture would go on. And chances were that I would eventually break and do anything the Assembly wanted. Or maybe their brainwashing magic would work better on me.

The dagger gleamed in the light of the sconces on the wall.

I didn't reach for it.

I'd been wrong. I wouldn't do anything to stop it. I wouldn't kill another person, not even Klara.

I'm sorry, I said telepathically. *I just can't do it.*

More pain came. The Guardians weren't happy that I'd denied them again. They focused on Artur, and Guardian Skalski made sure that I knew it was all my fault and it all could have been avoided. I knew he was right so I didn't try to distract myself and fixated on Artur's pain.

Later, I lay curled on my side, squeezing Artur's amulet, unable to sleep again. I was startled by a voice in my head:

Are you okay? asked Artur.

I stifled a burst of hysterical laughter. In what scenario would I be okay right now?

I'm sorry, I said. *I could have stopped it.*

I won't let you apologise for not killing someone, little fox.

Even someone who repeatedly hurt us?

Do you believe that people are fundamentally good or bad? Do you think we're unable to change and can be condemned like that? And even if you'd killed her—do you really think that would have been it and they would have let us walk away? If they discovered that they can use me to motivate you to murder someone, can you imagine what they would have asked you to do next? Wiki, you know what sort of power you have and they must realize it too, by now. It wouldn't have ended there.

They hurt you because of me.

They hurt me because they're cruel bastards who enjoy hurting others. And they would have done it regardless of anything you would or wouldn't do.

I sniffled and wiped at my eyes.

What happened? I asked. *How did they catch you?*

It was stupid. We were staying in Gdańsk, waiting for you to pull this impossible heist. I was going mad knowing something went seriously wrong, that your mum's plan was…ambitious to begin with, and that they were hurting you. We had a fight and I went outside to cool off and they got me.

Shit. So…it's not some sort of silly rescue attempt?

I wish.

Well, I don't, that would have been really stupid. But I'm sorry.

The door to the cells creaked open and I froze. No, it was too soon. They'd barely let us rest.

But why would they let us rest if they planned on breaking me?

We repeated the charade twice more. Two more times I was dragged to Klara's cell and offered a chance to kill her and end it all. Twice more I denied. Twice more, Artur paid for my refusal, while the Guardians kept saying how easy and comfortable my life could be if I just listened. How they'd take care of everything, how all will be well. But I didn't listen.

Do you know what I'd like now? asked Artur one night.

To not be tortured by the de facto leaders of the magical community because your queer-platonic partner won't murder someone to save you?

We've been through that. If you do it, it will never end. And what I'd really like is to be on a warm, summer meadow, to feel the magic flow gently from the Earth. To feel the sun on my skin.

I'm sorry.

You're not keeping me here, little fox. And no, murdering Klara wouldn't have changed that. Tell me what you'd like now.

My mind was blank. I didn't believe we'd ever see the outside world unless I did the very thing that Artur didn't want me to do.

I want it all to be over, I said. I couldn't think of anything else.

Artur was silent for so long that I thought he'd fallen asleep.

I slept with Damian, he said.

I smiled, surprising myself that I was still able to feel anything beyond fear and pain.

How was it?

Good? I mean, thanks to our bond I can almost understand why sex is such a big deal to some people.

I'm glad you could experience it. And it doesn't seem like you're having a bi-crisis?

No, thanks. Ace crisis was hard enough. Besides, I thought I might be bi long before I knew that ace was even an option. I guess biromantic ace has a nice ring to it?

It does. It...never would have worked between the two of us, right? I mean sex. Not that I think that our relationship isn't awesome but...

I know what you mean. And I don't think so, either. Or it would have been very different.

Is it bad if that's what I really like about us?

Not at all. I like it, too. And just in case you're worried, unless it's something that you want, it doesn't have to change. That was about Damian, not about us. I'm still very much on the team "we can watch a film or we can have sex, it doesn't really matter."

I think—I started, ready to share my thoughts about my own potential aroaceness when steps echoed down the dungeon. I closed my eyes and took a deep breath, resigned to relive the same nightmare.

"Let's go," said Guardian Skalski. "The Assembly is ready for the trial."

I was in the Assembly Room again, squinting at the light coming through the tall windows. Mateusz and another sorcerer held me between them and threw me to my knees in front of the Guardians. On the other side of the room, two more sorcerers guarded Artur. In between the two of us kneeled Klara, also fully guarded. The Guardians towered over us in a semi-circle like a red sea.

At least the Twardowski's scriptures were still here. Apparently, the Assembly's ego was more important than security.

Good. At least even in the darkest moment, I could count on the egos of white cis men.

"We gather here today to stand trial to two members of the magical community guilty of highest treason against the magical world," started Konrad, addressing the Assembly. "In front of us we have an unregistered hybrid of a highly dangerous and illegal mixture of Guardian and sorcerer blood. Daughter of known insurgents, her father was executed by the Assembly eighteen years ago for his unspeakable crimes against the community. She followed in her parents' footsteps and she's guilty of the murder of Guardian Stanisław Kromer in a plot to destroy the magical protections in the area. Together with her fellow sorcerer here, they've destroyed the protections over an entire territory, exposing hundreds of thousands of people to demonic attacks and starvation. In doing so, they revealed the existence of magic to the greater population, undoing hundreds of years of work to protect our community. They are also responsible for insurgent attacks in Gdańsk, including starting fire at the airport and causing traffic accidents on the motorway. Despite numerous chances to correct their way and use their magic in a productive manner, they have refused to change or show remorse. They represent the worst in the magical community and serve as a warning for what happens when magic isn't controlled."

"We haven't found a single redeeming quality about them," said another Guardian, repeating the script from Klara's trial. I almost didn't hear him, overwhelmed by my list of crimes, blood roaring in my ears.

"It's against our duty to allow people like them to roam the streets and endanger our world," said Guardian Skalski. "The sorcerers have shown no remorse, no hope of changing their ways. It is a recommendation of the Assembly to execute them on spot. All in favour?"

All the Guardians raised their hands.

Faced with a list of everything we'd done, I almost agreed with them. Or I would have, if I'd been there alone. But Artur was kneeling across the room from me and I could feel the absolute terror squeezing his insides.

"Klara Elżbieta Nowacka," said Guardian Skalski, approaching her with a pillow holding a dagger. "The Assembly has decided to give you a chance to redeem yourself. Kill the traitors, prove your loyalty to the Assembly, and your sentence will be lifted."

Fear squeezed my throat like Filip's icy hand as Klara accepted the dagger. No. No, no, no. She stood up and approached me. Sharp pain erupted on my skull as one of the sorcerers guarding me pulled on my hair to tilt my head back and expose my throat. Klara's knife gleamed in the candlelight.

The door to the Assembly room opened and Klara's hand faltered.

"How dare—" started Guardian Skalski, but he was interrupted by a sorcerer who just entered.

"Apologies to the Assembly. But the eighteenth Guardian just used the right of blood to enter the building and is demanding to join the proceedings."

FORTY FIVE

Zuzanna strode into the Assembly Room, her steps echoing in the great hall. She wore her beet red cloak and the Guardian's ring gleamed on her finger. The Children of Weles had taken it from me after my mock fealty, so I didn't know how Zuzanna had recovered it. She squeezed the hand with the ring on a bloodied tissue and more blood dripped to the white marble floor as she walked but she paid it no mind.

What was she doing here? How did she get here?

Was her presence a good omen? Was it our chance to get out?

"It has come to my attention that the Assembly has been holding trials despite not being complete," said Zuzanna, her voice cold and loud. "There are only seventeen of you here."

The sorcerer behind me released his hold and Klara lowered the knife, their eyes trained on Zuzanna. I took a deep breath. I couldn't be distracted. I needed to get the Twardowski scriptures and get us out of here.

I put my hands in the pocket of my hoodie. The shard of the crystal bracelet was still there.

"Miss Kromer, you have been formally dismissed from your position in November last year," said Konrad. "You have been notified of that fact. You yourself have given up your Guardianship and made no attempt to restore protections in your area after the breach. Indeed, no one has heard from you since the sky had broken, which leads the Assembly to the conclusion that you've been at least partially responsible for it. You are no longer a member of the Assembly and you are not permitted to partake in the proceedings."

"If that's true, how did I enter this building?" challenged Zuzanna.

"We are all sorcerers," I whispered. Klara glanced at me. "And we can all be free."

I flung myself forward, tackling her to the floor. The dagger fell from her grip with a loud clang and skidded across the floor. I didn't go after it. Instead, I dropped the piece of crystal in Klara's hand.

"Don't let it go," I said.

I gambled everything on a hunch that her desperation to escape would be greater than her hatred towards me. She was our only chance. It had to work.

Strong hands wrapped around my arms and heaved me off Klara. I struggled, but they held me firmly.

Klara looked at me wide-eyed. After a moment, she gave me a small nod. She squeezed her hand around the crystal before anyone else could notice it.

"I'm really tired of your insolence," said Guardian Skalski, shaking his head. "Let's stop this foolishness once and for all. Dear Guardian Assembly. Can we agree that Zuzanna Kromer, the former Guardian of Bydgoszcz, is guilty of jeopardizing the safety of the realms, which resulted in ripping her territory away from Jawia for the duration of six weeks? Have we all witnessed her repetitive refusal to accept help in guarding her territory? Have we all witnessed her outrageous claims against other members of the Assembly? Do we find her guilty?"

All Guardians raised their hands.

"Then it is agreed. Ewo, if I could ask for your assistance."

Guardian Skalski nodded at a sorceress standing by the door. Before I could understand what was happening, reality blurred, and my mind slowed. Everything around was fuzzy and the sounds seemed to come from a great distance. Hands pulled me towards the centre of the room, but my body didn't feel mine, my steps awkward and our steps too loud in the big room. I was barely aware that Artur, Zuzanna, and Klara joined me there, surrounded by sorcerers and Guardians.

"There's a time-honoured tradition of consequences for magic-users who can't abide by the common laws," said

Guardian Skalski, his words jumbled in my brain. "We haven't had to resort to it since the treason of Igor Kromer. Perhaps it's only fitting that his sister and daughter will meet a similar end."

Something rough wound around my arms and then legs. Artur, Zuzanna, Klara, and I were so close now that we were almost leaning on each other. Strong, familiar smell filled the air. My muscles still felt weak, out of my control, but the fog in my mind lifted.

Artur, Zuzanna, Klara, and I were bound together, standing in a puddle of petrol. I yanked on the bonds but the others stood still and I didn't have the energy to move all of us. They must have still been under an influence of whatever magic was at work here.

"Miss Potocka, you will have the honour of being the executioner," said Guardian Skalski.

Foreign magic pushed on mine, trying to coax it up. Terror squeezed my heart and I trembled. I knew what they were trying to do. Just a spark would be enough for us to burn. More magic pushed on mine and I fought against it with all I had, but the Assembly knew my magic too well, had too many ways to control it. It was only a matter of time before I lost.

I'm sorry, I said telepathically, squeezing my eyes shut. I didn't want to see what was about to happen.

I hoped Artur could hear me. Or maybe not. Maybe it was a small mercy that he wouldn't be fully aware of burning alive.

Then, with a powerful crush, a full-length window exploded into a thousand pieces. Screams erupted as a demon with powerful red and black wings dove inside and flew straight towards us. Aysun grabbed my jumper, bringing us eye to eye, hers flashing red. My magic stilled. The ropes around us unwound as I was lifted into air by some invisible force.

"It's not her fault!" shouted Zuzanna in English. "Someone else is controlling her magic."

I dropped to the floor, petrol splashing around, its stench overwhelming. Artur pulled me into his arms and I clung to him, trembling.

Aysun was here. Of course, she was. Of course, she'd come to save Zuzanna.

Aysun dove for the Guardians but before she could reach them, a ring of fire erupted around us sealing us off. Fire roared and I jumped away from the petrol, dragging Artur with me, but our shoes were covered in it. Not only shoes—there were splashes of petrol on my dirty, worn-out jeans as well.

I was shaking, magic tickling my skin. The flames shot up all the way to the high ceiling, leaving us no room to escape, not even with Aysun's wings. Sweat poured down my face but all I could think about was staying away from the fire. If so much as a spark flew in our direction, we'd erupt in flames, just like the Guardians wanted. I didn't know what to do. Water? No, maybe not. How does one stop a petrol fire? With a blanket? A fire extinguisher? It was something I was supposed to know. Why didn't I know it? We were going to die because I didn't know this simple thing that people should know, how—

Artur squeezed my shoulders, magic tickling between us, grounding me. I squeezed his hand. At least I got to enjoy our bond one more time before it was over.

Aysun was looking at the fire, as if hoping to find a weak spot. She sheltered Zuzanna with her wings and that stirred my memory.

She'd used my magic to save us before.

"Please stop it," I said in English to Aysun, taking off my amulet.

Aysun turned to me, her red eyes meeting mine. I nodded my consent again and my brain calmed, my frantic thoughts stilling. All I could see were Aysun's red eyes as her magic took hold of me. My magic pushed on me again and I let it free. Within seconds, the flames were smothered.

A line of sorcerers stood between the Assembly and us. My magic stifled and small flames appeared around us again. But Aysun wouldn't have that. She flew towards the sorcerers and, with one gaze, lifted all seven of them off the ground. Screams erupted as the sorcerers threw their arms wildly around, as if trying to swim in the air.

"We're on the same side," said Artur, stepping towards them. "Just let us go and it all can be over once and for all."

I knew what he was doing but we didn't have time for it. It was our one shot to get out of here. If we played our cards right, the Guardians won't be able to hurt anyone again. The sorcerers in their service would be free.

We need the scriptures. Now.

A clapping sound echoed down the hall. I turned to look at Guardian Skalski, blood roaring in my ears.

"What a beautiful performance," he said. "I'm pretty amazed, Miss Potocka, it's been a while since I've met a sorcerer half as entertaining as yourself."

I fisted my hands and stared him in the eye. I could make him suffer, like he'd made us. I could make him cry and beg. I could make him burn. Magic sparkled on my skin, begging for release.

"Your reign is over," I said. "Now, sleep."

The Guardians fell to the ground in a mass of red cloaks.

A wave of sympathetic pain blinded me and, for a second, I thought that using magic hurt again. Then pain faded and I my mind cleared. I whipped around. Artur was crumbled on the floor, the Twardowski's scriptures next to him.

I sprinted to him, throwing myself to the floor. My hands were shaking, my heart pounding, and I murmured protective spells under my breath. He was breathing.

The Guardians must have known I'd try to get to the scriptures again and put protections around them.

"Wiktoria!" shouted Zuzanna.

My head jerked up just in time to catch a ring she threw at me with my magic. I put it on my finger and wrapped my arms around Artur, Twardowski's scriptures squished between us. I caught Klara's eye across the room and pulled on her magic, shadows growing around us. This time when the shadows reached for me, I welcomed their ice-cold embrace.

The last thing I saw was Zuzanna flying off with Aysun.

FORTY SIX

SEA SOUGHED, THE WAVES BEAT LEISURELY AGAINST the shore. It was dark, but the Gdańsk's skyline glimmered on the horizon in a thousand colourful lights, reflecting in the sea. I kneeled in the sand, welcoming the cold, cold wind on my skin. My fingers squeezed the Twardowski's scriptures to my chest. Artur lay in the sand next to me and I leaned over him. He was still breathing and I couldn't see anything wrong with him—no blood or unnaturally bent limbs. The bond between us was quiet and it didn't seem like he was in pain.

I shook his shoulder, but he didn't react.

There was a soft thump and I flinched, magic blasting out. Klara screamed.

"Sorry," I said. "You startled me."

"Why did you get me out?" she asked.

I shrugged. It wasn't like I would have left her at the Assembly's mercy.

"You didn't kill me," Klara stated the obvious. "Why?"

"Just because I don't like you, doesn't mean I will murder you in cold blood."

"I almost did."

"I know. You also kept me prisoner and tortured me. You used my magic against my will. You turned half of my community into stone. You kidnapped Artur and had him tortured by empaths. You've done so many horrible, inexcusable things. But it doesn't mean I'd kill you."

Klara shook her head.

"A thank you would have sufficed," I murmured, but Klara didn't answer.

I didn't have energy to fight with her. I needed to know what was wrong with Artur and how to help him. I needed to find Karina and Damian. I hoped they were still in Gdańsk, I hoped they hadn't done anything stupid.

I clasped Artur's right hand. I didn't know if it would work, but I focused on the magical warmth of the ace ring he'd got from Damian. I reached out through the bond.

We're on the beach in Jelitkowo, I thought over and over, hoping Damian could hear.

"Are you planning to stay here and wait for the Assembly to catch you again or the sirens to eat you?" asked Klara.

"You're free to go," I said. "Honestly, I don't ever want to see you again. Hitchhike to Croatia or build yourself a hut in Bieszczady, I don't care. Go and enjoy your life but stay out of my way."

Klara was silent for a moment, then she nodded. She threw me one last look, then her silhouette disappeared in the shadows again.

I was left alone on the beach with an unconscious Artur, wind howling in my ears, magic sparkling on my skin. It hurt, my skin feeling overly stretched and sensitive even to the lightest touch, but I didn't hate it anymore. I'd grown into that power and I liked the feel of it. If anyone approached us now, a demon or a Guardian, my powers would keep us safe. Which was good because with all the magic flowing through me, I was like a magical beacon.

I wrapped my arms around myself, squeezing the Twardowski's scriptures to my chest as I shivered in the cold. My jacket had stayed at the Assembly, but at least I had Artur's hoodie. Artur also wearing just a jumper. But then an idea budded in my head. I focused on my link to Damian and thought about feeling warm. Magic listened immediately, my skin warming up enough to keep me comfortable. I grabbed Artur's hand and coaxed the warmth to flow into him.

Encouraged, I played on. I coaxed the wind to slow down around me. I still wanted to feel it, I wanted to know I was outside, facing the elements, but it didn't need to blast into me with such force.

The wind around us slowed.

What else could I do? I looked down at Artur, but I didn't know anyone with healing magic. I didn't want to risk hurting him. Instead, I focused on our bond and imagined Arrow tearing across the sky towards me. I smiled, seeing the illusion of my baby dragon, but my eyes grew wet quickly, so I wished the illusion away.

I blinked fast and took a deep breath. I needed to hold myself together just a bit longer.

Magic sparkled stronger on my skin, encouraging me to use it. I stared at the sea in front of me. Could I control water? I knew Dawid had elemental powers but I'd never seen him control water. It had been a long while since I'd seen him, but I was willing to try.

I focused on the sea, let its soughing fill my ears. My heartbeat slowed to match the waves. On an exhale, I coaxed the water up. It started off with a tiny stream, but I pulled and pulled until a wave as tall as me rose suspended in front of me, waiting for my next move. Magic danced on my skin and filled my lungs as I stared, taking the wave in, the full extent of my power slamming into me.

I could do anything.

No one would hurt us again.

I let the water gently down and the sea soughed again.

"Wiki!" shouted Karina.

I spun around to see two figures running towards us across the sand, the bond firing up between us.

"What happened?" Damian asked, kneeling next to Artur. He leaned over him to check on his breathing, his hand checking for the pulse.

"I don't know." I kneeled next to him. "I think there

were some protections around the Twardowski's scriptures. I felt his pain before he blacked out."

Damian pulled out a familiar golden potion from his pocket. He cradled Artur's head and poured a little into his mouth. After a couple of tense moments, Artur coughed. He blinked a couple of times, then looked disoriented around.

"We got out," he said.

I didn't respond, only squeezed him close to me.

"Good, at least we didn't have to resort to true love's kiss," said Damian, putting his arms around us.

Karina joined in and for a few long moments we were just a tangle of arms and legs, pulled together close, magic jumping happily between us. I was torn between feeling grateful that we were all together again and feeling overwhelmed by all the magic on my still oversensitive skin.

Soon, I promised myself. I'd be able to enjoy our bond soon enough.

"I still have that," I said, lifting my left hand. The black crystal bracelet gleamed on my wrist and I couldn't stand it a second more.

"Can I?" asked Damian.

I nodded and he closed his hands around my wrist, over the bracelet. I flinched as it heated up, but then there was a crunch and the crystal broke. Damian took the pieces and put them in his pocket.

"I don't trust them to just lie out here," he said.

Then he swung down his backpack and took out a familiar jar of rosemary poultice. He smeared a thick layer around my wrists, magic sparkling between us. Gods, I hoped he hadn't felt what was happening to us at the Assembly. I couldn't feel him. I hoped he hadn't been exposed to all of that.

Damian's fingers didn't linger—he either noticed my reluctance to touch or he was back to his no-nonsense self. Then he moved over to help Artur, spreading the poultice on his bruises.

I felt what they did to you, said Damian, and it took me a moment to realize he spoke to me telepathically. My eyes widened.

Our bond is growing closer, I said.

Otherwise we wouldn't be here. Let's only imagine what we'll be able to do years from now.

I looked up at Artur and Karina. Years. It was almost all over and we had a future to look forward to.

"Let's make the Assembly pay," I said.

We sat in Aunt Eliza's car in the parking lot, eating veggie kebabs and sharing a huge bag of fries, and reading the Twardowski's scriptures. They started with an account of the deal between Twardowski and a devil, followed by pages upon pages of different magical rituals Twardowski had tried—from simple healing magic to summoning the ghost of a dead queen and restoring youth to our city's mayor. Details of entrapping and channelling other's magic. Lists of sorcerers with abilities that had caught Twardowski's interest.

Payment notes for magic performed for others, including king Sigismund II Augustus. Things that normally would have been fascinating to learn but I was jittery to just get things over with.

But we couldn't be too careful.

Yes, Mum had said that we needed to destroy the scriptures. And it wasn't that I didn't trust her—that was a complicated issue—but it'd been nineteen years since she'd read the scriptures, before the Assembly had taken them away. We had one chance to get it right and after the fiasco with Laura's ritual, we weren't taking any chances.

"Here it is," said Karina.

We cuddled closer together, reading the last page in the scriptures. It was written in different handwriting than the previous ones. I squinted, trying to make sense of the loopy handwriting.

"It's Latin," said Damian. "To no one's surprise."

"Thankfully the internet works," said Karina, taking a picture of the last page with Google Lens.

The translation appeared on her screen.

"Looks straightforward enough," said Damian. "And confirms what we already know. Can I lead the ritual?"

We walked back to the beach and went through the familiar motions of preparing the ritual. We drew the circle in the sand, its edge touching the sea, and prepared the fire torch on the other side. When it was done, I placed the Twardowski's scriptures in the middle. We stood at the edge of the circle, holding hands.

Magic sparkled stronger between us and I focused on our bond, cherishing it.

"Gods and demons, we call on you to listen," said Damian. Warm magic washed over me and I squeezed his and Karina's hands harder. "Sława Wam. Weles, god of oaths, god of magic, we're here thanks to you and we ask you to bear witness to our ritual. We stand before you as the Circle of Four to right the wrongs of the past. We are here to return the knowledge that wasn't for the humans to take and to restore the magical balance. It should have never been up to humans to make decisions that impact the worlds that we all inhabit. We are here to even the balance once more."

Karina took out the fire torch. Together, all four of us, closed our hands around it and we touched the flame to the scriptures.

"With this sacred fire, we release the past," said Karina. "The time of the Guardians is over. Let the magical balance be restored."

The Twardowski's scriptures burst into flames, and Karina stuck the fire torch back in the sand. We watched the volume burn, magic creeping on my skin. And then the smoke rose, stinging my eyes. I coughed and blinked and when I opened my eyes again, my heart caught in my throat because I was standing at the edge of the circle alone.

No, not alone. There was another figure standing across from me. I couldn't fully make it out through the smoke but

I recognized the bull's horns on the god's head.

Weles.

A shiver ran down my spine, and I bowed before the god of magic.

The god walked towards me and images flashed in my mind. Weles distracting Perun so I could reach the firebird, Weles sending Arrow to catch me when I fell from the oak tree, Weles telling me to go to Nawia and allowing Karina and me to wander through his land, retaining our human bodies, and return to Jawia afterwards. We would have never made it this far without the god's help.

"Thank you," I said. "Um, Sława Ci."

But then I saw more images. Guardians, cloaked in red, closing the Jawia from Nawia. They stood in a circle on a beach at night, four of them, not unlike us, holding their hands to the sky and chanting in Latin. A group of sorcerers, clad in black, kneeled in front of them, their heads bowed. One of the Guardians, a short, wide-shouldered man with brown hair, held a thick volume of the Twardowski's scriptures and read from them. And as they chanted, the ground underneath moved and stilled. The magic in the air died. The sea calmed. And they smiled, the heavy rings shaped like the letter S on their fingers gleaming in the moonlight.

And then I saw myself like I was not long ago, standing by the sea, magic sparkling on my skin, more powerful than ever. It made me feel safe, but it was against the magical balance for one person to bear so much magic. And my magic had never been mine to begin with. I had the Guardian's magic, bought at the high cost that we were trying to repay now. There was a sorcerer part in me, but I had no abilities of my own and even if I had, I wouldn't have been able to keep them.

Weles touched my forehead and the sparkle of magic on my skin died once and for all.

FORTY SEVEN

THERE WERE HANDS ON ME, TOUCHING MY FACE, LIFTING me up.

"Wiki," said Artur.

"Hi," I said, forcing my eyes open.

I was disoriented. One second, we were doing the ritual, then Weles was there, and now here I was, lying in the damp, cold sand. The sea soughed gently, splashing onto the shore. Above us the sky shone with bright, shifting colours. Fear froze me for a second before I realized it wasn't another break in the sky—it was the northern lights.

"Oh gods," Artur said, squashing me against his chest. His arms trembled around me, his breaths uneven.

But it wasn't right.

"Wait."

465

I pulled back and put my hand on his arm. Nothing happened. There was no sparkle of magic.

No. Sparkle.

I took a deep breath, trying to remain calm, but as I took in Artur's widened eyes I knew it wasn't just in my head. I couldn't feel the bond between us. I couldn't feel his emotions.

Can you hear me? I asked telepathically.

Artur didn't respond. He pulled me against his chest again, hugging me close, his face hidden in the nook of my neck.

"Can you feel anything? Can you feel our bond?" I asked.

"No," said Artur.

"Have you seen Weles?"

Artur nodded.

"He made sure I'd never be able to use magic again," I said. "That was my sacrifice, my payment to save us from the gods' wrath. No one should have power like that, that's against the magical balance."

"He took my magic, too," said Artur.

I looked over at Karina and Damian. My cousin nodded.

"It's gone."

For a moment the silence was disturbed only by the sea soughing and a car driving in the distance.

"The Circle of Four's purpose has been fulfilled," said Damian, startling us. "It's over now. Our bond is gone."

We watched the northern lights dance in the sky in silence. When we heard voices of people flooding to the beach, we returned to Aunt Eliza's car and sat in the parking lot, numb, unable to move.

"Where do we go?" asked Karina.

"Where did you stay for the past days?" I responded with a question.

Karina started the engine and drove us towards a flat that Dawid and Darek arranged for our Circle of Four from some sorcerer friends. As we left the parking lot, we passed more people walking towards the sea.

"They're the sorcerers of Gdańsk," said Artur.

"Should we try to escape silently, or…?" asked Karina.

Someone noticed us and pointed towards the car.

"Hey!" they shouted, and I flinched.

"Wait," said Artur.

Karina stopped the car. Then, with a telling look at Artur, she pressed the button to lock us in.

"What did you do at the beach?" asked the person.

"Let them be, Cyprian," said another sorcerer. "They aren't our community, they are just kids."

But Cyprian shook his head. "No, that's Mariusz Rydgier's kid. Their city has been cut off for months after a magical accident."

"Are you certain? I can't sense any magic from them."

"Yes," said Artur, lowering the window. "I'm Artur. And we've just destroyed the Guardian system."

The two sorcerers stared at us open-mouthed. One of

them giggled, but it came out harsh, more hysterical than funny.

"That's blasphemous," said Cyprian.

"They've been abusing the magical system for centuries. They've taken the magic from us and from these lands. If it continued, it would have soon disappeared forever but now it's back. Go and celebrate. We need to get some sleep now."

Karina put her foot on the gas and we drove out of the parking lot just as the shouting started. "They've done to our city the same thing they've done to theirs!" was the last yell we heard before we left the sorcerers behind.

We got to the rented flat. Artur and I collapsed on the sofa while Karina and Damian took the bed. We passed out almost immediately, drained of energy. I didn't know how long I'd slept before I startled awake, my heart pounding so hard as if it wanted to escape my chest. There was a steady weight pressing across my abdomen, pinning me down, and constricting my lungs, making it hard to breathe. It took me a confused moment to realize it was just Artur, and I tried to relax into his touch, to listen to his steady, warm breath against my neck, but my body was begging me to flee.

I trusted Artur. We'd slept together plenty of times. Yesterday, I would have killed to be able to hug him. But my brain wouldn't listen. I tried to move Artur's arm off me, but he just shifted, putting even more weight on me and pushing me into the wall, and I couldn't breathe, *couldn't breathe—*

"Wiki?" asked Artur, his voice sleepy.

"Let me go," I whispered, my voice unfamiliar to me.

Artur shifted, taking his arm off me, and I scrambled away so fast I fell to the floor, banging my knee painfully on the sofa's side. Fighting to breathe, I scooted across the floor and put my head between my knees. Acid burned my throat, and I swallowed the nausea.

Breathe, I told myself. *Breathe.*

"What's wrong?" asked Artur, his voice sounding as if it was coming from a great distance. "How can I help you?"

I don't know, I thought. *I don't know, I don't know, I don't know…*

But he couldn't hear my thoughts anymore and my lungs squeezed more and I gasped for breath but the air wouldn't come in and oh gods, I didn't survive so many demonic and sorcerer attacks to die here and now and…

"It's a panic attack," said Artur, his voice still muted in my ears. "You'll be okay, you hear me? Just breathe."

I dug my fingers into my hair, pressing my nails into my scalp as Artur counted the breaths for me. I don't know how long it took for my heart to slow down and my breaths to even out. When I no longer felt like I would drop dead any second, I brushed the tears out of my eyes.

"I'll bring you some water," said Artur. "Or would you prefer tea?"

Water, I thought and immediately closed my eyes as my heart squeezed painfully.

He couldn't hear me anymore.

"Water," I repeated out loud, my voice hoarse.

Artur's steps retreated and the door squeaked closed. Soon, he was back, handing me a cold glass of water. I took a few sips and pressed the glass to my forehead, enjoying its coolness on my burning skin.

"Thank you," I whispered.

"Are you feeling a little better?"

I nodded, not trusting my voice. Adrenaline was slowly dying off, leaving place for exhaustion. My muscles were shaking as if I'd just run a marathon or climbed an oak connecting the worlds.

"I can go if you want space," said Artur after a pause.

I lifted my head so fast I spilled some of the water on my t-shirt.

"Please stay. Please," I said, not caring how pathetic I sounded. "Please don't leave me."

Artur sat on the floor, his back leaning on the sofa, giving me space but close enough that he could touch me if he stretched his arm. My eyes were still watery and my stomach squeezed and, gods, I couldn't go through it again—

"I won't leave you," Artur said, his voice gentle. "It's okay. I'll stay. For as long as you want me to, I'm here. I just wanted to check in."

"I'm sorry I panicked. It has nothing to do with you, okay? I trust you. I do. But I was asleep and I couldn't feel our bond, and I guess my brain panicked."

"You don't have to explain yourself. It's okay."

"It's not okay. Everything is far from okay."

Artur sighed, staring at the wall behind me.

"I know."

When I woke up again, the sky was getting dark. There was a pillow between Artur's and my side of the couch but Artur's side was empty. I wouldn't have been surprised if I'd scared him off last night.

Maybe that was how it ended. Our bond was gone, our mission completed, there was nothing holding us together anymore.

My heart pounded harder as I ignored the nausea and got myself out of bed and walked towards the kitchen. Artur and Damian sat at the table; their eyes glued to a smartphone propped against a salt shaker.

"*...it was possessed!*" said the voice on the smartphone. "*A demon! Its eyes were pure white and it jumped at me but, bam!, I smacked it right on the head with my bag!*"

I drew closer, trying to get a better look at the screen. Artur jumped when I stood behind the boys, which made me jump, too. I frantically looked around, searching for the source of his alarm, heart in my throat.

"Gods, Wiki, you scared me," he said.

I stared at him, frozen. Until last night, it would have been impossible for me to sneak up on him like that.

"Hi," I said softly.

"Would have been a good thing to say when you enter a room," said Damian, never tearing his eyes away from the screen. He nursed a large mug of coffee, though, judging by the pale colour, most of it was milk.

"There are sandwiches in the fridge and we have some instant coffee, if you want," said Artur.

"The news…" I trailed off, unsure what to say.

"Yeah," said Damian. "The world is going to change now."

I took a piece of rye bread and put some cheese and tomato on top of it, listening to the news. More reports of demon sightings. Claims that people were performing magic on the streets—likely, the sorcerers we'd encountered hadn't been the only ones who had gone to the streets last night. Magic had returned to the world, but I wasn't part of the magical world anymore.

The thought was like a knife to the heart and I flinched. I looked at my sandwich and stood there, torn between joining Artur and Damian and running away.

I couldn't get the sorcerers at the beach out of my head. I'd trusted the adults to sort these things out, to prepare our community for what was to come. The Children of Weles had been preparing for that, they'd been supposedly sharing resources with others, but when had I started trusting them? I didn't want the magic-users to be caught unawares but now it was too late to worry about it.

Except I did worry. I worried a lot. What had we done?

How would this situation escalate? What if people rioted, what if sorcerers didn't want to live without the Guardians, what if the demons grew stronger, what if the gates to Nawia burst open again?

"The disturbances have been noted across Poland, with reports flooding in from Zakopane to Hel. Emergency services have been overwhelmed with intervention requests in all sixteen regions. The experts are debating whether the occurrences might have been staged by a religious sect or an influence of social media.

I leaned heavily on the counter and closed my eyes. Nausea rose in my throat, the whole world too much to take in.

"Wiki?" asked Artur, placing a hand on my shoulder.

There was no sparkle of magic. None at all.

I burst out crying.

FORTY EIGHT

I WAS SNUGGLED WITH A BLANKET, A CUP OF LEMON balm tea steaming in front of me. Nobody was watching the news anymore, and I was too tired to argue that I wanted to know what was going on. I *needed* to know.

"I have something for you," said Artur, sitting on a sofa next to me, careful to keep some distance between us. He handed me a drawing of a flying green żmij which was definitely Arrow.

My eyes teared up.

"When I was in Nawia, I had this dream. It was an alternate reality, we had a Jare Gody celebration, all of us, as a sorcerer community, and everyone was there—Zuzanna, my parents, even Igor, and Stanisław, and everyone was so nice and welcoming. And later you gave me a similar drawing as a birthday gift, with me flying on Arrow, with a bow and arrow in my hand, and the sky had the colours of the aroace flag." I sniffled. "I wanted to stay there. I didn't want to wake up."

"It does seem like a nice dream," said Artur, his voice gentle.

"We were friends, you know? Close childhood friends. We'd grown up together and everyone thought we should date, but we laughed at them and made bets about how many times Darek's mum would try to push us into each other's arms at a magical celebration."

Before Artur could respond, there was a knock at the front door. I jumped, even though Karina had told me we would have guests.

"I'll get it," Artur said and a few moments later the door opened and voices flooded the corridor. Rafi was the loudest, as usual.

"Vampire boy," I heard him greet Artur.

I put away my tea mug and straightened in anticipation.

"Wiwi, my child," said Dad, entering the room. He snatched me up in his arms and I didn't resist. "Are you okay?"

I didn't know how to respond. There was no good answer to that question. No one would have believed a "yes," but "no" would have meant more questions.

I shrugged.

"Tired," I said. It wasn't a lie—I was exhausted, barely able to keep my eyes open, my brain sluggish, but it didn't even scratch the surface of how not okay I was.

"You've done some amazing magic," Dad said. "You should rest."

He looked at the wall behind me, his gaze unseeing.

"I can't believe you managed to do it."

"Of course, they did," said Mum, entering the room. Unlike Dad who wore his regular winter jacket and jeans, she had a black sorceress's cloak on with a hedgehog stitched at her breast. "If anyone could have done it, it was them. I told you that magic had great plans."

I felt even more drained now. I didn't want to have this conversation. Not now, not ever.

I just wanted to sleep.

More people flooded into the room. Aunt Eliza scooped me into a hug. Looking over her shoulder, I noticed two more figures, clad in dark blue and I froze.

Gabriella. And Laura.

My heart pounded in my chest, my throat closing up and I bit my lip hard, trying to snap out of it and breathe. I didn't want a repeat from last night. Not in front of everyone.

"We're going to the Assembly," said Mum. "Well, the Sorcerers' Gathering, actually. We have a lot of things to discuss, it will be a long meeting. Especially after the disturbance last night."

"You mean us destroying the Twardowski's scriptures?" I asked. If I hadn't been so exhausted, I would have rolled my eyes. Disturbance was one way to call the whole reason I existed, and my mum should know it better than everyone, since it had been her plan.

"No. I mean the Children of Weles going after the Guardians in the aftermath."

"What?!"

It wasn't unexpected so I didn't know why I was surprised. The Children of Weles had been open about wanting to destroy the Guardians. They wouldn't rest until they—we—were dead. And last night had been a prime opportunity.

"Why has no one intervened? Were they just allowed to murder people?"

More blood. More blood on my conscience.

"They weren't," said Gabriella, stepping closer. "The local sorcerers realized what was happening and they stepped in. They managed to stop the worst in time. Both the Guardians and the Children of Weles are under arrest, pending the Sorcerers' Gathering."

"Where we need to head now," said Mum. "I just wanted to check if you need anything. Artur, if you want to come, your parents will be there as well."

Artur, who was standing in the doorway, his arms folded, nodded.

"I'm going, too," I said. "I want to know what happens next."

My parents exchanged looks. Artur eyebrows were drawn. I didn't need to read their minds to know they didn't think it was a good idea, but I didn't care. It was something I needed to do for myself. Besides, Artur had also just been to hell and back and nobody questioned if he should go.

So I repeated more insistently:

"I want to know."

There was another moment of silence.

"Maybe it's not the best idea," said Dad.

"Oh, now it's not a good idea?" I said, my voice rising, my hands trembling. "Now that you don't need me for anything else, I get to be a child again, sheltered at home? Now I can sit here and rest? No, thank you. I'm going."

There was a moment of silence.

"Yeah," said Karina, stepping to my side. "I imagine someone will have to explain what exactly had happened to stop the wild speculations. I guess we could stretch our legs a little."

"We should all go," said Aunt Eliza and I was grateful to have at least one adult on my side. "It will be good to show support, right?"

Since we were a big group, our former Circle of Four and Rafi took the second car. Karina had brought me a change of clothes to Gdańsk for which I was forever grateful. And once he'd realized I had no coat, again, Rafi lent me his jacket which I was not going to turn down. For a few moments we were in our little bubble again, even if we were going to the last place I wanted to be.

"Going there might be the stupidest idea we've ever had," said Karina. "And the competition is fierce."

"It's not too late to go back and sleep," said Rafi.

Of course, we wouldn't do that.

Karina drove us across the city, towards the old town. I took the passenger seat while the boys squeezed in the back seat. We passed a religious manifestation, with a crowd gathered around a church with candles, but compared to what had been happening in our city before the sky had broken, it was nothing.

I thought about what Zuzanna had said when we'd witnessed the first manifestation on the old market square. It was good people congregated like that. The Church was pretty good at protecting people from demons. And right now people needed all the defences they could get.

"Do you think it will be like back home?" asked Rafi. "Will they introduce the curfew, will there be soldiers on the streets?"

"I don't think so," said Artur. "It's nowhere close to the apocalyptic atmosphere we've experienced. The sky isn't broken. We aren't halfway to Nawia. And as far as I know no one decided to cut off Poland from the rest of the world, so we shouldn't face any major shortages."

"The electricity is working, too," said Karina.

"And, hopefully, we managed to appease the gods," said Damian.

Karina found a parking spot in a narrow street next to a construction site, a short walk away from the river I'd seen from my window at the Assembly. She put her arm through mine as we walked along the river.

Someone shouted, and I jumped. We stood frozen,

grouping close together, looking for a threat. Across the river a small child was pointing at the water. At first it seemed there was nothing there, but then a hand broke the surface and waved at the kid. The child shrieked louder but the parents paid them no heed and pulled them on. The demon—a rusałka—stuck out its head and grinned at us before disappearing under the surface.

"Slavic mythology is full of sex demons, isn't it?" asked Rafi. "I think we need a masterlist of who of us is at risk of which ones, so we know who to protect."

"It's duly noted you need saving from them all," said Karina.

"Hey, don't turn me into a stereotype!"

We speed-walked the rest of the way to a tall, brown tenement. Five tall steps led to the door, guarded on both sides by, characteristic to the city, sculpted dragons that spew water when it rained. There was a crowd of people in black sorcerers' cloaks around the entrance and we slowed.

None of us wore our cloaks. I wasn't sure if Karina and Rafi had theirs yet, and Damian would likely never get one.

And neither would I.

We looked at the sorcerers who were staring back at us.

"Any familiar faces?" asked Karina.

Artur shook his head. "I think I recognize some of them, but I don't know anyone's names."

"Well then, it's time to make friends," said Rafi, leading the way.

We exchanged looks and followed behind.

"Stop," said a sorceress standing by the door and my heart thundered. She was tall, with brown hair pulled into a bun on top of her head. There was a clover stitched into her cloak. "None of you are wearing the proper attire. And I sense magic only from you, whoever you are," she pointed at Rafi.

"We've used up our magic and we're waiting to recharge," Artur lied smoothly. It was weird not to feel the tell-tale pinprick of his lies. "We're from Bydgoszcz. We didn't expect to need our cloaks."

"That's an interesting story," said a sorcerer standing next to the woman. He was shorter than her and his cloak was adorned by a stitched snowdrop. His arms were crossed on his chest. "Coming from a cursed city that's been cut off for weeks after the biggest magical upheaval we've witnessed in centuries. Some might say it sounds suspicious."

"Well, whether you like it or not, I'm a sorcerer and this is a Sorcerers' Gathering."

Artur pulled out my amulet from under his clothes and showed it to the sorceress.

"I recognize the amulet," she said. "But Ludmiła doesn't have a grandson or nephew that age."

"The amulet is mine," I said, standing next to Artur. I pulled out his blackbird amulet from under my clothes. "This one is his."

"Hey, aren't you the girl from the video with the flying stone eagle?" asked the man and it took everything in me not to react.

The sorceress looked between us, silent for a moment.

"I'll get Ludmiła," she said at last and disappeared inside.

"I guess we'll follow," said Rafi, throwing a glance at the man.

At first it seemed like he might protest, but Rafi towered more than a head over him and, after throwing us a sideways gaze, he didn't stop us as we walked in.

We entered a narrow wooden staircase which made my skin crawl. I fisted my hands and forced myself to walk on.

"Artur," I said, as we climbed the steps. "I'm sorry about earlier."

"Please, don't be. It's okay. Trust me, I know it's a tough adjustment."

His tone was flat and I couldn't read his emotions. And I would have given a lot to know how he felt. Did he think it was an effort worth taking or was it all over?

I squeezed his blackbird amulet under my jumper.

"Of course, it's tough," said Karina, startling me. "You've never learnt how to communicate like normal humans. You relied on your bond so much to read each other's emotions and thoughts. And communication is *hard*. And no, you won't always get it right, but that's normal. You will have to readjust and it will take time."

We didn't have a chance to continue the conversation as we reached a tall double door marked *Assembly Room*. It was open, welcoming us in, even though my skin crawled at the memory of that room.

But this time, the room was bustling with people dressed

in black sorcerers' cloaks and a few in dark blue of the alchemists. No red cloaks stood out in the crowd, though a part of me kept expecting a Guardian or eighteen to make a great entrance.

What if they still had some power? More importantly, what if the people would still listen to them? What if it was all one big trap?

No matter how hard I tried, I couldn't remember anything from the long hours spent with Zuzanna in the ritual room.

Karina squeezed my hand.

"It looks like Węgliszek's castle, doesn't it?" asked Damian

I nodded. "I had that thought, too. Do you think he's done it on purpose?"

"Oh, definitely."

"Artur!" shouted Beata, tearing across the crowd to get to her son.

She closed him in an embrace.

"I brought you your cloak," she said, pulling it from her bag. "Aleksandra told me you might be here. Oh, Artur, was it really you?"

Artur nodded. He tried to get the cloak from his mum's hands but she held on.

"Why would you do that?" she whispered, looking around to make sure no one was listening. "Didn't we bring you up to respect the Guardians? To protect the community at all cost? If it was the girl—"

"We did it to protect us all," said Artur. "We did it to save the magic."

He took his sorcerer cloak from his mother's hands and put it on.

"I can't even feel your magic," Beata said.

"Any other part of me that you'd like to criticize?"

"I don't think you understand the scale of the trouble you caused. It's not some small magical accident. This is serious. It changes everything."

"Good. Now we have a chance to move on. And I hope that one day you'll realize it."

Beata shook her head.

"I wish you'd kept your head down."

"Nothing ever changes if you just keep your head down and play along. I'm glad I didn't and I'm ready to face the consequences."

Artur brushed past his mum and we followed behind, Beata throwing us a nasty look. I caught up to him and squeezed his arm.

"That's nothing," he said quietly. "Let's wait until she finds out I lost my magic."

I searched for something to say but I didn't have any comforting words to share.

"There they are!" shouted a sorceress who'd interrogated us on the staircase. She was walking fast towards us. "How did you get in?"

Following her was an older woman with long grey hair braided back. She wore a black cloak with a hedgehog stitched on.

My heart stuttered as I scanned her face, because it was familiar even though I'd never seen her before. She had my mum's eyes and mouth, but she was half a head shorter.

The sorceress scanned me back, her eyes lighting with recognition. She smiled.

"That's my granddaughter," she said confidently. "Definitely sorcerer blood, unless you want to question my place here, too."

She stepped towards me and, after a heartbeat, I met her halfway. She squeezed me hard.

"It's good to finally meet you, Wiktoria," she said.

"At least she could have bothered with the proper attire," murmured the sorceress who'd refused our entry. "No respect for tradition. And what about the rest of them?"

"I'm a witch," said Damian, his tone a challenge.

"A witch?!" repeated the sorceress, her voice raised.

"I dare say that the meeting today will be about breaking away from tradition, don't you think?" asked the older sorceress.

The sorceress didn't have a chance to respond as we were joined by my parents and Aunt Eliza. Mum stood tall in her sorceress's cloak but Dad and Aunt Eliza wore their usual clothes.

"Finally, we've been looking everywhere for you," said Mum. "I thought you'd wait outside."

"We wanted to make friends," said Rafi. He nodded towards the elderly sorceress. "And we made one."

Mum's eyes flew to the woman next to me, then widened in shock.

"Mum?" she said.

"You'd expect me to miss the first Sorcerers' Gathering?" asked the woman. "It's as if you don't know me at all."

Mum's eyes clouded and her hands shook as she walked towards the woman and threw her arms around her.

"It's been so, so long, Oleńka," whispered the woman. "You've grown so much."

Then she looked at my dad.

"And Adrian. I'm glad to see that you're still together."

She hugged him as well. Then she pulled back and looked at our group.

"Come on. Let's find a good spot and get comfortable, I have a feeling it will last long."

Just then a gong reverberated off the walls. I stumbled and Damian and Rafi caught me simultaneously. Rafi held on to my arm, weaving it through his.

"Let the Sorcerers' Gathering begin," said a loud voice.

FORTY NINE

"**W**HAT EXACTLY HAPPENED LAST NIGHT?" ASKED A sorceress with short blonde hair who stood near the centre of the room.

"Marlena Dudzik. She's been right hand to our Guardian," murmured the older sorceress—my *grandma*—into my ear.

I looked at Karina, Artur, and Damian. Karina knew how to read me and Damian's body language skills were close enough to mind-reading. But I hoped Artur had understood me as well.

"We destroyed the Twardowski's scriptures," I said, my voice loud and clear.

People turned to stare at me and my heart drummed harder in my chest. Everyone in the room apart from us had magic and I'd just drawn a target on us. But it was important that people understood what exactly had happened.

"Isn't that the girl from that video?" asked someone in a loud whisper, but they were shushed.

"Raise your hand so everyone can see you," demanded Marlena.

I did. I was quickly followed by Artur, then Karina, and Damian.

People parted around us, giving us space. All apart from my family. Rafi, Dad, Mum, Aunt Eliza, and my newfound grandma all stayed by.

"Tell us what happened," said Marlena.

"We're the Circle of Four," I said, my voice echoing off the high ceiling. "We'd been given a chance to save the magic from disappearing from this world. And last night we did just that. We destroyed the Twardowski's scriptures to restore the magical balance. Master Twardowski sold his soul to learn how to entrap magic-users' power. The Guardians have been using his knowledge for centuries, taking away our magic without consent, destroying the magical balance. Now that knowledge is lost forever. Don't you feel stronger already? Magic is coming back to this world."

Voices started to raise but Artur raised his, talking over the people:

"The Guardians have been trapping our power for centuries, syphoning it away. We had maybe one generation left until magic disappeared for good from this world."

"You let the demons in!" someone shouted.

"Demons are part of the magical balance," said Karina. "And they aren't necessarily bad. Don't you remember domowiki? Or żmije, who granted us powers? Humans, demons, and gods used to coexist together, magic moving freely between the worlds. This era is back now."

"Is that what you've done to your own city?" shouted someone else.

"Skybreakers," said someone else, repeating the name that Filip had called me in front of the Assembly.

"That was a sabotage by the Children of Weles," said Damian. "And some of them are still around you. I'm not saying you should kick them out because they have some good plans for what comes now, for the future without Guardians. and we will need the help of all magic users. It will take entire communities to make sure we stay safe. But you should be aware that many of the Children of Weles are extremists and they've done some horrible things to our community."

"The Guardians lied," I said. "They told us over and over that without them, the world would be devoured by demons. That they are singlehandedly keeping us safe. They called themselves the Guardians of Realms, for fuck's sake. But people lived for centuries before the Guardians and, in the other parts of what used to be the Polish-Lithuanian Commonwealth, people lived for decades after the Guardians. What happened in our city was a sabotage, yes, and a world thrown wildly off-axis by powerful magic. Not because we lost a Guardian but because the borders between Jawia and Nawia broke down. What happened last night was the world coming back to the magical balance."

Voices rose again, people screaming at each other, blending into a mass that was impossible to understand. Soon, it became clear no one would listen to us anymore.

Which was good because I had no more energy to spare.

I spotted Mateusz across the room. He gave me a small nod, and I dropped my eyes to the floor.

The gathering lasted long into the night and not much was decided. People shouted and argued over one another, unable to make up their minds. We stuck to the back of the room, cuddled close together. Every once in a while, my grandma would whisper a comment in my ear, telling me who someone was or who made a good cheesecake.

I didn't have a heart to tell her I wasn't the greatest fan of cheesecake anymore. Just like I wouldn't mention that I'd lost magic for good, that this was likely the first and last time we'd participate in a magical event together.

I'd hoped to see the future of the magical community that night, but I'd been naïve. The chaos of the Sorcerers' Gathering made it clear it would take a long time for the magic-users to organize themselves.

At least people were already preparing smaller, family- and community-based protections against the demons. They also hoped to start passing the most important warnings to the non-magical community: don't wander alone after dark. Don't go to the forest at night, and never go to the forest alone. Don't swim before Midsummer Eve. Remember that demons can't cross the running water. Well, at least the lesser demons that people were more likely to encounter. And with some notable exceptions like sirens and rusałki.

Another good result was that the Guardians were temporarily on house arrest as the sorcerers debated what to do with them. The Children of Weles were arguing strongly for trial and execution but, thankfully, most of the sorcerers were against it. Nobody wanted to start the new era with bloodshed. And some hoped that the Guardians would still step in and bring the world back to the way it used to be.

At long last, we left the Assembly building. I never wanted to go there again. We were by the river, when Laura shouted "Watch out!" before tackling me to the ground. We tumbled down to the pavement just as air whooshed above us in a powerful blow.

"What…" I started saying, disoriented, but my mum already zeroed in on the perpetrator.

"How dare you," she growled, approaching the sorcerer who hadn't wanted us to come in.

"You will leave my granddaughter alone," said my grandma, appearing by his side.

"They destroyed the world as we know it."

"They saved magic," said Mum.

Laura helped me up to my feet and I gave her a feeble smile.

"Always saving our asses, hm?" I asked, but I was shaking.

Laura smiled back.

"Let's go," said Karina, pulling me away. "We want to put as much distance between us and these people as possible."

We marched quickly down the river. My parents soon caught up to us.

"We booked a night in the hotel," said Mum. "The conversation will continue tomorrow and likely for many more days, if not months. But I think it was a good start. Are you good to stay at your flat for one more night? You have Aunt Eliza's car so you can get back home whenever you want to."

We said goodnight and my parents walked towards the old town.

"Mum, wait," I said.

She stopped and looked at me, waiting.

"There was a price to pay for restoring the magical balance," I said. I didn't want to hide it from her. I didn't want to give her false hope, to imagine futures that wouldn't be. "I paid with my magic. I don't have magic anymore. None of us do"

Mum looked stricken, her eyes widened. She put her hand to her mouth.

"My parents don't know yet," added Artur.

There was a moment of silence. A car engine sputtered in the distance and I flinched. I dug my fingernails into my hands, trying to ground myself.

"Thank you for telling us," said Dad, squeezing our shoulders. "I know it will be a tough adjustment, especially for you, Artur. But I'm sure it will all work out in the end. Maybe it's for the better, maybe it's time for you to move on."

My heart hurt, but I nodded. Slowly, we walked back to Aunt Eliza's car and we drove back to the rented flat.

I slept with Karina and Rafi, clinging to the edge of the bed. I didn't want to take the middle, afraid of a repeat from last night. I needed a proper night of sleep, not to wake up panicking.

The joke was on me. I didn't sleep much at all and once the sun had risen, I got out of bed and walked to the kitchen.

Artur was already there, preparing instant coffee. His hair was damp and he wore the glasses that he'd got from his mum at last night's gathering.

"Do you want some coffee?" he asked instead of a hello. I nodded.

"You couldn't sleep?" I asked.

"I had trouble sleeping before it all started. Our bond made it easier, the way we shared dreams…" Artur closed his eyes and took a deep breath. "I already miss it. And with everything that has happened my mind pretty much doesn't shut up. So yeah, I guess sleep is off the table for me."

He handed me a blue mug. The handle was cracked but what counted was the precious insides. Coffee. What wouldn't have I given for coffee a week or two ago?

What wouldn't have I given to be back there now?

"There's a bakery around a corner," said Artur, blowing

into his scalding hot coffee. "Do you want to go with me and get some pastries?"

The honest answer was no. I was exhausted, and I wanted to be out of Gdańsk. I wanted to curl up with my coffee on the sofa and never get up.

But Artur's voice was slow and uncertain, making my heart ache. I wasn't the only person who'd lost something two nights ago. I wasn't the only person who'd been broken by the events of the past weeks.

I nodded. We put our mugs aside so the coffee could get a little cooler and more drinkable. We put on our shoes and jackets (I borrowed Rafi's again) and walked out into the winter morning.

We walked in silence, taking in the first rays of sun. The bakery was just a two-minute walk away and we bought enough pastries and bread rolls to feed our group three times over. When we rounded a corner towards our building, I said:

"Artur? I know we lost our bond but you didn't lose me, okay? I'm still here, for as long as you'll have me. And…I thought back to what I didn't have time to say to him in the Assembly's dungeons. "I think I might be ace. Probably aro, too. But Damian got really into my head because he made me realize that I was scared of admitting it to myself. I was just thinking about all the 'shoulds.' And then, in this demonic apocalypse craziness, it was the last 'normal' thing I could cling on to. Despite our relationship and despite our Circle of Four. Despite all the evidence pointing to the contrary. I think it's because it's so difficult to imagine an aspec future. Which is stupid because I had the best support system I could ask for. I had a relationship that fulfilled all my needs. And now…"

I snorted, blinking away the tears.

"Not normal," said Artur. "You told me that yourself. It's not normal, it's normative."

I smiled sadly. "I'm still here, little fox. Can I hug you?"

I nodded.

Artur put his arms around me. We stood together for a few heartbeats, our hands awkward, hesitant. There was no warmth of magic between us, just the warmth of another human on a cold winter morning. It wasn't the worst feeling in the world.

"I'm here for as long as you'll have me, too," Artur said, releasing me from the hug.

He offered me his hand and I squeezed it. I still missed the tickle of magic between us, it would take me a long time to get over it. But maybe I didn't have to try to face it alone. Maybe, magic or not, we could make it work.

FLATY

THE CLAVICHORD CAFÉ WAS SILENT AND EMPTY, sunlight streaming in through the windows faded with age. Dust floated around, sparkling in the sun. The floor was mostly empty, the air didn't smell like coffee or bread. We'd removed the majority of the broken furniture and only two armchairs remained intact. The mural with the forest filled with demons was still there, reminding me of my time in Nawia. I avoided looking at it.

It was chilly inside. I couldn't feel the tenement's magic anymore.

Zuzanna walked slowly around the café. It was the last time she would see it—she'd signed the papers to sell the tenement the previous day. The tenement was bought by an older, rich sorcerer, who would probably carry on the Clavichord Café as a community space for the magic-users.

But Zuzanna wouldn't be welcome there.

"It's bittersweet," she said, resting her hand on the back of her favourite black and white armchair. "I hate this place so much. I wanted it to be home so badly, even though it rejected me over and over. But I'd been resigned that I'd eventually have to come back here. I've never expected it to happen so early, but maybe in thirty more years. Maybe it would have been different then."

"You can visit," said Mum. "It doesn't have to be a goodbye forever."

"I think I've had enough of the Guardians. No, it's good to have this burden off my shoulders. To have my future filled with possibilities."

Zuzanna walked over to the mural with the demons, a small smile on her face.

"You came for us," I said, joining her. "At the Assembly. You saved our lives."

"That was the least I could do," she responded. "You were taking too long. You'd been gone for days, we knew that you must be trapped. Besides, it all almost went very wrong."

"You knew that Aysun would come."

"Yes. But I didn't expect the Guardians to almost burn us alive before then."

I shivered. I could almost smell petrol in the air.

"How did you get into the Assembly?"

"The right of blood. I didn't know if it would work, but I needed to try something. I had the ring and the

Guardian's blood flows through my veins. Apparently it was all I needed."

"So if Igor had stolen the Guardian's ring, my parents wouldn't have had to make a pact with the devil?"

"Maybe yes, maybe no. He'd never been sworn in as a Guardian. My fealty had failed, but I was at least half-sworn-in."

I ran my finger along the Baba Jaga hut in the painting.

"Do you remember anything about the Guardian magic?" I asked after a couple of moments. "Do you remember what we used to do here all day?"

Zuzanna shook her head.

"No. That knowledge is now gone and the world is all the better for it."

The bell above the door rang as Aysun opened it, her and Zuzanna's suitcases by her side—Aysun's pink one and Zuzanna's black, with a heart-shaped, glitter sticker with stripes in shades of orange, white, and pink. I would have bet anything that Aysun had stuck it there.

The black suitcase slowly unzipped itself and a small head covered in grey hair popped up. Aysun reached into her tote bag and retrieved a cookie which she gave to the domowik. He took the offering and zipped himself back up in the suitcase.

I hoped he'd enjoy living in Berlin together with Aysun and Zuzanna.

"We have to go if we're to catch the train," Aysun said in English.

Zuzanna nodded. "It's a goodbye then. Thank you for

everything, and I'm sorry for how our acquaintance started. And I want to be very clear on one thing—you didn't kill my family. My brother was killed by the Assembly and my father by the Children of Weles. Both of them were very interested in the curse for different reasons, but it wasn't your fault. And I don't want you to ever think otherwise."

She moved towards the door, but I stopped her. I pulled her into a hug.

"Goodbye," I said.

Later that afternoon, the Clavichord Café filled with sorcerers. Some wore their black cloaks, others stuck to civilian clothing. A couple of kids chased around the room, laughing, but the adults were mostly silent.

"Welcome everyone," said my mum. "We're here to discuss how to continue protecting the city now that the Guardians are gone."

"And just who do you think you are to suddenly lead this meeting?" asked Beata.

"Someone has to do it." Mum shrugged. "If you volunteer to do it instead, you're welcome to take over. But what really matters is the contents of the discussion and not who starts it."

"That's what you say now. And then what, you'll expect us to elect you our next leader?"

"That's precisely what we need to discuss, Beata. How we move on. Personally, I'd prefer to see us as a collective rather than a group with a structured hierarchy. We need as many people as possible helping out to keep the city and the surrounding areas safe. But it's just one of many options."

"And why should we go on with your idea?" asked the sorceress who'd helped Beata interrogate me.

"You don't have to. I'm just putting it out there to start a discussion. That's the beauty of the Guardian-less system, no one will force us to choose one way or another. We will decide together."

"Beauty? You're calling this utter disaster a beauty?" asked a middle-aged sorceress, her voice high-pitched. "At least seven hundred people died already, and it will be a miracle if hundreds more don't die as they're left vulnerable to the demons."

"That's why we should be discussing how to save them," said Tomasz. "Whatever we decide on, it will take a collective effort."

"And why do you assume we have time and energy for that? When are we supposed to do this between our jobs and taking care of our families?" asked Beata's friend.

My head pounded, and I tuned the discussion out. My lungs squeezed, making it difficult to breathe and I dug my fingers into the chair I sat on.

Everyone in this room apart from me had magic. It was probably stupid of me to come. Artur's parents didn't let him and he didn't fight them on it even though I wished he was here with me.

No, that was selfish. I was glad he didn't have to feel

what I did. We were responsible for the mess they were in, but we wouldn't be able to help them anymore. Our job here was done, even if it didn't feel like it.

"It's her fault," said an older sorcerer, pointing at me.

The angry glares around said that he wasn't the only one to think so.

"No," said the most unexpected voice. I did a double-take to look at Beata. "It's the fault of all the Guardians across history. And ours, for not realizing what was happening, for not questioning it, for not acting sooner. But what happened had to be done."

The meeting dragged on as Mum, Tomasz, and Darek presented alternative systems that different territories took up after overthrowing the Guardians. The magical collectives in Belarus, democratically elected sorcerer councils in Ukraine, and so on. I only half-listened to them—apart from the interruptions, it wasn't anything I hadn't heard them discussing before in our kitchen. It shouldn't have been a surprise that Mum would throw herself fully into rebuilding the magical society. I knew it was everything she'd dreamed of when she was my age. But I was still only getting to know that part of her.

I hid in the corner, trying not to attract the sorcerers' attention. Dawid cast me a wary look every once in a while, checking if I was okay.

"Hi," whispered Laura, appearing by my side.

I straightened. She wore her pink jumper and a pair of jeans. Her long, black hair streamed down her back. There was a single pink carnation behind her ear.

"Hi."

"At least you didn't flinch this time."

I closed my eyes, already exhausted with this conversation. "Can you blame me?"

There was a moment of silence.

"No. I know I can't."

I nodded. At least we were on the same page.

"I should have trusted you," Laura said. She nodded at the scene in front of us, the magic-users discussing their future, no Guardian among them. "I mean, you got us here. We didn't manage to do that."

I shrugged. "I'd say you managed to change things rather epically. Getting us to break the sky and all."

Laura was silent for a few moments.

"I've never meant for things to go that far. I didn't know so many people would be hurt. And I didn't want to hurt you. I know it doesn't mean much but—"

"I believe you."

We stared at each other. A small, hopeful smile showed on Laura's face, but she quickly wiped it away.

"It can't happen again," I said. "No one would listen to me, not anymore. Not that they ever valued my opinion. But everything depends on what happens now and we can't let things get so bad again. It was supposed to be a better world, with magic safe and all magic-users treated equally. But so many things could go wrong."

"There are a lot of good people here and we're already a community. They've been through a lot and change is never easy. We need to heal from everything that happened and that will take time, but we'll get there."

"Trust won't be rebuilt overnight."

"No. But we'll make it work." We looked at the magic-users debating in front of us. "Would you like me to read your future?"

There was one more thing that needed doing. Karina and I strung up homemade bunting in Aunt Eliza's flat, while Artur helped with balloons. A cake which I'd baked cooled in the fridge so that the frosting wouldn't melt. It was chocolate with more chocolate and chocolate on top. Aunt Eliza gave us a bottle of vodka and a whole collection of juices to mix it with, then left to meet Gabriella.

"Ah, happy seventeenth birthday to me," said Rafi, looking around the living room.

"You aren't supposed to say that to yourself," said Karina.

"I think since it's a very delayed birthday party, I'm allowed," said Rafi.

It was a weird party by Rafi's standards. Normally, he'd have invited his classmates, people he knew from martial arts, and any and all casual acquaintances. Now it was only the four of us. I wasn't sure if Damian had been invited, but in either case, he was in Poznań.

"Will you sing for yourself as well when I bring the cake?" I asked, walking towards the kitchen.

He didn't, so we sung *Happy Birthday* for him and

cheered when he blew the candles. We helped ourselves to the cake and made drinks.

"Look, I can make it bubbly!"

Rafi put his hands on his glass and soon enough the drink bubbled up so much it almost poured out of the glass.

He was the only one of us who still had magic. He was learning more and more under Gabriella's tutelage.

Artur froze, his eyes on the glass. I squeezed his shoulder. Karina spoke up first, breaking the tension:

"Why would you think it's a good idea to make vodka bubbly?"

"Don't diss it until you try it."

They bickered for a while but, after a second drink, Karina announced she had to go to bed. She had a lot of studying to do the next day as she was trying to catch up on school to pass her final exams in time in May.

Rafi looked at Artur and me.

"That's a really sad party," he said. "Do you want to watch *Star Wars*?"

FIFTY ONE

FOR THE HOURS, DAYS, WEEKS AFTERWARDS, I KEPT expecting something to happen. For the door to my room to burst open, the windows to explode, the shadows to pull me through, the fire to erupt from me and engulf the room. I jumped at every little noise, ready to fight or run. I wore shoes inside, much to my mum's disapproval, just for an occasion like that. My showers were as brief as possible, and I was hesitant to change into my pyjamas because I needed to be ready to run.

Every time I opened a book, I waited for someone to interrupt. Every time I started a show on Netflix, I expected the internet to die.

But nothing happened.

It took us a while to get our flat back into a liveable condition. When we first came back, with Dad and Tomasz as a back-up, the place had been raided, furniture destroyed, books thrown to the floor, all the food gone. Mum suspected the Children of Weles, but it could have been anyone desperate for food.

"Dinner is ready!" shouted Mum.

I pulled the duvet over my head, blocking her out, my eyes peeled on the screen in front of me. I was watching a sitcom that I didn't find funny but, somehow, I was already on the fourth season, even though I'd started it only yesterday. I blamed Netflix for launching the next episode before I could muster enough energy to switch it off.

There was a knock and the door to my room was pushed open, but I didn't leave my hiding place.

"Wiki," said Mum. "Dinner is ready."

"I'm not hungry," I said.

"We made pizza."

"I'm still not hungry."

Mum sighed. "Did you eat anything today?"

"Yes."

I'd had a handful of cereal and a yoghurt drink. My stomach was too tightly knotted with anxiety to eat.

"Please come," said Mum, her voice pleading. "Just for a bit. Tomasz is here and Darek and Dawid came over as well, they would be happy to see you."

I weighed my options, but decided that humouring Mum would cost me less energy than continuing this conversation. She might even leave me in peace for some hours. I paused the series and crawled out from my bed. Artur's grey hoodie lay on the back of my desk chair and I pulled it over my t-shirt. That was all the effort I could make.

Tomasz looked immaculate as ever, in one of his usual crisp shirts. He took out the pizza from the oven and set out the plates for the five of us. He behaved as if it were his home, and, to be fair, he'd been spending a lot of time here. Darek and Dawid sat side by side and Darek was opening a bottle of wine.

"Wiktoria," Tomasz said, offering me a smile. He put a piece of mushroom pizza on a plate in front of me.

I plopped down on a chair next to Dawid and pulled my hood over my greasy hair. I pushed my hands into the big pocket at the front of the hoodie.

"We need to find a way to get through to the former Children of Weles," said Mum, taking a piece of pizza off the baking tray and biting into it.

"I don't think they consider themselves 'former' anything," said Tomasz.

He ate his pizza with fork and knife. Of course he did.

"They have some good ideas," said Mum. "They've been preparing for the Guardian-less future for a long time. We need them on our side."

"No," said Darek. "We need them to realize there are no more sides."

"It doesn't matter how good their ideas are if they keep undermining everything we're trying to do," said Dawid.

"They just need to understand that Weles isn't coming back," said Mum. "At least not in the way he did when the sky was broken. This is our reality now. Maybe if they knew no one will disturb them when they worship their god…"

"They know that," said Darek. "But that's not enough for them because they want all of us to worship him together."

I half-listened to their conversation until I could excuse myself and hide in my room again. The world was readjusting around me, getting back on course, and I was left behind. And the distance between us kept growing because I had no energy or real will to chase it.

I didn't know what I was supposed to do now. My life purpose, my reason for existence had been fulfilled. The Circle of Four bond had been broken, my magic gone. I couldn't go back to the life I had, and I didn't know how to move on. I was stuck. One of the first things I'd done after the world stabilized was to beg Tomasz to write me a doctor's note to get me out of school. I wasn't eighteen yet, so I was obliged by law to go to school, but I'd done only a month of the second year of high school. There was no way I'd catch up on all the months I'd missed and I was in no shape to try, so it was obvious I'd have to repeat the year either way. And I couldn't even stand the thought of sitting in class when getting out of bed was too much work most of the days.

Artur had dropped out as well—or rather the school had given up on him, too many absences to catch up on and the IB program was especially strict on that. It was easier for him as he was legally an adult. Damian had suspended his studies as well. Karina was the only one of us who'd been brave enough to return to school and to try to catch up, so I didn't see much of her.

I spent my days watching Netflix. I mostly stayed in bed, curtains drawn, sometimes relocating to the living room when Mum was away. Artur was with me most of the time, staying overnight so often that he had his own toothbrush in our bathroom.

"Just make sure she eats something, okay?" was all Mum had to say about that.

I was so relieved he was there, but it didn't stop surprising me that he kept coming. I missed our bond; I missed how warm and secure it made me feel. But I started to appreciate that Artur himself had a similar effect on me—I trusted him and I could count on one hand all the people I fully trusted these days. I felt safe and peaceful around him. When reality became too much, he stayed up all night with me, watching extended editions of *Lord of the Rings*. And there was a lot to be said about having a warm embrace to retreat into when the edges of the world started to blur.

That night I couldn't sleep, my mind spinning too much, too fast. Tears kept falling from my eyes and when I got a grasp on myself, I decided to make myself a cup of camomile tea. I walked into the living room to see that Artur was still up, his drawing pad in his lap. Sleeping together in my narrow bed had been fine when we shared the bond and craved physical touch but nowadays it was too crowded, so Artur usually slept on the living room sofa.

When he saw me in the doorway, he brushed his eyes with his hand. His eyes were red. He'd been crying, too.

"Do you want a hug?" I asked, sitting next to him.

Artur nodded and we cuddled in silence for a long while.

"You first," I said at last.

"I…really miss magic? It has always been a given in my life, the one thing to fall back on even when everything else was shit, and now it's gone and I'm not sure how to move on. Home is difficult, too, my parents aren't used to the idea of their child losing magic. I guess that's what happens when you get together only to create a new generation of sorcerers, you get upset when they conveniently lose their powers, even if it was to preserve magic. And I'm really worried about you, too."

I was silent for a beat, my heart drumming in my chest.

"I'm surprised that you keep coming here. That everything is over and you're still here."

Artur didn't respond immediately. He held still, as if he could still sense my emotions, as if he could still read my mind, but instead overthinking what was the right thing to say.

"Would it be easier if I wasn't?" he asked, the uncertainty clear in his voice.

"No." I squeezed him closer, wishing for even a tiniest sparkle of magic, for the comfort it used to bring me. "I'd sink without you, and it terrifies me."

These were the sort of words that belonged only to frightened whispers in the dead of the night. I wasn't used to speaking things like that out loud, because I'd never needed to. But I needed him to know how vital he was to me, how he was the only thing keeping me together, and how scary it was. Especially since in the end people always left me.

"It's okay to accept support from others," said Artur, his hand running up and down my spine. "But…it terrifies me, too. I can't be the only thing keeping you going, little fox. You need more than that."

"I have nothing more to give. I'd done what I was supposed to do, the whole reason for my existence is over. I used to be a burden on everyone around because of my magic and now I'm useless because I don't have magic anymore."

"Living isn't something you have to earn. It's not about what you have to give. You don't have to be useful, whatever that means, and you don't have to be palatable to others. You're a whole person without magic, too. I know it's difficult now, but it's not forever. I promise you that. The worst is over."

"But the future is empty. Everyone else is moving on and I'm stuck in my room, without any sense of direction. Everything takes too much energy."

"Wiki, you've been through so fucking much. It's okay to take time to recharge. It's okay to not leave your bed for a few weeks. It's okay to not have answers when your world has been turned upside down over and over and over. It's okay."

"But everyone else *is* moving on. Karina and Rafi are finishing school. Damian found a job. My mum is basically running the magical community. I know you're struggling, too, but you're also all over the place, drawing, reading, running every day, bringing fresh pastries from the bakery… and I'm stuck."

"You'll find these things, too. I promise that one day, soon, things will bring you joy, will give you purpose. You just need to hold on."

I didn't answer, hiding in his embrace.

"You need to promise me one thing," said Artur, his voice slow, measured. "Whenever you feel like that, you need to tell me, okay? Or anyone else. You can wake me up whenever you need to, I promise it's fine, I promise you that I want to know how you feel. Okay?"

"Okay," I said. "Do you want tea? I came out to get some tea."

Things were difficult and the days went on forever. I didn't understand why they dragged when I just wanted them over. Wasn't time supposed to be healing?

"We could go have pizza?" proposed Artur one afternoon.

I was lying on the sofa, staring at my laptop.

"We can order it online," I said.

"We could go for a walk?"

"I've had enough walks around this city."

"Cinema?"

"I'm literally watching a film and you're interrupting."

Artur sighed, brushing his hand through his hair.

"Wiki, please let me take you out of here. At least for ten minutes."

"If you want to go, it's okay. I'm not holding you here."

Artur leaned his forehead heavily on his hand, but he didn't say anything. I didn't feel his emotions but something vital squeezed inside me. I was disappointing him. He was worried. I needed to make an effort if I wanted to keep him around.

Maybe I didn't deserve him. Maybe he was finally realizing how much better he could do.

If I kept pushing him away, he'd leave.

My stomach squeezed tighter.

I paused the superhero film I was watching. It wasn't like I particularly enjoyed seeing another American production portraying people with an accent like mine as villains. Though I knew a lot of people in the magical community would agree we were villains.

I didn't believe in villains and heroes anymore. Life wasn't nearly as easy.

"Artur," I said. He squeezed his eyes shut but I continued, "I can't be out in this city. I really, really can't. But…can we visit Damian?"

Artur raised his head, his eyes searching mine.

"You want to go to Poznań?"

"Maybe? Yes?"

"Now, or do you want to give him a heads up? No, never mind, come. Let's go, I'll text him on the way."

FIFTY TWO

Leaving my safe bubble was more difficult than I'd have admitted out loud. Panic squeezed my throat as we caught a tram to the train station and waited for the next connection to Poznań.

"How do you feel about hand-holding?" asked Artur as we sat on a bench on the platform.

"What? What do you mean?"

Artur shrugged but his cheeks reddened a little.

"Well, it's something we used to do a lot to share magic. And I wondered if you're okay with that if there's no magic involved. And PDA in general, I guess." There was a beat of silence. "And by PDA I mean hugging."

"I don't know," I admitted. "Do you want to try?"

Artur put his hand on mine. It was still weird not to feel

the sparkle of magic between us, but it wasn't unpleasant. I liked the way his hand shielded mine, how our fingers locked, linking us together. How he kept me warm in the cold winter air.

"It's nice," I whispered.

A little smile stretched Artur's lips and he squeezed my hand.

The train ride was a lot. So many potentially threatening sounds, so many people to keep an eye on. I tried using Artur's headphones, but not hearing everything around me only made me more anxious.

The barriers between Nawia and Jawia had been blurring since we'd destroyed the Guardian system. Everyone knew the demons would be back. I hadn't seen any since the rusałka in Gdańsk, but I'd heard people on the news speaking of the creatures they'd encountered.

When we arrived in Poznań, I was exhausted and my head was beginning to throb.

"Damian is at work, but his flatmate can let us in," said Artur as we made our way towards the tram stop. "Or we can go to the cinema and watch a film before Damian finishes his shift."

Cars zoomed on the street, people pushing past us. Someone's bag bumped into my side. So many people going in all directions, as if the world hadn't been thrown off its axis. As if everything was all right.

I opened my mouth then closed it. We weren't home anymore, it was an uncharted territory.

"We can go watch a film and wait for Damian."

Damian was waiting for us in front of the screening room when the film finished. He pulled us into a hug and we held on for a long while.

"I don't like surprises, but this is a good one," he said. "I'm taking you for drinks, come on."

Artur glanced at me and I shrugged. I wasn't at my best, but I wasn't dying to hide either.

To my surprise, Damian took us to a board games bar. It was cozy, with low lights and big tables to spread up games and boxes upon boxes upon boxes lining up the walls. *The Lord of the Rings* soundtrack played in the background. We had overly sweet drinks and a huge basket of fries to share while we played *Ticket to Ride*. We didn't talk much but we soaked in each other's company.

We spent two enchanted days in Poznań, with Damian showing us his favourite spots when he wasn't at work, watching films together, and playing games. But it couldn't last.

"I don't want to go back," I said.

Artur and Damian exchanged a look.

"You don't have to," said Damian after a couple of moments. "You can stay for a bit."

And so I did. Artur had to return for his mum's birthday and Damian had to go to work, but I didn't mind staying alone. I borrowed a book from his collection and hid among the many plants filling his room. Even though he'd disappeared for months, his flatmate had done his best to save them. He'd even paid Damian's rent, hoping he'd be back, which was extremely generous—or naïve, even under the extraordinary circumstances.

The sun flooding through the windows was beckoning me, so I pulled on my trainers and ventured outside, walking down the baroque streets of Poznań old town, around the castle, exploring little bookshops and parks. The cobblestones weren't spattered with blood, the shadows weren't heavy with memories. It was a whole new world, full of possibilities.

When Damian got back, we made pasta and watched Netflix together. Half an hour into the film, after we were done with our food and put the bowls away, Damian leaned his head on my shoulder.

"I miss it," he whispered after a few moments.

"Our bond?"

"Well, yes, that, too. But I meant all the platonic closeness, having people right there for you, no matter how bad things got. All the casual physical touch that is neither romantic, nor sexual. Fuck, if you told me a few months ago that I'd willingly cuddle with someone, I'd have laughed you out of the room. It's just so rare, so precious to have a platonic connection like that."

I leaned my head on his.

"I miss it, too."

In many ways, it was easier with Damian. We'd never

relied on our bond that much. With Artur, we had to reassess our whole relationship, renegotiate every little touch and boundary, and each day I worried that with our bond gone, it would become too obvious that I didn't match the intensity of his feelings.

"It's…is healing a cheesy word? Well, it feels good to know that our emotional levels match and you don't feel about me in a way I can't reciprocate," I said.

"Aro alliance. If you decided to pick up that label."

"I…think so?"

"Good. Well, I understand what you mean. You know that Artur and I are talking things out, too, right? In the past that would have been an automatic 'no' from me but seeing how he behaves around you and how he respects your boundaries despite the emotional mismatch, or whatever you called it, well, that gives me hope. Though it's also different because in our case it's about finding the balance without feeling like we are each pushing another into something he doesn't want."

"I hope you'll figure it out."

I looked at all the plants, crystals, and moon charts scattered around the room.

"You still practice magic, don't you?"

"Once a witch, always a witch. It's more of a spiritual thing, you know? It's about your relationship with the world around you. And our time as the Circle of Four only helped me learn to appreciate it more."

"And…it's something that can be taught, right?"

Damian lifted his head from my shoulder to look at me.

I held his gaze.

"Yes," he said. "You'd have to forget a lot of what you've been taught by the other magic-users, but yes. I would really like to share it with you."

My stay in Poznań planted a seed of hope. I thought I was getting better. But the moment I stepped back home, everything slammed into me again, paralysing me in place.

"You can't just run away across Poland without telling me," said Mum instead of a hello.

"You knew I went to Poznań."

"Because *Artur* messaged me! I'd like to hear that from my own daughter. I'd like to have a say in big plans like that."

"So what, you'll lock me in the house again like when I was a kid? Keep me away from everyone? Maybe you want to take my books so, god forbid, I don't think that magic exists?"

Heart pounded hard in my chest. I knew I was being unfair, but I wasn't sure I cared. If Mum couldn't see my pain, I wanted her to feel it.

"Wiki—"

"I fulfilled my life's purpose and now I'm just standing in your way. I'm sorry that all the shit you put me through took its toll, I'm sorry I can't just shrug it off and move on. I know you'd be happier if I wasn't here—"

"That's not true. Don't put words in my mouth."

"I won't let you lock me here again. I've done what you wanted me to do and all I want in return is space to live."

That night I couldn't stop crying. All the progress I made in Poznań evaporated; all the hope was gone. I was stuck, unable to move, unable to see any options. Artur tried to talk me through it, but his words were muted in my ears.

In the end, he picked up his phone.

"Who are you calling?" I asked.

"Tomasz."

I stared at him through my tears.

"Wiki, I don't know what to do, okay? I don't know how to help you. I'm in above my head."

"No, please, don't. Please, I'm sorry."

"Don't be sorry. I told you—Tomasz? I'm sorry about the late hour it's just that—Yes…yes, it is." He turned towards me and said: "I'll be right back" before leaving the room.

That was it. The final straw. I knew it was coming, I knew it couldn't have lasted forever. Clever of fate to give me a little hope like that and then snatch it all away.

Everything. Was. Gone.

"Wiki."

My head snapped up as Artur touched my arm. I hadn't realized he'd come back. He showed me a small bottle filled with inky blue liquid.

"I won't make you drink it. But Tomasz recommends that you do so you can get some rest until morning. Does it sound okay?"

I nodded and soon blackness swallowed me whole, tears still running down my cheeks.

I woke up groggy and disoriented. The blinds were down so I couldn't tell if it was light outside. My lips were parched and I stumbled out of bed. I squinted at the bright light filling the flat as I made my way towards the kitchen.

Tomasz sat at the table, drinking coffee with Artur.

I stood frozen in the doorway.

"I'll leave you two alone," said Artur.

I let him walk past me. A few moments later, the door to the flat clicked close.

"Don't be angry at him," said Tomasz. "He did the right thing."

"I don't want to talk to you about my emotions."

"I don't expect you to. And I'm too entangled in your life for it to be fair. But I have a therapist friend who is ready to talk to you online tonight, to see if she might be a good match for you."

"Is she a sorceress?"

"Not a sorceress but she's well-aware of the magical community, demons, gods, all of it. So you could freely talk to her about everything you might want to talk about."

I shrugged. It wasn't like I had anything left to lose.

"Sure."

~~I'm so, so sorry. Please don't leave me~~
~~Please come back~~
~~I'll try, I'll keep on trying, I'll do whatever it takes but please don't aba~~

I typed and retyped and deleted with shaking fingers. Tomasz had left and I tried to make myself look semi-human and now the frantic energy in me was competing with the part that was telling me to just accept it.

A key turned in the lock and I stiffened. Artur walked into the kitchen, planted a kiss on my temple, and put a bag with a local bakery logo on the table in front of me.

"Did it go okay?" he asked, pouring himself a cup of coffee. When he noticed I didn't have any, he poured a second cup for me.

"You…went to get pastries?"

"I thought you could use some chocolate."

The tears I'd been trying to hold back now started falling freely.

"I didn't know if you'd be back," I whispered.

"Why wouldn't I be?"

I stared at him. Artur stared back, his head tilted.

"I'm afraid I can't read your mind anymore," said Artur after a few moments.

I struggled for words.

"Because of everything," I said after a few moments. "Because of last night. Because I'm a mess and you're in above your head and—"

"Hey. Hey, hey, hey, no. Come here." He coaxed me out of my seat and into his arms. "Yes, I was in above my head. I am. That's why I called Tomasz. Because you need professional help from someone who knows what they're doing and how to help you. But that doesn't mean I'm giving up on you, okay?

It's the opposite. I want you to have every possible tool and chance to build your life back the way you want it. And I'll be with you every step of the journey, as long as it takes."

"Really?"

"Yeah. In fact, I sort of have a plan. And I hope you'll like it."

On my eighteenth birthday, when the local magical community was preparing to celebrate the spring equinox, Karina drove Artur and me to Gdańsk before daybreak.

"I have a gift for you," she said, as she stopped her mum's car at the airport drop-off area.

She pulled out a little linen bag from her pocket and handed it to me. I pulled out a long silver chain. The airport lights reflected from a green stone carved into a little dragon. The details were breathtaking, from minuscule scales to sharp claws at the end of its paws.

It looked every bit like Arrow.

"Thank you," I whispered, pulling my cousin into a hug. I blinked back the tears as I hung the pendant around my neck.

"I also put a bottle of prosecco in your suitcase. You definitely can't afford alcohol there. Damn, I'm not even sure if they'd sell it to you."

Karina leaned between the seats to hug Artur, too.

"Don't forget to have some fun, okay?" she asked as we took our bags from the trunk.

As the sun rose, I was on a plane for the first time. I hadn't set the airport on fire this time and the plane didn't fall. The excitement of it all almost made me forget how different my eighteenth birthday had looked in the alternative reality I'd glimpsed in Nawia.

I didn't want to dwell on it. I knew how impossible that vision had been. The community, the strong sense of belonging. The magic. People who weren't here anymore and people I was better off without.

But maybe some pieces were possible to reclaim.

"Artur?" I asked, drawing his attention away from his e-reader. "Can you braid hair?"

It had been Artur's idea. He'd schemed with my dad, who was happy to help him out. Dad had found us a room to rent in a collective across the street from where he lived and arranged us temporary jobs, packing online orders into boxes at a company where his flatmate worked. None of us acknowledged it, but it was clear that Dad thought the same way we felt—that we needed time away from our city, from the whole magical community, and from my mum. And Artur needed time away from his family, too.

It was impossible to heal while we were still stuck there, reminded every hour of every day about everything that had happened. Of everything we'd lost.

We fell into the new routine easier than expected. The salary, which made our eyes go wide when we'd first heard, was enough to pay for our room and food and to save up a bit. We usually worked different shifts, missing each other in the room we shared. Artur would still be asleep when I'd wake up at five a.m. and often I'd be already asleep before he came back from his shift. He'd make sure I had lunch to get back to or even get me a surprise breakfast snack and I'd leave him dinner in the fridge. When we were together, we were mostly too exhausted to do anything after standing up and carrying boxes all day, so we'd snuggle up and watch Netflix. On an odd day off, we'd go out and explore Bergen and its surroundings, hiking in the fjords. Inspired by the level of activity of the Norwegians, I finally started to train up my running skills. I didn't have magic anymore so it wasn't stupid to finally learn to run from trouble. I wouldn't be taken by surprise by another apocalypse.

The routine was exhausting but it turned out to be what I needed. Just this extra push, the necessity to get out of bed and get dressed, and work, had changed everything. The work was mindless, but it gave me a sense of purpose and the routine put me at ease. Packing online orders wasn't life-changing, but it showed me that I could still do something, get things done.

Artur came out to my dad on our first evening in Bergen. We were having pizza and prosecco from Karina in a small birthday celebration in my dad's kitchen. He shared his flat with Ahmad, an Afghan man in his late twenties who'd arranged for our temporary jobs, and a Norwegian person in their fifties, Sigrid. They both took a piece of pizza and Sigrid raised a glass of prosecco in my honour but they didn't linger, leaving us alone in the kitchen.

"I want to be clear about our relationship," said Artur, swirling the prosecco in his glass. He raised his eyes to look at my dad. "We aren't dating. We don't call each other boyfriend and girlfriend. I guess we're closer to best friends. Maybe what we had was all just magic, maybe all that's holding us together now is so much shared baggage, but… we just fit together. And I'd do anything for Wiki. And also I'm asexual."

Dad clasped Artur on the shoulder.

"Thank you for telling me." He smiled. "Is there any word you use to describe your relationship that you want me to use?"

Artur and I shared a glance.

"QPR?" I said. "We call it a queer-platonic relationship. And I'd call Artur my queer-platonic partner or partner-in-crime. So, I guess 'partner' works."

"It's a word for a non-romantic committed relationship," said Artur.

"But, also, I mean, almost everyone calls us boyfriend and girlfriend," I rushed to add, my stomach clenching. "So it's not a big deal."

"It upsets you every time they do," said Artur. "So it's sort of a big deal."

"I know what a QPR is," said Dad. He smirked at our astonished looks. "I'm not that old and I have an internet connection. Also, you know I was in a poly triad when I was not much older than you, so I know a thing or two about amatonormativity." A small smile worked its way to my face upon hearing this word from my dad's lips. "So queer-platonic partners it is. Not a problem. And you, my dear child, will stop belittling yourself to try to fit into other's narrow-minded worldview."

He looked at me sternly and I nodded. I took another sip of my prosecco to swallow the emotions bubbling in me.

"Does your mum know?" he asked.

I shook my head. I pulled on a stray string of hair that had fallen out from the crown that Artur had braided around my head.

"Do you want her to know?" asked Dad. "Should I correct her if she says something?"

The horrible truth was I didn't care. I glanced at Artur.

"It's fine with me if you tell her."

"I don't mind either," said Artur.

Later, in the privacy of our room, Artur took out a flat object wrapped in a colourful paper. He bit his lip as he handed it to me.

"You don't have to pretend to like it," he said, as I started unwrapping it. "It's just something you mentioned when we first met and I couldn't get this idea out of my head. I talked to Laura and Darek and they helped, coming up with more stories and filling in the blanks. I know that considering everything it might not be welcome so don't feel any pressure to keep it."

I held a large book. The cover was a bit lose, clearly

handsewn. It was framed by two drawn oak trees which shined gold. A fox walked between them. The title in the middle was also handwritten and read "Tales from the Magical World." I glanced at Artur, who was staring at me, anticipating my reaction, his eyes big. I opened the book and browsed pages upon pages of beautifully illustrated, handwritten stories.

I knew both the art style and the handwriting.

"That must have taken you *weeks*," I said, leafing through the book.

"I started when you were in Nawia. We had a lot of time with nothing to do."

The book started with the story of how the world was created. The illustrations showed the breaking egg and two gods, Perun and Weles, on a boat in the middle of the ever-sea. Then there were more stories, some familiar, like the one about King Popiel who'd been eaten by mice, the tale of Master Twardowski—the legendary version, not the truth—or the legend of the dragon of Kraków. Many more I'd never heard before.

"But as I said, it's okay if you don't like it," Artur babbled on. "I knew it was risky. But you said that you'd do horrible things to get your hands on the stories I grew up with and, well, I didn't want you to have to do these horrible things."

I looked him in the eyes.

"It's perfect," I whispered.

FIFTY THREE

1 SEPTEMBER, POZNAŃ

It was a small, cluttered flat, with piles of books, crystals, candles, and plants and moving-in boxes all around. You could hardly walk around without tripping on an odd book or a plant that's been moved in the way. We made sure the plants didn't cover the windows too much, so that as much light could stream in as possible. The kitchen window sill was covered in all sorts of herbs, especially thyme, and potted tomatoes, peppers, and green beans, all thriving and climbing towards the sun. There was a pot of strawberries, too. And outside there were the flowers—cosmoses, daisies, asters, and lavender. A rainbow flag hung proudly from the window, spelled by Damian to withstand all sort of hate attacks—and our neighbours hated it with a passion. A moon calendar hung on a wall, next to a display of pictures: Dad, Artur, and I at Bergen Pride, Artur and I hugging under an ace flag and Dad waving a smaller pan flag; Karina, Artur, Damian, Rafi, and I at the summerhouse; me walking into the Brda river and flipping off the person holding the camera, because, honestly, a girl could walk into the river just to swim but they wouldn't stop teasing me. There was also a large drawing of a żmij with green, shining scales and golden eyes, and different pride stickers.

The cupboards were stacked full of non-perishable foods. That was something we couldn't just switch off, calculating how long we could survive for if the city got cut off. And then we'd just bring more cans, more flour, more *chocolate*. Yes, half of the cupboards was coffee and chocolate.

We might have been in a different city but the fear was all too real, the past too close to let go of.

"Are you ready?" asked Artur, adjusting his tie. It was the morning on the first of September and warm light streamed through the window, promising the summer still wasn't over, even if our holiday was. Ciri was wagging her tail at his feet.

"To relive my worst nightmare? Absolutely not."

I nursed a cup of coffee in one hand and looked at a half-eaten toast in another. I got the crumbs all over my white shirt but I couldn't care less about it. If it stained, I'd wake up Damian, annoy him until he magically cleaned it for me. There were many perks of having a witch for a flatmate.

We were all learning Damian's magic now, but he'd had years of practice while we needed to unlearn and re-evaluate our relationship with magic. We were no longer the Circle of Four, not in the magical sense, but a coven in the making.

"Remember what you told me when we first met?" asked Artur.

"That I think you might be a werewolf?"

Artur smiled. It was good to see him smile, even if I knew he still struggled without magic more than any of us.

"No. I mean, that would be a plot twist, but no. You told me you want to go into medicine. Do research. Study in the very city where you live now. Discover how magic is possible, if some humans have actual predispositions for it."

"I'm pretty sure I didn't tell you half of it. You've lifted it off from my mind."

"Either way, something tells me there might be quite a lot of funding for research like that right now. But before you get there…"

"You need to finish high school," finished Karina, appearing behind my back. "Also, a werewolf, really? I thought we agreed Artur's a vampire."

"It's *two years*," I moaned. "Two years of memorising tonnes of useless information that I'll forget as soon as I pass the exams, two years of tests and essays and math equations, two years of reading sexist, racist books by dead white men and writing about how they perfectly describe what it means to be Polish. Two years of being around *people*."

"Oh no," Karina deadpanned. "You might even make friends. Horrible. I'd imagine living without parents might make you wildly popular. Besides, you'll be the oldest and everyone will use you to buy all the alcohol for at least half a year until your classmates start turning eighteen."

I sighed and Artur and Karina exchanged a glance over my shoulder.

"Okay," said Artur, putting his hands on my shoulders, looking into my eyes. "If you really don't want to do it, it's okay. You don't have to. You can make your own decisions and you're over eighteen so no one can force you to go to school. You can wait one more year. You can finish high school later in life. You don't have to finish high school at all, it's not the end of the world. And there are vocational schools, too. If you need more time, we won't hold it against you. You have all the possibilities in the world and I'll do everything to keep it that way."

I dropped my gaze to Artur's shoulder, the intensity of his eyes burning me.

"Will you help me with maths?" I sniffled.

"Yes. Of course. And physics. And English, though I think you'll be more than fine. And you'll slay science."

"I'll read through all your Polish essays," said Karina. "And did you know that Damian is good at German? We can also bully him into making you second breakfast."

"I can try," I said. Then, because, in lieu of having a magical bond, we were working on talking about our emotions out loud in this flat, I added: "I'm scared."

Karina and Artur squeezed me between them. Ciri rushed to join us, yipping and jumping to not be left out.

"High school is scary," agreed Karina, propping her chin on my shoulder. "And restarting it in another city is even scarier."

"But they celebrate Rainbow Friday there," said Artur.

"And if you survive the beginning of the school year ceremony, we can go to Malta Lake afterwards. We'll sit on the grass, eat pizza, and enjoy the sun. But, also, if you decide to stay home or if you run away halfway through, we can still do it. How does it sound?"

"And we'll watch *Empire Strikes Back* afterwards," I added.

"Nice try. Absolutely not," said Karina. "Wednesday evenings are for board games. But we can watch it tomorrow."

I took a deep breath. The future was still a scary and big unknown but we had plans. I was surrounded by people I could rely on, who understood me on a level that no one else ever would, and who'd have my back no matter what. It was a good start into doing what I wanted to with this life.

"Okay," I said. "I can try."

We stood in a human sandwich for a moment longer before Artur and Karina released me and I could finish my coffee. I brushed the crumbs off my shirt and twisted the talisman on a red string that Damian had tied around my wrist. Karina fluffed up my hair, freshly cut and dyed pink by her last night, and adjusted the collar of Artur's shirt.

"Don't forget to take a selfie for our picture wall," she said as we pulled on our shoes.

Artur took my hand and we ran downstairs into a sunny September morning, making it just in time to catch a tram.

ACKNOWLEDGEMENTS

I've never expected to wrap up a trilogy, and I can't believe it happened. Over a decade spent with this world has come to an end, even if the books started becoming less of a pile of notes and more book-shaped only a few years ago. A bunch of thank yous are in order to everyone who helped make it happen.

Firstly, to my amazing team at Fractured Mirror. Thank you for creating a new home for my story, it means the world to me. This book would quite literally not be here without you.

To Noah and Shimaira, who believed in this story from the very beginning and never gave up on me.

To Kristel, who listened to unending rants and breakdowns caused by this story and helped me through it all. I would have never finished it without you.

To Kai, for remembering that a dragon needs horns. Arrow is eternally grateful to you.

To my amazing beta readers: Maraia, Merle, Moa, Nora, and once again Kristel. Thank you for helping me out with my piles of questions and sorting out the loose ends.

To all the book reviewers, anyone who mentions my book to a friend, asks for it at a bookstore, or includes it in a bookstagram recommendations list—thank you, thank you, thank you! Word of mouth is the most powerful tool in book selling and I'll never be able to thank you enough so just know that it means the world to me.

To spAcers, the ones who've been there from the beginning and the new ones—thank you for creating a community I've always dreamed of.

And to you, who is reading it—because what are the odds that an indie book, much less third in trilogy, would make it beyond my circle of friends? Thank you for sticking around for so long.

ABOUT THE AUTHOR

Anna grew up in Poland and lived in a number of countries before settling in Sweden. She spends more time in imaginary worlds than in the real one. She grew up on a mixture of Polish legends and original Grimm fairy tales, which she channels into fiction. She's also a dog lover. She is easiest to find on her Instagram, where she talks about books and goes into queer-feminist rants.

https://twitter.com/_AnnaKirchner

https://www.instagram.com/rattletheshelves/

https://www.goodreads.com/author/show/
20197623.Anna_Kirchner

annakirchner.author@gmail.com